NEMESIS

NEMESIS

CATHERINE COULTER

G. P. PUTNAM'S SONS | NEW YORK

Doubleday Large Print Home Library Edition

This Large Print Edition, prepared especially for
Doubleday Large Print Home Library, contains the complete,
unabridged text of the original Publisher's Edition.

PUTNAM

G. P. Putnam's Sons
Publishers Since 1838
An imprint of Penguin Random House LLC
375 Hudson Street, New York, New York 10014

ISBN 978-1-62953-557-9

Printed in the United States of America

**This Large Print Book carries the
Seal of Approval of N.A.V.H**

To my incredible other half,
who continues to pour his heart
and brain into my books.
Thank you for this very special book.

—CATHERINE

To sleep, perchance to dream...
For in that sleep of death,
what dreams may come.

—HAMLET

ACKNOWLEDGMENTS

To Angela Bell, FBI Office of Public Affairs. You continue to keep me on the straight and narrow, and I thank you. Soon we need to go for drinks.

Nichole Robson, SM guru,
Trident Media Group

Emily Ross, SM guru,
Trident Media Group

Brianna Weber, SM guru,
Trident Media Group

You three women did so very much to promote **The Lost Key** on social media. (Yes, that's what SM means, not S&M.) My thanks. I can't wait to see what you do with **Nemesis**.

And finally, and always, my bows and kudos and everlasting thanks to Karen Evans, my own personal guardian angel who's always there for me, always in my corner, ready to take on anything. Always. Thank you, Karen.

NEMESIS

1

JFK Airport
New York City
Wednesday afternoon
Mid-May

The airport security line slowly inched forward, nearly sixty passengers stoically weaving back and forth in the ritual strip-dance everyone knew and put up with. At least Sherlock didn't have her Glock with her, so she wouldn't have to fill out a gazillion forms. Her meeting with the lead federal prosecutor in an upcoming murder trial had lasted six and a half hours, and probably would have gone on longer if she hadn't simply gotten up and said she had a plane to catch. She couldn't wait to get home and throw a football with Sean, if the plane took off at a reasonable time, that is. She looked forward to downing a cup of Dillon's knock-your-socks-off coffee, and having him sing to her while he scrubbed her back in the shower.

Out of habit she studied the faces, the eyes, the clothes, and the body language of those around her, guessing what people were thinking, planning, where they were going. Home? Business? Rendezvous? She knew one thing for sure: they were hoping as she was that flights wouldn't be delayed or canceled. The woman ahead of her sighed. "All I want to do is get home, jump in the tub, and wash off all traces of Mickey Sturgiss."

Sherlock said, a smile on her face, "A wild day with Mickey?"

The woman rolled her eyes. "A deposition for a slime bucket who should be deported to Mars."

Sherlock laughed. "You're a lawyer?"

"Yes, but not this idiot's lawyer. I was doing his lawyer a favor. Believe me, I'll make sure he knows he owes me big-time." She stuck out her hand. "Melissa Harkness."

Sherlock shook her hand. "Lacey Sherlock. Come to think of it, I could do some washing, too."

"Don't tell me you're a lawyer, too?"

"I'm FBI, actually." Melissa Harkness was on the heavy side, in her thirties, and she was carrying a large briefcase in one hand and a black tote the size of one of Jupiter's moons in the other. She looked like she might be dragging, but her bright eyes were filled with intelligence and interest.

Her laugh at Sherlock's name started them off, and soon they were talking about Sherlock's dad, a federal judge, and Sherlock's job as an FBI agent, as the line slowly snaked its way toward the TSA folk ensconced on their high stools, checking each ticket and ID.

Sherlock noticed a tall man a couple people ahead of Melissa. He was standing stock-still, as if frozen in place. The man behind him had to nudge him, unheard of in an airport security line with everyone wanting to move forward quickly. He was dark-haired and on the thin side. What caught her eye was the fact that his lower face was bone white, as if he'd recently shaved off a full beard, perhaps that very morning. He looked calm, but she saw his hands were trembling as he pulled off his black loafers and placed them in a bin. Something was off. She watched him shrug off his coat and start on his belt.

Then, without warning, he turned, shoved aside the two passengers behind him, and grabbed Melissa around the neck. He pulled something out of his briefcase—it was a grenade. He waved it around, all the while backing away, pulling Melissa with him. When people around them realized what was happening, there were screams and shouts, everyone focused on the grenade held high over his head now, a finger through the safety ring. He yelled, his voice shaking as badly as his hands, "That's right, it's a grenade!" He screamed at the TSA agents, who were now speaking into their walkie-talkies, several of them moving toward him. "Nobody move! Your X-ray isn't much use now, is it? It doesn't matter I'm not lily-white!" He pointed the grenade at a tall black TSA agent who was trying to flank him. "Or black! All of you—stay away or she dies, along with the rest of you." He stopped moving when he felt a concrete pillar behind his back.

A TSA agent called out, only a bit of a wobble in her voice, "Sir, put the grenade down and we can talk about what you want."

He laughed. "Really? I know how you idiots operate. Even without this grenade, you'd probably have taken me to one of your little rooms and ordered me to strip down, treated me like a criminal—that's because you target men who look Middle Eastern, and that's profiling and it's against the law." His voice was near a scream now. Sherlock heard a French accent over-lying the British clip, with a trace of Farsi or Arabic. "Because I'm dark and wear a beard?" Had he forgotten he'd shaved it off? "Don't come any closer or we all die right now!" He tightened his hold around Melissa's neck. Her hands were pulling at his arm, her face turning blue.

The TSA agents were slowly flanking him as he talked. Sherlock knew airport security would arrive at any second, all of them trained to deal with such a threat, but it didn't matter. They weren't here yet. She was on the spot, a few feet away from him, looking right into his eyes. His arm was still around Melissa's neck, his finger still hooked around the grenade's ring. One pull and a whole lot of people would die, herself included. Her heart kettledrummed in her chest; the spit dried in her mouth. There was an instant of dead silence, only the sound of his hard, fast breathing. She called out, her voice calm and easy, "Sir, what do you want?"

He locked on Sherlock's face, tightened his death grip on Melissa, and held the grenade toward her. "Who told you to talk, you stupid woman? Get back with the rest of the mutts and shut up!"

"Sir, you obviously knew you couldn't get a grenade through X-ray, so you planned it this way. Why? What do you want? What if they simply let you leave?" She wanted to see how tight his hold was on the grenade ring, but she forced herself to keep her eyes on his face.

He screamed at her, "Shut up or you'll be the first one dead! You agents, stop moving around, do you hear me? Any more of you take a step toward me, I'll toss the grenade right in front of you!"

The TSA agents stopped in their tracks, their eyes moving from him to Sherlock, and always back to the grenade he held in his shaking hand. The passengers stayed still as stones, as they'd been told, hardly breathing, watching, praying. Sherlock heard a distant cacophony of voices, either running away or swarming closer to see what was happening. **Not good.** Airport security was beginning to inch toward him. He juked this way and that, trying to keep an eye on the agents. His eyes narrowed, sweat beaded on his face. What had he planned to do? Sherlock felt rage and fear rolling off him. Yet he hadn't pulled the pin. Why? Was he having second thoughts, or was he waiting to make some kind of statement? She saw it clearly on his face, he was struggling with himself, trying to rev himself up to kill as many people around him as possible, Melissa included. That was certainly what he'd planned when he'd taken off his shoes and set them in the bin. They didn't matter then because he knew he was going to die.

She looked at Melissa's face, at her eyes. She was terrified, but she was there, ready to do something if she could. Sherlock said to her, "What's your name?"

He was distracted and automatically loosened his hold. Melissa sucked in air. "Melissa Harkness."

He was looking at Sherlock now, focused on her. **Good.** "And what's your name, sir?"

"None of your business!" He raised the grenade higher, ran his tongue over his lips, and tightened his hold on Melissa's neck again.

"Why don't you let Melissa go? She didn't do anything to you. Maybe I can call your wife, you can speak to her and to your children."

"What are you talking about? You know nothing about my blessed wife. For you to even speak of her is an abomination." He kept swinging the grenade around to force airport security guards and TSA agents back.

Melissa was beginning to choke again, her fingers pulling against his arm.

Sherlock spoke quickly now. "Does your wife expect you to die today and kill dozens of innocent people along with you? Does your wife even know what you're doing? Where is she now?" She saw the security team moving even closer and she smelled fear, a raw corrosive in the air, from everyone around her, especially from him. He was as frightened as Melissa. She had to stop this now.

"I told you not to speak of her. I'm a British citizen, not some poor sod from Pakistan or Iran you can manipulate." He laughed, a scary laugh that was filled with derision and something buried deep, something that made him what he was, and something deeper, a kind of desperate bravado. He was trying to convince himself to accept his own death. "I'm from London—that decadent city they call Londonistan. We will fight until we control the whole world, in the name of Allah."

What idiot taught you that? It sounded like he'd practiced saying it, exactly that way. **Why?** "Despite what you said, I don't think you want to die. If you throw the grenade, that is what will happen. You'll die and you'll never see your family again. Do you want to be nothing at all in the flash of a second?"

2

Sweat bathed his face, and his hands trembled so badly Sherlock wondered how he could keep hold of the grenade ring. He bared his teeth at her. "You shut your mouth."

Sherlock smiled. "You throw the grenade and so many bullets will hit you from airport security, your body won't be able to hold itself together. Your wife won't be able to recognize you because your face will be blown off. Maybe she'll recognize your sock, the one with the hole in it."

He glanced down automatically at his foot and Sherlock ran at him. "Melissa, drop!"

Brave Melissa threw all her weight forward, pulling the terrorist with her. He struggled with her, off balance, and his finger slipped free of the grenade safety ring. Sherlock took two fast steps, reared back on the heel of her foot and kicked his right wrist, heard the bone crack. He screamed and dropped the grenade. Everyone froze, watched the grenade hit the floor with a loud thump and begin to roll. There was mayhem—yelling and people running to get as far away from the grenade as possible, pushing others out of their way, some of them falling to the floor, a stampede, and over it all security shouting, "Everyone get down! Get down!"

The terrorist was holding on to his wrist, cursing her, but he didn't come at her, he lunged for the grenade. Sherlock ran after him, kicked him hard in the kidney. He whooshed out a breath as he fell forward onto his hands and knees, hissing in pain as he crawled toward the grenade, now fetched up against a security counter. She prayed none of the security officers would lose it and shoot, since she was so close to him now.

She yelled at him, "Don't do it!"

He twisted back to look at her, fear and desperation glazing his eyes, screamed curses, and dove for the grenade, his good arm outstretched. She kicked him in the head. He fell forward, sprawling away from the grenade, but still Sherlock saw his fingers reach out and pull the ring free of the grenade. Thankfully, the safety lever stayed attached, still in place, but for how long?

Everyone remained frozen in place, terrified, all eyes on the grenade.

One, two, three agonizingly slow seconds —nothing happened.

She didn't have handcuffs, so Sherlock planted her foot on the middle of his back and pressed down. "Listen to me, get hold of yourself. If you don't move, the grenade might not explode and you might survive this."

The man was heaving for breath, murmuring over and over something she couldn't understand. A prayer? To Allah? His eyes were tightly closed, one hand still pressed to his head where Sherlock had kicked him. He wasn't moving now. His other hand lay palm up three inches from the grenade.

He was weeping. He said in a whisper, "You've ruined it all. Now they'll die because of you." She leaned close, heard him whisper over and over, "Bella, Bella." A woman's name, his wife's name?

"Who's Bella?"

He didn't even see her, didn't see anything beyond himself and what had happened.

She heard the loud buzz of voices all around her, but she ignored them. She looked up to see a man striding toward her, airport security officers flanking him, guns drawn. She'd recognize a Big Dog anywhere. He had to be the chief of security here at JFK, ex-military, tall, built, straight as an oak, with white buzz-cut hair. He yelled to all the huddled passengers, "Do not panic. TSA agents will escort you away from here right now. Slowly, that's right. Clear the area!"

As Sherlock lifted her foot and stepped away from the man, a half-dozen security agents covered him, picked him up, and dragged him away.

Big Dog shouted, "Okay, Security, back behind that concrete column!" and he led them all briskly away from the grenade, pulling Sherlock with him.

A mustachioed man trotted up. "Pritchett, bomb squad—it's a grenade? Was the ring pulled?"

Sherlock said, "Yes, about four minutes ago. The safety lever's still in place."

"I see it. What a stroke of luck. It could also be defective, but let's not take any chances. Chief Alport, move your crew back another dozen feet."

Pritchett said into his portable radio, "Grenade, ring pulled four minutes ago, safety lever still hanging on, could be defective. Let's not take any chances. No frag bag, bring in the PTCV."

Sherlock said, "PTCV?"

"Portable Total Containment Vessel."

Sherlock watched along with everyone else as a few minutes later two members of the bomb squad, looking like green space aliens in their heavy protective suits, walked clumsily to the grenade. One of the men was pushing a large white cylinder on wheels, maybe four feet high, nearly four feet wide, with an opening in the center front.

They studied the grenade, then, after instructions from Pritchett, gently lifted it with long-handled prongs and eased it inside the vessel. They closed the opening, rotated the cylinder. There was a huge collective sigh of relief.

Pritchett said to Big Dog, "You took a big chance getting that close, Chief. I'd say an extra Mass is in order."

Sherlock and the chief watched Pritchett follow the two suited men wheeling the containment vessel toward an emergency exit. The security people gave them wide berth. Twenty feet short of the doors, there was a loud muffled bang. The containment vessel box shook, but it held.

No one moved for a second. Then Pritchett yelled, "Guess the safety lever fell off, or the grenade wasn't defective after all. Talk about a bit of pucker action. You can bet that's going to make the news."

The chief let out a big sigh and crossed himself.

Sherlock saw he was still stiff as a board, the muscles in his arms and back knotted with tension, but now he was smiling at her. Sherlock turned to him. "It's a pleasure to see a Big Dog in action."

"Big Dog?"

She lightly laid her hand on his forearm. "Yeah, I'd recognize you guys anywhere. My husband's a Big Dog—you're a rare breed. But I gotta say that was way too close." She stuck out her hand. "FBI Special Agent Sherlock."

He shook her hand. "Guy Alport, chief of

security in this nerve-fragging zoo. A pleasure to meet you. My people were telling me about this crazy woman who faced him down, got right into his face, and kicked the crap out of him."

Crazy, that was about right, but Sherlock only smiled and turned away when his people crowded around him. She prayed she'd never be tested like that again. She went looking for Melissa Harkness and found her outside the doors, surrounded by security, airport employees, and passengers. Behind her, she heard an alarm sound, then the loudspeaker: "Everyone will leave the terminal by the nearest exit. The terminal is closed until further notice."

What had she expected? She wondered when she'd get home. Probably in the next millennium. The security people saw her, let her through. She lightly touched Melissa's shoulder. "You did great, Melissa. You brought him down, saved the day."

Melissa Harkness grabbed Sherlock and hugged her close. "Thank you so much. Even my ex-husband thanks you." As she hugged Sherlock close again, fiercely, she whispered in her ear, "The jerk might even send you flowers. I'm his golden goose, after all." Then she grinned. "I don't think I'm going to go on that low-carb diet yet. My weight came in handy today."

"Don't you change a thing, you're perfect." Sherlock drew in a deep breath. "We all survived." She turned when a black-suited agent called out to her. She said to Melissa, "Sorry, no bath for either of us for a while. Now the fun starts."

3

FBI agents from the New York Field Office took the terrorist from the TSA guards and airport security while Homeland Security agents and NYPD officers weeded out gawkers from witnesses and herded them to several conference rooms. It was an alphabet soup of agencies, all wanting to take charge. Sherlock knew that the FBI—namely, the New York Joint Terrorism Task Force—would take the lead, because the resident FBI agent at JFK would have called them right away. She also realized the adrenaline rush was bottoming out, also knew this was long from over. She and Big Dog were separated, each taken to a room to be interviewed. The last she saw of Melissa, she was in the middle of a knot of agents.

Sherlock was escorted to a small security room filled with TV monitors and compu-ters and seated at a battered rectangular table. She was handed a cup of coffee and introduced to two FBI agents. They turned on recording equipment and started right in, going over and over what had happened, why she was in New York, what exactly the terrorist had said to her, his affect, his accent, his tone of voice, what she believed his intentions had been, and on and on it went. Sean would earn his college degree before she was finished answering questions. She heard agents talking about the airport reopening again soon, after security was certain there were no threats in the offing. Wouldn't that be a nice surprise? She no longer wanted to flop her head onto the table and take a snooze. It was a remote possibility she'd even get home before midnight, if only someone would pull the plug on all the questions. The door opened and she was instantly aware of the eerie quiet in the terminal. There were no passengers hurrying to their gates, nothing at all.

A woman came in and marched directly over to Sherlock. "I hear you're FBI."

"Yes, Special Agent Sherlock." She held out her creds.

The woman studied her creds, handed them back, and stood over her, arms crossed over her chest. She was about Sherlock's age, with straight dark hair to her shoulders, a milk-white face, a body honed to muscle and bone, and no humor at all in her dark eyes. She looked severe and tough as nails in a black suit, white shirt, and low black pumps, but when she spoke, her voice was quite lovely, lilting, with a hint of Italian music. "That name, you've got to be kidding me."

Sherlock had to laugh. "My dad's a federal judge; it suits him even better. Criminals and defense lawyers do a double take."

"I'm Supervisory Special Agent Kelly Giusti, New York FBI. Why didn't you keep out of the way and let the agents do their job? They're all very well trained for exactly this sort of thing."

Sherlock gave her a sunny smile. "I was right there when he grabbed Melissa. No choice."

"What you did was stupid."

"You're sure right about that. Put a big question mark in my day, that's for sure. Tell me, Agent Giusti, what would you have done in my place?"

Giusti stared at her. Was that a crack in

that severe mouth, a meager smile trying to burst through? "I guess I'd have been as stupid as you." They shook hands. "I heard most of your interview on my way over. Do you think he was going to try to get through security with the grenade? To blow a plane out of the sky?"

Sherlock said, "It seems like a pretty stupid thing to attempt. I know, I know, knives and guns still could get through, but it'd be unusual."

"Maybe you're underestimating your fellow humans' capacity for stupidity. You forget that numbskull Brit who tried to get the bomb in his shoe to go off?"

Sherlock laughed. "And thanks to him everyone walks barefoot through security now. The thing is, our guy didn't even try to go through X-ray, even though it looked like he was going to. I mean, he'd taken his shoes off and put them in the bin. No, he pushed two passengers out of the way, grabbed Melissa, pulled out the grenade, and started yelling. I'm thinking that was his plan all along. He said to me that I'd ruined it all, and that means to me that something else may be going on here, somewhere else."

"All right, let's say this drama was a smoke screen for something else. Chief Alport immediately began checking throughout the terminals. As of three minutes ago, nothing hinky was reported anywhere else at JFK, which is why they're going to reopen soon.

"It's possible there's nothing complex at all here. It's possible he's a lone wolf who came here to blow up at the security station, but he couldn't bring himself to do it before you disarmed him."

"He also said a woman's name—Bella. His wife?"

"You mean a final good-bye?"

"Maybe."

Giusti opened her mini-tablet. "The passport he had with his boarding pass identified him as Nasim Arak Conklin, thirty-six, address in Notting Hill, London, not one of the popular Muslim neighborhoods, like Newham, for example. I wonder why he was living there.

"We don't know anything more yet. I'm betting the passport isn't forged. There'd be no need for it, not if he or his handlers set him up to do exactly what he almost did—blow himself up along with as many passengers as he could take with him. We'll know soon enough; his fingerprints are being run through the system now. He hasn't said a word yet. Evidently he did all his talking to you." She rose. "The name Bella—I wonder if it might start him talking again. But it's no concern of yours. The upside of what you did is that no one got hurt, and we nabbed ourselves a suicide bomber."

"And the downside?" Sherlock asked.

"Once the terminal opens again and you leave the protection of this room, the media is going to eat you alive. When Chief Alport was outside the terminal, the media swarmed all over him. He was going down for the third time when he threw you under the bus."

Sherlock closed her eyes for a moment. "It isn't going to be fun, is it?"

"How fast can you run?"

Sherlock laughed. "I should call my husband before he hears about this and strokes out."

Giusti's cell buzzed. "Giusti here." A short pause, then, "You've got to be kidding me!" And she was off and running.

4

St. Patrick's Cathedral
New York City
Wednesday afternoon

Maddix Foley, vice president of the United States, took a quick look at his watch, then resumed his vigil, his eyes on the white rose–covered casket on its gurney in front of the beautiful altar three rows in front of him. Inside that lovely ornamental box lay the remains of New York's senior senator, Cardison Greiman, a longtime party force who'd ruled the Senate with a personality like a nail-studded hammer until his face had hit his desktop in his own Senate chamber five days earlier, right after he'd lost the vote for a bill the president particularly wanted passed, and he was dead from a heart attack. A pity about the bill, but then again, it was likely Card's successor would pick up his hammer and doubtless use it handily. Foley had liked the old buzzard, who'd claimed in drunker moments that he could show the lead in the TV series **House of Cards** a thing or two. Foley thought that could be true.

There was organ music—Bach, Foley realized—overlaying the low conversation of nearly eight hundred mourners here to pay their final respects, punctuated by an occasional sob from Mrs. Greiman, who'd been diagnosed with Alzheimer's two weeks before, which had shaken Card Greiman to his core. In Foley's opinion, it was the realization of losing his wife after more than fifty-plus years that had brought on Card's heart attack. Now it was Eleanor Greiman who was left to grieve him instead. Foley wondered if it wouldn't have been more merciful if she'd been further gone so she wouldn't now have to know the soul-wrenching grief.

Foley sighed, looked again at his watch. It was after five o'clock and the funeral mass should have begun five minutes ago. Cardinal Timothy Michael Dolan would be leading in the priests and altar boys and deacons, ritual incense filling the air from their swinging thuribles, and Card's final send-off would begin. Foley saw one of his

Secret Service agents speak into the unit on his wrist. He must have spotted Cardinal Dolan, which meant they were about ready to get Cardison Grieman's last big show on the road. He turned in his seat and looked down the long nave toward the narthex.

In the narthex, altar boy Romeo Rodriguez was swallowing hard, praying he wouldn't throw up, not with His Eminence Cardinal Dolan six feet away from him, looking resplendent in his vivid red cassock. The Cathedral's rector, Monsignor Ritchie, was at his side, Father Joseph Reilly behind him. Romeo realized Father Joseph was looking at him, and he looked worried. Romeo had the horrible feeling he looked as bad as he felt and he was going to hurl after all. He swallowed again and tried to distract himself, saying a Hail Mary, concentrating with all his might. He'd been a full-fledged altar boy for only seven months now, and it was Father Joseph who had recommended that he be a part of the service today. It was a great honor, his father had told him over and over, and his mother had kissed him and told him how proud she was that he would be carrying out his duties at this great man's funeral. But now his stomach twisted and cramped and he knew he couldn't hold it any longer. He was going to throw up.

Now.

Romeo ran to a small closet few people ever opened, next to the closed gift shop annex. He barely made it inside before he fell to his knees and heaved beside boxes of gift shop supplies. He felt a hand on his shoulder, steadying him. It was Father Joseph, and his deep, soothing voice told him it would be all right, he didn't have to go in with them, all he had to do was breathe lightly and relax. Romeo dry-retched, sat back, and held himself perfectly still. He felt like his stomach was hollowed out. Then he saw a large backpack stuffed into a corner of the closet. "Why is that here, Father?"

"What? Oh, the backpack. Some parishioner must have put it here, probably forgot it. Romeo, I have to leave you soon, the service is beginning—"

Romeo pulled the backpack toward him and opened it.

Both the boy and the priest stared down at it in horror.

5

Father Joseph Reilly had been a medic in the first Gulf War, gone through two tours of duty before all the death and savagery he'd seen there had turned him back to his true calling. He knew instantly what he was looking at in that backpack, grabbed Romeo, dashed out of the closet, and yelled to the Secret Service agent who stood by the huge bronze doors. "Bomb, I've found a bomb with a timer, to go off in twelve minutes!"

The Secret Service agent verified it was a bomb, then went into action. Vice President Foley reeled with the information, then got himself together. Before his Secret Service agents could hustle him out, he dashed to the ambo with its microphone and spoke out loud and clear to the eight hundred people who stared around, alarm on their faces. In a deep, calm voice, he told them to evacuate the cathedral immediately and get as far away as possible.

There was no stampede, only a sense of

urgency, as lines formed and moved quickly at each of the exits. Foley thought he smelled fear in the air.

People poured out through the huge bronze doors onto Fifth Avenue and out the back of the cathedral onto Madison Avenue. Police cruisers began to block off a two-block perimeter because there was no time to erect physical barriers. Police officers yelled and waved scores of shoppers, pedestrians, and onlookers away from the cathedral as mourners poured out the doors to join them. Still, it would take time to move the hundreds of bodies to safety, too much time.

None knew this better than Vice President Foley. He'd insisted his Secret Service agents bring Mrs. Greiman with them, so an agent had simply picked up the old lady in his arms and carried her. Foley was now standing with her across Fifth Avenue at Rockefeller Center, surrounded by agents and three NYPD cops, well away from the cathedral.

Foley prayed no one would be killed, prayed the bomb squad would get here in time to defuse the bomb before it caused massive destruction to one of the most revered religious landmarks in the world. Where was the bomb squad? New York City had the fastest bomb squad response time in the nation. Where were they? And shouldn't there be more cops? Soon now it would be too late, and all the beautiful stained-glass windows inside St. Pat's would be shattered, its incredible art destroyed. It seemed to Foley that everyone around him was thinking the same thing. An eerie silence fell as they stood and waited, Foley praying as hard as he had when he'd heard his son had been in an auto accident three months before. They all stared at St. Pat's, at the final lines of mourners racing to safety. Was everyone out now? He stood stiff beside Mrs. Greiman, holding one of her gloved hands while her daughter held the other; she didn't quite understand what was going on.

Foley couldn't believe what he was seeing. He stared, appalled to see Cardinal Dolan, Monsignor Ritchie, priests, and deacons wheeling out Senator Greiman's coffin. Some of them carried objects from the altar, a monstrance and the tabernacle holding the Eucharist. The cardinal walked calmly alongside the gurney, helped lift it down the steps and into the street, pushing it faster now, to safety, the senator's grandson and the police joining them. Foley had the insane urge to laugh. He knew how much Card would have enjoyed all that attention. He didn't know it, but in his death, Card had become a symbol. Perhaps they were all symbols, and symbols counted.

Where was the bomb squad? Not that it mattered, because there was no time left, Foley thought, no more time.

Father Joseph knew time was fast running out. He'd heard a Secret Service agent tell another that the New York bomb squad and upward of one hundred cops were at JFK because of a terrorist incident, and they weren't going to make it back in time. A second bomb squad wasn't going to make it, either. Was there enough explosive to gut the cathedral? Bring down the scores of concrete pillars?

Father Joseph and everyone else were wondering the same thing, but he knew the cathedral better than they did. He imagined the terrorist bomb tearing through the

sanctuary and the Baptistry, and all the
chapels that would be destroyed. At least
there would be no loss of life in God's house
today.

Father Joseph slipped across the street
and inside a doorway. He looked beyond
the Altar of Saint Elizabeth to the Lady
Chapel, and he knew he wasn't going to
let this happen. He couldn't. He ignored
the two cops who were yelling at him
from the street to move back out of the
cathedral, and he ran toward the closet. He
grabbed the backpack and ran, flinging
open one of the side front doors onto Fifth
Avenue. As he ran out, a cop yelled at him
but didn't try to stop him. He started running
beside him.

Oddly, only the senator's big black hearse
remained at the curb; everything and everyone else were well away. **Thank you, God.**
There was a blur of sounds around him,
thousands of horns blaring from distant
drivers who had no clue what was happening, people shouting, police yelling at
him, screaming at him to drop the damned
backpack and run, but he didn't. He hurled
the backpack as far as he could onto

Fifth Avenue.

The bomb exploded in midair just beyond the hearse, the concussion from the blast so powerful it hurled Father Joseph and the policeman next to him back toward the bronze cathedral doors. Even as he struck his head, Father Joseph saw one of the hearse doors fly through the air and land against the sidewalk, not a dozen feet away. The force of the explosion was so tremendous that shards of metal—were they nails? Bolts?—were spewed high into the air and were still falling on the street and on the police cruisers, some of them landing in the crowds behind them. There were shouts of surprise, of pain, people scrambling to move farther away. He looked down at himself and over at the policeman next to him to see how badly he was injured. The police officer was propped up on his elbows beside him, shaking his head, staring at the mayhem around them, and then their eyes met. "Are you all right, Father?"

Father Joseph nodded even though he knew shards of metal had torn through his cassock and into his body, but it didn't matter. They'd both survived. "And you?"

"Yes. You've a brave man, Father."

"So are you." They smiled at each other. Father Joseph saw the cop was an older man, maybe close to fifty, his face scored with years of life. He took one of the officer's hands in his. Together they watched.

Foley heard ambulances, sirens blaring, saw scores of paramedics making their way through the crowds, saw several of them on their knees beside Father Joseph and the cop who'd come running out of the cathedral with him. He saw a young altar boy in his white cape run to Father Joseph and fall to his knees beside him. He saw the priest speak to the boy, take his hands, squeeze them, saw the boy's lips moving in frantic prayer. The agent beside Foley told him it was the young altar boy Romeo Rodriguez who'd alerted them to the bomb. He saw the paramedics didn't try to send the boy away.

The cathedral hadn't suffered much damage at all, from what Foley saw, just some chips of concrete gouged from the huge front pillars. It was less important than the lives saved, but a huge relief nonetheless. The hundreds of millions of dollars spent on the restoration of one of New York's greatest icons hadn't been wasted. Father Joseph Reilly had saved St. Pat's and the little boy had saved eight hundred people, himself included. Foley would be sure the President thanked both of them personally. He called the President to update him as he was hustled to a limousine on Sixth Avenue.

Time passed, only slowly now that the danger was over, and Foley thought, wasn't that odd?

Kelly Giusti pushed her way through the crowd. Only forty-three minutes had passed since the terrorist attack at JFK and now the bomb at St. Pat's. She knew from the information that had come through her earbud so far, there had been injuries, but nothing fatal. Giusti wondered if there was such a thing as a miracle. Then she felt a wash of rage so great she couldn't catch her breath. So many people could have been killed, the incredible interior of the cathedral damaged, and dozens more killed at JFK. Giusti wasn't Catholic, but that didn't matter. She raised her eyes heavenward and thanked God for Father Joseph Reilly and Romeo Rodriguez and the FBI agent at JFK. She had Nasim Arak Conklin under wraps. She was going to wring him out. He had to know about both attacks; they were two halves of the whole. He had to know who had planned them.

6

Rayburn House Office Building
Washington, D.C.
Wednesday, earlier in the day

Outside the third-floor office of Virginia congressman Burt Hildegard, George "Sparky" Carroll, a handsome young man dressed in his best suit, white shirt, and red tie, was wearing a face-splitting smile so wide his molars were on display. He was so pleased, he looked ready to dance, not that anyone would notice. The endless long hall before him seemed to go on forever, and was jammed with staffers, lobbyists, secretaries, visitors, and committee members pouring in and out of doors to add to the traffic, everyone on a mission. **Mission.** He liked the sound of that. **Mr. George Carroll to Houston, I've completed my mission, ready for liftoff.**

Sparky jostled against two big men who looked like bodyguards, hastily begged their pardon, and allowed himself a single small skip. But he could whistle, and as he wove his way through scores of people back down that endless institutional hallway toward an exit somewhere and a grumpy security guard, he did whistle, nice and loud, an old tune he knew, "I've Got the World on a String."

No one paid him any mind. Everyone was hurrying somewhere, jostling one another, carried along by the sound of low conversations.

Thanks to Sparky's intense study of his granny's prized copy of **The Power of Positive Thinking**, he'd pumped himself up, made his presentation, and, glory be, Congressman Hildegard had signed on the dotted line. A contract for two years to cater all the congressman's home district functions, a minimum of three dozen. He could hear his granddad's old cash register cha-ching in his head.

Best of all, was he ever going to get laid tonight. He knew Tammy was probably carrying around her cell, waiting for his call. He'd buy her flowers, maybe lift a bottle of champagne from the storage room. Tammy had always believed in him, long before they'd gotten married four months before, a month before he'd inherited his father's catering company, Eat Well and Prosper. He loved the name because his dad had raised him on **Star Trek**. His dad's lasagna, now **his** lasagna, had made Eat Well and Prosper famous. Congressman Hildegard had even mentioned how much he'd loved Milt's lasagna and his signature garlic toast, now Sparky's lasagna and **his** signature garlic toast.

He was still whistling when he reached for his cell phone to call Tammy. He punched in her number, heard the beginning of the first ring, then her excited voice, "Sparky! What happened? Did the congressman sign our contract? Sparky, talk to me, tell me everything."

He was grinning wildly into the cell as her words tumbled over one another, but before he could speak, a man ran right into him, shoving people out of the way, and pressed him back against the wall. Sparky felt a hit of cold as something sharp sank into his chest. It was more odd than painful, the feeling of his flesh splitting open, and then agony ripped through him, unspeakable, and he knew, he **knew**, he was dying. Sparky dropped his cell phone and began to slide down the wall. Vaguely he heard Tammy yelling his name. She sounded scared and he hated that. He heard people screaming around him. Then he didn't hear anything at all.

7

Georgetown
Late Wednesday afternoon

Savich heard about the terrorist incident at JFK a minute after it happened. He was in the Porsche, driving from Langley back to Georgetown after a meeting with some brass who wanted the FBI to pull their butts out of a bind. He liked to be owed favors, particularly by the CIA, and had complied.

He had only a minute to think about calling Sherlock, knowing she could have been in that security line at JFK, when his cell sang out Billy Ray Cyrus's "Achy Breaky Heart."

"She's all right," Ollie Hamish said immediately, his voice hyper-excited, "she's okay, asked me to call you because she had to shut her cell down. Go home and watch the news. You won't believe this, Savich," and Ollie rang off before Savich could ask him what he wouldn't believe.

Savich felt fear for her swallow him. No,

Ollie said she was okay. What had happened? He speed-dialed Sherlock, got voice mail.

He heard about the explosion at St. Patrick's Cathedral as he pulled into his driveway. It was like the newspeople didn't know which one to talk about first, both were so horrific. They had few specifics except that no one, miraculously, had been seriously injured, either at JFK or at St. Patrick's.

When Savich ran through his front door, he heard the TV and slowed. He didn't want Sean to see him scared out of his mind. But Sean wasn't around, only Gabriella, and she was glued to the TV.

She said, never looking away from the screen, "All the news stations are going back and forth with video from both JFK and Saint Pat's. Nearly everyone there took a video with their phone, plus all the security tapes of both attacks. There's even footage shot from Rockefeller Center looking down on Saint Patrick's Cathedral, all the people hurrying out, the priest throwing the bomb, all the mayhem after the bomb exploded." Gabriella looked up, saw he was pale as death. "No, no, Sherlock's okay, Dillon. Don't worry. Sean's playing football with Marty at her house. I didn't want him to get scared watching this." She gave him a manic grin. "Wait till you see her—Sherlock's a hero. They're showing her picture. You won't believe what she did." She flipped the channel and the two of them watched a priest throwing a backpack, saw it explode in midair, saw the priest and a cop hurled back with the power of the blast, and then the station switched over to JFK and he saw a picture of his wife.

He was shaking as he listened, couldn't help it, until his cell phone blasted Billy Ray Cyrus again. It was Sherlock. "Dillon, I'm okay, I promise. I was with the FBI agent when she got a call about a bomb at Saint Pat's and she took off. The airport will reopen, when, I'm not sure, but I'll call you when I'm ready to get on a plane home. I've got to go, Dillon. My cell will be on voice mail. Text me if you need to reach me." And she punched off.

He closed his eyes against the enormity of what could have happened. **She's all**

right. He turned back to the TV when the anchor began talking about her again. He saw her in real time being escorted out of a conference room, walking, talking, unhurt. Dozens of media microphones surrounded her as she walked out of the terminal; they yelled out questions, asking how she felt, what had happened in there, what she'd said to the terrorist, what he'd said to her, although they had to know already, calling her a heroine, but she only shook her head and kept walking. Then she paused, faced all of them, and said, "Everyone did their jobs today and thankfully no one was seriously hurt. That's all I'm free to say now. There's an ongoing investigation, and an FBI spokesperson will answer all your questions when they can."

The media stayed with her, nearly on top of her, shoving their mikes in her face. Three men in dark suits, obviously FBI agents, finally pushed them away and escorted Sherlock to a waiting Crown Vic, past all the media, the cameras, and the gawking passengers who were huddled outside the terminal. Through it all, she stayed expressionless, except when a reporter yelled out if she believed the bomb at St. Patrick's Cathedral was connected to the grenade attack here at JFK. Her face went pale. Her expressive eyes went from stark to emotionless as she closed it down and said nothing, kept moving. As he watched the whole incident at the airport on a cell-phone video a passenger had posted, he felt a gamut of emotions, staring with rage at what he saw happening, to roiling fear when Sherlock engaged the terrorist, and he actually heard what she said to him, then relief so profound he shook with it. And pride, he could have burst with pride. It was over and she'd survived.

He watched the Crown Vic pull away. **Where were they taking her?**

Every TV station was going back and forth from JFK to St. Pat's, newspeople on scene, so excited to be at ground zero, they were nearly stuttering. They had huge news stories to tell right on top of each other. Naturally, they tied the two incidents together—it was a time-honored terrorist strategy, wasn't it? To get the first responders out of the way of the prime target, St. Patrick's Cathedral? If it hadn't been for the bravery of Father Joseph Reilly, a former Gulf War vet turned priest— and on and on it went. He saw Romeo Rodriguez, the altar boy who'd found the bomb in barely enough time, a thin, white-faced little boy, maybe three, four years older than Sean, and cameras showed him close up beside the priest, his small hands clasping the priest's.

Homeland Security put every airport in the nation on high alert. But how would they protect the large historic cathedrals? There were so many to choose from, if a terrorist was bent on destroying prime symbols of Western culture and civilization. Savich took calls from Director Comey; his own boss, ADA Jimmy Maitland; and every member of the CAU; Sherlock's parents in San Francisco; a few FBI agents in New York, Nicholas Drummond among them; and the chief of security operations at JFK, Guy Alport. Savich had watched him being shotgunned with questions until he'd looked ready to bolt or shoot them all. Alport called to tell him Sherlock was scary good, that Savich was a lucky man to have that woman. He said he wanted to meet her husband, the guy she called a Big Dog. He laughed, then sobered immediately. "That priest at Saint Pat's, I'd sure like to hire him, but God beat me to it."

Finally, Savich set his cell to vibrate, put the landline on automatic message, and fetched Sean from next door.

When he finally heard from Sherlock at eleven o'clock that night that she was on her way home—hallelujah—he left Gabriella to watch Sean and left for Reagan National Airport, surprised her flight was only three hours late. At last he saw her walk past the luggage carousels, a bulging black FBI briefcase in one hand, a small black hand-bag in the other. Even from a distance he could see she was exhausted, running on fumes, but when she saw him, her face lit up. A few people recognized her, but she didn't acknowledge them, kept her eyes straight ahead, never looking away from his face.

When Savich finally got her into the Porsche, guarded by airport security in a no-parking zone, he revved the sweet engine and pulled away from the curb, relieved to see no reporters. He said nothing until he could exit the airport. He pulled her against him, held her tightly until she reared back in his arms. "I'm okay, you can see I'm okay. Do you know what, Dillon? They gave me a first-class seat on the flight home and three bottles of champagne. The flight attendants wrapped them in napkins so they wouldn't break and I stuffed them in my briefcase. Do you know some people even asked for my autograph on the plane?"

He laughed, told her she should take a bath in all that champagne.

On the way home he told her about the calls from President Gilbert and Vice President Foley, and perhaps most important, the call from the CEO of Virgin America, offering Sherlock free lifetime first-class tickets to wherever she wanted to go. He wondered if the Pope would invite Romeo Rodriguez to the Vatican for a private reception, Father Joseph to accompany him, once he recovered from his injuries.

He saw she was still wound tight, knew it would be good to get her mind off New York, and so he told her about the bizarre murder at the Rayburn House Office Building earlier that day. The victim was a young man who'd been stabbed through the heart with an Athame—pronounce that a-tha-may, he'd been told—a ritual knife used in witches' ceremonies, quickly identified by the medical examiner as it had been conveniently left stuck in the victim's chest, complete with his killer's fingerprints. As for the man who'd stabbed him, he'd been brought down immediately by several people in the hallway and held for the police. Savich's boss, Jimmy Maitland, had called Savich because the murderer claimed to have no memory of what had happened and because the ME said he'd never before seen an Athame used as a murder weapon.

"Mr. Maitland said I shouldn't be surprised he called me. I interviewed the guy, name's Walter Givens, an auto mechanic from Plackett, Virginia. He's unmarried, but has a serious girlfriend, likes beer and hanging out with his friends. He was terrified, no faking that, and he has absolutely no memory of killing anyone. He said he finally came to when a half-dozen people slammed him down on the floor. The young man he killed was George Carroll, the owner of a catering company called Eat Well and Prosper in Plackett, Virginia. He said he'd known Sparky—that was George Carroll's nickname—since they were kids and his family had moved to Plackett. He liked him, sure, he liked him, everybody did, and he was a real good cook, especially for a guy. When I showed him the Athame, he claimed he'd never seen it before in his life. It looked weird to him, with those ugly dragon heads on the handle. He didn't want to touch it. I'll show you a photo—it's called a Dual Dragon Athame, seven-inch blade, carved dragon heads with red ruby eyes."

"Did this Walter Givens really not remember? You're sure about that?"

"Yes, I'm positive. Frankly, he isn't smart enough to fool anyone. Dr. Hicks agreed. He believes someone was strong enough to hypnotize him into committing murder, something Dr. Hicks had a difficult time believing. He wanted to hypnotize Walter, but Walter refused, he was too scared to let someone else fool with his brain." He paused for a moment. "Actually, I don't think I've ever seen anyone as scared as Walter Givens was."

"Can't say I blame Walter, not after what happened to him."

"But we have to know how it all came about. Maybe we can talk Walter into the hypnotism tomorrow. Do you know Dr. Hicks patted my hand, told me to figure out how to convince him?"

"Both the victim and the murderer are from the same town? Plackett, Virginia?"

"Yes. Plackett's a small town about thirty minutes northeast of Richmond, two thousand souls or thereabouts." He paused for a moment. "Both the murdered man, Sparky Carroll, and Walter Givens, his murderer, from the same town—it's got to all tie in with this ritual witch's knife, this Athame."

"So we have a pissed-off witch on our hands and Sparky Carroll somehow got on his bad side?"

"Sounds like it."

"I saw an Athame once," Sherlock said, her voice slurring, she was so tired. "I think it was medieval. It was pretty."

Pretty? That brutal knife with its ruby dragon eyes staring out had looked alien to him, and malevolent.

Savich pulled the Porsche into the garage, turned in his seat, cupped her beloved face between his hands, leaned forward, and touched his nose to hers. "You scared the crap out of me. I love you." He kissed her, and took her whispered "I love you, too, and I'm so happy to be here saying that to you," and when her eyes closed, her mouth still smiling, he finally let go of his fear.

Savich lay on his back, staring at the dark ceiling, Sherlock's head on his shoulder. She was boneless, and slightly drunk, with half a bottle of champagne in her bloodstream. Savich wished he'd drunk more champagne, maybe he'd be snoozing, too, but no, his brain was stone-cold sober.

Bless her heart, she hadn't had time to think about consequences, but Director Comey had. He'd assigned an assistant to handle all the media requests that would be flooding in to the Bureau. He'd also sent two agents to keep the media vans away from the Savich front yard and driveway. He'd laughed, suggested Savich and Sherlock might consider visiting Canada for a while, maybe take Romeo Rodriguez and Father Joseph with them.

Maybe Banff, Savich thought, his exhausted brain finally beginning to fuzz over; he'd like to visit Banff in western Canada. Maybe swim with Sean in Lake Louise. Need a wet suit for that. Did they make wet suits small enough for Sean? Sure, they did.

Savich's last thought before he fell asleep was how it had been possible for some-one to invade Walter Givens's mind, convince him to murder Sparky Carroll, and then make him forget all of it. And why murder him in the middle of the hallway of the third floor of the Rayburn House Office Building with a witch's ceremonial knife?

8

Reineke Post Office
Reineke, Virginia
Thursday, 5:15 a.m.

Ellie Moran was a twenty-five-year veteran
of the Reineke post office, a woman as
stalwart and plain as the boxy red-brick
building she worked in. It sat proudly in the
middle of High Street, sandwiched between
the sheriff's office and Donut Heaven.

Ellie knew everyone in town, and most
of their secrets. She liked to think of herself
as the hub of the Reineke gossip wheel.
She might not be the postmaster, but she
made the place run, and when the new
postmaster showed in town the year
before, he figured out what was good for
him fast enough and fell into line.

She'd learned nearly every job and did
each well, but her favorite was greeting
the first early truck from the distribution
center in Richmond that delivered the big
rolling metal OTR package containers. She

liked the predawn, enjoyed watching the sky get lighter and lighter as she wheeled the OTRs in from the dock inside the post office and unloaded them into the route hampers. She knew all the contract drivers from the private service the post office used, knew the sound each of their big trucks made as they backed up to the dock to unload the five to ten big OTRs that held up to fifty parcels each. Brakey Alcott was driving the truck this morning. He was young enough to be her son, always sucking down coffee like young people did to stay awake so early in the morning. Usually they joked back and forth as he pushed off the OTRs onto the loading dock, and he usually gave her a wave and called her beautiful as he headed back out again. But there were no jokes today. He was quiet, sort of nervous, and couldn't wait to wheel the OTRs onto the loading dock and get away. She tried a joke, one of her best ones about the foul-mouthed parrot and the freezer, but Brakey didn't even seem to hear her. **Girl trouble,** she thought; she'd bet her new Skechers it was girl trouble.

She wheeled in the first OTR, released and lowered the side of the cage, and began unloading the parcels, tossing each one into its proper route hamper, never getting it wrong. She'd been scheme-trained years before and that meant learning every street, every address, every route. She'd never been tested, but she thought she probably knew every resident's name, except the new ones. When she finished she'd head for the employee lounge with its brand-new Keurig K-Cup machine for a cup of tea. She'd be alone, it was even too early for Eddie Hoop, the mail sorter, to show up and brag about the American postal system, the best in the world, blah, blah, blah, a tune he never tired of singing.

She hummed Justin Bieber's "As Long as You Love Me" as she worked, her movements smooth and fast. She wheeled in the sixth and last OTR, this one filled to the top. She carefully lowered the side so the packages wouldn't go flying off to the concrete floor. She lifted out a long, narrow package, read the address, and tossed it into route hamper eight. She paused to look at a small parcel addressed to Mrs.

Lori Bamburger. From Victoria's Secret, another pair of black lace undies that would be returned. Lori always ordered them two sizes too small.

What was that black stain nearly covering the address? She touched it—dry and smooth. Had a clerk at the distribution center spilled something on it? It was still legible, so she tossed it into the hamper and lifted out the next package. There were more black stains, drips and smears and smudges. She frowned. What was this stuff? She lifted out the next parcel.

And screamed.

9

Savich House
Thursday morning

When Savich's cell blasted out Billy Ray, he'd been dreaming, not about Sherlock and the madman at JFK, but about walking through a stark white room whose walls were covered with mounted Athames, all their blades dripping blood, hundreds of them, some handles old and elaborately carved, others simple black-painted wood. The problem was he couldn't find his way out.

Special Agent Jeremy Haimes, the SAC of the Richmond Field Office, was on the line to tell him about a murder in the Reineke post office. "The man yesterday, Savich, the one who was murdered in the Rayburn Office Building—I've got another dead man and he's from the same town—Plackett—and he was also stabbed with some kind of ceremonial knife. That's why I called you."

"Jeremy, you said the body is in a post office in Reineke? How far is that from Plackett, Virginia?"

"About twenty miles southwest of Plackett."

"Do you have an ID?"

"Yes, and this is tough. He was a cop. His name was Kane Lewis, an older guy, a paunchy grandfather, well liked. He was the sheriff's only deputy, had been for eighteen years. That's all I know so far. Everyone's really shaken, as you can imagine. Can you come, Savich?"

When he, Sherlock, and Sean came downstairs half an hour later, it was to shouts from the front yard, where a half-dozen reporters were barely held in check by three FBI agents. A paparazzo had gotten close enough to snap a shot of Sean in his Transformers pajamas, staring at them out the window, a good catch. Most everyone remembered he was the kid whose video had gone viral at the San Francisco Symphony Christmas show. Savich scooped Sean up, pulled the curtains tight across the window, and took him into the kitchen as Gabriella was coming in through the back door with an FBI escort.

Forty-five minutes later Savich and Sherlock were driving to the Reineke post office.

Savich stood over the metal parcel cage he'd been told was called an OTR, looked at the boxes scattered around it on the floor, streaked and smudged with blood like abstract paintings. Only the packages beneath the body had kept the blood from dripping out of the OTR. He looked down to see the body of an older man with a circle of gray hair around his head. He was torqued into a tight fetal position —difficult because he was heavy—his arms pulled between his legs. No deputy's uniform. He wore a long-sleeved flannel shirt, old jeans, and ancient brown boots. Impossible to tell what sort of man he'd been—if he'd enjoyed jokes, if he'd loved his family, if he'd been honorable—that was all wiped away, gone in an instant, when the Athame was stuck into his heart. There had to be people out there already worrying about Kane Lewis, wondering where he was. They'd find out soon enough. Savich imagined he'd been a pleasant-looking man, but not in death. No, not in death.

Savich touched his fingers to Lewis's neck, his cheek. He'd been dead when he was dumped into the OTR, but for how long? Maybe two, three hours? More? He looked at the long knife sticking out of his chest. Jeremy Haimes was right. It had something of the look of the ceremonial knife in Sparky Carroll's chest, but was much plainer. Its ebony wooden handle was carved with two sickle moons, no outfacing dragons with ruby eyes. He'd seen Athames like it in that long white room in his dream the night before.

Agent Jeremy Haimes introduced them to the manager of postal operations and a postal inspector both hovering on the periphery. Both were older, shaken up and trying to hold it together, and of no help.

Several people who saw Sherlock did a double take, then were all over her with compliments and endless questions. She was polite but learned quickly to shut them off by saying only, "Yes, thank you. Now we have Deputy Lewis to attend to."

Savich and Sherlock heard the James Bond theme "Nobody Does It Better," and turned to see the postmaster, Mr. Mantano, turn away to answer his cell. When Mantano hung up, he walked back to them, careful not to get too close to the OTR, cordoned off by yellow crime scene tape, newly arrived forensic techs working around it. "As I told Agent Haimes, Ellie Moran, the employee who found the body, called me right away. I came down, verified that a dead man was in an OTR, called my boss in Richmond. She called the postal inspector, who called the FBI in Richmond. Everyone was here by six-thirty. I've kept all our employees away from that OTR—"

Sherlock asked, "What's OTR mean, Mr. Mantano?"

He blinked at her, shook his head. "I've been with the post office for fourteen years and I don't know." He called out to another employee, then another. No one seemed to know. "It's been in the PO lingo so long no one remembers, sorry."

The manager of postal operations said he thought it meant "over the road," as in transport. There was nervous laughter.

Dr. Krowder, the Richmond ME, with three assistants in his wake, shook hands with Haimes, Savich, and Sherlock, told Sherlock she was a pistol and wanted her autograph, then bent down to examine the body. "I sure don't like seeing this after a lovely breakfast of scrambled eggs," he said over his shoulder. "This is nasty, Agents. This knife—I've never seen one like this before."

"I saw one similar to it yesterday. It's called an Athame," Savich said. "It's a ritual knife used in witches' ceremonies."

"I don't imagine you see that every day. You're here from Washington, Agent Savich, so I presume you know something about this knife?"

"Yes."

"Do you know what's going on here?"

"Not yet."

"Wait, that murder yesterday in Washington. The news said something about a ceremonial knife used to kill a man. Was it like this one?"

Savich nodded.

The sheriff was a tough-looking old buzzard and he looked angry. He said, "I've known Kane Lewis for thirty years, met him after I first became sheriff back in the eighties. Tough as nails and everybody knew it, but folks in Plackett liked him better than the sheriff. Lucky for the sheriff, Kane didn't want to run against his boss, always saying life was too good for him to screw up his karma. He had a half-dozen grandkids." He smacked his fist into his palm. "I hope you have some ideas on what kind of monster would do this."

"Not yet, Sheriff."

Dr. Krowder straightened and stepped aside for a tech to snap photos of Kane Lewis.

"I'd say he's been dead about six hours. Looks obvious what killed him, but I'll let you know anything else I discover during autopsy. Sheriff, I'm real sorry about the deputy. I guess you're going to be the one to speak to his family?"

"Yeah, me and Sheriff Watson of Plackett, that'd be the right way to do it. A case of the devil you know—Kane's murder is going to shake up Watson, even though he was jealous of him, hated it that every-one liked him better and respected him more. You know someone as long as he knew Kane Lewis, it burns a hole, you know? Oh, yeah, Sheriff Watson was also Kane Lewis's brother-in-law; Kane was married to his sister, Glory. What a mess." He shook their hands and walked away, muttering to himself. He turned back to Savich. "This is the second victim murdered with a ridiculous witch's knife. What's going on here, Agents?"

"We'll find out," Savich said.

Watson, Sherlock, and Haimes watched the techs wheel out the big OTR. Savich didn't think it would fit into the ME's van and wondered how they'd get it to the morgue.

Sherlock said, "Dane and Griffin are going to the trucking company that's under contract by the post office, to interview Brakey Alcott, the driver who delivered the OTRs early this morning." Sherlock pulled out her tablet. "Brakey's real name is Joseph. Says here on his Facebook page that he ended up with the Brakey nickname after he stopped his dad's pickup too fast at age sixteen and sent his dad through the windshield, broke his dad's neck, but thankfully he pulled through.

Brakey's twenty-four years old, fairly new to the job, but reliable and well liked. The truck company can trace his movements."

It didn't matter that she'd been involved in a terrorist attack only hours before, Sherlock knew how to focus. She knew what to find out and she did it fast. Savich said, "Time is the key here—the killer stabbed Deputy Lewis, then he had to get his body into the truck, bury the body in an OTR and cover it with parcels, relock the truck and skedaddle before Brakey Alcott arrives. All this with no one noticing. So had he planned all along to use Brakey's truck? The killer took a really big risk, and for what? Our finding the body looks more like a blunder to me, by somebody on the inside."

Sherlock said, "Ellie Moran said Brakey Alcott seemed off this morning, and her eyes implied more than that, right, Jeremy?"

"Maybe, but please remember she's got a reputation for gossip, I hear, likes a good story. Count on Deputy Lewis's murder being all over Reineke by ten A.M. and all over Plackett by noon."

Savich and Sherlock left Special Agent

Jeremy Haimes and walked back to the parking lot behind the post office. Savich said as he opened the Porsche's passenger door for Sherlock, "Why set up this elaborate, bizarre way to get rid of the body? Why go to the trouble of burying him under parcels bound for the Reineke post office? It's complicated, obviously requires intimate knowledge of the postal operation. And it puts Brakey Alcott right in the center of the spotlight. If the murderer could have forced Brakey Alcott to stab Deputy Lewis in front of half the town and then forget all about it—as Walter Givens did yesterday in the Rayburn building—why not deliver Brakey up to the world, too?"

Sherlock said, "Let's stop and talk about it at that café I saw on Jackson Street. We can have some tea. Truth is, I'm still a little wrung out from yesterday, and a short rest would be nice."

Forty-five minutes later, Savich was drinking the last of his tea when Special Agent Griffin Hammersmith called. "Brakey Alcott, the driver, always stops six miles out of Richmond at a small diner off the highway called Milt's. He's in there when it opens, stays for ten minutes, drinks two black coffees, eats one bear claw, chats up the waitress. He goes back for lunch on most days. He's nearly got her ready to go to the movies with him.

"The truck is locked at the distribution center after they fill it up with parcels, and it stays locked until he unlocks it to deliver the OTRs to the Reineke post office, his first stop of the day.

"I checked the lock—not tampered with, which means our killer had a key to the truck. So how'd he get it? The private con-tractor the Richmond distribution center uses is the Paltrow Trucking company. The drivers are hired by the trucking company, but the trucks themselves are left at the distribution center, except when they need servicing.

"The truck keys are left on a board inside the truck bay. The OTRs are loaded up early in the morning, between three and four A.M. Then the drivers simply pick up their keys on the way out. It's a close-knit group, so making a copy of the truck key would be difficult unless everyone knew you, so I'm thinking one of the drivers or an employee."

Savich said, "So no report of any strangers around within the past week?"

"No. In fact..."

Savich smiled into his cell. "Spit it out, Griffin."

"It seems to me the killer has to be connected to the post office or to the trucking company. No one else would know their operations well enough, know the schedule and all that. So I'm thinking Brakey Alcott, for whatever reason, has got to be connected, maybe even be the killer, otherwise the whole operation has too many unknowns. If Brakey doesn't pan out, I'll move on to the other employees at the distribution center and the post office, but I'll tell you, Savich, it feels like he's at center court."

Savich said, "But unlike Walter Givens, who killed Sparky Carroll in front of fifty witnesses, this murder was an attempt to hide the killer's identity. When you find Brakey Alcott, Griffin, see if he, like Givens, has no idea that he even could have committed the murder. Keep it low-key,

Griffin—you need his help, that sort of approach, very nonthreatening. If you think he's another dupe like Givens, you need to keep him close, so take him back to the Hoover Building.

"Keep in touch. Sherlock and I are going to interview George 'Sparky' Carroll's wife. Then we'll head back to Washington, see what Brakey Alcott has to say."

"We'd never be thinking about it like this except for the Athame murder weapon."

He was right, and Savich wondered who had such power to make two men kill and not remember doing it.

10

26 Federal Plaza
New York City
Thursday morning

Special Agent in Charge Milo Zachery faced the roomful of agents from an alphabet soup of agencies—FBI, Homeland Security, JFK security, NYPD, NSA, ATF. There was relentless pressure from every level—his bosses, national leaders, the press—but the urgency each of them felt came from knowing there could be other attacks, and soon. The president had spoken to the nation two hours after the attacks yesterday, and the vice president, obviously still shaken, spoke eloquently of what it was like to be at ground zero.

Zachery told them to ignore all that, to make their own part in the investigation their entire focus until it was over. "Our nation is at risk, and we're all on edge, at our airports and public spaces, and even in our own churches—and it will go on until we get it cleared up." Zachery remembered 9/11, the shock, the outrage, the misdirected anger at anyone who looked Middle Eastern. This time there had been no deaths; this time both attacks had failed spectacularly. "We won this round, so maybe that's why the usual groups aren't lining up to take credit, but the threat remains real, people. It's up to us to close this down. I know you're sleep deprived already, I'm on hyperdrive myself from all the coffee flowing through my veins." He paused. "Maybe that's as it should be." Zachery introduced some of the key people around the table, and turned things over to Kelly.

Special Agent Kelly Giusti stepped to the head of the long conference table, loaded with open laptops, tablets, notebooks, coffee cups, soda cans, and trays of Danishes, now mostly crumbs. At least she didn't feel like roadkill after a long hot shower on the sixteenth floor, but she felt fatigue nibbling at her again. She took another sip of coffee so strong she could taste it on her teeth. She felt her brain snap to and looked quickly around the table at the twenty-plus agents watching her. Many of them looked to be in the same shape she was, but it didn't matter, they were focused and ready, running on adrenaline and anger at what the terrorists had tried to do at JFK and St. Patrick's Cathedral.

She clicked on the big wall screen to show them a dozen different photos of Nasim Conklin. "Your packets have all the information we have so far on Nasim Conklin—his background, his family. Let me say up front that he doesn't fit any known profile of a terrorist. He's a thirty-six-year-old dual French and British citizen, Syrian mother, British father. He recently relocated to London from Rouen, France, following the death of his father in London. His family is wealthy, his father the owner of a very successful chain of dry cleaners in England that Nasim is in the process of selling.

"Conklin lives in a nice area, Notting Hill, in London. He has a wife and three children under the age of eight. He has a website as a freelance journalist and he's written articles about the European economy that have appeared in **Le Monde**. He's also a member of a think tank that consults with the French government on Middle Eastern issues. We don't know much yet about the specifics of this.

"So the question is why did a man like Nasim pull a grenade out of his pocket in the security line at JFK yesterday? Nasim and his mother are both Muslim, but Nasim has given every indication of being westernized. He's married to a French Catholic woman. Nasim's mother, though, worships regularly at the South London Mosque, a mosque that has been under MI5 surveillance for over a year. Their theory is that Nasim stuck his toe in the water there. If so, that's where he could have come into contact with the people who set him up to be the goat in the JFK operation. MI5 suspects this mosque is a recruiting and fund-raising center for jihadists. It's run by Imam Al-Hädi ibn Mīrzā, a charismatic fifty-eight-year-old firebrand fundamentalist. They say he could talk a lizard off a rock, he's that persuasive. They suspect he skims off the top of the donations that pour in and takes in a good deal of unreported cash. You'll see in the profile that he's arrogantly outspoken and believes he's above British law. As of now, despite their suspicions, the Brits don't have enough proof to arrest him."

Kelly nodded to Agent Gray Wharton, a longtime agent, computer genius, and friend. He badly needed a shave, as did most male agents in the conference room, and a change of clothes.

Gray cleared his throat. "MI5 should be able to ID Nasim on their surveillance video if he was ever at the mosque.

"So here's what we know. Nasim Conklin flew into JFK on Monday of this week, cleared customs. We see him pulling his single carry-on outside the terminal. A man we haven't yet identified joined him and escorted him to a large black van. They got in and drove toward the airport exit. They were not spotted on any further webcams or traffic cams, so we haven't been able to track him from there. So we have no idea where he stayed Monday or Tuesday night or who gave him the grenade he used at JFK on Wednesday. He had no cell phone on him, only his passport and two hundred dollars in cash. According to his passport, he left France once in the past three years to attend his father's funeral in London. In other words, no terrorist training camps. We're in the process of getting his cell phone and landline records in London.

"His family flew into the U.S. on Tuesday to Boston's Logan International, cleared customs, and walked out of the terminal, escorted by two unidentified men who were also on the plane. We see them being taken to a black SUV, the license plate muddied so no identification is possible. Both the men were wearing hats and sunglasses, making facial recognition impossible. We found two men on the flight who checked in with forged American passports. The passports are excellent forgeries, but the ID photos were altered. We believe they were the family's handlers.

"As Agent Giusti said, our working theory is that Nasim was indeed the goat. He was forced into the attempted suicide bombing at JFK to keep his family alive, and that his family was being held hostage by the terrorists. They may still be in the Boston area, since that's where they landed. In your packets, you have photos of the Conklin family. Mrs. Conklin doesn't look frightened, so she was probably told she would be joining her husband. She may have had no idea what her husband was being forced to do. It's possible the family is no longer alive, I mean, Nasim did fail in his mission. Kelly?"

Kelly nodded. "We need to verify that Nasim Conklin's only motive was to protect his family. So far we haven't found anything to indicate otherwise. The question then is: Why did they single Nasim out? We need to examine his phone records, talk to his contacts and acquaintances, check his e-mail and Internet activity, his financial history, learn more about his family life and religious beliefs.

"And in the last few days: Where was he staying? Where did he get the grenade? Who did he speak to during the day and a half he was here in New York? What is the significance of the name—Bella—as it isn't his wife's name? Could it be the code name of their operation? Agent Valicky at the NSDA is checking the chatter on that. If we find out where he stayed, we might find his cell phone.

"We need to follow Conklin's path in the past six months, identify who he spoke to, who he met with. And we'll check in to his mother's activities as well. MI5 is all over much of this. Your packets spell out a specific focus for each of you.

"Some of you will be working on the bombing at Saint Patrick's. It's obvious Saint Patrick's was the real target and JFK the diversion. Unfortunately, we have less to go on there. We have feed from three webcams and two traffic cams that show a man we believe to be of Middle Eastern extraction carrying a backpack directly into Saint Patrick's two hours before the bomb was found by Romeo Rodriguez. He's wearing a cap and sunglasses. We haven't identified him yet." She turned on a video feed. "You'll see here we have a small part of his jawline and nose, so there's still a possibility facial recognition will help, if they can match these features to a known terrorist. There's not much point releasing that partial to the public, though.

"We're looking for witnesses who may have seen him before he entered Saint Pat's or when he came out. Also, if the bomber stayed around, there are hundreds of cell-phone videos, plus all the webcam footage we're hoping will identify him.

"We need to know if this plot is the brainchild of Al Qaeda, ISIS, or a smaller radical group. It appears to come out of London, so that's our focus, particularly the South London Mosque and Imam Al-Hädi ibn Mīrzā , until we know for sure otherwise. Agent Drummond"—Kelly nodded to him, and Nicholas gave a little wave—"is our liaison with MI5. He'll be updating your data packs periodically as we learn more about what's going on in London.

"You may have heard a brief discussion about the question of a lawyer for Mr. Conklin. The word has come down. There will be no lawyer for now. We have sole custody. We've decided to take him to a safe house for the benefit of all. The location is classified." She paused, didn't want to admit this, but she had to. **Suck it up, Giusti.** "Here it is. So far Conklin refuses to say anything. He keeps insisting he wants to speak to Agent Sherlock, the FBI agent who brought him down at JFK. However, we will continue working on him. I'm confident we'll get him to open up."

"If he doesn't, will Agent Sherlock be joining the operation?" Nicholas Drummond asked.

How odd it was to hear a British accent coming out of an FBI agent's mouth. Kelly said only, "We'll see."

An agent from Homeland Security said, "We haven't even discussed the possibility that the attack on Saint Patrick's Cathedral could have been an attempt to assassinate the vice president of the United States. There were also a number of high-ranking state and federal politicians and businesspeople there."

SAC Milo Zachery rose. "A good point, Arlo. We have considered this possibility and have assembled a small group of agents to look into this. We want to cover all bases. Now, all of you know what to do. Communicate any questions or suggestions you have directly to Agent Giusti." He looked at each face. "It's feet-to-the-coals time, people. Good luck and thank you."

11

Plackett, Virginia
Thursday morning

On the drive from Richmond to Plackett, Sherlock took a call from the medical examiner who'd just completed the autopsy on Deputy Kane Lewis. Straight up, the knife to the chest had killed him. Also of note: Deputy Lewis had been a longtime drinker, and his cirrhosis was getting serious. He'd had a blood alcohol content of .25, enough to render him nearly unconscious when he'd been stabbed. "I doubt he felt a thing when the knife went in, so that's something. No need to let this get out in town, though. His family doesn't need to know."

Families, particularly the wives, always knew, Sherlock thought. About other women, and certainly about too much booze.

Savich said, "You know Sheriff Watson will find out about Lewis's being drunk. At least he wasn't on the job.

"Sparky Carroll didn't have anything in his system when he was murdered yesterday in the Rayburn Office Building. He had no defensive wounds, either. He knew his attacker, Walter Givens, but there were so many people in the hallway I doubt he saw him until it was too late.

"Burt Hildebrand wasn't a happy camper when Mr. Maitland turned over the Sparky Carroll investigation to us, but what with the Athame being the murder weapon and Walter Givens not remembering anything about it, I suspect he was also a little relieved.

"He took the chaplain with him to break the news to Sparky Carroll's young widow, Tammy, yesterday afternoon. He said it was tough, she was a mess. He couldn't interview her because her mother and her two sisters wouldn't let him. None of the three, however, could believe Walter Givens had done this. They'd known Walter forever, he was a sweetie, the mother's words, he fixed their cars and charged them peanuts.

"I think we'll do better today," Savich continued. "Tammy Carroll's had some time to get herself together, to reflect on what it could mean that Walter Givens killed her husband with a witch's ceremonial knife and has absolutely no memory of it.

"I texted pictures of the Dual Dragon Athame to Professor Hornsby at GW. You know him, he's the theoretical physicist who's also a practicing Wiccan—a Wicca expert, I've been told."

"I met him once. He sort of stared at me, shook his head, didn't say a word. He looks like Ichabod Crane."

Savich laughed, flipped on his blinker, and smoothly passed an eighteen-wheeler. "You probably terrified him. He's not known for his social abilities. In any case, he called me right back, told me the Dual Dragon Athame is unusual. It's not medieval, despite all the ancient-looking elaborate carving on the handle and the dragon heads with the ruby eyes, which, he assured me, were real. He believes it was forged no more than a hundred years ago, probably much less. It's old enough, though, to be part of a generational collection belonging, most likely, to a Wiccan family. He was appalled when I told him it had been stabbed into a man's heart.

"He assured me that for Wiccans the Athame isn't a weapon, isn't even used to cut up herbs. It's only used for ritual purposes. He laughed because he said he was clumsy and told me he made sure his knife blade was dull. He showed me photos of Athames. Most are very plain, black handle, unadorned, many made of stone, the key being to keep the material natural. Most have a four-inch blade. All Athames are straight, double-edged blades. The length of the blade of this Dual Dragon Athame is seven inches.

"Hornsby told me a Wiccan's Athame is his most important tool, that it's tied intimately to its owner's energy."

"What does that mean?" Sherlock asked. "It's all symbolism?"

"This is what I remember his saying. The Athame serves as a conductor of the wielder's energy—that is, it directs his energy outward, like a beam of light. And supposedly controls it. What that means, I'm not sure."

"Did he say any particular Athame was considered more powerful than another?"

"No, they're all individual, they all draw

their power or their energy from their owners."

Savich pulled off I-95 and onto the 123, and turned right at the Plackett exit some ten miles later. Soon they were on the main street of an old country town with a road sign boasting a population of 2,102. Many of the buildings were turn of the last century and looked a little shabby. But there was charm as well, and a central square with a hundred-year-old stone courthouse surrounded by maple trees. A small pond with a dozen ducks sat off to one side.

The home of Sparky Carroll and his wife, Tammy, was in the middle of Pine Nut Street, a solidly middle-class residential neighborhood parallel to Main Street. Oaks and maples had thickened up nicely for late spring, the sky was blue, and a slight breeze stirred their hair as they walked up the flagstone driveway to the ranch-style home. It was perhaps ten years old, and well maintained, the grass freshly mowed, pansies planted in narrow beds in front of the house. Savich was glad to see there were no cars in the driveway. He'd called Mrs. Carroll, asking to speak to her alone.

A perfect pocket Venus answered the door. She was barely five feet tall, curvy, with long straight brown hair and brown eyes red from weeping. She was painfully young. Savich and Sherlock showed her their creds, introduced themselves.

"We are very sorry for your loss, Mrs. Carroll," Savich said. "Thank you for seeing us. We really need your help."

Tammy didn't say anything; it seemed her throat had been clogged with tears since she'd heard all the shouting and screams on her cell when Tommy had called her. She'd known, she'd known something terrible had happened. She turned away on her small feet and showed them into a long, narrow living room with windows across the front, the thick green draperies pulled tightly shut, shadowing the room.

She waved a small white hand. "Please, sit down. May I get you something to drink?"

"No, thank you," Savich said. "We're fine." He walked over to her and gently took her small hands between his. "We will find out why Walter Givens killed Sparky, Mrs. Carroll."

Tammy blinked up at him. "But didn't

Walter tell you why?"

"Walter has absolutely no memory of killing your husband. He has no idea why he even drove to Washington, why he even went to the Rayburn Office Building. When he came to, I guess you could say, he did remember that Sparky had told him he was making his big pitch to a congressman yesterday, but he couldn't explain what he'd done. He was so horrified and scared because his memory of what happened is simply gone. We don't think he's lying. Please, sit down, Mrs. Carroll."

Tammy Carroll slid her tongue over her lips, nodded, and eased down on what was obviously her husband's big TV chair. She scooted to the edge and sat stiff, her back board straight, like a schoolgirl, her hands on the knees of her jeans. "Call me Tammy. I've been thinking and thinking, but still, it doesn't make any sense that anyone would stab Sparky, much less Walter, one of his best friends. And you said Walter doesn't remember? You mean he blocked out what he did because he felt so bad about it after he—" She swallowed.

Savich said, "All we know is that Walter

doesn't remember. Do you know of anything between them, a business dispute, a fight over something, jealousy, anything that might explain Walter stabbing your husband?"

"No, no, nothing." Tears brimmed over, snaked down her face. Sherlock leaned forward, her voice low and soothing. "Mrs. Carroll—Tammy—how long have you known Walter Givens?"

Tammy swallowed her tears, drew herself up. "Walt and Sparky and I grew up together. I met them when I was in the fifth grade and they were in the eighth. Despite the age difference, despite the fact I was a little girl, we all became friends. We were together all through high school. Walt wanted me to go out with him in high school, but Sparky and I were already getting serious. But it didn't matter. It didn't break anything up, we were still friends, you know? That's what doesn't make any sense. Walt is—**was**—one of Sparky's groomsmen at our wedding." She paused, then raised tear-filled eyes to Savich. "That was four months ago. Four months. I'm only twenty and I'm a widow."

She lowered her face in her hands, her shoulders shaking. Sherlock walked to the big chair and sat on the wide leather arm. She pulled Tammy against her, rubbed her hands up and down her back. Tammy's arms came up around Sherlock's back. She pressed her face against Sherlock's chest. "I'm so sorry," Sherlock whispered against Tammy's shiny hair. "So very sorry. We will find out what happened, I promise you. But you need to help us, Tammy. Can you do that?"

Slowly Tammy quieted, finally released Sherlock. She raised her face. "I'm sorry to fall apart again. It's just that—"

"It's okay, don't worry about it." Sherlock patted her arm and walked back to sit down on the brand-new burgundy leather sofa. "Have you ever heard of an Athame?"

"Yes, sure. My mom has two she made herself. She buried the first one she made to ground its energy."

This was a surprise. Savich said, "Your mom's a Wiccan?"

"Yes. Like my grandmother and one of my sisters. My mom's Athame has a plain flint black handle, ugly, really, but she keeps it sparkling clean for all her rituals, won't let anyone else touch it, says she couldn't connect to the spirit of things if she didn't have her Athame. I don't really know how she believes all that stuff, and to be honest, I don't really care."

"What's your mom's name?" Sherlock asked her.

"Millicent, Millie—Stacy, that's my maiden name."

Savich handed her his cell phone. "Do you recognize this Athame?"

She looked at the knife, raised stricken eyes to his face. "This isn't the Athame that killed—"

"No, no, it's one that's similar, that's all."

She shook her head. "The only Athames I've seen are my mom's. This one looks old, really old, doesn't it, back to when knights were riding around and knocking each other off their horses, right? Are those dragon heads?"

"Yes."

Sherlock asked, "Are there many practicing Wiccans in Plackett, Tammy?"

"I've heard my mom say she wishes there were more around here and that many of them go back at least two generations. She said my grandmother raised her in Wicca, told her Mr. Gardner from England taught them everything way back in the fifties. Gwen—she's one of my sisters—well, neither of us ever got interested in any of it, so Mom didn't force it on us. She and my other sister will celebrate Litha—that's the summer solstice—next month. It's a time of great joy for them, it's a popular time for handfasting. That's a Wiccan wedding. I know that because she said she wanted Sparky and me to celebrate a handfasting with them next month, at Litha. Sparky didn't know what to say when she asked, but he agreed.

"My daddy thinks it's all crazy nonsense, so she doesn't push it. He told her he'd join her at Litha if they could have wild sex in front of the fire." Tammy smiled, a ghost of a smile, but still a smile. "She smacked him. For her, Litha is a time of celebration, a spiritual time."

Savich asked her, "Is Walter Givens a Wiccan? His family?"

"Not that I know of. Wiccans don't advertise, you know? That's what my mom told me. Most people around here are like my dad—screwy in the head about Wiccans, my mom says." She made a screwing motion at the side of her head. "So Wiccans tend to keep quiet about their beliefs, and their ceremonies. They don't advertise."

"Can you tell me the names of other practicing Wiccans in town?"

Well, I know the Alcotts for sure. They say they're Wiccans outright. My mom told me in a real hushed voice once that she doesn't have much to do with the Alcotts. She seems a little bit scared of them. I know that sounds weird, but I think it's true. My mom does feel things, know things," Tammy added, a touch of embarrassment in her voice.

"What do you mean, Tammy—what things? Can you give me an example?" Sherlock leaned forward, her eyes on Tammy's face.

"I don't know that much about it, Agent Sherlock. I never paid much attention. I'm sorry."

Savich said, "What about Brakey Alcott? Is he involved?"

"Brakey? Not that I know of. Brakey usually keeps his head down, stays out of trouble. Brakey's a nice guy, a little shy. He wasn't all that good in school, but nice, you know? He's a year older than Sparky." Her voice hitched, her small hands clenched. She raised liquid eyes to Savich's face. "He **was** a year older than Sparky. It doesn't even seem real. Sparky was only twenty-three."

After a couple moments Tammy raised her head again. "Brakey's an Alcott, and he'd know all about the gossip about his family. How could he not? Why are you asking about Brakey?"

"It has to do with Deputy Kane Lewis," Savich said. "Did you or Sparky know him?"

"He's been here forever, even before I was born. I knew him better when we were kids and he was always giving us a hard time if he caught us at Milson's Point over on Route 7." She blushed and swallowed again. "He nearly surprised Sparky and me once. It was close. I don't really like him, but my folks do, all the parents do. Why do you ask?"

As Savich spoke, Sherlock watched

Tammy Carroll closely. "Deputy Lewis was found at the Reineke post office this morning stabbed through the heart with another Athame. Like Sparky. I'm sorry. He's dead."

Tammy Carroll couldn't take it in. She stared at Savich, through him, really, and quietly, without a sound, she slid from the sofa to the floor. She hadn't fainted. She lay curled up on her side, not crying, not making a sound, simply staring ahead of her.

12

Criminal Apprehension Unit
Hoover Building
Washington, D.C.
Thursday, early afternoon

Savich opened the door to the interview room on the third floor of the Hoover Building, down the hall from the Criminal Apprehension Unit, the CAU. Griffin had Brakey Alcott waiting for them there. He'd picked him up chowing a hamburger at Milt's Diner. Griffin told him if Brakey was worried about anything, he didn't show it at the diner. He was chatting up the waitress big-time. But he was scared now.

Savich said, "Mr. Alcott, I'm Agent Savich and this is Agent Sherlock. You've already met Agent Hammersmith." He nodded to Griffin, who sat at the end of the table, leaning back in his chair, his arms crossed over his chest, looking as stern as possible. Sherlock knew that look would never work on a woman. Griffin was too handsome.

Brakey Alcott was slight, and skinny as a parking meter. He had to top out at under one hundred and forty pounds, if that. He had beautiful light green eyes, an artist's hands—slender, with beautifully tapered long fingers. He was wearing a large silver ring on his fourth finger, a dark sapphire sitting high in the middle. Not a sapphire. Closer up, it looked nearly black. He was nervous, sweaty, his elegant hands moving, clasping, unclasping in front of him on the table. Savich and Sherlock sat across from him.

Brakey said in a sweet Virginia drawl that crawled with fear and confusion, "Agent Savich, Agent Hammersmith hasn't told me much of anything. I was eating my hamburger at Milt's when he came up to my table and told me I had to come with him. I'll tell you, people really looked at me weird then. I'd heard about Deputy Lewis getting killed and being found in the Reineke post office, but he told me somebody put his body in an OTR that was on my truck. I swear I didn't have anything to do with that."

Brakey jerked forward in his chair when he realized the three grim-looking federal agents didn't believe him. "Listen, I swear, I don't know anything about poor Deputy Lewis, only what I heard at Milt's. Everybody was talking about his being dead, and looking at me funny. Even Laurie was nervous, brought me my hamburger medium rare instead of my usual well done, but I didn't mind. I knew she was upset about Deputy Lewis, like everybody else. And then this agent came in. Everybody saw him haul me away. It's my hometown." He paused and focused on Sherlock, came out of his chair. "Wait, I know you, ma'am, I saw you on every single TV station yesterday—you took down that terrorist at JFK, kicked him to the ground. You're Agent Sherlock." He beamed at her.

"Thank you, Mr. Alcott, but that was yesterday. Today I want you to tell us about the dead man in your OTR. And please, don't waste our time telling us you have no idea how Deputy Kane Lewis's body got there."

"No, no, honest, I don't know." He nodded again toward Griffin. "I already told him I didn't know he was there. Really, I had no clue. I'm as shocked about it as everyone else. I mean, I've known Deputy Lewis all my life, I always liked him—"

Savich interrupted him, leaned forward, his voice hard. "You're expecting us to believe that? You're telling us the murderer simply happened upon your truck while you were in Milt's Diner having your two cups of coffee and a bear claw this morning? There's no trace anywhere of someone trying to break into your truck, no sign of forced entry on the truck doors, and you've said you never leave it open. And if someone did get in without your knowing about it, they somehow stuffed Deputy Lewis's body into an OTR, even covered the body with parcels, while you were sipping your coffee? You can't be stupid enough to think we don't know it was you who killed him."

Brakey's mouth opened, closed. He whispered, "Somebody did it somehow. I swear I don't know anything about it."

Savich came out of his chair, leaned forward, grabbed Brakey's shirt in his fist. "Since it's obvious you were involved, the real question is, what were you thinking? If you didn't want to get caught, what you did was idiotic. Was it a mistake? Did you panic after you stabbed Deputy Lewis? You stuffed him in the OTR, threw parcels on top of him, and went back to making your daily delivery to Ellie Moran at the Reineke post office? Did you leave that OTR there by accident, or were you too panicked to think straight?"

Brakey looked white as death, horrified, shook his head back and forth. Savich let his shirt go. Brakey leaned back as far as he could in his chair.

Savich slammed down a photo of Deputy Kane Lewis. "Look at him, Brakey. This is what a man looks like after you stab him in the heart."

Brakey Alcott stared down at the photo, gulped once, twice. "He's really dead, Deputy Lewis is dead. I liked him, more than that dickhead Sheriff Watson—" Brakey shot a look toward Sherlock. "I'm sorry, ma'am, but he is one, really, but I shouldn't have said a bad word like that." Brakey looked from one to the other. "You think I did this to Deputy Lewis? No, I'd never do that to anybody."

"If that's true, you've got to help us prove it," Sherlock said. "Where were you last night, Brakey? What did you do?"

Brakey blinked at her. "Last night? I tried to get Laurie from Milt's to go out with me, but that didn't happen, so I went home and watched TV with my mom and grandma. We were watching the news, and that's when I saw you, Agent Sherlock. Jonah, one of my brothers, he came over for a while, brought his kids over like he often does. Both my brothers live on our property, in their own houses across the yard from us.

"After they left, we all went to bed. That's it, I swear it to you. I went to bed and I slept all night, woke up when the alarm went off at a quarter to four this morning."

He was telling the truth. Brakey Alcott wasn't a good enough actor, Savich knew, to be lying. He had no memory of what he'd done. And he couldn't know that Walter Givens, the man who'd stabbed Sparky Carroll in the Rayburn Building corridor, had said the same thing. The press, thankfully, didn't know that yet.

Savich placed photos of the two Athames in front of Brakey. "The one on the left is called a Dual Dragon Athame; the other one was used to stab Deputy Lewis to death. Where did you get that one, Mr. Alcott?"

"I didn't. It's not mine!"

Sherlock sat forward, her voice soft like Glinda the Good Witch's. "But you recognize both Athames, don't you, Brakey? I mean, your family are Wiccans, right? Are these Athames in a collection in your mom's house?"

He shook his head violently. "No, really. I'm not sure. I've seen a lot of them. You should ask my mom, she'll tell you."

And now Brakey was lying. Was he protecting his family? Savich saw he was ready to fold down, from ignorance and fear, and too much knowledge.

Savich rose. "I would appreciate speaking with your mother, in fact. And your dad?"

"My dad died six months ago, in an auto accident on route 123. My mom's still getting over that."

"I'm sorry. That will be all for now, Mr. Alcott. I'll have an agent drive you back to Plackett. I'll be stopping by later this afternoon and talk with your family."

Savich nodded to both Sherlock and Griffin, and out the door they went, leaving Brakey to sit as still as a block of wood.

13

Plackett, Virginia

The newly widowed Mrs. Lewis wasn't alone. As Savich turned off First Avenue onto Briar Lane, they saw cars parked in the driveway, at the curb, across the street, stretching almost a block in both directions. The Lewis house was a simple two-story, maybe fifty years old, with a two-car carport attached. It looked comfortable, like an old armchair that had sat through years of ball games. The house could use a paint job and a lawn mower. Oddly, it didn't seem like neglect, it seemed like a choice that fit the house's and the owners' personalities.

Savich parked the Porsche a block away. As they walked back to the house, he said, "Quite a crowd. That might actually help us get Mrs. Lewis alone."

An older man who answered the door didn't move, gave them a suspicious look. "Who are you?"

Sherlock gave him her sunny, guileless

smile and showed him her creds. "Special Agent Sherlock, and this is my partner Special Agent Savich, FBI." Savich showed the man his creds. "And you are, sir?"

"Sheriff Ezra Watson." He looked over his shoulder at the living room full of people. "I'm showing in people who want to pay their respects. There's no excuse for you people to come here today. Glory—Mrs. Lewis—and the family aren't in any shape for questioning. Why don't you come back, or call my cell later. I can tell you what you need to know."

The sheriff wasn't wearing his uniform. He was in a shiny black suit that looked like it hadn't been worn in a long time and was now a size too small. He was nearly bald, sported a comb-over of light brown hair. His long, seamed face was grim, his mouth tight. It had been a rough day for him, Savich thought. He didn't look like a man pleased with life or his fellow man. Savich stepped into his space and said, his voice pleasant, "I wish we could do that, but we have a job to do, Sheriff. Would you like to introduce us to Mrs. Lewis, or should we go in and introduce ourselves?"

He's measuring me for a coffin, Savich thought. The sheriff stared and stood his ground, barely holding his simmering anger in check. Sure, the sheriff was on edge, his deputy had been murdered that morning, but Savich wondered if the man didn't always act this way.

The tension lifted when a woman in a purple dress with a pleasant, no-nonsense face and hair drawn up in a bun on the top of her head said from behind the sheriff, "Ezra, who is this?"

The sheriff turned slightly. "They're FBI agents. They shouldn't be here. You should be with your family and friends."

"I shall do both. They need to speak to me, I understand that." She stepped around him, dismissing him rather like a dog, Sherlock thought. Mrs. Lewis was in charge, no doubt about that. She stuck out a graceful hand. "I'm Glory Lewis."

They shook her hand, showed her their creds. She was a large woman, but not fat. She looked vital and fit, and quite in control of herself. Sherlock asked, "Is there somewhere we can speak in private, Mrs. Lewis?"

"Certainly. There's no one in the den.

Follow me." Mrs. Lewis led them through a knot of people into an overly warm hallway and living room. Most of the people stopped talking and tracked their progress across the room. She paused in front of two younger women whose eyes were red, grief and shock clear on their faces. They both had the look of their mother, but not her composure. Two men, their husbands, Sherlock thought, stood like guard dogs behind them. Mrs. Lewis paused. "These are my daughters, Angela and Cynthia. Agents Savich and Sherlock. They're here to talk to me about your father."

Angela nodded, then whispered, "You're that FBI agent from JFK."

"Yes, I am," Sherlock said, then, "But that's not important now, is it? We're very sorry for your loss."

Savich saw Mrs. Lewis was tapping her foot, anxious for them to get away from her daughters. He nodded to them, took Sherlock's arm, and followed Mrs. Lewis into a small, old-fashioned den behind the kitchen. Photos lined the fireplace mantel and covered every surface. Sherlock recognized Angela and Cynthia in photos from when they were younger, smiling, happy, with their husbands and kids, and dozens of photos showing them as infants and toddlers and young children.

"Forgive my brother," Mrs. Lewis said. "He tends to use a hammer when a tack would do the job. My husband always knew when to use the tack." She smiled impartially at both of them, pointed to a sofa. "Can I get either of you something to drink?"

"No, thank you, ma'am, we're fine," Sherlock said. "Sheriff Watson is your brother?"

Mrs. Lewis nodded, eased down across from them on a tatty love seat. "Yes, he is. Are you sure neither of you would like anything?"

"No, thank you, ma'am, we're fine," Sherlock said. Was Mrs. Lewis so focused on being a hostess, to occupy her mind with something, anything but what had happened to her husband? Her eyes held only a hint that she'd been crying, but she allowed herself no overt sign of grief. Of course she was much older than Tammy Carroll, experienced in both life and death.

And everyone dealt with grief differently.

"This morning we were told there was no love lost between your brother and your husband," Savich said. "Is this true?"

"As you can tell from all the multitudes out there, Kane was well liked. He kept an eye on those people's kids, especially, kept a tally of who they were and what he caught them doing. He started that up right after he found our youngest—Angela—parking with a local boy." She smiled toward a photo of her dead husband, younger in the photo, smiling really big, wearing his uniform, a gun in its holster. "Kane rarely told on them, but the parents knew he was watching out for them. You've met my brother, all gruff and by-the-book. He's never learned how to get along with people as well as my husband did."

"What did your husband think of him?"

"Kane would come home some days, laughing at Ezra being in one of his moods, Agent Savich. He'd say Ezra must be wearing shorts that were too tight again.

"You have to understand we moved here years ago when Ezra's wife was dying of cancer, back in the eighties. They had no children to support Ezra while he took care of her, and they needed us. After Connie's death, Ezra was never the same, poor man, but still Kane did what he could to humor him. I think Kane felt sorry for him, thought he was doing the best he could. He honestly didn't mind that Ezra was his boss. Kane wasn't usually bothered much about anything, and that's a fact."

But it bothered you, didn't it, Mrs. Lewis? Sherlock thought. **You wish your husband had had more of a backbone, like you do.**

Glory looked vaguely around the room, folded her hands in her lap. "I don't own a black dress. Purple was Kane's favorite color." She gave a little shudder. "He bought this dress for me. That's why I'm wearing it. Tomorrow it will go again to the back of the closet."

"Mrs. Lewis," Sherlock said, leaning toward this composed woman, "are you're saying your husband didn't have any enemies?"

Glory Lewis looked down at her folded hands, then back at Sherlock. "He was a police officer, and that means he had to get involved with angry people, even arrest them sometimes. But he had no enemies I'm aware of. As I said, as everyone in my house will tell you, Kane was a sweetheart, easygoing, always had a ready smile for everyone."

"Mrs. Lewis, are you aware your husband was a heavy drinker?"

"Agent Savich. I assure you, I am neither blind nor stupid. Was he drunk when he was killed?"

14

Yes, he was," Savich said, "very drunk. Do you know where your husband was last night, Mrs. Lewis?"

"He told me he had a Lion's Club meeting, but I knew he was headed for one of the three bars out on I-66." She shook her head. "He always used breath mints before he came back into the house, as if I wouldn't know he was drunk as a skunk. He wasn't a young man anymore, and I worried for his health. But he thought I was nagging him if I said anything to him about it.

"I went to bed last night the same time I usually do. Kane and I had separate bedrooms because of his snoring, so I didn't know he hadn't come home until my brother woke me up early this morning to tell me he was dead." Her voice stayed steady, without a hitch.

"Did your brother know your husband drank?"

Glory Lewis smiled at Savich, a sad,

accepting smile that said it all. "Sure, Ezra knew, not that he would worry about him. Ezra would say Kane is his own man, and if he runs off the road, that's his business. I think he was more worried about what the townspeople would say if that happened. Did Kane's being drunk have anything to do with his death—his murder?"

"We don't know that yet, Mrs. Lewis," Sherlock said. "But I have a question for you. Are you a Wiccan?"

"**What?** What did you say? What sort of question is that, Agent Sherlock?"

"I know it's an unusual question, ma'am, but we need for you to tell us—are you a Wiccan?"

"Wiccan? No. Kane and I have attended the Plackett Bible Church in town every Sunday for almost thirty years."

"Do you know any practicing Wiccans in Plackett?"

"Well, there is a small group in and around Plackett, I've heard. I mean, there are a few of them everywhere nowadays, aren't there? I hope God's grace touches every-one searching for whatever peace they can find in this world, but I'm not the kind to look for it in herbs and chants and symbols. But really, I've never paid them much mind. Now that you mention it, I remember my eldest daughter, Cynthia, was flirting with the idea of becoming a Wiccan when she was about fourteen. Read about it in the library. She was just getting interested in boys then, and I suggested she'd find them more fun than burning candles and drawing circles in the dirt and shivering in the woods. She never raised it again."

"Do you know the Alcotts, Mrs. Lewis?"

She cocked her head at Savich. "Sure I do, Agent Savich. This is a small town. Everyone knows most everyone else. I remember Kane investigated Mr. Alcott's unfortunate death six months ago. It was a hit-and-run."

"What did your husband discover, Mrs. Lewis?"

She cocked her head again, showing only mild interest. "He found some skid marks, nothing they could identify, and that was all. Kane told me it seemed to him the driver who struck Mr. Alcott stopped completely, panicked, and drove away. They never found who it was."

"Then you know Mrs. Alcott," Savich said.

"You're asking me this because you believe Brakey killed my husband." Her voice was flat, matter-of-fact. "No, don't deny it, you have only to step into my living room to know everyone is talking about it. Not in my presence, of course. Did Brakey kill my husband?"

"Your husband was killed with an Athame, Mrs. Lewis," Savich said. "A Wiccan ceremonial knife. You're aware, naturally, that Sparky Carroll was also murdered yesterday in Washington. He was also murdered with an Athame. We're investigating what Brakey Alcott's involvement was now, Mrs. Lewis."

Glory Lewis stared at them. "You're saying that Sparky Carroll and my husband were killed by the same person? But isn't Walter Givens in jail? What is it you're saying, Agent Savich?"

"Again, I'm not at liberty to speak about our investigation yet, Mrs. Lewis. I'd appreciate it if you talk to us about the Alcott family."

"But Walt Givens—he's only a boy, like

Brakey. They're both younger than my daughters. Everyone was so upset about Sparky and Walter Givens, no one understood, and now my husband. They're saying Brakey's had to have done it. Ezra said you'd arrested him. But Brakey's such a nice boy, always has been. He and Kane liked each other, and as far as I know, Walter Givens never had anything against Sparky Carroll. You want to know about the Alcotts because of Brakey?"

"Brakey Alcott is not under arrest. But please tell us what you know, Mrs. Lewis."

"Well, I've known Deliah for as long as Kane and I have lived here, thirty years come the fall. I know they didn't have much money. Then about twenty years ago, they found natural gas on the property, sold off the rights, and they haven't worked in town since. They're quite well off. They stay mostly to themselves, maybe because Deliah doesn't like people talking about them. She's always been pleasant to me, and so have her sons. Well, there is Liggert, her eldest. My husband said Liggert can't hold his liquor, turns into a loudmouth and hits people. He's spent several nights in jail." She paused, smoothed the purple skirt of her dress. "I imagine my husband was at the same bar and had to arrest him."

"Was there ever any trouble between the Alcotts and your husband? Other than with Liggert?" Savich asked. "Or any bad feelings between the Alcotts and Sparky Carroll and his family?"

"Certainly not, that's absurd. My husband was friends with all of them, even Liggert, except on the nights he had to arrest him. As for Sparky Carroll, he was a nice boy, too. He had ambition, wanted to make the catering business his dad started even bigger than it was under Milt Carroll, his father, who was also a good friend of Kane's. Milt started Eat Well and Prosper, they call it"—she rolled her eyes—"back in the eighties." She looked down at her clasped hands again. "I knew Sparky's mom, Rachael. They hardly ever let her cook a meal, she told me, and it bothered her, not being asked to cook for her family. She died two years ago, bless her soul.

"You know as well as I do that every town has its criminals, Agent Savich, its share of greed and violence. That's what

Kane's job was about. But neither of those boys are criminals."

"Do you know who some of your husband's drinking buddies were, Mrs. Lewis?"

"I have no idea, Agent Savich." Her voice was prim, and her chin went up in the air. Savich doubted anyone would be talking much more about Kane Lewis's drinking in the Lewis home.

15

Alcott Compound
Plackett, Virginia
Thursday, late afternoon

Savich and Sherlock stopped for pizza at Country Cousin's in downtown Plackett. Everyone in the eatery was talking about Sparky Carroll and Deputy Kane Lewis. Savich doubted there had ever been a murder within living memory in this small town, let alone two. No one approached them, which was a relief, except the waitress, and it was obvious she was brimming with curiosity, but she held her tongue.

Thirty minutes later they were driving out of Plackett and into rolling hills thick with oak and pine trees. Sherlock opened her tablet. "There are three generations of Alcotts in residence, including grandma, who's eighty-three and wheelchair-bound. She is Deliah Alcott's mother-in-law. Deliah's three sons and their families live with her, Brakey the youngest, then Jonah, and Liggert, the oldest. Liggert's an odd name. I looked it up. The etymology's obscure, but it may come from Serbia, go figure that."

"Do we have anything else on the late Mr. Alcott's hit-and-run accident six months ago?"

"Let me see. Okay, the police report put the accident about one hundred yards outside this—let's call it a compound. Mr. Alcott was walking the family dog on the side of the highway when he was hit. The dog stood barking over him until someone stopped. He stayed guarding Mr. Alcott until the police arrived, and that would be Deputy Kane Lewis. As you already know, Deputy Lewis only found skid marks, but nothing to identify the vehicle or the driver."

The Porsche's GPS told them to turn right, and soon they were looking down a long gravel driveway at a distant cluster of houses. It was indeed a compound, with a larger two-story house set in the middle. On either side of the big house were single-story ranch-style houses. All three houses were set close to one another, as if privacy wasn't a priority. All three were well maintained and backed up to an oak and pine forest.

Savich turned smoothly onto the driveway. Sherlock said as she took it all in, "Brakey must have given them all an earful. That was smart to tell him you'd let him go if he agreed to let us come speak to his family."

"Hopefully his family goes along with it." Savich stopped in front of the main house, which was charming, with a wraparound porch and a half-dozen chimneys that gave it a 1940s look, even though he knew it had been built in the past fifteen years. It was painted white, with dark brown trim. Flowers filled pots on the wide porch, hung from baskets from the porch beams. Trees crowded next to the wide expanse of lawn, and the smell of freshly mowed grass was heavy and sweet in the air. There were four children playing football in the front yard, all of them shouting, laughing, running around like berserkers. An old woman in a wheelchair sat on the porch, knitting in her lap, rocking slowly back and forth, watching them over the rims of her half-glasses. The children stopped playing abruptly and huddled together in a knot, staring at them.

A little boy called out, "Wow, that's a beautiful car, mister!"

"It's not just any car," an older boy of about eight said. "That's a race car." Savich had to smile.

"Well, we've made a hit, Dillon," Sherlock said, and patted the Porsche's roof. "Would you kids like to come over and look at it?" It was lovely here for these kids, she thought, the smell of freshly mowed grass in the fresh spring air, no exhaust fumes anywhere. The kids gathered around. "I like red," said a little girl wearing hand-me-down blue jeans she hadn't grown into, rolled up to her ankles, a football pressed tight against her chest. "Are you here to visit grandma?"

Savich looked again at the old lady. He'd never seen a wheelchair that rocked before. She said nothing, only stared over at them, rocking back and forth. They walked right up to her, the kids following after Sherlock. "Good morning, ma'am. I'm Special Agent Dillon Savich, FBI, and this is Special Agent Sherlock. We're here to speak with the Alcott family." Both he and Sherlock pulled out their creds.

She gave them a quick look, still rocking, and finally allowed a small lipless grin. "What a pretty boy and girl you are," she said in a lovely drawl, sweet and slow as syrup. "Brakey said you'd be coming, said he'd made a deal with you. We let you talk to us and no jail for him. I bet you drove all the way from that wicked city of Washington here to make Brakey come clean. Why, that boy's a sweetie, innocent as a lamb. You want to get the goods on him? Well, you won't. He wouldn't even play tackle football in high school, couldn't bring himself to hurt anyone or anything. So you need to keep looking because your bad guy isn't my Brakey. Tanny, get back, you don't want these fancy law people to step on you."

The little football girl took two steps back, but she never stopped studying them, never stopped easing closer. There was curiosity and awareness in her light green eyes well beyond her years, Savich thought, as if she knew some things most people didn't. Savich sighed. She was a little girl, that's all she was, a pretty little girl.

Sherlock looked closely at the old lady. She was all bone and parchment skin, domed purple veins riding high on the backs of her hands. She couldn't weigh more than ninety pounds. Her snow-white hair was pinned in a knot at the back of her head, the several bobby pins she'd poked into it looking ready to slide out, because there wasn't enough hair to hold them in place. But when she'd spoken, beneath that drawl was hot spice and vinegar. "Yes, ma'am, we came from the wicked city," she said. "And we'd appreciate any help you can give us."

The old lady rocked and creaked. "I heard you visited with Glory Lewis today. I'll bet the entire town was there, stuffed into her living room, eating all the casseroles they carted over. Kane was that popular. Now, Glory, she's tough, lots tougher than Ezra and Kane put together. Ezra, he's the sheriff, you know. You don't want to cross Glory. If you do, you're in deep trouble. Ezra's the same way, but Glory's better at hiding it."

What did all that outpouring mean? "Yes, ma'am," Sherlock said, "there were a lot of people at the Lewis house. I didn't see any casseroles, though."

The old lady smiled at them again, showing off the complement of white teeth too big for her mouth. "We're all willing to help you with your job, Angela, so long as you aren't here to haul poor Brakey off to the federal jail. He's a sweetie, like I told you, wouldn't step on a spider, that boy, not even if his mama asked him to. Stick a knife in Kane's chest? No, not Brakey."

"Mother? What—oh. You're the federal agents, aren't you?"

Savich nodded, introduced himself and Sherlock again, showed her their creds. Unlike the old lady, Mrs. Alcott took each of their IDs and studied them carefully. "Brakey told us he saw you on television yesterday, Agent Sherlock. And now you're here."

"Yes, ma'am. You're Brakey's mother? Mrs. Deliah Alcott?" It was an unnecessary question because it was obvious. The resemblance was pronounced—the same pale green eyes, the same tilt of the head, only Mrs. Alcott's hair was a much darker brown than her son's. Her hands were like Brakey's, too, slender and fine-boned, with

long, tapering fingers. She was a handsome woman, yes, that was the word for
her. She was taller than her boy, Brakey,
and straight as a sapling. She was dressed
casually in a long, gauzy summer dress,
with sandals on her narrow feet, her toe-
nails unpainted. There was no gray in her
dark brown hair, though Sherlock knew
her to be fifty-five years old. She wore her
hair in a thick braid that hung nearly to
her waist. The necklace she was wearing
caught Sherlock's eye—a necklace made
of different stones. Did the stones have a
particular meaning to her? She looked,
Sherlock thought, like a Wiccan should—no
artifice, natural, and proud of it.

"Yes, I'm Deliah Alcott. Brakey had a
moment to call me, tell me he'd made a deal
with you." Her chin went up. "We will talk
to you, but if you make any threats against
Brakey, I will call our lawyer. Do you understand?"

"Yes, ma'am. We understand. No threats."

"Why do you drive an expensive car like
that?"

Savich merely smiled. "Is Brakey here?"

"Yes, he is. He's with his brother Jonah.

We've been watching the news channels about the investigation of the terrorist attacks in New York City, and then these murders happened—Sparky Carroll and Kane Lewis—and both live right here in Plackett. It's hard to believe—horrible, really. What is worse is that an Athame was used in each. That makes it unbearable, because it makes everyone in town look at us differently, with suspicion, and it's not right or fair.

"I understand why you would think Brakey was involved because of where Kane's body was discovered. But there is simply no reason for Brakey to do such a terrible thing to Kane Lewis. Brakey's known him all his life. He liked him. Listen, Brakey's only a boy, twenty-four years old."

"Now, Morgana, I knew a twelve-year-old girl who smacked her own sister with a shovel, killed her dead. Age doesn't have anything to do with it. I already told them Brakey wouldn't hurt a living thing. He's like you, now, isn't he?" And again, a wide, full smile with all those gleaming teeth. Was that mockery in those rheumy old eyes?

16

Don't call me Morgana, Mother," Deliah Alcott said. "You're going to confuse these agents. I don't know if you've properly met. This is my husband's mother, Ms. Louisa Alcott."

The old woman gave them another big smile. If Sherlock wasn't mistaken, there was a twinkle in her faded old eyes. "No, you don't want to put shackles on poor Brakey," she repeated. "If you're wondering, I'm not Louisa May Alcott. I'm not that old. Maybe someday."

"It's a fine name," Savich said, "a name to be proud of."

"My middle name isn't May, like you're expecting, it's Lorna, as in Lorna Doone. My mother was a witch like me, but she loved her classical romances, even though she was always muttering about how foolish the characters were, how if they knew some witchcraft, they'd be less stupid."

"So you're from a long line of witches,

Mrs. Alcott?" Savich asked her.

"Oh, yes, we go back further than the silly Wiccan stuff Morgana spouts."

"My name isn't Morgana, Mother."

The old woman shrugged scrappy shoulders. "Sounds better than Deliah. Morgana was a wicked woman, a powerful woman. Look what she did to poor Arthur, twisted him up but good, didn't she?"

Down the rabbit hole. Savich said to Brakey's mother, "Mrs. Alcott, may we come inside, speak to you alone?"

She looked out over the four children now hooting and hollering again, Tanny throwing the football to Jenny. She called out, "Time to go home, kids." The kids whined about it not being dark yet, but Mrs. Alcott held firm. She turned back, eyed them. "Very well. My boys are in the den. We can talk in the living room."

"But what about Daddy?"

"Jenny, he'll come when the TV newscast is over," Mrs. Alcott said. "Go now, scat, your mama is waiting."

One by one, the children trailed off, splitting up into pairs as they went to their own houses, each looking back over their shoulders. Deliah looked down at the old lady.

"Go on with the agents, Morgana. I like it out here alone, no more noise from the children. The crickets will be out soon. A fine time of day."

"I'll be right inside if you need me," Deliah said. "Don't call me Morgana." **Her daily litany?**

She led Savich and Sherlock through an ornately carved front door. There was a brass pentacle hanging from it, at least a foot long, the five brass points of the star within the circle polished to a high shine. **Some kind of protection charm?** Sherlock wondered, and saw a pentacle hanging in each of the front windows, smaller than the one on the front door, but as highly polished. Fresh flowers adorned the entryway, set inside a large iron container with three legs that looked like an old-fashioned cooking pot or cauldron. There was a smell of incense in the air.

Mrs. Alcott waved them into a country-style living room filled with oversized furniture. Sepia photos dating back to the late nineteenth century covered the walls.

The impression was charming, in spite of the strange bric-a-brac scattered around the room—feathers, seashells, jars full of herbs, an incense burner, and a crystal sphere set in isolated splendor on top of an antique marquetry table.

Behind a big television Sherlock saw a set of bookshelves with a mishmash of paperbacks. She could make out some of the titles nearest to her—**The Magic of Crystals** and **Encyclopedia of Herbs**. She saw a box of tarot cards on a table by the sofa, more Wiccan trappings.

Deliah noticed them looking around. "The objects you see are part of our tradition. We call them tools. We're proud of them, have no reason to hide them."

She went still, faced them, arms at her sides. "I know you believe my son is a murderer. You've terrified him. Now, if you would tell me what you wish to know, perhaps we can be done with this, you will leave, and I won't have to call my friend Eileen over." Her voice rose. "Eileen is the family lawyer. Believe me, she wanted to be here, and is willing to act as Brakey's lawyer."

Savich saw the weight of the world looking out at him through Deliah Alcott's eyes. She was tense and angry and was no longer hiding it. He knew her husband had died only six months before, and now her son was in deep trouble. He said, "We're here to gather information, Mrs. Alcott. We realize you're a Wiccan. We also know that one of a Wiccan's tools is a ceremonial knife, an Athame. I'm sure Brakey told you that each of the murdered men were killed with an Athame. Brakey said he doesn't remember anything about last night. Can you help us with that?"

Her look was suspicious, as if she was parsing each word Savich said, but she nodded. "Yes, Brakey told me about the Athames. I can't begin to understand that. All I can say is that someone is trying to throw the blame on us. There's no other answer. As to his not remembering anything from last night, this complete loss of conscious self—I have no answer for that. Believe me, I wish I did.

"But for anyone to think that Brakey, or any Wiccan, would murder someone with an Athame—it is unthinkable, impossible.

Using an Athame for violence is anathema to us." She actually shuddered, looked faintly ill. "Listen, I'm not lying to you. Both my husband and I come from families of Wiccans, so all of us are quite familiar with those traditions, even those of us, like Brakey, who have chosen a different path. My husband was an amazing man, he..." Her voice fell off, her grief too close to the surface. She caught herself, cleared her throat.

"The first rule of Wicca is to practice kindness, to do no harm so that no harm will return to us. We believe our karma guides each of us to use our powers to heal ourselves and others, not destroy them, not murder them."

"What sort of powers do you mean?"

"You believe energy exists in a physical sense, Agent Savich. We believe everything in the natural world is a form of energy, people included. Wiccans strive to become ever more aware of that energy, more at one with that energy, by celebrating the rhythms of the moon and the sun, the seasons, the powers within nature and ourselves that people have worshipped as deities through the ages.

"You're looking at some of our tools around you; many are common everyday items you are familiar with. We use them in our rituals—dance, music, chants, all to heighten our awareness of how we fit into the spirit of the natural world.

"Sure we believe in magic, but even magic is natural. Did you know that, Agent Savich? There's nothing supernatural about it. Our magic is about using our own personal power, and with the help of the divine power, we direct energy toward what we visualize, perhaps something we desire, something we need. Despite the prejudices and fairy tales about us, we are not so different from you as you think."

Savich said, "Mrs. Alcott, perhaps you are right and someone is making it appear a Wiccan is responsible for these murders. Perhaps it is someone who doesn't share your values, perhaps someone you unwittingly harmed."

"Yes, yes, that is obvious to me." She paused, drew a deep breath. "We are not idiots, Agent, we fully recognize there are those who profess belief but do not believe. But Brakey is not one of them. He has harmed no one, on purpose or without realizing it. It cannot be a question of revenge. We strive to focus on what is life-affirming and positive. We do not attempt destructive magic, nothing intended to hurt or exploit anyone. There may be some-one capable of violence in any group, but for me? The evil of what was done, it terrifies me. And it terrifies Brakey. And that is how I know Brakey simply could not have done this, that it must be someone outside of us."

"Mrs. Alcott," Sherlock said, "you said your husband was a witch. We understand he was killed by a hit-and-run driver?"

Deliah looked away from them. They knew she was trying to hold herself together. She swallowed, turned back. "My husband —Arthur—was a gifted man, a spiritual mentor and a powerful witch, but he was kind and honorable, he never hurt anyone. I think Brakey learned that from him. I'll never understand why the person who hit him didn't stop, why he didn't help Arthur."

They heard Ms. Louisa's creaky laugh from the doorway. She was waving a knitting needle toward her daughter-in-law. A balding man in his early thirties stood behind her wheelchair, pushing her in. "You speak of Dilly like he was the grand poobah of witches, Morgana. Dilly swayed and twisted like a clothesline in a stiff breeze, you know that. Yes, he was a good witch, but he had no backbone. Weak as water, was Dilly."

17

"Dilly?" Sherlock asked her.

"Arthur Delaford Alcott was his birth name," Deliah said with a frustrated look at her mother-in-law. "Only she called him that ridiculous name—Dilly. This is my son, Jonah Alcott. Jonah, these are FBI agents Savich and Sherlock. You know Brakey."

Brakey moved from behind Jonah to stand stiffly beside a well-used brown leather recliner, hands in fists at his sides, his face white; he was obviously scared. Sherlock nodded to him. "Mr. Alcott."

"Sir. Ma'am. Agents."

Brakey's older brother Jonah walked over to them, sleek and confident, and asked to see their creds. He frowned over them, then said in their general direction, "I don't know what you think you're doing here, or how you can think Brakey murdered Kane Lewis. That's really stupid."

"Don't be rude, Jonah," Mrs. Alcott said automatically, probably a lifelong habit.

"It's an insult to Wicca to accuse us of

murdering people, Agents, and that's what you're doing. Our first and prime rule is to do no harm. My mother must have told you that already."

Coming from Jonah, it sounded like a clipped party line, memorized to recite to the uninitiated. "So you're a Wiccan yourself, Mr. Alcott?" Savich asked him.

"Yes, I practice the Craft."

Brakey broke in. "Dad never talked about any of it in front of us kids. He never celebrated any of the rituals with anyone, didn't pay any attention to craft tools like candles and stone, you know? Neither does Liggert. I think Dad agreed with Liggert. He laughed at Mom for dancing around in a white robe around a fire, chanting at the full moon."

Deliah said, "I will tolerate no more disrespect from you about your father, Brakey. You didn't know him, didn't know the essence of him. I know you are scared. We are all scared. But that doesn't give you the right." She turned back to Savich. "You asked about my husband. Yes, it's true, he didn't feel comfortable practicing some of the ways of Wicca."

"He was a witch," the old woman said. "A witch, no fancy trappings."

Deliah Alcott cleared her throat. If she wanted to smack the old lady, she hid it admirably. "Being a witch was a private matter for him. He didn't take part in any public displays of what he was or what he believed. But what he accomplished, what he could do, was incredible. He never disdained my beliefs."

"Can you give us an example?" Sherlock asked.

"Example? Well, after that big tornado in '09 that caused so much damage near here, he put a protection spell around the houses to keep us safe. There have been five more tornadoes since then, causing damage all around us. But not here. His spell still lives with us."

Jonah said, "The last tornado hit down across the road from our driveway, but no closer."

The old woman cackled. "Incredible, was he? Dilly protect himself, did he? A car comes along and bam! Knocks him aside the head and kills him. Even though he had a crystal in his pocket, so the Deputy Lewis said." Dilly's mother snorted. "He was weak," she said again, and she rocked faster, the knitting needles clacking loud in the still room. "He was my son. I know what he was made of. You ran all over him yourself, Morgana."

"My name isn't Morgana, stop calling me that!" Mrs. Alcott's teeth clenched. She looked about ready to belt the old lady. Was it like this between them all the time? The old lady pushed and pushed until Mrs. Alcott finally cracked? Probably so, for years and years now. Sherlock wondered if Mrs. Alcott had ever been tempted to send an evil spell her mother-in-law's way, against the Wiccan rules or not.

She sighed. "I was named after Deliah Mecala, a name I'm proud of. She was a witch who lived in these parts over a hundred years ago, a great healer who worshipped the Goddess of the Air and the Wind. I still have what we would call her **Book of Shadows** today, you see, and that's how I know."

Ms. Louisa never looked up. She kept on knitting, her clacking needles a constant drumbeat.

Jonah Alcott said, "I don't think Dad's protection spell kept the tornado out. I think Dad turned it away himself. It was headed right toward us, and then it wasn't."

The old lady said, "No, Jonah, it wasn't your daddy who turned away that cyclone, it was me." She looked up. "And there was Tanny—that's Liggert's oldest. She'd just planted a garden all by herself. I didn't want her to get upset if it was destroyed."

Off the tracks. Savich said to Brakey, "You said your father didn't use any tools of the craft. That includes an Athame? Did he own one, perhaps a collection of them?"

Jonah waved an impatient hand. "So the murderers used Athames. Anyone can buy them really cheap on the Internet. It doesn't mean anything."

Brakey leaped on that. "Jonah's right, it doesn't mean anything. No, I never saw my dad with an Athame. I don't own one, either."

Deliah Alcott said, "Brakey told us you had pictures of the Athames?"

Savich pulled out his cell phone and called them up. He handed the cell to Mrs. Alcott. She stared at them blankly, no signs of recognition, he was sure of it, unless she was really good. She raised her eyes to his face. "The first one, the Dual Dragon, it's not used often, at least by Wiccans I know. It's quite old, isn't it? The other is quite simple, probably handmade. That's what's favored by most Wiccans."

Savich passed the cell phone to Jonah. "Have you seen either of these two knives before?"

Jonah shook his head no.

Savich handed the cell to Ms. Louisa. She hummed as she looked at each of them. "Yes, what Morgana said is true. And Jonah's right, you can buy 'em anywhere nowadays, and isn't that something?"

Savich asked again, "Do you keep a collection of Athames here, Mrs. Abbott?"

"No. As I told you, an Athame is a very personal tool, Agent Savich. If something happens to it, then you would make another one. Neither Brakey nor Jonah as yet have made their own personal Athame.

"Listen, I assure you Brakey doesn't know anything about any of this. He grew up with Sparky Carroll, grew up with Deputy Kane Lewis watching over him. As I've said before, perhaps someone is leading you to

suspect a Wiccan for their own reasons."
She sighed. "But then Walter Givens isn't a
Wiccan, yet he used an Athame. Why? And
Deputy Lewis's murder—why an Athame?
This is all very confusing."

"Yes, it is," Sherlock said. "Mrs. Alcott,
isn't it true that Wiccans believe they can
influence other people's behavior, even
control it?"

"We do believe our higher magic can
influence events and the people involved in
them, but we do it only with their consent,
and only in their interests, not ours. Again,
we do no harm."

"But do some ever try it even without
consent?"

"Well, sometimes, rarely, a binding spell
may be necessary."

"A binding spell?" Savich asked.

"A binding spell," Deliah said patiently,
"is to prevent another witch from doing
mischief. Otherwise, influencing someone
without their consent would be unethical—
abhorrent, really—to a Wiccan."

Brakey said, "Mom, remember that time
Ricky Tucker told me you were a witch and
should be burned at the stake? Said it all

over town?" Mrs. Alcott didn't say anything, simply pleated the soft material of her dress. "Made me mad and I told him so, but he laughed at me, said it was true. A week later, Ricky drove his daddy's truck into the old oak tree at Clemson Fork, broke his legs and knocked himself out. Ricky thought you did that."

"That's only ignorance talking, Brakey, you know that. It was an accident, pure and simple." She said to Savich and Sherlock, "Brakey's father and I have heard just about everything over the years. An absurd comment by a teenage boy wouldn't concern us at all. As far as I know, Ricky's father had nothing to say about it."

Ms. Louisa said, "It's true Ricky's daddy never said much about the broken legs or the concussion, but he was real mad about the truck." Ms. Louisa raised her eyes to Savich and gave him a big white-toothed grin. "It was totaled. He grounded Ricky for a month. Didn't matter because Ricky was in bed with two broken legs. The truck wasn't insured."

Deliah said, "I think you'll agree we've been very cooperative with you, Agents.

We kept to Brakey's bargain with you. My boy Liggert is the only one who couldn't be here. He told me it was wrong not to have Eileen, our lawyer, here."

"Liggert's a smart boy," the old lady said. "One thing about Liggert, he'll always do the needful." Ms. Louisa cocked her head to one side, stared at them, but didn't stop knitting, the low clacking a constant rhythm. Sherlock wondered if it drove her daughter-in-law mad. It would her.

"We're nearly done here, Mrs. Alcott," Savich said. "I have one final question for Brakey." He turned to Brakey, who looked back at him like a trapped deer. "I believe you when you say you have no memory of Deputy Kane Lewis's death. We have a way to help you remember. I want you to come to Quantico with us, and our expert, Dr. Hicks, will hypnotize you. He can help you find out what happened to you, help us all find out. We can end this once and for all, Brakey."

"He didn't kill anyone!"

Sherlock said, "Mrs. Alcott, someone did, and the fact is Brakey had to have been there, and he has no memory of it. We need to find out, for everyone's sake. And Brakey can tell us what happened."

Jonah said, "That's bull. You can probably get him to say whatever you like."

Sherlock said to Brakey, "No, that isn't true. Brakey, it's not dangerous, and it's the only way for you to get past this."

"No!" Mrs. Alcott shook her finger at them. "No hypnotism. I will not allow you to poke around in Brakey's unconscious mind. I forbid it. Your father would forbid it, Brakey."

Sherlock said, "Mrs. Alcott, your son is twenty-four years old. He is an adult, he can answer for himself. Unless he helps us, we'll have no choice but to arrest him. The preponderance of evidence is against him."

Deliah looked like Sherlock had slapped her. She lowered her voice, pleading now, "Brakey, you don't want to do this, you don't have to do this. I can call Eileen, she can help you. They cannot force you to do this, do you understand?"

Brakey looked thoughtful, then straightened, squared his shoulders. "Agent Savich, I didn't lie. If I killed Deputy Lewis, I don't remember doing it. I need to know, you're right about that." Then he looked at his mother and suddenly he looked like a little boy. "I don't want to go to jail, Mom, I don't."

Jonah Alcott stepped forward. "I think Brakey had some kind of fit, and maybe he killed Deputy Lewis in some kind of fugue state. If that's what happened, they're not going to be fair. They'll have you signing a confession, Brakey, right then and there, and you'll go to jail for a long time. I agree with Mom. Don't do this."

"Your brother's right," Mrs. Alcott said. She walked swiftly to her son, took his head between her hands. "Brakey, look at me. You do not want to do this."

Brakey's hands came up to rest on her shoulders, strong hands, Savich saw, strong enough to bring down a man, stab him in the heart. "I've been so scared, Mom, but more than anything I can't stand not knowing what happened, not remembering. Now I can know. Mom, they believe I killed Deputy Lewis. You heard them, they could arrest me and convict me anyway, surely you can see that. What if they're right?

"If I killed a man I should be punished for it, that's what you believe, it's what Dad believed. I'm going to find out what really happened."

Sherlock said, "Mrs. Alcott, Dr. Hicks is an expert. He'll help us find the truth. Let me say we have reason to believe Brakey may not be responsible for Deputy Kane Lewis's death. Someone else is. Allow us to prove that. Brakey wants the truth. You should, too."

"When can we do this?" Brakey asked, his voice thin as a reed.

"Tomorrow morning, Mr. Alcott, we will send someone to drive you to Quantico. We will meet you there."

Ms. Louisa looked up at her daughter-in-law, nodded toward Savich and Sherlock. "Seems to me these pretty young people think something very strange is at work here. Sounds interesting, doesn't it? If their shrink wants to dig into Brakey's brain, let him. Who knows what he'll find? Maybe a murderer, or maybe a boy who doesn't know his elbow from his knee."

18

Savich House
Georgetown
Friday night

It was late. Sherlock was asleep, her hand over his heart, her breath warm against his shoulder. Savich kissed her hair, breathed in her scent, and closed his mind down. He fell asleep and into a cold so brutal his bones were going to shatter. Fast as snapping fingers, the cold was gone, and he was standing in a small, circular clearing in the middle of a thick pine-tree forest, the thick-needled branches spearing upward, nearly meeting overhead. It was full-on night, yet oddly he could see around him as if it was twilight, the darker night hovering indistinctly in the billowing shadows at the edge of the trees.

He was alone beneath the motionless sentinel pines with no idea of where he was. He was naked but he didn't feel cold, and surely that was strange, because he could make out small patches of snow. He realized he didn't feel the rocky ground beneath his feet, and he felt a stab of panic. He had to be dreaming, but why would he dream this? And if he was conscious of it, knew he was dreaming, surely he could change the dream. That's what a conscious dream was, wasn't it? Could he bring himself out of it? He willed himself back into bed, wrapped around Sherlock, pictured himself kissing her neck.

Nothing happened.

Another shock of panic. He calmed. **Relax, go with it.** It wasn't as if he had a choice anyway.

He sniffed the air, smelled smoke. He couldn't remember actually smelling anything in a dream before, but now he could. It was burning wood, off to his right. He walked toward it, along a wide trail through the trees and the undergrowth, noticed again that he didn't feel the brambles on the trail under his feet, though he walked right over them. He reached out to touch a pine tree, but his hand went through it. He drew back, slashed his hand through the tree again, harder. Nothing there. He knew then this wasn't a dream. His subconscious had nothing to do with this. No, it was something else. Was he in some sort of hologram?

Something or someone else was in charge of his spirit-walk thought these woods and toward the unknown. He felt a presence, a presence he knew he should fear. **What do you want from me? Why am I here?**

Savich stepped out of the pines and into another clearing. An ancient stone tower stood before him, lichen growing thick on the stones. He saw two rough-cut skinny windows covered with what looked like animal hides. **Why this bizarre tower?**

He raised his hand to push the knob on the large black door, paused. Slowly, he laid his palm against it. He was surprised. It was solid, the wood rough against his palm. Savich shoved and the door swung open. He stepped into a magnificent Moorish-tiled entryway with a soaring ceiling so high he couldn't see the top. The smell of smoke was strong inside, as if the air itself were burning, making his eyes tear. The stone beneath his bare feet felt icy cold and as solid as the door. Very well, for whatever reason, inside this tower, he wasn't insubstantial, he was real.

He felt a sudden blast of arctic air. What was that—a touch of the spurs? Had he broken a rule? Whose rule?

He slapped his hands to his arms for warmth and looked around. He had to admit it was an awesome illusion, a vast space replete with Gothic trimmings. There were rush torches fastened to the stone walls, but they weren't lit. **Couldn't you manage that?**

Some twenty feet beyond him, wide stone steps led upward, fading into the roiling shadows in the distance. They looked well worn, as if centuries of heavy booted feet had marched over them. There was a solid stone wall on his right and an arched stone doorway on his left. He walked through it and into a room from the past, filled with dark, heavy, richly carved furniture, like he'd seen in an old castle near Lisbon. There was a blazing fireplace large enough to roast a cow, which blew out blue puffs of smoke. He walked over and reached out his cold hands to the flames, but they held no heat, no warmth at all, like a moving picture of a fire. There were dark beams crisscrossing overhead, but no windows, only large faded tapestries of medieval hunting scenes on the walls.

The air was oppressive, heavy, but the thick smell of smoke was now gone. He felt something stir behind him. It was the presence he'd felt in the forest. It was here. He turned slowly, but there was no one there.

He called out, his voice clipped and impatient, "You went to a lot of trouble to bring me into this elaborate dream with you. I smelled your smoke and found you, as you wanted me to. Time for you to show yourself and stop showing off."

Savich heard a laugh, a man's deep laugh, not the sort of laugh you'd join in. It was crude, mocking. He turned toward the arched doorway. It was no longer empty.

A man stood there, his hands crossed over his chest. He was swathed in a hooded black robe with long, billowing sleeves. The robe seemed to twist and swirl around his dark boots, as if stirred by an unseen wind. A thin gold cord was tied around his waist, the ends dangling nearly to his knees. His face was long and thin, his head covered by a hood. From what Savich could see of his face, he was pale, with long black hair that spilled forward from his hood onto his shoulders. He looked like an ancient scholar, or perhaps a monk from an old religious order who might have worked in a dark tower like this. He'd seen pictures of witches in robes like that, dancing in their ceremonies, their faces exalted while they chanted to the heavens, carving the air with sharp-bladed Athames.

"You are not frightened," he said in a deep voice. "I admit that surprises me. I brought you here to instruct you about what you're going to do for me."

His voice was resonant yet strangely hollow, like an old recording played too many times. He sounded faintly European. Savich said, "You mean the kind of instruction you gave Walter Givens and Brakey Alcott, to stab their friends?"

"You're quite intuitive, I see. Perhaps that is why you are not as afraid of me as you should be. You realized quite quickly my beautiful forest wasn't a dream, that I had eased into your mind, created this splendid setting to bring you into."

"I should be afraid?"

"You will do as I say, as they did, whether you are afraid or not. Before we are done here, you will revere me, worship me. And you will remember nothing."

Savich waved his hand around him. "I don't see much to be afraid of, actually. Look around you. You couldn't manage to get the lighting right, so many shadows, so many blurred corners in your tower. And you couldn't provide heat, either, could you?

"Worship you? If you don't mind, now I'm too cold."

The hooded figure didn't move, stood with his black cloak swirling about his ankles. If Savich wasn't mistaken, he looked surprised at the mockery. What would he do? Savich hated to admit it to himself, but he was afraid. He had no idea what would happen if he were killed in his mind. Would his body die as well?

The witch, or whatever he was, cocked his head to one side, sending more of his black hair to fall out from under his hood and slide along his face.

"Enough of this melodrama. Who are you

and what do you want?"

"My name is Stefan Dalco. I have told you what I will do."

"Is that name part of this Romanian fantasy? Who are you, really? How does all this concern you?"

"I will kill you before I allow you to find that out. You are not here to question me. I brought you here to stop all these questions, whatever it takes. And I will."

"You say you have that power, yet you're afraid to tell me who you are?"

Savich felt a burst of anger from Dalco, so real he almost smiled. "You are nothing like the others," Dalco said. "They could not think beyond their fear, they could not reason. For a time they believed they were mad. Yet you remain yourself, even here. You are not a witch, you are something else entirely. There are not many like us, you know."

"If that's the case, you can stop looking like a Hollywood villain from a melodrama. Why don't you pull your hood back, show me your face?"

A pause, then a stiff voice: "I provide the trappings one expects to see. These hands, for example"—he raised narrow hands with bulging purple veins and long, thin fingers, their nails filed to a point. "A fine touch, don't you think?"

Savich didn't answer. He was looking toward the medieval tapestries. Only now they were large dirty-brown woven rugs hanging on the walls, as if Dalco had lost concentration and the hunting scenes had disappeared. **Interesting.** Was Dalco really strong enough to hold him here? Until when? Until he died?

He looked back at Dalco. "Why did you kill Sparky Carroll and Kane Lewis?"

Savich knew he wasn't wrong; a spasm of pain had crossed the shadowed face. **For what?** Dalco said, "All you need to know is that they deserved death. At my hands, as do you for your interference."

Dalco took two steps toward him, raised a hand that held a long black-handled Athame, and hurled it at Savich, but Savich had already fallen to his side and jerked one of the big chairs in front of him. The Athame struck the wooden back and sank deep, not three inches above his head.

He had no weapons, nothing to protect

himself. He heard Dalco's harsh breathing. "You are too arrogant, too proud to spare. You will not give up. I will not let you destroy me."

He saw the flash of another Athame in Dalco's hand. He was coming closer and he would kill him this time. Savich focused, pictured Winkel's Cave in Maestro, Virginia, a place he'd dreamed about several times, a place where he and many of his friends could easily have died. He pictured both of them standing in the large chamber beneath a ceiling of incredible stalactites.

Suddenly they were both standing in the cave.

Dalco stood very still, staring at the walls. "How did you do that?"

Savich had no answer, for either of them. He'd simply willed both of them out of Dalco's illusion and into one of his own. It had worked.

Dalco said, his voice thoughtful, "You've done this before, haven't you? And you didn't tell me."

"Why should I tell you anything? Would you like to be buried here in my cave, Dalco?" Savich pointed to the wall. "Look at your own personal coffin I fashioned especially for you."

Dalco looked at a coffin carved into the stone, his name carved in large letters on it. He stumbled, then seemed to get hold of himself and jerked back to face Savich, shaking his head back and forth. "No, this can't be possible." He looked panicked, turned and started to run, and suddenly everything disappeared.

"Dillon! Dillon! Come on, wake up!"

It was Sherlock's voice and she was shaking him, slapping him. He was gasping for breath, drenched in sweat.

"Come on, wake up. You've had a nightmare, a doozy."

He grabbed her wrist, pulled her down close to his face. "I'm okay now. Thanks for waking me."

She wrapped her arms around his neck, pulling him up, kissed his nose, his mouth, held him hard against her. "Was it because of what happened in New York?"

"Actually," he said slowly as he pulled away, "it wasn't." He stroked her wildly curling hair from her face. "I know who killed Sparky Carroll and Kane Lewis. His name is Dalco. Stefan Dalco." He kissed her again, pulled her tight against him. "It wasn't a dream. He brought me into this elaborate dream setting. He talked to me. He tried to kill me."

Sherlock studied his face in the dull gray dawn light. She tasted fear and relief, a heady brew. "You stopped him."

"Yes. This time." He knew there would be a next time. And what would happen? In the silence of the early morning, he could still hear the faint echo of Dalco's voice.

The alarm went off, and they both heard Sean running down the hall toward their bedroom, ready to take on the day.

19

Criminal Apprehension Unit
Hoover Building
Washington, D.C.
Friday morning

Sherlock had just reached her desk in the CAU when her cell belted out "Born on the Fourth of July."

She glanced at the caller ID. Now, this was a surprise. "Hello, Agent Giusti."

"I heard you and Agent Savich have already been assigned another high-profile case, the stabbing in the Rayburn Building. You've got half of us proud of you, the other half jealous."

"We try our best," Sherlock said. She wasn't about to elaborate. Her mind had been turning in circles since Savich had told her what had happened to him. "What can I do for you, Agent Giusti?"

When Giusti finally spoke, the words sounded like she was having to pry them out of her mouth with pliers. "The terrorist at JFK—Nasim Conklin—as you know. He won't talk with us, refuses to speak with anyone but you. So I need you to come up to New York immediately."

"I've seen you in action, Agent Giusti. You'll get Conklin to beg to talk to you, no doubt in my mind."

"You'd think, right?" Again, a pause. "Look, I know you're busy with your current case, but I'm ready to throw in the towel. My boss is, too. We have to get Nasim to talk, Agent Sherlock, and it looks like you're it."

Sherlock didn't want to leave Dillon, not after last night. "Here's the thing—" she began, but Giusti rolled right over her.

"Actually, it's not up to you, Agent Sherlock. There's another consideration in calling you up here. We're going to take you out of the public eye for a few days. The terrorists behind Conklin know he spoke to you at JKF, and it's not a big leap to assume they'd be happy to see both of you dead, as payback for sending their operation into the crapper. Both of you might be targets, Nasim because he failed. You know as well as I do it would be a public relations coup for the terrorists if they succeeded in killing you in particular, and we're not going to let that happen. So please be careful until we have you safely here with us in New York. As for Nasim, we've got him hidden away as safe as a baby.

"My boss, SAC Zachery, has spoken with Mr. Maitland and he's given his thumbs-up. He's arranged for one of the FBI Bell helicopters out of Quantico to bring you up to New York. We'll meet you at the East Thirty-fourth Street Heliport. Bring clothes for, say, three days."

Well, that's that, Sherlock thought, as she stared at her cell. She had to hand it to Giusti, she'd gone about it the right way, gone right up the ladder on both ends, leaving her no choice. She thought of Dillon, of this mad psychopath on his hands and in his head, and knew he wouldn't be happy about it, either, a vast understatement.

"Very well. I'll be at Quantico in two hours," Sherlock said to the cell phone, since Giusti had already hung up.

20

Friday, late morning

Special Agent Callum McLain was standing next to the helicopter at Quantico, chatting with their pilot, J. J. Markie, a fireball who told stories about how he'd flown a heli-copter into the heart of hell in Afghanistan, mixed it up with the devil, and flown back out whistling, when Sherlock drove onto the tarmac in her trusty Volvo. Sherlock had met Callum—Cal—a couple times, and liked him. He was smart, funny, and no-nonsense when he was focused. He was a big guy in his early thirties, buff and well dressed in a dark suit, white shirt, his Glock doubtless clipped to his belt. She saw he was wearing black boots, not wing tips. She was glad Dillon had picked him to accompany her. She hadn't argued because she knew it was important to him, to do all he could do to keep her safe.

"Agent Sherlock? Good to see you again." She and Cal shook hands and he took her overnight bag. "Been about four months, since that barbecue the director gave at his house for a bunch of agents."

Sherlock smiled up at him. "I remember the special dishes he made for the vegetarians, especially that grilled corn on the cob, one of Dillon's favorites."

"Worked out. I got his share of barbecue ribs. You and Savich had your little boy with you—Sean, right? Do you know, I'd like to have one like him someday?"

Markie poked him on the shoulder. "To pull that off, you've got to find an unsuspecting woman first, McLain. Congratulations, Sherlock, on bringing down that terrorist at JFK, amazing what you did. My daughter Ruth says she wants to be an FBI agent like you when she grows up. I asked her if she was going to curl her hair and dye it red to match yours. Not a problem, she told me, she'd already picked out the exact shade. She wants to start karate tomorrow."

"How old is your daughter, J.J.?"

"The little pistol turned six last week." He looked down at his watch. "You guys ready to go? I'd like to get this bird in the air. We don't want to keep New York twiddling their thumbs."

When they were buckled in the back seats, their headphones clear, Markie gave them the safety rundown. Then, "A little under an hour to the helipad on Thirty-fourth Street. We've got a nice wind on our tail pushing us north."

They rose slowly to about fifty feet, banked and headed northward. Minutes later, Sherlock was looking down at dozens of white granite buildings and monuments, the Potomac lazily curling around them, the Washington Monument spearing toward the clouds. She said into her mike, "Cal, if you didn't know, Dillon asked Mr. Maitland for you specifically. He said you'd have my back, that you have no fear, which is really not that reassuring if you think about it. I thought you'd like to know, though."

No fear? Yeah, he liked the sound of that, but then he caught Sherlock's crooked smile. "My boss told me both of you wanted someone with you from our house, not some New York cowboy you didn't know. I gotta tell you, Sherlock, to be involved in this particular terrorist investigation, to actually be in on the chase, it's more than

I hoped for. Trust me, I'm going to be your second skin."

That sounded good to her. Cal studied her, then lightly touched his hand to her arm. "Not that you need me. They ought to be showing that JFK video of you at Quantico, how you got the terrorist's attention right away, engaged him, distracted him. The woman he grabbed—Melissa Harkness—she was impressive, too, the way she saved herself. I told my brother he ought to give her a call, ask her out for a cup of coffee. He's with Treasury, harmless and single. Someone like her might do him good."

"I hope he follows through. Melissa deserves a really good guy. He might have some competition, though. I spoke to her this morning. She's blooming, enjoying her coworkers drooling all over her."

"I wonder why the terrorist is insisting on speaking only to you? I mean, you beat the crap out of him. If a woman did that to me in front of the world, the last thing I'd want to do is have a nice chat with her."

"Everyone's wondering the same thing. Maybe it's a case of the devil he knows, or maybe the devil he'd like to strangle if he gets the chance. I'm expecting Agent Giusti to bring us up to date on the investigation and give us an idea of what to expect before I sit with him."

Cal said, "If he does try to strangle you, I'd appreciate it if you'd let me take him apart this time."

"Well, okay, I can hold myself back, let you get your licks in. Oh, yes, Agent Giusti doesn't know you're coming. She's probably already assigned another agent to protect me."

"Another body who can shoot a gun can't hurt. I heard Giusti's got quite a rep as a badass in the New York office, and that's saying something, since a lot of them are yahoos."

"You have the same rep, Cal. That's one of the reasons Dillon wanted you with me."

He looked surprised. "Me? A badass? Nah. Now, Giusti, I've never met her, but like I said, I've heard some things. I expect she'll try to take me down a notch—or two— if she can manage it."

Sherlock pictured Kelly Giusti's ramrod-straight back and squared shoulders, remembered the small smile she'd finally managed to coax out of her. "My money might be on her, Cal. She's tough, smart, and focused—hmm, sounds like you, doesn't she?—except I'm not sure she has your sense of humor. Yeah, I think you can expect some grief from her. So could Darth Vader. I'm sure you'll both be professional about it, right?" And she punched him in the arm.

"No worries, I'm the very definition of the word." He fell silent and drummed his fingertips on his knee. "I heard Savich didn't like your getting involved in this. Can't say I blame him."

All Sherlock said was "He wasn't thrilled." Dillon had been silent, which meant he was afraid, not about what he was dealing with, but for her. He'd held her so tight she felt her ribs creak. She'd leaned back, held his face between her hands, and kissed him, twice. "I love you. I will be all right. I'll call you as often as I can." She had time only to call Sean, tell him she had to leave, a couple of days, no more. New York? He'd asked her to visit FAO Schwarz and buy him something very cool, like Captain Munchkin's new video game with the river trolls.

21

East Thirty-Fourth Street
New York City
Friday afternoon

It was a beautiful afternoon in New York City, the sun glistening off the East River. Their helicopter flew low over the river toward the thick traffic on FDR Drive. J.J. set them down smoothly on the Thirty-fourth Street helipad. As soon as they were away from the helicopter, J.J. gave them a grin and a wave, and lifted off.

Agent Kelly Giusti, with the wind from the rotor blades whipping her dark hair around her head, strode forward and shook hands with Sherlock, then turned to stare at Callum McLain, a dark eyebrow arched, a look Sherlock admired and had never managed. She was impressed. Giusti said, "Who is this?"

Sherlock gave her a sunny smile. "This is Special Agent Callum—Cal—McLain. He's in counterterrorism in Washington, so the two of you are automatically on the same team."

"That remains to be seen," Giusti said, her dark hair settling into a wild tangle around her face. "Why is he here?"

Cal waved his hand. "Hello, I'm standing right here."

Giusti never looked away from Sherlock and Sherlock never dropped her smile. "Like I said, Cal's in the counterterrorism section. Mr. Maitland assigned him as a liaison to our office and to assist in the investigation. We know him and trust him to protect me. Can't have too many experienced hands, right?"

Cal gave Sherlock a sideways glance. She'd heaped some tribute on his head, but he didn't think Giusti was buying it. She was looking at him like the Wisconsin lineman who'd slammed him into the ground so hard he'd almost broken his throwing arm. Odd how he'd pictured her older and heavier, with maybe a cell phone bud hooked to her ear and a thin mustache on her upper lip. She was the very opposite—tall, dark-haired, about his own age, almost as tall as he was, wearing black pants and jacket, a white stretch cami, and a lanyard around her neck with her shield. Even though her hair was all over her head, the rest of her was stiff and straight. And would you look at those dark laser-beam eyes—talk about pinning a guy. He wondered if she ever laughed.

He smiled, stuck out his hand.

Giusti shook his hand. "I suppose I could get in trouble if I dumped you in the East River, McLain, so stick close to Sherlock. If anything happens to her, we're both screwed forever and I will personally cut off your most beloved body parts—if you live."

"That's a bit harsh," Cal said.

Sherlock said, "Trust him, Agent Giusti, Cal's not going to let anything happen to me."

Giusti turned to the older man who stood at her elbow. "Agent Sherlock, Agent McLain, this is Special Agent Erwin. Pip was supposed to guard you, Sherlock."

The two men eyed each other. Pip Erwin said, "You look tough enough. Are you fast on your feet?"

"Yes," Cal said. "Maybe as fast as you once were."

"Good to hear," Erwin said, "because I ain't wired to be a bodyguard."

Cal liked the looks of Pip Erwin, black wing tips and all. He was pushing fifty, looked fit, a sharp dude in his regulation black Fed suit. He took in the world through intense dark eyes, darker than Giusti's, harder even, like a man who'd seen most everything and couldn't be surprised, his cynicism fairly dripping off him. Then again, Giusti was younger and she looked like nothing would surprise her, either.

Giusti waved them toward a big black SUV. "We've got to get going. We're heading out straight away to Colby, Long Island. We're keeping Nasim Conklin there in a safe house."

Erwin eyed them in the rearview mirror as they climbed in. "Hey, interesting name, Agent Sherlock. Any relation to that Holmes fellow?"

"I believe he's somewhere back there in the family tree."

Erwin smiled at that. It changed him utterly. "You get lots of that, don't you?"

"It's been a while. Thanks for reminding me of my roots."

"How are you faring with the media, Agent Sherlock?"

"Both of you, call me Sherlock and him Cal. It'll take some time before they get tired of camping out in our neighbors' front yards. But now I'm in New York, where no one expects me to be."

Giusti pulled two tablets out from a leather briefcase and handed one to Sherlock. "There are classified files on there for you about our investigation thus far. I didn't know you were bringing Mr. Hot Dude, so he'll have to look over your shoulder. They're updated regularly. You can fill yourselves in on some of what we've learned about Nasim Conklin on the way."

"That's Special Agent Mr. Hot Dude," Cal said, and was sure he saw a corner of her mouth kick up.

Sherlock turned on the tablet, and she and Cal dug in as Erwin pulled out his opaque aviator glasses and got the behemoth running. Cal smiled as he watched him negotiate the insane traffic like a bomb squadron leader, ignoring the obscene gestures from taxi drivers screaming at him in languages he didn't understand. It wasn't long before they were on the Long Island Expressway.

After reviewing the info, Sherlock looked up at Giusti. "So there's still no definite link between the bombing at Saint Pat's and Conklin's grenade attack at JFK?"

Giusti shook her head. "Other than the timing, no, though there's no doubt in any-one's mind. It's a classic, pulling first responders and resources in one direction, then attacking in another.

"You'll see we have a partial facial of the bomber at Saint Pat's, but no ID. He was careful. Cell-phone videos are still being turned in and posted, but we don't have more than that yet. We've found traces of C-4 in the crater the bomb left at Saint Pat's, right in the middle of Fifth Avenue, and we're trying to trace it. It wasn't a low-tech, homemade bomb. This was well planned."

"I'll bet that's made New York really pleasant now," Cal said. "All that rerouted traffic."

"Nothing short of a nightmare," Erwin said, looking back at Cal. "And you wouldn't believe the gawkers—tourists, for the most part. New Yorkers take one look, go home, and order Chinese takeout."

Cal said, "This bomber Sherlock will be interviewing, Nasim Conklin. Your theory is he was coerced into lobbing the grenade at JFK? He was threatened with the murder of his family?"

Giusti nodded. "You'll see from the profile there's no other likely conclusion. We've found no suspicious electronic communications, not in his e-mail, Internet activity, or phone records, no evidence he might be capable of this. Every professional contact who knows him agrees this was way out of the blue. If he really is an operative, under deep cover for some purpose, blowing himself up would be a waste of a good resource."

"They expected him to die at the airport," Sherlock said. "And we'd never be able to find out who forced him there."

"Correct," Giusti said. "MI5 video surveillance records have confirmed Conklin did visit a radical London mosque, the South London Mosque, on three occasions in the past two weeks, twice in the company of his mother at afternoon prayers and once alone. Nothing unusual in that, except that the mosque is run by Imam Al-Hädi ibn Mīrzā, who is radical enough to be capable of this. MI5 has had him under surveillance for some time. Nasim Conklin's mother, Sabeen Conklin, has attended the mosque for several years, seems to admire the imam and his bombastic rhetoric, his relentless recruiting efforts, his calls for a jihad against the West despite her big, lovely home in Belgravia. She lawyered up immediately, won't answer any questions."

"Using family as leverage, another common practice," Cal said. "I wonder about Conklin's mom, though. I can't imagine she'd put her grandkids at risk to be killed—or her son, for that matter."

Erwin said, "We don't know what she knew or knows. She's not talking. MI5 hopes she might roll on the imam if the grandkids are hurt, but like you, I can't imagine she'd knowingly sacrifice her own son."

"Agreed," Sherlock said. "My guess is she didn't have a clue about much of it."

Giusti said, "We suspect Nasim's mother disapproved of Nasim's wife, Marie Claire, since she is French and a Catholic. But you're right, it's a stretch. Since Nasim won't talk to us either, we assume he's more afraid of the people holding his family than he is of us. And yet he demanded to speak to you, Sherlock, for some reason. It's going to be up to you to convince him to open up. We may be able to help him if he tells us what he knows. You've got some time to think about it. We're coming up to Great Neck, and it'll be another forty-five minutes in the god-awful traffic before we exit at Colby."

Erwin said, "My stomach's rubbing against my backbone. I know a good deli in Great Neck. Anyone want a sandwich?"

22

On the way to Quantico
Friday morning

Savich carefully steered the Porsche around an eighteen-wheeler, accelerated, and seamed back between two cars. Traffic would lighten later as they approached Quantico. It was a day you were happy to be alive. The sky was a clear blue, no summer heat yet to blanket Washington, but it would come. He wished Sherlock were with him, especially this morning, but she'd been pulled back to New York to interview Conklin. He'd promised her he'd take another agent with him to Quantico for Brakey's hypnosis, and she'd known it would be Griffin for the simple reason that Griffin would believe what had happened to Savich the previous night, without question. She'd known he'd take the leap of faith. He himself was gifted.

Savich looked over at Griffin sitting beside

him. Not only was he gifted, he was very smart, ferocious in his dedication, and intuitive, some of the reasons Savich had asked him to transfer from the San Francisco Field Office to Washington. He knew Griffin would be well able to see the possibilities and the problems of the psychic they now faced. It didn't hurt that he was already involved in the case and knew Brakey. If Savich was right, Griffin would hear Brakey describe exactly the scene Savich himself had been drawn into under hypnosis.

He'd started telling Griffin about it this morning in the office as if he was telling him a dream, about the pine forest, about following the smell of smoke to the ancient tower, about Stefan Dalco appearing. Griffin had listened, sure, but it wasn't until Savich had baldly told him it wasn't a dream but an illusion created for him, probably exactly what Walter Givens and Brakey Alcott had experienced before they'd become murderers, that Griffin's eyes had blazed—no other way to describe it. As Savich had hoped, he wanted to know everything. Savich took him through it, step by step.

Griffin was quiet now, thinking about everything. He said matter-of-factly, more to himself than to Savich, "What do you think would have happened if Dalco's knife had stabbed you?"

"I don't know what would have happened, but I'll tell you, Griffin, the illusion had substance, it felt real."

"And you believe it's the same illusion Dalco used on Walter Givens and Brakey Alcott."

"Yes, a variation. Dalco came after me for a very different reason than Walter or Brakey. Dalco came after me to kill me. He wanted the investigation stopped."

Savich shook his head. "We don't even know all that much yet. Doesn't he realize you'd simply pick it up where I left off if something happened to me?"

"It wouldn't be the same, and you know it. It's amazing what you did, Savich— changing the scene to Winkel's Cave. Maybe it saved your life."

"Maybe. Or maybe Sherlock did when she started shaking me and slapping me to wake me up."

"We know it had to be Brakey who killed Deputy Lewis. It would have been an insane risk for anyone other than Brakey, even in the dark. But Dalco said nothing about why he chose Brakey? Why Walter Givens?"

Savich shook his head, settled the Porsche behind a Volvo like Sherlock's that cruised right at the speed limit. "I think Dalco, as our Brit friend Nicholas Drummond would say, is barking mad. He has his reasons, though. Revenge, perhaps. The deputy may have been unlucky enough to arrest him or someone he cared about very much, and his murder was payback. Why did he use Brakey? I don't know yet."

"How did you do it, Savich? How did you escape Dalco?"

"I concentrated with everything in me on that huge chamber in Winkel's Cave. I don't know who was more surprised when we popped right there, me or Dalco."

They passed a hitchhiker, a gnarly-looking bearded man with a backpack and banged-up leather boots. Griffin said, "It sounds amazing. And scary. Now, you think Brakey's going to tell us about a pine forest and a tower? That he'll remember Dalco telling him to murder Deputy Kane Lewis?"

"I'm betting on it, which means Dalco, whoever he is, is living in or near Plackett, Virginia, and that Deputy Kane Lewis and Sparky Carroll have something in common with him, something that made both of them his targets. Dalco said they deserved to die, so whatever it is he believes they did was enough for him to murder them, or rather manipulate Brakey and Walter into doing it for him."

"Both Brakey Alcott and Walter Givens are young," Griffin said. "Did Dalco pick them because he found them malleable, suggestible? And the Athames, Savich, they're common to Dalco and to both murders. And the Alcotts own them, you know they do. All of this is somehow connected to them, no doubt in my mind. Dalco knows them, interacts with them, at least he does Brakey. Did you and Sherlock meet the whole family yesterday evening?"

"Not the eldest son, Liggert. As for Mrs. Alcott—Deliah is her name—I know to my gut she was lying, I just don't know what about, exactly. You know the Athames aren't traceable, unfortunately. Still, Brakey and Walter Givens had to have got hold of them somehow, somewhere. I doubt a search warrant to search the Alcotts' houses for a pile of Athames would help us; you know they're long gone by now."

"Maybe Brakey will tell us," Griffin said. He shook his head. "If the Alcotts are involved, why would they have made Brakey the obvious suspect? Why bring our focus right to him? Dalco didn't seem to care about Walter Givens, made a huge flashy statement by having Walter stab Sparky Carroll right inside the Rayburn Building. But Brakey? Why would the Alcotts want to implicate Brakey?"

"If Brakey doesn't fill in the blanks, we will need to speak to more people in Plackett; it's the only way forward to find the tie-in between Sparky Carroll and Kane Lewis and find our way to whoever's behind these murders. We'll also check with the sheriff, examine Deputy Lewis's arrest files. Maybe there'll be something there." He said, "Why not have the sheriff do it?" In a minute flat, Savich was speaking to Sheriff

Watson. He identified himself, then posed the assignment to Ezra Watson.

"Good, I need something to do, something that counts. Everyone's talking nonsense— aliens and terrorists, and that's because they're afraid as well as upset about the two deaths. This I can understand and work with."

"How is your sister doing, Sheriff?"

"Glory keeps pestering me to do something and I keep telling her that it isn't my case, that there's nothing I can do, that she should call you." He paused. "But now I've got something to sink my teeth into. I'll get back to you, Agent Savich, if and when I find something that could help. Do you know anything yet about the two murders?"

"Yes, but it's not solid enough yet. I'll be speaking to you, Sheriff, and thank you for your help."

Savich rang off, checked the rearview mirror. "I'm glad the cops aren't around to pull me over for using my cell while driving."

"Since you're driving a Porsche," Griffin added, "they'd haul you right to the hoosegow." Griffin's smile faded quickly. "Stefan Dalco—did you try to trace him?"

"There's no record of anyone by that name entering the U.S. He's not a citizen, either, not by that name. I can't very well give a drawing of Dalco to the press and to Metro. His appearance was as much an illusion as the rest of it. I did have Jesse make me a sketch of his face to show to Brakey. His face may not be his own, but his illusion is, and I hope Brakey will confirm that for us."

"You know we got the tracking record from Brakey's truck in this morning. The morning of the murder, he went directly from the distribution center to his usual route, no detours. He'll have to tell us himself where he killed the deputy and where he put his body on the truck. And why.

"I still find it amazing that Dalco could suggest or order or manipulate two people, whatever their ages, into killing another human being."

Savich gave Griffin a quick look. "I think Dalco scared them to death. Maybe even more, I think it gave him a thrill."

"But you bested him, Savich. That's got to have knocked him back on his black-booted heels, don't you think?"

"Maybe for now, but I know we have to move quickly. If we don't find out who Dalco is, I can't begin to predict what he'll try next. Kill someone else who's offended him? I do know, though, that he's coming after me again."

Griffin smiled at him. "If—when—he does, you call me."

23

Jefferson Dormitory
Quantico

Forty-five minutes later, Griffin and Savich sat quietly and watched Brakey Alcott relax back in the comfortable chair, draw in a deep breath, and stare straight ahead through Dr. Hicks, his eyes blank. "I'm seeing him walk right up to me, his face so close I can feel his cloak brushing against my leg, see the black hairs in his nose. He called me by my name, Brakey. I swear I could feel his thoughts probing at me, like fingers reaching into my pocket to take my wallet." Brakey shook his head back and forth, moaned.

Savich leaned forward, lightly touched Brakey's shoulder. "It's all right, you're safe. He's not going to hurt you. All right? Tell us what he said to you, Brakey."

Brakey stilled. "He said I was going to have a dream, a very vivid dream, and this dream would be my chance to avenge a great evil. It would only be a dream, but I had to do it perfectly. He told me that in the dream I would get out of bed and get dressed, drive to The Gulf, the old bar out on Route 79. It would be crowded and I would order a beer and wait in the back, near the bathroom exit. Deputy Kane Lewis would be there drinking with all his buddies and I would follow him when he left but not let anyone see me. When we were alone in the parking lot and he was nearly to his car, I would call out his name, and when he turned, I would stab an Athame into his heart. I would carry his body exactly one hundred steps into the woods and I would dump him there." Brakey's breath hitched, speeded up. Savich lightly rubbed his hand. "It's all right. I know this is difficult, but tell us the rest of it."

"He told me several times not to let anyone see me. He put his right hand on my forehead and told me I would wake up soon, and when I awoke I would be in that dream, my next dream, he called it.

"I guess I was shaking my head because he said again it would only be a dream, a dream that would teach me about justice.

I felt his words wrapping all around me, taking over from me somehow. They became my own words, as if I'd said them myself. I did wake up and I got dressed right away, snuck out so Mama wouldn't hear me. He told me the Athame would be on the front seat of my car, and it was. I drove right to The Gulf."

There was horror on Brakey's face at what he saw now. "I stabbed him. It was easy, the Athame slid right into him. He was so drunk I don't even think he understood what was happening. His blood spurted out at me, all over my hands, my face, my clothes, and I knew it wasn't a dream, it was real. Deputy Lewis—I knew him all my life and he never did anything to me, and yet I'd killed him. And I knew then it wasn't a dream, he was dead because of me. Do you know he just weaved there before he fell over? He didn't say a word, didn't make a sound, he just looked surprised. I couldn't believe what was happening. I pushed on his chest, but he was dead." Brakey's voice broke.

Griffin said, "Brakey, you didn't carry Deputy Lewis into the woods like you were told to, did you?"

"All I could see was the blood and him lying there on the ground. I couldn't think anymore, I only knew I had to do something. I couldn't leave him there on the ground and so I put him in my car trunk and I started driving. Do you know I drove to the distribution center without even realizing it? I snuck in and got the key to the truck I was driving the next morning and I put him in one of the OTRs. I don't know why, I just did it, and I pulled some packages on top of him.

"I drove home and cleaned up and got rid of my bloody clothes. Nobody heard me. My brain started flying this way and that. I didn't know what I was going to do when it would be time to go back to the distribution center and pick up my parcel delivery truck. I knew Deputy Lewis was lying in the back of the truck and he was dead." Brakey fell silent. He lowered his face in his hands and sobbed. "That man, Dalco, he said it would all be a dream, but he lied. It wasn't. I killed Deputy Lewis." He raised his face, wet with tears, and looked at them blindly. "I must have dozed off, because the next morning when the alarm went off, I drove to work and delivered the OTRs to the Reineke post office. I had no idea he was in one of them. I had no memory of any of it."

Savich leaned in close. "I want you to listen to me now, Brakey, and believe me. It's Stefan Dalco who's the monster, not you. He's responsible for killing Deputy Lewis, not you."

Brakey was shaking his head back and forth. "I don't want to kill anyone else, I don't. What if he comes back again? What if he comes back tonight?"

You won't stand a chance. Savich knew if Brakey went home remembering Dalco and his dream, remembering he'd stabbed Deputy Lewis, it would be all over Plackett in a flash and Dalco would act. Dalco had to be close to Brakey, close enough for him to put an Athame in Brakey's car. He'd be putting Brakey in imminent danger. Savich made a decision. He leaned close to Dr. Hicks and spoke.

Dr. Hicks gave him an I-hope-you-know-what-you're-doing look and said in his calm voice, "When you wake up, Brakey, you will not remember being hypnotized, you will not remember anything you said to us. You will remember only what you already knew when you came here this morning. You will not be frightened. When you wake up, you'll do exactly what Agent Savich tells you to do. Do you understand me, Brakey? Good. I want you to wake up now."

Brakey blinked, looked from Dr. Hicks to Savich, then to Griffin. "I'm ready for you to hypnotize me. Why are we waiting? Is someone else coming?"

"Listen to me, Brakey," Savich said. "Sometimes hypnosis doesn't work. But you don't need to worry, we won't arrest you. You are obviously trying to help us. If there's anything else you want to tell us, or anything unusual happens to you, call me." Savich wrote his cell number on a card and put it in Brakey's pocket.

"Okay, I can do that. Wow, you couldn't even hypnotize me." Brakey's face fell. "But we still don't know what happened. I'm guilty of killing Deputy Lewis, you said, I've got to be. Why aren't you going to arrest me?"

"Because you're helping us, Brakey. You

will have to wear an ankle monitor, though. It's for your safety."

Brakey blinked at him. "For my safety? It's so you'll know where I am all the time, isn't it?"

"Both," Savich said. "We need to know where you've been, if you don't remember again. Agent Hammersmith will take you home once we get it fitted. I suggest you don't say anything about our meeting here at Quantico to anyone in Plackett. As for your family, feel free to tell them you can't be hypnotized." He paused, then, "Brakey, can you tell us if Deputy Lewis ever busted Sparky Carroll for any reason?"

"Sparky? No, Spark's a straight arrow, always has been. I mean, the guy cooked, Agent Savich."

"So far as you know, Sparky was never drinking at The Gulf when Deputy Lewis was there?"

"No, it was Sparky's dad who drank— Milt Carroll. He started drinking all the time after his wife died of cancer. He was at The Gulf a lot. Milt could still cook like a dream, didn't matter if he was roaring drunk. But Sparky only drank now and then, usually beer. He stopped that after his dad died of cirrhosis a few months ago. He was a really good guy. A lot of us are really going to miss him."

"I know, and I'm sorry," Savich said.

Brakey's face went blank. "Walter fixed Sparky's first car, an old Chevy his father gave him, when he was in ninth grade. By the time Walter was fourteen, he could fix anything on wheels. That's what Walter does now, too, and he gets paid more than I do working for the distribution center."

Griffin asked him, "So Walter and Sparky were always friends? No falling-out of any kind?"

"Never. They drag-raced all through high school, out on Old Pond Road, hooting and hollering. Walter stabbing Sparky in that office building, Agent Savich. I just don't know. What happened to me and Walter? Will I ever know?"

24

Colby, Long Island
Late Friday afternoon

Erwin exited the Long Island Expressway and headed to Colby. "About twenty-five thousand people live here, mostly retirees in houses too big for them. And about as many squirrels, ducking golf balls all over the golf courses. Good place for a safe house."

Giusti said, "The house is at the end of a long block. It's quiet and private, an easy perimeter. And yes, lots of squirrels."

"And too many oaks and maples," Erwin said. "I could get to someone in that house, no problem."

"Yeah, so you've told us, Pip. But you'd have to find us first and have feet as light as those squirrels." She turned to Sherlock and Cal. "Pip thinks he can walk in a room without anyone hearing him. What does your wife say about that?"

"All June ever said was she'd never cheat

on me, not worth the risk of getting caught. Really, Kelly, I'm only saying there are too many spots for snipers in those trees. We can't cover them all. If we lose Conklin, that's how it'll happen."

"Everyone knows that, Pip. We have to deal with the site we have until they move us again, which will be soon. Nasim's safer here than in federal lockup, without a doubt. No one followed us here, you and I made sure of that. Not that anyone would have known to follow us, in any case."

They pulled to a stop at the curb of an out-of-the-way 1960s clapboard house at the end of a cul-de-sac. It was a weathered gray that needed serious touch-ups and maybe a new roof. It looked passable for the neighborhood, though barely, and didn't call attention to itself. A fence enclosed the property, about six feet high, and Cal wagered it was alarmed, maybe electrified. Would anyone wonder about seeing a fence like that around such an ordinary, nondescript house?

Pip Erwin was right to worry about all the oaks and thick maples—not those on the property, where they'd been cleared near the house, but on the lots around it. The house windows were mostly small, at least, their curtains pulled. A deep porch surrounded the house, no doubt alarmed. Cal knew there had to be cameras discreetly placed, as well as motion sensors and listening devices. He wondered how often squirrels and rabbits tripped the alarms and made the agents inside skip a heartbeat or, worse, get complacent about them. Giusti was right, though. It would be difficult to get past them all. And only a few people could possibly know Conklin was here.

Giusti's cell rang out the theme from **Star Wars**. Cal perked up, pleased at that bit of whimsy from Ms. Commandant.

She answered and spoke low. "Four of us, Pip and me and Agents Sherlock and McLain up from Washington. No sign of pursuit coming out of the city. Pip stopped off for sandwiches to make sure."

And here Cal had believed hunger the motive for the stop for sandwiches. It was standard procedure.

A buzzer sounded and a discreet gate swung open. Erwin drove the SUV through with inches to spare on each side and stopped behind an old Chevy, beige and boring, not too new and not too old. Cal didn't see a single agent. **Good.**

An agent opened the front door, came out to stand on the porch. He wore jeans and a Kevlar vest over a white T-shirt, an open shirt on top, a Glock held at his side. He shook hands, introduced himself as Elliott Travers.

He showed them inside the small house, closing and locking the door behind them. Before he said anything else, he walked to a front window, pulled back the dark curtains an inch, and looked out. He stepped back, nodded to Giusti, and called out, "Jo, no worries. All clear."

A female agent wearing jeans and a blue Giants sweatshirt, doubtless with a vest beneath it, strolled into the living room, nodded to Erwin and Giusti. She was about Pip's age, fit, with salt-and-pepper hair and shining blue eyes. Cal could imagine her cheering at the top of her lungs at a Giants game. "Back's clear." She smiled at Cal and Sherlock. "Welcome to our humble abode. I'm Jo Hoag." She stuck out her hand. "It's a pleasure to meet you, Agent Sherlock. What you did at JFK—you made all of us in law enforcement proud. Kelly told you Nasim will only speak to you. He won't tell us why, keeps repeating he wants to speak to the redheaded agent from JFK. You'd think you'd be the last person he'd ever want to see after what you did to him."

She turned as another agent who looked to be in his forties and built like a fireplug walked into the room. "And this is Arlo."

Agent Arlo Crocker stuck out his hand, shook theirs. "I thought we could talk him around, but no, he insists it has to be you, Agent Sherlock. You guys want some iced tea before Sherlock has a go at him?"

Sherlock shook her head. "Not right now, Arlo. I'd really like to speak to Nasim right away."

Giusti said, "Look over there, Sherlock."

Nasim Conklin sat in front of her on a high-definition monitor hung at eye height on the living room wall. "He's in the back bedroom," Jo said. "You see he's shackled to a chair, watching TV. He watches the news. Other than that he reads—

newspapers, magazines, whatever we give him. He doesn't sleep much, hasn't eaten much. When he's not reading or watching the news, he sits there looking like the world is over. I suppose it is for him, and he knows it. He leaves that room to use the bathroom, and the half-hour we gave him outside last night when it was full-on dark."

Giusti said, "We'll wait out here."

Jo escorted Sherlock to the back bedroom, unlocked the door, and pushed it wide. "Nasim, here's your Agent Sherlock," she said, and stepped aside to let Sherlock pass. She started to close the door, but Cal shook his head and followed Sherlock into the bedroom. It was a small room with little furniture; a single bed in the middle was covered with a dark blue spread. Nasim Conklin had to ask to be moved from the chair to the bed, and those were his only choices. A pile of magazines, books, and newspapers was beside him.

Sherlock walked directly to Nasim Conklin and stopped in front of him.

"Hello, Nasim. I'm still amazed the grenade didn't blow us both to bits."

He slowly raised his head, stared at her,

his eyes shining with intelligence, but also with pain. Agent Hoag was right. Nasim Conklin looked like he knew this was the end of the road for him. But how he'd gotten to this point, that was what Sherlock had to find out.

"No," he said, his voice matter-of-fact. "I don't think you were close enough, but you'd have had to wash me off you." He gave a laugh, raw and bitter. "That is if I'd had courage enough to use it." He spoke in fluent British English, but with a French accent, and something else. She knew his origins were Syrian.

She sat down on the edge of the bed. "It did blow eventually—thankfully, in the bomb box."

She saw his hands were cuffed loosely together in front of him, fastened to a belt he wore, allowing him only enough movement to turn book pages and scratch his nose. The wrist she'd broken at JFK was in a thin cast.

"I could have thrown it at you, watched you explode into a million bloody bits right before my eyes."

"Now, there's a visual," Sherlock said.

"I've got to say, I'm glad you didn't."

He nodded toward Cal, who stood against the door, his arms folded over his chest. "I don't want him here. Make him go away. Just you."

"Pretend I'm not here," Cal said.

"You her bodyguard?" Nasim rattled his shackles. "I can't do much of anything to her now."

Cal leaned back against the closed door, his arms still crossed over his chest. "As I recall, you couldn't do much of anything to her the first time."

Nasim smiled, let it fall away. "A pity, perhaps, but you're right." He studied Cal for another full minute, then turned back to Sherlock.

"Why didn't you talk to the other agents, Nasim? Why me?"

He looked at her full-on and said simply, "Because you don't fear death."

25

The words hovered in the still air between them. Sherlock didn't know what she'd expected him to say, but not this. She shook her head. "You're wrong, Nasim. Everyone who has both feet in this world fears death."

"But you came after me regardless."

No one had asked her about that. "Actually, the truth is pretty simple. Everything happened so fast. I only knew I had to stop you from killing Melissa and all those other innocent people. My job is to protect, you know that."

"You even remember that woman's name —Melissa. I should never have grabbed her. I should have thrown the grenade and ended it."

"But you didn't."

"I failed at the airport because I was afraid to die."

"Perhaps it wasn't fear that stopped you. Perhaps you couldn't convince yourself to kill all those people."

He began picking his thumbnail. "I heard the agents talk about your little boy. You have both a husband and a son, yet you acted, knowing you could die. Don't you care about what would happen to them? How they would grieve for you?"

Where was this coming from? Did Cal and the agents in the living room wonder as well?

Then she understood. "My husband and my son are the center of my life. You have a family, children, you know what that means. What I don't understand is what drove you, what you hoped to accomplish. You are an educated man, a journalist. Nothing you've written or done suggests you are a terrorist or a jihadist. You have no ties we could find to any terrorist organization, no history of speaking out for their cause or defending what they do. You've led a peaceful life, an admirable life; you love your wife, your family.

"So tell me, why did you take a grenade to JFK intending to kill dozens of people?"

"I had no choice."

"Because they took your family from you, didn't they?"

"How did you know that? How very stupid of me. By now you know my youngest son has a birthmark behind his knee. You know everything about me, don't you? And about my family?"

"Not yet. But we do know your wife, Marie Claire, arrived in Boston with your three children three days ago. We have identified two men on the plane with them as having forged documents, very good ones. They were seen on airport security cameras leaving the terminal with your family."

"So you don't know where they are?"

"We saw them in a black SUV leaving the airport exit, but we have nothing else. Not yet."

"Do you understand I had no choice? That I acted as you would have acted if someone held your husband and your son hostage, would kill them without a thought?"

There was no point in contradicting him. Sherlock said, "How long did they have your family before they sent you to JFK?"

"Three days and three nights."

"Endless time to let your fear of their dying

gnaw at you, to let you feel the grief of losing your family if you didn't explode the grenade. Endless time to live with the knowledge of your own death."

"They are ruthless and cruel, but all that makes no difference now. I am prepared to die, I will die. My only hope is that you will find my family before they are murdered."

"You are under our protection here, Nasim. You're safe here, you know that."

"You Americans overestimate your-selves, Agent. My safety no longer matters to me, in any case. Even after I die, I fear for what they will do to my family."

There was no doubt in his voice. He was certain he would die soon. "Tell me how all this happened to you, Nasim. Tell me who it was who put you here."

"I will tell you all I know if you swear you will do everything in your power to find my family. Swear you will not let your govern-ment sacrifice them because they are of no value to them. I will tell you then, no one else. You."

"I swear it, Nasim. I will personally take part in the hunt for your family. And we will hunt for them, you can be sure of that."

He studied her face, slowly nodded. "You will not have much time."

"Take me through it, then, Nasim. How did they approach you?"

"Approach me? I was walking home from the market on Lancaster Road when two men wearing nylon masks threw me in the back of a van. I never saw the driver. They struck me whenever I tried to move, didn't say a word to me. They chained me in a dirty warehouse somewhere that smelled of rotten fish, left me there terrified, not knowing why this was happening to me or whether they would kill me.

"When they returned, always three of them, always in their masks, it was only to bring me enough food and water to survive. They wouldn't speak to me or answer any of my questions, ignored my plea to call my wife so she would know I was alive and arrange for a ransom, hit me again if I said too much. From the few words they said, it was obvious they were Arabic. When they spoke in that language, it was with a Syrian accent. I might recognize their voices, perhaps, but that is all.

"After two days they sat me down and

the man with the strongest accent told me I would be taking a trip to New York, said they had an assignment for me there. He showed me photos of my family on a smartphone, surrounded by men in masks, played a video of my wife, terrified, pleading with me to do as they asked. They had my passport, so I knew they'd taken my family from my home, since all my papers were there. He said I would learn later what I would be doing there, but that if I failed, they would murder my wife and my children."

Nasim paused, looked down at his fisted hands. "The man told me he would do it himself, strangle each of them in turn, bury them all together in a single grave. I believed him. I demanded to speak to my wife, demanded proof she was alive. They said I could speak to her only after we were all in New York. That way no one in London could find them, even if I got word to someone. They had me purchase tickets for all of us myself, even left me alone during my flight to New York.

"A man approached me at Kennedy, took me to a waiting van, blindfolded me, and drove away. I believe there were three men.

They did not speak, except for the destination: Queens. They held me in a small apartment there, I don't know where in Queens. I spoke with Marie Claire for the first time that night. We spoke in French until one of the men struck me in the ribs, said we had to speak English. They let her tell me they were still all right, that they had made it to America. I heard my children in the background."

Nasim Conklin looked toward the single window, darkened by the curtain pulled tightly over it. "They took the phone away. That was the last time I spoke to my wife."

"You say 'they,' Nasim. You obviously saw them. Do you know who they were? Can you describe them, or the van?"

"There were three of them, their accents Syrian, like the first three. They were about my age and older. They looked pleasant and well dressed, all three in slacks and jackets. They were polite; their English was quite good. The license plate on the van? I didn't see it."

"I will show you photos, see if you can identify them."

"Yes, I will try. I do know they had British

passports, but perhaps they were forged as well."

"And it was only then they told you what you had to do? Explode a grenade in the security line at JFK?"

He nodded. "Right after they took the phone, the nightmare became worse than I imagined. They showed me the grenade, showed me how to make it explode, and handcuffed me to a cot in the back room, expecting me to sleep. Of course I could not sleep at all. It was then I overhead bits and pieces of their conversation through the closed door, in Arabic. They didn't realize I could sometimes hear them. That was when I heard them use the word **Bella**, a kind of code word for what they were doing. They mentioned a man they called the Strategist—there is no Arabic word translation, so they used the English. I don't know who he is, but they spoke of him respectfully, almost reverently—as their mastermind or leader. And one of the men—his name was Rahal—mentioned a name, Hosni, called him his brother and Hosni was here in the United States, and was helping them. He laughed a bit. Do you think Hosni Rahal might be important?"

Sherlock's heart kicked up. "Hosni Rahal. We will search for him. You have no idea at all who the Strategist might be?"

Nasim shook his head. "Other than the one who seems to have planned this Bella project, I have no idea. Those were the only names I heard. I do not know if that will help you."

"The question we need to focus on, then, Nasim, is why did this happen to you in particular? Who picked you out to do this, and why? If we can discover that, we can find them, and perhaps your family."

"I have hardly thought about anything else. What did I do, what did my family do to deserve this? Why didn't they send one of the many misguided souls who are eager to die for jihad, someone they had thoroughly trained, rather than take the risk of choosing someone like me? I froze, didn't I?"

"Exactly the question. Could they have picked you because they thought you couldn't be connected to them? Expected that you would die without even knowing who they were? Or perhaps it was also something personal, someone wanted you dead?"

"I have no mortal enemies, so far as I know."

"When they first took you, though, you believed it was for ransom? Because you were selling your father's business and you would shortly be very rich?"

"That is true, but there is only my mother. Why would she want me dead?"

Sherlock nodded. "All right. Go back with me, Nasim. You returned to London about six months ago?"

26

He nodded. "Yes, about six months ago, after the death of my father. My mother, Sabeen, took his loss very hard, begged me to move to London. To be honest, Marie Claire and I were happy in Rouen, both of us settled and looking forward to our future there. But my mother needed me, asked to have her grandchildren back in her life, and there was the family business in England to attend to."

"She couldn't come visit your children, stay with you in Rouen?"

"She and my wife, Marie Claire, do not like each other. My mother never approved of my marriage to a French Catholic, was especially upset about my children being raised Catholic. You see, my father was an atheist, and he allowed her to raise me in Islam. I lapsed in my beliefs long ago, and she was pushing me to come back to my faith."

"And your father?"

"My father disapproved of us for different

reasons. He owned a very successful chain of dry-cleaning stores, all over England and Scotland. He expected me to join the business with him, and when I told him I had no interest, that I wanted to be a writer, a journalist, instead, he was very angry. He severed ties between us."

He shrugged. "Then he was dead and I felt I had no choice but to return to London, at least temporarily, and so we moved the next month. We found an apartment near enough to visit my mother but far enough away to suit my wife. Marie Claire was worried what my mother would say to our children about their religion if she left her alone with them.

"I told my mother I intended to sell the stores as quickly as possible. I was surprised she said she'd been very involved in the business for a number of years. She begged me not to sell the business, that I didn't have to be involved at all. I could simply hand over the running of it to her. But I refused. I wanted nothing to do with the chain, I admit it, in part because I still felt great anger at my father for what he'd done to us. To me, my father's business was an albatross around my neck. Besides, I soon had conglomerates lining up to make offers, and I had already been asked by the **London Herald** to write for them."

"Surely your father must have realized your mother would want to keep the chain. Why did he leave his business to you?"

"My father always did exactly what suited him. For some reason, he must not have wanted my mother involved in the business any longer. I don't know why. He must have known I would sell the business if he left it to me. In any case, he didn't beggar her, don't get that idea. He left my mother three houses and a great deal of money.

"Dealing with my mother was the difficult thing. I wasn't in England more than a week before she was asking me to visit the South London Mosque with her and meet with the imam, Al-Hädi ibn Mīrzā is his name. I finally agreed, for my own reasons, let me be clear about that. I was curious what it would be like to revisit my religion after so many years. The imam was all she could talk about with me—how wise he was, how his fire would bring Islam to the world, and the world to Islam. He was a genius, she said, at helping Muslims who had lapsed into the ways of the West with the greater jihad, their personal struggle to fulfill their religious duties. She was smitten.

"Finally I visited with Al-Hädi ibn Mīrzā after prayers. He certainly had charisma, seemed comfortable speaking with people like me. He listened carefully to my concerns about the faith, blessed me for searching for my true path, invited me back to speak with him.

"To my surprise, the imam suddenly asked me over tea, to reconsider selling my father's business. He said it was important to Islam that devout women like my mother continue in positions of power in England, that she was a pillar of the mosque and he needed her support. My mother obviously put him up to it, and it angered me. I was not very polite when I told him it was not his affair, and that it had nothing to do with Islam. He lectured me for a bit about my responsibilities, but when he realized he wouldn't convince me, he bowed his head and apologized. I did as well, for being short with him. He changed the subject, spoke of my success as a journalist, and asked if I was interested in writing a piece about some of the young local men he had recruited to the faith. He said it might help me find my way.

"I told him I would think about it, that I'd only just moved to London and needed time. That was all that was said. I have thought back to that conversation many times, but I don't know if that meeting with the imam had anything to do with this."

Sherlock said, "MI5 already had the mosque and the imam under surveillance, Nasim. We knew you had been there. We'll know to ask questions about your father's business now. You were right to be upset, to suspect something."

"Let me say that my wife, Marie Claire, was far more upset than I." He paused, a memory bringing a quick smile. "She'd been against my going to the mosque with my mother in the first place, called it 'sticking my foot into my mother's tent.' She called my mother, told her to stop trying to manipulate me using the imam, that selling my father's business was my decision and she could keep her nose out of it. As you can imagine, my mother didn't take this lying down. She screamed that Marie Claire was a worthless Crusader harlot, that she, my mother, would not rest until I returned to Islam. Needless to say, they haven't had any contact with each other since then.

"You might laugh, but it hasn't been easy for any of us." He paused again, another smile playing around his mouth. "Marie Claire can be ferocious."

When he looked up again, he whispered, "Do you know what is most painful for me? Realizing that Marie Claire, however she tries, cannot help herself or our children. And I am useless to her.

"You have heard everything I know. And you will use it to help my family. I am sorry it wasn't more."

"Did you have any idea you were a diversion, Nasim? That Saint Patrick's Cathedral was the prime target? That the vice president of the United States was inside the cathedral when the bomb was planted? And other high-ranking members of our government?"

"No, I didn't know. I did believe, though, there would probably be other attacks. Why a grenade in a security line if there was no more to it than that?"

"You never heard any of the men who took you speak of the vice president? Or any other American names?"

Nasim shook his head. "I only heard the word **Bella**—and as you know, that is Italian for beautiful. I can't imagine their calling Vice President Foley beautiful. I suppose now they meant the beautiful cathedral, other cathedrals as well? They are prized symbols, are they not, monuments revered for their beauty?"

"Worse, they are effective targets for terror. If you can't feel safe in a church, where are you safe?"

"Yes. Who would risk attending a place of worship if someone might blow it up? I pictured the incredible cathedral in Rouen, lying in rubble. It would be an awful thing."

Sherlock said, "Until we find them, we can't know what they will try to do next. Do you think there is any chance they will release your family?"

"Not while I am alive, in your custody. While my family is alive, they control me. These people know no mercy, no forgiveness, no understanding. They are like dogs. They defecate and move on. I pray my family is not already dead." He raised hopeless eyes to her face. "I pray also that I am not being a fool to believe it possible."

She brushed against the cuff on his wrist. "You have done the right thing, Nasim. If it is possible to help them, we will."

Nasim looked down at his shackled feet. "They took me outside for a half-hour last night, when it was dark, to breathe in the fresh air, to let me feel I'm alive. I look forward to that. May I ask you to bring me a pen and paper now, so that I may write a note to my family? I will trust you to give it to them, if it is possible."

"Yes." As she rose, he said, "My kidney still hurts, but I don't have any more head-aches. Perhaps you are out of practice."

"I thought I kicked you hard enough to give you a right proper concussion, maybe a short hospital stay. I'm glad I didn't." She smiled at him, waited for Cal to follow her out, and closed the door.

Was that a laugh she heard?

27

When Sherlock and Cal returned to the living room it was to see Jo raising a cup to Sherlock. "Well done."

Giusti was rubbing her hands together. "We've already notified MI5 about this nom de guerre—the Strategist. We have nothing in our records about him. I've put out a call to find anyone by the name of Hosni Rahal, get us a location."

She looked at Sherlock. "I'm sorry for Nasim. We won't let him die, we won't let that happen, but I fear for his family as much as he does."

Cal said, "Seems to me Nasim asked the best question—why him? This imam? And why? MI5 needs to do some digging into the imam's finances, his dead father's, his mother's. There's got to be something there."

Pip Erwin sipped his iced tea. "I still wonder why Nasim trusted only you, refused to speak to the rest of us. Just you, Sherlock."

Sherlock said, "I think he wanted to tell someone, and I was the one he felt a connection to. It's strange, though, how convinced he is he will die soon."

Giusti nodded. "He clearly does. I don't think there's a terrorist within a hundred miles of this place, but I'm tempted to tighten security even so. Perhaps we should keep him in the house tonight."

"He was so looking forward to being outside," Sherlock said. "It would be an opportunity for me to talk with him again."

Cal was standing next to the front window, his arms crossed over his chest. "Come on, you guys can't really be thinking about taking him outside every night, among all those trees? Have you looked through an infrared sniper scope, like the Ares 6? Attach that to an H-and-K and you're in business from hundreds of yards away. You can't take that kind of risk, especially if Sherlock is with him."

Jo Hoag walked to Cal, put her hand on his shoulder. "Cal, I've walked the grounds, and there are only a few spots that would be vulnerable to a sniper. We never let Nasim walk that way."

"There are people who want Nasim dead, he's right about that," Cal said. "He failed them, and he's a major loose thread, a threat to them. I would be moving him room to room, never on a schedule, and no outside jaunts, ever. As for letting Sherlock out with him, I veto that."

"Your objection is noted," Giusti said. "However, McLain, you're not in charge here, I am."

Cal got in her face. "My job is to follow my own orders where her safety is concerned." He looked from Pip Erwin, to Jo Hoag, to Arlo Crocker, and then to Sherlock. "If anything happens to you on my watch, Sherlock, my life won't be worth spit."

Sherlock said, "All right, I'll do as you like, Cal. I owe that to you." She didn't want to think about what Dillon would do if something happened to her; she couldn't think like that. There was always risk. And Kelly was right: who could possibly know about this place? "Everything having to do with Nasim is your call, Kelly. Now, does anyone know where I can find a pencil and paper for Nasim? He wants to write to his family."

An hour before dark, Sherlock and Cal sat down for dinner with Nasim in his room, the local news on TV turned down low. Nasim had asked for fast food, a hamburger and fries, his favorite food as a tourist, he said. They spoke of family. Sherlock learned Cal had three sisters, half a dozen nieces and nephews, and a mother who tapped her toe at him whenever she saw him. She wanted kids from him as well.

Nasim looked up at the camera and asked to use the bathroom.

Within a minute Agents Hoag and Crocker appeared in the open doorway. A visit to the bathroom after dinner seemed an established routine. Nasim rose.

Sherlock and Jo Hoag followed Crocker, his hand on Nasim's cuffs, to the end of the hall. Crocker took off the cuffs, opened the bathroom door, checked around the small room, and nodded. Nasim went in and Crocker partially shut the door.

Agent Hoag checked her watch. "Not long before it's dark enough to take him out to the front porch, if that's what Kelly decides. That's where we've got the best cover." They heard the toilet flush, heard water running in the sink.

There was a shot, then another, sharp and

very loud—rifle shots.

"No!" Crocker and Hoag were through the bathroom door in an instant. Nasim was leaning over the washbowl, staring at himself in the mirror. It was covered with a spray of blood, his blood. Nasim saw Sherlock's white face in the mirror and slowly sank to the floor, his hands pressed against his chest. He didn't speak, but his mouth formed the words **Save my family**.

Sherlock was on her knees beside him, pressing hard against a gaping wound in his chest. She saw blood pouring out of his shoulder where a second bullet had hit. "Nasim! Don't you dare die on me. Come on, keep your eyes open, stay with me!" Sherlock was dimly aware of the agents shouting, running, yelling into comm units. She heard more shouts from outside the bathroom window, more loud gunfire, but she wasn't listening. She was pressing her hands against his chest. But she'd seen his wound and she knew—she eased herself down over him, said quietly to him, "Nasim, you will not die, do you hear me, you can't die, not after all this. Stay with me!"

28

Nasim's thready heartbeat stuttered, slowed, and stopped. Blood no longer pulsed in his neck. Sherlock pulled him away from the wall, laid him flat on his back, and started CPR, pushing on his chest again and again, breathing into his mouth even after she felt Cal's hand on her shoulder. "He's gone, Sherlock. It's over."

She didn't stop, couldn't stop, not yet. She banged her fist against his bloody chest, breathed her breath into his mouth.

"Sherlock, look at his eyes."

Three fast shots rang out through the bathroom and shattered the tiles around them. Sherlock felt the hot, fast path of a bullet as it parted her hair at her left temple and crashed bits of tile onto her head. Two more bullets shattered yet more tiles and gouged out the rim of the bathtub. She flattened over Nasim and Cal slammed down over her, covering her as best he could.

There were shouts, more rapid bursts of

gunfire, then quiet.

They heard Jo Hoag yell out, "Thompson's down, but Elliott got the shooter!"

Cal whispered against her ear. "You okay?"

Sherlock looked up at him, nodded. "He's dead, Cal. He's dead, like that." She snapped her fingers.

Cal lifted himself off her, offered his hand, but she rolled to her side, balanced above Nasim, and stared into his empty eyes. "No," she whispered. She leaned down, touched her hand to his cheek. "We failed him."

"Come," he said, and finally she let him help her up. The front of her white shirt and her fisted hands that had banged against his heart were covered with Nasim's blood.

"Cal, your arm, it's bleeding."

Cal hadn't felt a thing, but he did now. A streak of pain slashed through his arm. He looked down at a spreading bloody stain on his shirt, pressed his hand against his upper arm. "It can't be bad, it's not bleeding very much. It's probably a through-and-through." Agents crowded into the bathroom, all of them talking at once. He heard Giusti's voice, turned to see her white face.

Sherlock looked over at her. "Nasim was right, Kelly. He said he was going to die here."

"I don't know how they found us." Kelly took a step into the bathroom. "Are you all right, Sherlock?"

"Yes, it's all Nasim's blood. But Cal took a bullet in his arm covering me."

"It's under control, no worries," Cal said. "He came close to taking Sherlock out, Kelly."

Jo Hoag yelled from down the hall, "Elliott shot the shooter right out of the tree, but he's alive! Thompson's okay, probably concussed. Paramedics will be here any moment. I'm going out to meet them."

Sherlock said, "Jo, wait. Have the paramedics tend to the shooter and Thompson. Don't bring them in here. Nasim's dead, there's nothing they can do." She drew a deep breath. "Listen, I don't think we want it to get out yet that Nasim is dead. Let's keep the terrorists guessing, at least until we find and hopefully save his family. Nasim didn't entirely trust the terrorists not to murder his family if he gave himself up and let them kill him, and I believe that's the reason he told me. I'm his backup.

"I don't trust the terrorists, either, so let's hold off—only a day, tops—give ourselves time to find his family. Then we can announce it and take the heat."

Kelly said, "We can't, Sherlock. We'd be crucified, accused of a massive cover-up, and that's the last thing—"

"You don't understand, Kelly," Sherlock said right over her. "Unlike Nasim, I believe once the terrorists know Nasim is dead, they'll kill the family. If they don't know he's dead, then maybe we have a chance. We have a name, Hosni Rahal. We can find the family." She stopped, looked down at Nasim again. His eyes stared straight at the ceiling. There was no surprise on his face. What there was was acceptance.

Kelly chewed this over. "All right, okay. I've got to call Zachery, clear it with him. A day, tops. We're looking for Rahal. If he's in the U.S., we'll find him and pray he's still holding the family." She looked down at her watch. "The crime scene techs and the ME are a half-hour out. Cal,

Sherlock, come into the living room. Before I call Zachery, we've got to figure out how this happened. We're lucky Elliott's such a great shot or it could have been worse. Do you know he could shoot a feather off an eagle's wing—"

Kelly realized shock was nibbling at the edges. She had to get herself together.

She saw Cal was shaking his head at her. "What?"

"This wasn't your fault." He'd wanted to blast her for this debacle but didn't because he knew she'd blast herself enough for all of them.

Giusti gave a scratchy laugh. "Then whose fault was it, Cal?"

"There's a lot to be done," he said matter-of-factly, "and you're in charge. You're the one everyone will look to."

"Yes, yes, you're right." Giusti nodded, sucked in air, rebooted.

Cal said, "Sherlock came closer to dying than any of us. I saw a bullet part her hair over her ear, scared me spitless. Those last shots were aimed at her and they came well after the shooter had to know Nasim was down. If he hadn't stayed in that tree to try to take Sherlock out as well as Nasim, he might have made it out of here. Point is, Sherlock wasn't a bystander, she was one of his targets."

Kelly looked like she'd taken a punch to the gut. "I'm very sorry about this. Why didn't you say anything?"

Cal said, "Nah, she'd never admit it to you because if she did, she'd have to spit it out to Savich."

She closed her eyes. "You swear your arm's not bad?"

"It's only a flesh wound," he said, and grinned at her. Cal saw it steadied her. **Good.** He knew Giusti had to be wondering about her career prospects in the FBI. She'd lost a major terrorist on her watch. Not good.

Sherlock said, "Cal, let me take a look at it. When the paramedics get here, they'll have to deal with the shooter and Thompson." She cleaned the wound with alcohol from the first-aid kit, then wrapped his arm in a soft white bandage. It didn't hurt all that much. Both of them were listening to the agents discussing what had happened, trying to figure out how it had happened. She said to Cal, "When we get to the hospital, they can take a look. As far as I can tell, all you'll need is Steri-Strips, Cal. You were lucky."

No, he thought, **you were the lucky one.** "You guys got any ideas on how they found Nasim?"

Pip Erwin shook his head. "I don't understand it. No one would break protocol and get us followed. I can't imagine there's a leak in the Counterterrorism Task Force."

Cal looked at Sherlock. "You know, don't you?"

"Yes, I think so. Remember Nasim kept repeating he was going to be killed, even though he was tucked away in a safe house? All he could talk about was that his life didn't matter, just his family's. Once he told me everything he knew, I think Nasim made it easy for them to shoot him. Did you notice the bathroom curtains were wide open? He did that to make an easy target of himself. He thought it was the only thing left for him to do that might let them live— that, and tell me everything. He figured he'd done everything he could to save them."

Kelly said, "So you think the terrorists

were still in control, that they'd convinced him he had to die, one way or the other, if his family was to live? But that leads to the question: How did they find him?"

Sherlock said, "I'm betting the ME will find a small wound hidden somewhere on Nasim's body, maybe his armpit or inner thigh. He'll find a low-power chip under the skin, a tracking chip. If I'm right, the terrorists have known where Nasim was every minute since he walked into JFK. With the chip, they could be sure he was walking into the security line and track him if he walked away."

Cal looked at her like a proud papa. He said to no agent in particular, "She's really good at this. I'll bet you she's right."

Giusti said, "Whether you're right or not, Sherlock, it still means we've been had. And not by some group of young men with box cutters or homemade bombs. These guys, whoever they are, who they represent, are stone-cold professionals."

Giusti's cell rang. She answered it, then hung up. "The paramedics took our shooter directly to the hospital. He's going into surgery to remove the bullet from his shoulder." She paused, pressed speed dial. "Time I spoke with Zachery." And she walked out the front door.

Sherlock called after her, "When the ME gets here, Kelly, he needs to find and remove the chip and leave it here, otherwise the terrorists would know Nasim's dead."

29

D.C. Jail
Washington, D.C.
Friday afternoon

The D.C. Jail was a grim spot in a beautiful landscape, Savich had always thought, at the end of D Street near the Congressional Cemetery, the Potomac at its back. Ten minutes after he'd showed his creds at the gate, he'd gotten permission from Warden Spooner to use the conference room. He was shown to a small utilitarian room with pea-green walls and institutional furniture where Walter Givens and his family had been seated around a large square table. Savich hadn't wanted to speak to Walter Givens through bulletproof glass, and when he learned Walter's family was visiting, he'd asked the warden that they all be moved.

Mr. Givens turned when Savich came into the stark room. He waved his arms around him. "I suppose we should thank you for this? Getting my boy out from behind that wall of glass with guards standing behind him?"

Savich introduced himself, showed his creds. "I thought this room would be better so all of us can speak together."

Mrs. Givens waved her fist at him. "Our lawyer found out you hypnotized Brakey Alcott. So if you're here to push hypnosis, Walter will not do it. I don't care if you take us all to the Ritz-Carlton."

"There's no need to have Walter hypnotized," Savich said. He motioned for Mr. Givens to be seated again. He was surprised to see a teenage girl in the room. It had to be Walter's seventeen-year-old sister, Lisa Ann. He smiled at her.

"I don't see what we have to talk about unless you've found out something," Mr. Givens said. "Walter still doesn't remember what happened with Sparky Carroll until that crowd of people tackled him in the hallway, told him he'd stabbed Sparky. We want to bring in doctors to have him tested, prove he had a seizure of some kind and was not responsible for Sparky's death. Can you help us with that?"

Twenty-three-year-old Walter Givens

looked pale after only two days behind bars. Worse, he looked leached of life, from the inside out. He was taking it hard. And why not? Two days ago, he'd killed his own friend, lost the thread of his life, and for all he knew, his own sanity.

Savich said, "We will conduct medical and psychiatric tests, and you will be allowed to arrange for your own. Your own attorney will arrange it. He won't need my help. I want you all to know I also think Walter wasn't responsible for Sparky Carroll's death. I'm going to try to prove that."

Mrs. Givens leaned forward toward Savich. "I knew it, I knew Walter couldn't have done this willingly. Do you know what happened to Walter to make him do this?"

"I hope to find out," Savich said, "and I hope you all can help me by answering some of my questions. I know you're worried —I would be as well—but I will need all of you to stay calm. Do not agree to any interviews, don't talk about this to anyone —that includes you, Lisa Ann. The tabloids and headline news sites would be happy to jump all over Walter's story, and that wouldn't help any of us. I would guess

Walter's attorney already counseled all of you not to speak to the media. Have you?"

"I told that pack of hounds what they could do with their microphones," Givens Senior snapped out. "Those vultures were even waiting outside when Lisa Ann was let out of her high school today, weren't they, sweetie?"

Lisa Ann was a very pretty girl with long, glossy brown hair that framed a heart-shaped face. She nodded. "It was horrible. This one overweight guy with a micro-phone in his hand yelled at me, and when I started running, he chased me, but not for long. He was bent over and heaving, he was so out of shape." She paused, licked some pale lipstick off her lips. "But I actually wanted to talk to them, tell them Walter wouldn't hurt anybody. He never even hit me once, even when I stole his shorts and hung them up in the girls' locker room at school. All he did was turn red in the face and tromp outside to Daddy's old Jeep and pop the hood."

"I changed the plugs," Walter said.

Mrs. Givens chuckled, shook her head. She had a glossy brown ponytail, the same color as her daughter's. "I fix hair in my home, Agent Savich, and one of my clients' daughters saw her do it. That's how Walter found out." She stopped cold, paled, then shook her head, as if disbelieving what she'd said.

Savich kept his voice calm, even. "I need you to tell me if any of you have harmed or angered or injured anyone in any way, anyone who might have a reason to strike out at you or your family." He saw they were confused, knew they believed Walter had suffered some sort of fit. "Indulge me on this," he said. "Are you in conflict with anyone, Walter? Mr. Givens?" He nodded toward Mrs. Givens and Lisa Ann.

Lisa Ann opened her mouth, then shook her head.

Savich leaned toward her. "What, Lisa Ann?"

"It just popped into my head, but it's silly. Tanny Alcott said she hated me. She hit me with a football once on purpose because I told on her."

"Whatever was that about?" her mother asked her. "Goodness, Tanny's only ten years old."

Savich said, "What did she do?"

"One day when I was visiting the grade school, I was in the restroom and there was Tanny, making fun of another little girl. She'd had leukemia and her hair was just starting to grow back because of her chemotherapy. Tanny said she wouldn't stop it when I asked her to and I couldn't make her, so I told their teacher, Mrs. Abrams. I called her a mean little witch. She gave me this freak-weird look and said she'd get me for that. That's when she said she hated me."

"Why did you call her a witch?" Savich asked.

"Everyone in Plackett knows the Alcotts are witches. Well, Mrs. Alcott says she's a Wiccan, so I guess she's not a bad witch."

Savich nodded, turned to Walter. "Has anything like that happened between you and any of the Alcotts, Walter?"

Walter shook his head, but Mr. Givens said, "Wait, Walter, remember when you were at The Gulf and got into a fight with Liggert Alcott?"

"Yeah, I remember. What happened was I saw him hit his kid, Teddy, outside the feed store last month and I told him to stop it. A week later we got into it at The Gulf. He was drunk, so Deputy Lewis hauled him off to spend the night in jail. He let me go because everyone backed me up, said Liggert was the one who started it."

"Walter," Savich said, "did Sparky Carroll ever harm the Alcotts in any way you know of?"

Walter thought, shook his head. "I'm sorry. Agent Savich, I can't think of a thing. He and Brakey and I were friends all through school. Sparky and I were in and out of the Alcott house when we were kids. There was never any trouble. We always thought the Alcotts calling themselves Wiccans was funny. Sparky and I drifted away from Brakey when we got older, you know how that goes. We had less in common."

Mrs. Givens said, "There's Liggert. He's older and a bully. He hits his wife, too, if what I've heard from my ladies is true."

Walter said, almost in a whisper, "Sparky was one of my best friends, ever since we were kids. How could I have killed him, Agent Savich? And why?"

It was almost the same question Brakey had asked him.

30

Plackett, Virginia
Friday evening

The front door at the Alcotts' flew open. "Brakey!"

Griffin recognized Deliah Alcott easily from Savich's description. She picked up her gauzy skirt and ran to her son, hugging him close. She ran her fingers through his hair, held his face between her hands, and asked him, "Are you all right, Brakey? Did you remember what happened? Why are you smiling? Did they prove you didn't kill Deputy Lewis?"

Brakey put his hands on his mother's arms, gently pushing her back. "I didn't remember anything, but it's okay, really. It turns out they can't hypnotize me, but they let me come home anyway. Agent Hammersmith brought me, and look"—he bent down and pulled up the leg of his jeans—"I've got to wear this ankle bracelet until they find out who killed Deputy Lewis.

That's it. Otherwise I'm free to do as I please, Agent Savich told me."

Deliah Abbott stared from that ankle bracelet to Griffin. She took Brakey's hand. "Don't show that bracelet off to anyone else, okay, Brakey? We don't want people talking any more than they already are."

Deliah Alcott turned fierce eyes to Griffin. "You're Agent Hammersmith?"

"Yes, ma'am." Griffin handed her his creds. "And you're Brakey's mom, Mrs. Alcott."

"Yes." She walked right up to him, got in his face. "Why is he wearing an ankle bracelet? Do you think he's going to run off?"

"We need to know where he goes, Mrs. Alcott, that's all. He's having trouble remembering, and there's a killer out there. It's for his protection, too."

"Bring him in, Morgana. I want to see the boy who's brought Brakey home, too," came a scratchy old voice from behind Mrs. Alcott.

Deliah gave Griffin a long look, then ushered him past the elaborate wooden front door with the pentacle hanging on it, over a wide threshold that would easily allow a wheelchair through it, and into the large entry hall that smelled faintly of sweet incense.

Griffin spotted the old lady Savich had told him about. Ms. Louisa, but not Louisa May. **What an old tartar** was his first thought. He studied her dark hooded eyes and wondered briefly if her dead son had had eyes, like hers. He introduced himself, shook her veiny arthritic hand.

"I thought the other one was a pretty boy, but you're really a looker, aren't you? What do you think, Morgana?"

Deliah Alcott shrugged impatiently, opened her mouth, but was interrupted by a man Griffin took to be Jonah wandering into the entry hall. He stilled. "You're back, Brakey. That's good they let you out. And who are you?" He stared hard at Griffin.

Griffin introduced himself again, showed his creds. Mrs. Alcott introduced her second son. While Jonah Alcott looked at them, the old lady wheeled herself into the middle of the living room, did a neat K-turn, turned off the motor of her wheelchair, and waved to them. "Well, come on in and tell us what all you smart folk think about the poor deputy's murder. It took you long enough to figure out some crook set up my poor Brakey."

Griffin followed Brakey and his mother into the large living room, redolent with the same sweet incense. Deliah Alcott didn't ask him to sit down. She didn't sit, either. She drew a deep breath. "I've been frantic." She gave Brakey a quick look, as if to reassure herself he was here and he was safe. "I sent you all the positive energy that was in me today, Brakey, to get you home." She turned back to Griffin. "So what is it you've got to tell me? What will happen to my son now?"

"Agent Hammersmith doesn't agree with me, Mom," Brakey said, "but I'm thinking how both Walter and I were drugged, and someone forced us to"—he couldn't get it out—"do what we did."

"But they don't know you killed Deputy Lewis, Brakey. They just don't have anyone else," Deliah said. "There's no proof, is there? So don't give in to them. Why would you even say you did something like that?"

"Because I can't remember and it was my truck and I don't see how anyone else could have gotten into it."

"Got you there, Morgana," Ms. Louisa said, and pulled her knitting needles out of the pile of bright green and gold wool on her lap. "You'd better be careful about what you say before you get Brakey into even more trouble."

Finesse it, Savich had told Griffin, and so he did the best he could. "Actually, Mrs. Alcott, Agent Savich and I believe someone managed to manipulate Brakey into murdering Deputy Lewis. It is this person we're looking for now, and we'd like your help."

He looked from Mrs. Alcott to the old lady to Jonah, the middle brother, who was now slouched against the fireplace, holding a deck of cards in his hand. Jonah said, "I thought you said Brakey couldn't be hypnotized. If that's the truth, then how could someone **manage** to talk him into killing Deputy Lewis? Is there any drug that can do that? Make you kill another person like that?"

How to finesse that? Griffin fell back on, "Sorry, Mr. Alcott, I really don't know the details. That's part of our investigation," to which Jonah Alcott snorted and started shuffling the deck of cards with one hand. He was quite good.

Mrs. Alcott was still standing facing him, her arms over her chest. Brakey had sprawled on an oversized chintz sofa. Ms. Louisa was knitting something he couldn't recognize, only the clicking sound her needles made filling the silence.

He said, "Do any of you know of anything Deputy Lewis and Sparky Carroll have in common that could have got them both killed?"

The Alcotts looked at him blankly. Deliah said, "Even if there was, even if you find something like that, I'm sure Brakey had nothing to do with it. You mentioned some other person. Who?"

Griffin pulled out his cell and showed her the FBI sketch of the man Savich had described to him, Stefan Dalco.

She froze. **Gotcha,** Griffin thought. He knew in his gut she'd seen him before. "You know this man, Mrs. Alcott?"

"No—I was surprised at how bizarre he looks, how foreign."

Griffin showed the photo to Jonah and

Ms. Louisa. They both shook their heads. "Would you show me the Athames you have in the house?"

"Jonah and I each have our own, but we don't have anything like a collection, Agent Hammersmith."

Brakey said, "We gave away Dad's collection after he died, right, Mom?"

"Who did you give the collection to, Mrs. Alcott?"

"I gave it to Millie Stacy." She paused. "That's Tammy Carroll's mother." Mrs. Alcott looked blindly at him. "She's Sparky Carroll's mother-in-law."

31

Colby Community Hospital
Friday night

Kelly Giusti was so physically tired she wanted to slide down the wall and onto the ancient Berber carpet in the waiting room. But she knew she wouldn't relax or sleep because she couldn't stop seeing Nasim Conklin's dead face. He'd begun as a mad terrorist in her mind and slowly morphed into a man whose life she realized had been taken over and flung away as if it meant nothing. He'd been a brave man, an innocent man they'd wanted out of the way. And he'd died not knowing why it had happened to him.

It was chilling. It didn't surprise her, but it did sadden her unutterably. In saner moments, she wondered if she was letting herself get too hardened at the advanced age of thirty-one. She'd seen so many evil human beings in her years in counterterrorism. What she needed now was some good news, like finding Hosni Rahal, the brother of one of the men who'd taken Nasim, or identifying the shooter, who'd been in surgery all this time. He'd carried no ID on him, not a surprise to any of them. They were running his fingerprints and photograph through the system, and she would have to wait. She looked over at Cal speaking quietly to Sherlock, probably consoling her about Nasim. From across the room Kelly could see the dried tears on Sherlock's face.

Sherlock's cell blasted out Brewer King's "It's a Cold Day in Hell," and she jerked up.

Kelly saw her look at the caller ID and draw a deep breath. She walked out of the room.

Sherlock saw the nurses' station up ahead and turned in the opposite direction. She closed her eyes. No way was she going to scare Dillon with the news that a bullet had barely missed splatting her head all over a bathroom. She knew the trick was to lie clean, with no hesitation. It was worth a try. She drew a deep breath, said without preamble, "Dillon, Nasim's dead. A sniper got him, at the safe house. Top secret for now, okay?"

A pause, then, "Yes, certainly. Are you all right?"

"Yes. Cal got a bullet in the arm; he was too close to Nasim when the bullets came flying through the bathroom window. He's okay, Dillon. I bandaged him up. The doctor in the ER said he was good to go with Steri-Strips and a tetanus shot."

There was a long moment of silence. He didn't believe her?

Then, "Talk to me. Did Nasim tell you everything he knew? Don't leave anything out, Sherlock."

"Nasim gave me a couple names, including someone with a moniker, the Strategist. He confirmed contacts with the imam Ali Hädi ibn Mīrzā in London, but nothing definite yet that connects the imam to the attempted blowing up of Saint Pat's." She told him exactly what Nasim said, and exactly what happened, except that she'd almost died. Dillon was quiet when she finished. "You did well. It's a good start. I'm sorry about Conklin. So how did they find the safe house?"

She could hear his brain working, sifting

through what she'd told him, and she kept going, fast. She told him about the GPS she believed the ME would find in his body. She told him about the shooter who was in surgery. "Kelly—Agent Giusti— is waiting on a call identifying him."

"You said Cal was shot because he was standing to close to Nasim. So where were you?"

Distraction time. "Close by, but really, I'm fine. Tell me, Dillon, what happened with Brakey Alcott and Dr. Hicks?"

The distraction worked. "It was as I thought, Dalco front and center. As you can imagine, Brakey Alcott is a mess. We've put a monitor on his ankle and Griffin took him home. He's going to speak to the family, see what he can learn. It's about all we can do, short of protective custody. I'm going to have to lay the facts out to our lawyers soon, see what they say. After they stop rolling their eyes.

"It sounds like they don't need you any-more. When are you coming home?"

Sherlock realized she was crying. She didn't make a sound, wiped the tears off her cheeks. "Oh, Dillon, the whole deal at

JFK—Nasim was supposed to sacrifice himself for his family and he was fully prepared to. He was brave, Dillon, he let himself be killed. I promised him I'd find his family. I have to do my best to keep that promise. We've got a lead, the name of a man who may be able to lead us to the family. And Kelly wants me here, wants both Cal and me involved."

Savich tried to keep his voice emotionless, but he didn't manage it. "Agent Giusti shouldn't be using you. She knows very well the terrorists would be happy to see you as dead as Nasim. It wouldn't be simple revenge for wrecking their plan at JFK, but a lot more than that. Killing you now would be a powerful message that they can eliminate anybody they choose, even you."

She felt a slick of fear in her belly, tried to quash it, to keep it from making its way into her voice. What would he say if she told him everything? "They may want that, but Cal and I won't let it happen. I don't have a GPS embedded under my skin. They won't get close. All I want now is to find Nasim's family alive. Give Sean a big kiss for me, okay?"

She knew he didn't like it, knew he wanted to argue. She wouldn't like it either if he were the one sitting in the hospital in Colby, Long Island. After a long silence, he said, "Yes, you know I will."

Her good-bye came flying out of her mouth. "You be careful, too, Dillon. Promise me you'll be careful. I love you."

"I love you more." A pause, then, "Don't ever forget, you're my mate. Keep Cal upright, okay? Otherwise he won't be any use to you."

He'd called her his mate. **His mate.** She liked the sound of that. She wondered if he'd fly up here, but she knew he couldn't, not yet. She had to remember to threaten Cal with mayhem if he dared mention that bullet.

As Sherlock walked back into the waiting room, Kelly's cell buzzed. It was the point agent in Boston. Kelly's heart speeded up. **Please, please.** She listened, felt her hope die, and punched off.

"What?" Cal asked her.

"The Boston Field Office followed up on a Hosni Rahal who lives in Plover,

Massachusetts, and has a Syrian brother on the no-fly list. Agents scoured the house for evidence Nasim's family might have been kept there, or any connection at all, but nada, zilch. The family appears to know nothing about any of this. In fact, Rahal claims he hadn't spoken to his brother for two years." She sighed. "At least that's what he said. They looked at his passport. He hasn't been out of the country in over five years. But that doesn't mean much of anything. They're going to keep him under surveillance."

"Sit down before you fall over," Cal said.

Kelly shook her head, leaned back against the pale green wall, not wanting to show any weakness, Cal thought. She stretched, trying, he knew, to keep herself upright and together.

"Really, Giusti. Sit down."

She looked back at him. "If I do, I'll go comatose." She fell silent, started worrying an opal ring on her thumb. It looked old. A family heirloom?

"Have you heard from the medical examiner yet?"

Kelly shook her head again. "It should be

soon. I told him to call me the minute he found anything like an embedded GPS chip. I guess Nasim never planned on going through the X-ray machine at JFK. They would have wanded him, maybe found the GPS. But maybe not, if it was mostly plastic." She looked down at her cell, as if willing the medical examiner to call her. Finally, she slipped it into her jacket pocket. She sighed. "I should have wanded him myself."

"Why?" Cal said, an eyebrow going up. "That isn't something you'd normally do. So why Nasim?"

"Shut up, McLain. I don't need logic right now."

He studied her pale face, saw the tension, the depression settling on her shoulders like a heavy weight. "I remember when my mom used to hug me when I was younger, telling me it would be okay. I wish she didn't live all the way over in Oregon. I could use one of her hugs right now."

Kelly gave him a small grin. How could he joke like that? She realized it was on purpose and she gave him another grin. It steadied her. "I remember my grandma used to hug me like that," she said. "After she died, my mom took over the big hugs." She didn't mention her college professor ex-husband, no support from him, either, when he'd been around. He'd hated it when she became an agent in the FBI, thought they were a den of right-wingers who wanted to control the world. Last she heard, he was filling all the smart young brains at Berkeley with how Mao had saved China, how he'd been maligned by the West. At least now he was surrounded by like minds.

Kelly waved her hand at Sherlock, who was staring down at her clasped hands. "I saw your kid on YouTube once."

"Along with the rest of the world," Cal said. "Sean's a pistol."

Sherlock raised her head. "**Pistol**'s a good name for him, all right."

"It shouldn't have happened, none of it," Kelly said. "I shouldn't have let it happen."

Cal yawned. "Let me know when you get powers like that so I can bow down."

"I was in charge. Nasim is dead. My fault."

"Yeah," he said, "I can see that. I'll be happy to send your boss an e-mail, maybe even write him a letter. And I'm always available for a hug."

He heard her hiss, then laugh, not much of one, but it still qualified.

Sherlock said, "I'm with Cal. A hug would be perfect about now."

Jo Hoag appeared in the doorway. "Our shooter's out of surgery, and stable. The surgeon took pity on us, said if we give it another ten minutes, he'll let us talk to him briefly in Recovery.

"Better yet, Kelly, we know who he is. His prints match a Jamil Nazari. Turns out MI5's got a file on him, but no one knows yet how he got into the country. He's a thirty-four-year-old Egyptian, at one time a member of the Muslim Brotherhood. He was a **muntazim**, which roughly means he was an organizer, in touch with the Brotherhood hierarchy. He was with them during the resistance to the military-backed regime. Bombings, kidnappings, they did it all. He's also a crack shot. He showed up in Algiers three years ago with his two sisters and his mother after his father was killed in a skirmish with government troops. He's thought to have joined one of the local militant groups. We'll know more soon about his family, his associates. Oh, yes, he's known to speak English as well as Arabic, and some French."

Sherlock jumped to her feet. "You got your pliers, Kelly?"

Cal said, "You're going to pull his tonsils out his ears?"

Kelly gave them all a manic grin. "Nah, I'm going to use my wiles on him. Come on, guys, let's go talk to Mr. Nazari." Kelly was suddenly a woman on a mission, the fire back in her eyes. **Good,** Cal thought, **she's got her mojo back.**

She laughed as her long-legged stride took her out the door.

32

Nurse Betina Marr buzzed them into the PACU and rounded on them. "You're the FBI, right?" She held out her hand and they took turns giving her their creds. "Okay. You're here to see Mr. Nazari. Dr. Baker said to let you in for ten minutes, no longer. Mr. Nazari's beginning to come out of anesthesia—talk about a happy camper, what with all the morphine cruising through him. His thinking's going to be muddled, so I don't know how you're going to get anything useful out of him. He's really a terrorist?"

"Yes," Sherlock said. "He killed a man tonight."

Nurse Marr's tone flattened. "Well, maybe, with all the drugs on board plus the residual effects of the anesthesia, he's groggy enough to spill something you want to know. We have one other patient in here. If something happens, though, do what we tell you and stay out of the way. Mr. Nazari's right over there. Good luck."

Jamil Nazari's bed was in the far corner of the room. The other patient was an older woman lying on a narrow bed, her head wrapped in bandages, smiling vacantly up at a nurse who was patting her hand.

Nazari was lying still, his eyes closed, as if he was asleep, an oxygen cannula in his nose. He looked uncomfortable taking shallow breaths, probably because it hurt to get in enough air with the large plastic bag coming out of his chest, draining pink fluid into some kind of vacuum pump. It was hard to hear him breathe at all over the noise the vacuum made and the hiss of the oxygen.

They moved around Nazari's bed, careful not to disturb the IV tubing and monitoring wires connected to his body. Kelly pulled the curtain closed for privacy. It was a tight fit, but she wasn't about to ask anyone to leave. All of them had a big stake in this. Kelly said quietly, "Please don't say anything, let me handle this."

Kelly shook his shoulders, said next to his ear, "Jamil, open your eyes. It's me, you lazy baboon, it's your sister. Wake up!"

He moaned, blinked his eyes, and frowned

up at her. "Jana, I do not feel good, Jana. Where is Mama?" His English was clear, though stilted, his accent heavily Arabic.

Kelly did her best to mimic him. "She's at home, you fool. Tell me what you've done, Jamil. Tell me right now or I'll make you very sorry," and she smacked him again on his shoulder.

"That hurt. You hurt me when we were young."

"You always deserved it. Stop whining and tell me what you did right this minute."

"I am thirsty."

"Tell me right now and I'll get you water, all right?"

"Yes, that would be good." His brain tripped off into the ether, and he fell silent.

Kelly shook him again. "Jamil, tell me about the man who sent you to shoot Nasim. Tell me about the Strategist."

"Ah, Jana, you always liked Hercule, didn't you? You wanted to marry him, but he wasn't interested."

"Yes, I liked Hercule. What is he doing now, Jamil? Where does he live?"

Something clicked in Jamil's glazed eyes. He blinked up at Kelly. "Wait! You are not

Jana, she can barely speak English. You cannot be—I remember. I saw you at the safe house, you are—" Nazari pressed his head against the pillow and yelled, "Help me! Help me!"

Nurse Marr appeared around the privacy curtain. She looked dispassionately down at Jamil Nazari, whose mouth was still open as he stared up at her. "Help me."

"You will have to keep your voice down, Mr. Nazari. You're disturbing our other patient."

"Wait, listen, they are going to kill me—"

"I'm sure you're mistaken, Mr. Nazari. It's the drugs making your mind fuzzy. They'll wear off soon now. You'll be fine. Trust me."

The nurse pulled back and Kelly came down close to his face again. "What's wrong, Jamil? Don't you want to talk with your sister Jana anymore?"

"You bitch! I don't want to talk to you!" Nazari let out another yell for help. Nurse Marr came back in and calmly punched a few buttons on his IV infusion set. In a few seconds, his head fell back and he was asleep.

"He was with it enough not to cooperate anymore, so I put him out again. Mr. Nazari won't be talking to anyone for a long while, so you might as well leave now, get a good night's sleep." She smiled at Kelly. "I heard what you did. Good work."

In the hallway outside Recovery, Kelly grinned madly and high-fived Jo, Cal, and Sherlock.

"Congrats, Giusti," Cal said. "We now have a name, and that's more than MI5 has."

"A name, we've got a name," Kelly said. "How many French Algerians can there be with a name like Hercule? And he knows Nazari's family, his sister Jana. We can have the family questioned, track their contacts."

Jo said, "It shouldn't take too long. Like you said, Kelly, there can't be many Hercules in Algeria. It's an odd name. You done good."

"At least we've got a good solid lead now," Kelly said.

"It's good for your career, too, Giusti," Cal said. "Hey, you wanna hug?"

33

Savich House
Georgetown
Friday, nearly midnight

It was late, after midnight, when Savich closed MAX down for the night. He'd tried every public record he could think of, but MAX had found nothing solid linking the Plackett murder victims, or their killers, other than what he already knew. He needed to do more legwork, speaking directly to people who knew both the killers and the victims. He'd call Sheriff Watson in the morning, see if he'd found anything promising. He lay in bed staring at the dark ceiling, hearing only the occasional settling-in moans the house made, sounds he knew, comforting sounds, but not comforting enough tonight. He missed Sherlock's head against his shoulder, her hair tickling his nose, her soft, smooth breathing against his skin. He was afraid for her, he'd admitted it to himself the moment her helicopter took off for New York. He hadn't told her that, but she knew.

He couldn't sleep, so he got up to check on Sean. It was something Sherlock would have done if she couldn't sleep. As he stood over Sean's single bed in his kid's room filled with bookshelves and posters of superheroes, he saw the pair of Sean's sneakers kicked off in the corner near his desk, his jeans tossed over the back of a chair. He could hear Sherlock's voice telling Sean to put his dirty clothes in the hamper and his shoes in the closet. It hadn't even occurred to Savich to remind him. Well, he got the taking-a-bath and brushing-his-teeth parts right. Savich had sung a song to Sean while he'd bathed, Sean joining Savich when he belted out "Let It Go." Savich had learned the words on his way to the Hoover Building that morning. Just in case.

He looked down at his sleeping son, his face bathed in the moonlight pouring through the window. He felt the familiar surge of love for this small human being, a part of him, a part of Sherlock. **Here we both are, Sean, trying to hang in without**

your mom. He cupped Sean's cheek. Sean lurched up, gave a sleepy snort, sent Savich a vague smile, and went limp again, snuggling his cheek into the pillow.

Savich tucked the covers around Sean's shoulders, lowered the window a bit. Sean liked to sleep warm. He walked back to his bedroom and lay down, pillowed his head in his arms, and willed himself to sleep. When it was clear his will wasn't doing the job, he turned on the bedside lamp and called John Eiserly with MI5. He had to do something to help Sherlock. The phone was already ringing when he realized it was five a.m. in London.

To his surprise, John answered his cell immediately, his voice a whisper. "Savich? Hey, it's past midnight in the colonies. Why aren't you sleeping? Wait a bit, let me get to my study. I don't want to wake up Mary Ann, not with our two-month-old daughter wrecking her sleep. I figure we've got another hour before Ceci wakes up again, demanding her next meal."

A minute later Savich heard John typing on his keyboard. He went through his apology, but John interrupted him. "I missed maybe a half-hour of sleep. I'm e-mailing you a photo of Imam Al-Hädi ibn Mīrzā so you have a clear face to put to the man. Wait, I'm an idiot, you must already have his picture, probably know as much about him as I do."

"Send it along anyway, John."

"Give me two seconds," John said. "Done. As of right now, we don't have anything for you on the Conklin family, except we've verified on our end they're in the U.S., maybe still around Boston, since that was their destination, but who knows? They could be in Florida by now."

Savich's phone signaled that he'd received an e-mail. He'd already memorized the imam's face—a compassionate face dominated by soft dark brown eyes that seemed to look right into your soul, a man to trust, to confide in, not the look of a fanatic who supported terrorists. The photo of the imam John sent was different. He wasn't wearing robes, and it was taken with him unaware and clearly angry at the man he was speaking to. His brown eyes looked hard as agates in the photo, a man you'd be wise to fear more than trust. Savich put the phone back to his ear and heard the sound of a baby crying. "Ceci's up," John said. "Mary Ann and I were talking about it today—terrorists going after our cathedrals. It scares and angers everyone. What's worse, even if we see to it this Bella project fails, they won't stop, you know that, not ever."

"John, you know as well as I do that if we can't stop the terrorists before they act, then we take care of them after they act, and then we have to move on."

"Yes, I know that intellectually, just as I know we can't live in fear of what they might try next. No, we can't live in fear. That would mean they'd won. I'll alert you right away if we find anything for you regarding this Bella project."

Savich said, "Do you have anything else new for me? Other than Ceci. Oh, yes, I can hear her. Fine lungs."

John laughed. "As for Ceci, she keeps Mary Ann and me at half-mast most days. The doctor assures us she'll start to sleep through the night soon. I don't believe it." He sobered. "You know I'll alert you right away if we find anything for you."

Savich wished him and Mary Ann the best with Ceci, rang off, and settled back against the pillow. He remembered Sean blasting out earsplitting yells at least twice a night, remembered how he and Sherlock had dragged themselves around for the first couple months.

He thought of St. Patrick's almost being gutted by a bomb, thought of the scores of mourners who could have died but didn't, thanks to a little boy who'd been sick to his stomach. He pictured the Basilica di Santa Maria del Fiore, the incredible duomo in Florence, imagined it empty, in ruins.

He managed to shut it down, finally, and fell deeply asleep.

At five-thirty in the morning, Griffin called. "Savich, Brakey Alcott is on the move."

34

Outside Reineke, Virginia
Early Saturday morning

Savich's Porsche cruised past the light traffic on I-95, no need for flashers or a siren. Griffin sat next to him, adjusting the map on a tablet in his lap as they approached the flashing red dot that signaled Brakey's ankle bracelet.

"I shouldn't have trusted Brakey to stay put. It was a bad call."

"I knew you'd think that, Savich," Griffin said. "You'd be telling me to move along, to let it go, if it had been my decision." He paused as Savich passed a huge beer truck, then said, "The signal is hardly moving now. Brakey's on undeveloped land with very little around it, probably forest, about a quarter-mile from the nearest road, according to this map. There could be a dirt road or a fire road near there, though. It's the boondocks, and guess what, the Abbott house is only about ten miles away, so he's staying close to home.

But why? What's he doing in the woods?"

"Whatever Dalco wants him to." Savich hoped that wasn't to murder someone else.

"Get off at the next exit. Savich, Dalco had to know we were tracking Brakey, didn't he? He knew we'd find him, knew we'd bring him back. Is he messing with us, showing he's in control?"

"I don't think that's dramatic enough for Dalco, too pedestrian. He thinks highly of himself, Griffin. He likes to show off."

"I'm worried it's Brakey who's in danger. Dalco could make him do about anything, even kill himself." Griffin paused. "Or try to kill us."

"He had Brakey wait until it was almost dawn so he could see what he was doing," Savich said. "Not much need for that if he'd told Brakey to stab himself with an Athame."

Savich slowed the Porsche as they turned onto a narrow country road that cut a winding path through the countryside. Houses were set farther and farther apart, mostly hidden by maple and oak trees. It began to rain. That was all they needed.

Savich turned the wipers on low, and they looked through the rain to the sound of that even metronome. "I hope we don't find Brakey's body in the woods, or anyone else's." Savich hit his fist against the steering wheel. "Why didn't Brakey call me?"

"I guess he couldn't." Griffin looked down at the flashing red dot on the tablet's screen. "Take that dirt road off to the left. We're close now."

The road ended at an open field at the edge of the forest. It was nearly seven o'clock in the morning, but it seemed earlier with the sky a pewter gray, spitting down a light warm rain. Savich pulled the Porsche as close to the edge of the field as he could.

They shrugged into rain ponchos and checked their Glocks. Savich looked over at Griffin. "Let's go catch us a madman."

35

The rain was coming down harder, warm against their faces, blurring the thick gray sky. It was weather for boots, not loafers. Thankfully, the ground wasn't soggy yet. The field had looked flat from a distance, but it wasn't. They had to cut around rocks, rises, and ditches that made the going slow. When they finally reached the edge of the woods, they saw a narrow overgrown trail ahead of them, weaving through a stand of tall pine trees pressed so closely together that very little rain got through.

"Brakey's in the forest, no more than fifty yards away. He's not moving, Savich."

They unholstered their Glocks, moved to opposite sides of the narrow trail, and walked slowly forward. They heard only the rustling of the leaves as the rain spattered off them, the scurrying of squirrels or field mice. There was no sign of Brakey.

The trail ended in a small clearing no more than ten by ten, the trees forming a nearly perfect circle. Savich froze. He knew this place—Dalco's dreamscape. All it was missing were scattered piles of snow and frigid air. There was even a faint smell of smoke. A nearby smoke stack? Savich saw a small stump in the clearing, on top of it Brakey's ankle bracelet.

Savich grabbed Griffin's arm. "It's a trap—get down!"

Both men hit the ground and rolled into the trees as half a dozen fast shots rang out. Dirt kicked up around them, and a bullet mangled the bark of a pine tree beside Savich's head. They returned fire blindly. Griffin knew if Savich hadn't seen the bracelet, they'd both be dead.

The shooting stopped.

"So far only one shooter," Griffin whispered. "A semiautomatic pistol. He's changing magazines. I put him at eleven o'clock."

"We'll flank him. I'll take the left about twenty feet out, then turn. One of us should be behind him."

They separated, moving as silently as they could, bent over from the waist, using the thick trees for cover. They heard another seven rounds fired in a burst, but behind them now, toward where they'd been crouched. The shooter was as blind as they were.

Did the shooter have a third magazine? Savich hoped it was Dalco himself, but he didn't think so. It wasn't his style to dirty his own hands. He hoped it wasn't Brakey.

Savich and Griffin waited and listened. There was an eerie silence now, no animals or birds were moving; even the patter of the raindrops on the pine needles had stopped, as if time itself was holding its breath.

The man couldn't be more than ten feet ahead of them, unless he'd been moving, too, trying to circle them. They saw only each other, no trace of movement in the trees. Savich wiped the rain from his face, whispered low, "Fan out wide."

Griffin heard movement from up above, from in the trees. He shoved Savich away from him as hard as he could. "Savich, he's above us!"

Shots rained down again, kicking up dirt and wet needles around them. They dove for cover, spraying suppressive fire into the tree above them even though they didn't see anyone.

Savich raised his head and shouted, "Up in the tree, you've used three magazines. You're nearly out of bullets, if you have any left at all. Climb down out of that tree and we won't hurt you. Do it now."

They walked back toward the tree, their guns fanning the branches. They saw no one until they heard a crackling sound overhead, branches rustling and breaking. A man crashed through the branches to land on Savich, taking him down hard. His Glock went flying. Savich twisted, looked up into a young face whose mouth was open, teeth bared, his eyes hard and nearly black with ungoverned rage in the rain-blurred light. Savich struck him in the throat with his fist, sent him careening backward. A teenager, he thought, wearing a ball cap, the bill pulled low over his forehead to protect him from the rain. He landed hard on his back, clutched his throat and wheezed for breath. Savich saw the pistol the young man had dropped at his feet. It was a Kel-Tec PF-9, seven rounds, not all that common. Where had a teenager gotten hold of it?

Savich thought the kid was down, but he jumped at Savich, a knife raised in his hand. He was slashing down with it viciously when Griffin shot him.

Griffin leaned over him. "Don't do anything but breathe." He said blankly to Savich, "He's only a kid."

Savich looked down at the boy, who was staring hard back at him. He didn't look like a would-be assassin, but he still had the look of blind hate on him, even with a bullet in him. Savich slammed his hand down on the wound on the boy's shoulder. He struggled and heaved. "That's enough! Stop it or you'll bleed to death. Now, who are you? Why did you try to kill us?"

The young man looked up at him, now he looked as if he was confused, his brow furrowed—in pain? In question? He opened his mouth, groaned and closed his eyes as his head fell back.

Griffin was on his cell—thankfully, there were bars—and called 911. When he hung up, he leaned down and looked into the slack young face. "How bad is it?"

Savich pressed bloody fingers against the pulse in the boy's throat. "Bad enough.

Go through his pockets. If he doesn't live in Plackett and know Brakey and Walter, I'll give up my season tickets to the Redskins. Thanks, Griffin, for saving my hide."

Griffin pulled a wallet out of the young man's jeans pocket. "His name is Charles Marker, and yes, he lives in Plackett. He looks younger, but in fact he's twenty-four years old, same age as Brakey. The ambulance should be here in ten minutes; we're a long way out."

Savich heard the anger in Griffin's voice, knew he was praying Charles Marker wouldn't die. "He would have killed both of us, if he could have managed it."

"The ankle bracelet," Griffin said. "Dalco had Brakey cut off the ankle bracelet and give it to Marker. Then he told Marker to lay it on top of that stump and wait for us, knowing we'd come. I don't know why he left it in clear sight. Why not hide it?"

The young man moaned, opened his eyes. They were dark blue now in the morning light. They looked clear before they widened and glazed with the shock of pain. "Why? Why did you shoot me? Who are you?"

His head fell back to the side. Savich was relieved he was out again. "Go, Griffin, bring the paramedics here."

Fifteen minutes later, Griffin led the paramedics to them. Savich raised his bloody hands when a paramedic pulled out a pressure bandage and took over for him. "You ride with him to the hospital, Griffin. I'll call Sheriff Watson, to meet you there." He looked up at the paramedic's grim face. "You think he'll make it?"

"A word to the Big Guy wouldn't hurt," the paramedic said. The two of them hefted Charles Marker onto a gurney and headed back out to the ambulance.

36

Colby, Long Island
Saturday morning

Special Agent Todd Jenkins sat outside Jamil Nazari's cubicle in the SICU, his hand resting lightly on his thigh, close to his Glock. It was already busy, even on a Saturday morning, a lot of new faces to learn after the shift change, new IDs to check before he let any of them near Nazari. He heard Nazari moaning as Nurse Collins checked him out, smiled when she said quite clearly, "You're getting all the morphine ordered for you, moaning won't get you any more." Everyone knew he was a terrorist and Todd had heard Collins say she wasn't going to put up with any guff from him. Todd thought about asking her out to dinner.

He looked over at a TV monitor tuned to a news channel on the far wall and saw a cut-in photo of Agent Sherlock labeled gutsy heroine of jfk, with a talking head from CNN next to the photo. He'd bet she'd be getting more than her share of grief from her fellow agents for having a moniker like that.

He saw a man walking toward him in a long white coat over black pants, an open-collared shirt, and no tie. He was tall, middle-aged but fit, not much hair left on his head. He wore a stethoscope around his neck and held a tablet in his hand. A second later, Todd was on his feet, his right hand on his Glock. **Wrong shoes.**

The man barely spared him a glance, kept walking to the central nurses' station, tossing off a comment to a nurse as he passed her. But his shoes—a doctor wouldn't wear black running shoes over white socks, would he? Well, it was Saturday and perhaps he'd been out running. Todd kept his eye on the man until he walked out of the SICU ten minutes later, whistling.

Todd was looking forward to getting relieved at eight a.m. The FBI had learned early on that it was difficult to stay focused doing guard duty for more than four hours at a stretch, particularly at night in a place like this, with so many people shuffling in and out. Besides the staff changes, there were the patient transfers, respiratory therapists, blood drawing teams, food delivery service, and the list went on and on. He'd studied them all carefully, assuming each of them was there to kill Nazari, until they proved otherwise. One dead terrorist in FBI custody was more than enough.

Todd heard Giusti's voice before he saw her striding through the SICU, Sherlock at her side, the other agent from Washington, Cal McLain, behind them. Giusti was smiling real big. What had happened?

"Hi, Todd. Any bad guys overnight?"

He started to tell her about the doc with the black sneakers, but thought again. He smiled. "Everything's fine."

"Silicon said to tell you she'll be here to relieve you in ten minutes. Stay sharp, okay, Todd?"

Todd nodded, reminded himself to talk to Nurse Collins after Silicon showed up. Silicon was really Special Agent Glynis Banks, a fanatic Trekkie. She liked nothing more than to yammer on about the silicon-based life-forms in her favorite old episode, earning that nickname.

The three of them slipped inside the cubicle, and he heard Agent Giusti say, full of bonhomie, "Good morning, Jamil. I hear you've been complaining quite a bit, unhappy with our fine service. Do you want to tell your sister Jana about all your grievances?"

They saw he tried hard, but Nazari couldn't get enough spit in his mouth to have a go at her. "You are not my beloved sister! Where is my lawyer? I have requested a lawyer. I do not have anything to say to you, to any of you. I want you to get out of here. Tell my nurse to bring me pain medication. I am dying of pain!"

Kelly clicked off on her fingers. "No more pain medication, you can't have a lawyer, and we're not going to leave. If you don't know, you can't have a lawyer because you're a terrorist. Now, you don't have to talk, but you will listen.

"Do you remember Agent Sherlock? She's the one who arrested Nasim Conklin at JFK, kicked him in the head, actually. You knew him. He's the man you were sent to murder, the man you did murder. Were you one of his handlers in New York? Were you one of the men who showed him how to fire off the grenade, who told him if he didn't sacrifice himself, his family would die?"

They could tell he wanted to yell at them, but he was in too much pain, something Kelly hoped would play to their advantage. All he could do was glare at Kelly.

"Alas, you're right, I'm not your sister Jana, though being your sister would make me so proud. I'm Agent Kelly Giusti, and I strongly recommend you rethink your options. You might want to consider me your confidante, your very best chance at staying alive.

"Nothing to say? Well, then, let me finish the introductions. This is FBI Agent Cal McLain. He's brought down a number of your brethren. He'd love to stuff your teeth down your throat. I'll tell you what, though. I'll hold him off you for the time being, unless you really piss me off."

Jamil cursed her under his breath again, but without much heat. He turned his head away from them.

Kelly leaned over him. "Jamil, come on, now, don't be rude. I really do think it's to your benefit to hear what I have to say about your future.

"Let's start off with a first-degree murder with special circumstances, attempted murder of federal officers, conspiracy to commit terrorism—already more than enough for the death penalty. Or we could send you up for life without parole in a maximum-security federal prison, which might be worse, given what prisoners think of terrorists. It's right up there with child molesters. Or, if we really want to be cruel, Jamil, we could arrange to send you back to Egypt. I'm sure you wouldn't enjoy the experience of what they call questioning and punishment."

At last she got a response. He whipped his head back around to stare up at her. "Your threats are ridiculous. You Americans do not know anything. I've listened to you, now go away. Leave me alone. No, get that stupid nurse to give me morphine."

"Then again," she said right over him, "we could simply let you go, after we let it out that you gave up the Strategist's first name, that you told us all about how he's a family friend from Algeria. How long do you think you would last before your own comrades found you, sliced you up like a Christmas goose? Without our protection, it would be over like that." She snapped her fingers in his face.

"So the FBI would protect me if I talked." Jamil sneered. "Like you protected Nasim from me?"

"We know your people embedded a GPS chip in Nasim's body, the chip you used to find him. Yes, we failed Nasim, but do you know he wanted you to shoot him? He made it easy for you, so he could save his family.

"You're a murderer, Jamil, a coward, a puppet whose strings are pulled by the Strategist, by Hercule." She leaned down again, said against his cheek, her breath feathering his skin, "Still, I am willing to make a deal with you. There are two things I can do for you. First, think about what your family could do with one hundred thousand dollars. All you have to do is tell me the last name of this man your sister Jana wanted to marry. How long ago was it,

Jamil? Ten years? Longer?"

He gave her a thoughtful look. "You said there were two things you would do for me. Money—one hundred thousand dollars for my family—and what else? What is the second thing?"

Kelly touched her hand to his arm, right above an IV line. "You won't be executed. And the biggie? I won't let it be known you're a terrorist, so the other prisoners won't stuff a bar of soap down your throat in the shower. Hey, I've got a couple photos we believe might be the Strategist taken at Heathrow, one at Gatwick. You want to take a look for me?"

"Heathrow? The Strategist would never fly in one of those places where people are cattle, herded through the ridiculous security, and the cameras everywhere, he wouldn't—" He closed his mouth, turned his face away from her.

He didn't see her quickly smile toward Sherlock and Cal. "Come on, now, Jamil, if you do not tell me Hercule's full name I really don't have any impetus to want to keep you breathing, do I?"

His mouth remained tightly seamed. He

stared up at the ceiling, ignoring her, ignoring all of them. Finally, he said, "Do you think I fear for my fate after ridding the world of that useless scum Nasim? Nothing but a rich little whiner, who'd forsaken his religion, turned his back on what he should have willingly done for our cause. I have not. I will put my trust in Allah, not in you.

"I do not care what you do to me. I would never give up the Strategist. He knows already that I have been wounded or killed, and he trusts me to keep silent, and I will. You will never find him. He will stay a ghost, a shadow, until he is ready to kill whichever of you he chooses. He is a great man, a man to follow." He looked at Sherlock. "He was surprised to hear you were visiting with Nasim again, woman. He was already angry with you. Now he will avenge me." He looked at each of their faces. "He will kill all of you."

37

Alcott Compound
Plackett, Virginia
Saturday morning

The rain had stopped, but dark clouds hung low, no sunlight to penetrate the thick trees surrounding the three Alcott houses. It would rain again soon. There wouldn't be any children outside playing football on this dreary Saturday morning.

Savich turned off the Porsche's engine in front of the main house. When he pressed the bell, it played the beginning of what sounded like a Gregorian chant, without the voices. Savich knew whoever was here had to have heard the Porsche, but there was no sound from inside the house. He tamped down on his anger, anger because a young boy had tried to kill him and Griffin only an hour before and that boy was now in the hospital. And someone in this house knew exactly who did it.

He rang the bell again. Oddly enough, the

chime didn't start at the beginning, it continued on with the same chant. It brought to mind monks at matins, or perhaps witches in a circle around a bonfire.

He finally heard footsteps, the sounds of children's voices.

A man he didn't know jerked the door open. He was big, mid-thirties, muscular, with the look of an aging football player or prizefighter. He was wearing faded jeans, a flannel work shirt, old worn boots. It had to be Liggert, the bully who'd tried to beat on Walter Givens. He looked a lot like Jonah, both bruisers, probably resembled their dead father, only Liggert was running to fat. Savich hadn't yet met Liggert, because he drove a truck for Alcott Transportation out of Richmond and had been gone for two weeks. Jonah worked in the front office, probably being groomed to run the company someday. Savich had wondered why that was. After all, Liggert was older.

"Yeah, what do you want? We're having breakfast and we're not buying anything you're selling." Savich heard lots of mean beneath the velvet southern drawl.

"It's Agent Savich," Deliah Alcott called from behind her son. "Let him in, Liggert."

Liggert gave Savich a look that threatened mayhem and stepped back. He turned on his heel and walked away down a long corridor, and didn't look back. Deliah Alcott said, "Are you here about Brakey's ankle bracelet? It must have fallen off his ankle and he can't find it anywhere. He wanted to call you about it, but I told him it was too early and he should keep looking, he'd find it somewhere. But now you're here."

Voices sounded from behind her. Deliah said, "Everyone's in the kitchen, eating pancakes. It's a Saturday-morning tradition. So are you here about the bracelet?"

"Yes, I'm here about the bracelet."

"Then come on in. Are you hungry?"

Pancakes, she'd said. "Yes, I'd like that, Mrs. Alcott. It's very kind of you." Savich followed Mrs. Alcott down the long back corridor.

The Alcott kitchen was enormous: a long pine table stretched down the middle of it, covered with a bright blue tablecloth. Brakey sat at the table with the rest of his family, eating pancakes, but his head was down. When he looked up to see Savich, he jumped to his feet, nearly knocking his chair over. "I was going to call you, Agent Savich. My ankle bracelet's gone! I swear I never tried to take it off. I swear!"

"I know," Savich said, "and you don't remember getting out of bed, is that right?"

"No, no. I'm sure I didn't get out of bed."

"Then don't worry about it, Brakey. Sit down and enjoy your breakfast."

He looked around the table, pulled out his creds, and handed them around. He introduced himself to Liggert's wife, Marly, and to each of the six children, listened to their names. All looked under the age of ten, he thought, with Tanny the oldest. He looked into her strange green eyes. She was one of Liggert's children. The other children had grown quiet, not knowing what to make of him, but Tanny was staring at him hard. Liggert sat at the head of the table, his wife, Marly, a thin, anxious-looking young woman, on his right. Jonah was next to her. Where was Jonah's wife?

Savich said to Jonah, "Your wife doesn't like pancakes?"

"She's working, the feed store in Plackett.

She's the assistant manager."

Deliah clapped her hands. "Children, everyone sit down, more pancakes coming up. Tanny, please set a place for Agent Savich. He will join us."

She turned back to spoon more batter into two big flat skillets. Everyone listened to the batter hiss and sputter.

Liggert said, "Why'd you come back so soon? It's about Brakey's bracelet; you're not here for Mama's pancakes."

"That's certainly a side benefit," Savich said as he sat down next to Deliah Alcott's place at the other end of the table. Tanny slid a plate with three stacked blueberry pancakes in front of him. Savich breathed them in, smiled up at her. "They smell great. Thank you, Mrs. Alcott."

Ms. Louisa sidled her wheelchair into the kitchen and pulled up close to the table, a child on either side of her. She nodded to Savich and said in a scratchy drawl, "Well, Marly, did I lie? Isn't he a looker? As for you, Liggert, don't go all huffy and stick your knife in his gullet just because Marly appreciates the look of the man. That wouldn't be polite." She grabbed a bit of a child's pancake, and stuffed it into her mouth. She laughed. "At least let him enjoy his breakfast first."

"That isn't funny, Mother," Deliah said as she flipped another pancake.

Marly sent a nervous look at her husband, who was busy forking down a pancake, ignoring her and ignoring his grandmother.

Ms. Louisa said, "The boy's here for a reason, Morgana. I'm helping him out. So now you've met both of Dilly's older boys, Liggert and Jonah. They're buff and loud and tough, aren't they? Their daddy was as tough as they were once, but later on he wasn't, not at all. Like I told you yesterday, Dilly was weak."

"That's not fair, Mother," Deliah said patiently as she turned another pancake. "He was the strongest man I've ever known. After the first Gulf War, he simply couldn't abide violence." She said over her shoulder, "He was in Iraq. It…changed him."

"It changed a lot of people," Savich said.

Ms. Louisa cackled. "But would you look at how Dilly bit the big one. He didn't croak it like a man should, he got him-self run down by a stupid car and a driver who didn't care enough to stop and see if he was still breathing. It's a cruel world, Morgana, a cruel, cold world. You should be glad two of your boys can take care of themselves."

Brakey burst out, "I can take care of myself, Grandma, most of the time. Agent Savich is here because he thought I'd escape, isn't that right? You know what happened to my ankle bracelet, don't you?" He suddenly fisted his hand around his fork. "I didn't kill anyone else, did I?"

38

No one died, Brakey." Savich turned to Deliah. "Sorry about breakfast, but please tell Tanny to take all the children into the living room. I don't think they should be here for this."

She gave him a long look, then nodded toward Tanny, who started to protest. Deliah overrode her. "Everyone take a last bite. The pancakes will be here when you get back. Now all of you go with Tanny to the family room. Watch TV, all right? I'll call you when you can come back."

After the children had filed out of the kitchen, Savich said, "I showed all of you except Liggert the drawing of Stefan Dalco." He called up the photo on his phone, handed it down the table. Liggert only glanced at it, shook his head, impatient.

Savich looked around the table. "I believe one or more of you know who this man is, you recognize that sketch but aren't telling me. Why? Because you want to protect this person who calls himself Stefan

Dalco? He is one of you, or someone you know? I have seen this man. He is a psychic and he appeared to me in a dream as he did to Brakey and Walter Givens, and now Charles Marker. Dalco wanted Sparky Carroll and Deputy Kane Lewis dead, and he told them what he wanted them to do, forced them to commit murder and then forget all of it."

Brakey said, "Charlie? What does Charlie have to do with this? Is he all right?"

"Charlie Marker is in the hospital, Brakey. He has a gunshot wound, and he's in surgery. He tried to shoot Agent Hammersmith and me a little while ago in the pine woods about ten miles west of here. Charlie obviously got the bracelet from you early this morning, though you don't remember that. He used your ankle bracelet as the lure to get us to follow him into those woods.

"Charlie will probably pull through, but like you, Brakey, and Walter Givens, I'm sure he won't remember anything. Dalco sees to that; it's one of his orders.

"Again I know one or more of you know this murderer, or you are this murderer, and I intend to find out which of you it is."

"This is nuts," Liggert said, and half rose from his chair.

"Sit down!"

Liggert's face filled with rage, but he saw violence in this FBI agent and he slowly sat down again.

Jonah stared at Savich, his head cocked to one side. "Charlie Marker shot at you, this morning, in some woods ten miles west of here? That stand of thick pines, next to the field they cleared?"

Savich nodded.

"It sounds like the McCuttys' land," Jonah said. He looked around the table. "My grandfather used to own that land. All of us know it very well, but so do most people in town. Agent Savich, you can't really mean you think one of us got control of Charlie's mind, made him try to kill you? Come on, I mean, that's crazy."

"It sounds crazy, yes," Savich said, "and Stefan Dalco is afraid I'll prove it. He's afraid enough to try to kill me. He won't succeed."

Deliah was on her feet, her palms pressed flat on the table. "It's frightening to think anyone has such powers, especially for a Wiccan. I believe that if this person does exist, the evil he does will be returned to him, his own powers will be turned back against him. I wish we could help you find him. You know I would do anything I could to help Brakey. The simple truth is we can't."

Savich said, "You can't? And what does that mean? I see, it's the Wiccan party line. Don't get involved, trust that bad people will have their evil turned back on them. Karma in all its glory." He banged his fist on the table, rose. "One of you knows full well what's going on here, possibly all of you. I will find out." Savich looked at them dispassionately, then he turned on his heel and walked out of the kitchen.

39

**Aboard the TGV, Train à Grande Vitesse
North of Lyons, France**

Twenty-Four Kilometers
The newly appointed French Ministre de l'Économie, Marcel Dubroc, drummed his long, thin fingers on the armrest of his solo seat. He wanted to enjoy some rare privacy, and so his aide Luc, with his interminable notes and suggestions, sat behind him. Still too close. He could still hear Luc on his cell phone, wallowing in his mistress's voice, no doubt gloating about being the new power behind the throne.

Marcel looked out the window at the straight shot of highway running parallel to the high-speed rail track. At three hundred kilometers an hour, the highway, the trees, and the fields beyond passed in a near blur. He saw a beautiful red Ferrari, guessed it was traveling at two hundred kilometers an hour. It looked like it was going backward.

He saw an attendant place a plate of croissants on a passenger's table and realized he was hungry. Why not celebrate a bit? He could hardly jump out of his seat, shout, and wave his fist in the air. He drew a deep breath, settled back in his seat to enjoy the moment, and ordered an espresso and a croissant.

He'd won. He'd planned to head this office for the past five years, had worked hard to achieve his goal, and at last the power, the influence, the public exposure were his. It hadn't quite settled into his bones yet, the actual knowledge he'd finally arrived, but it would, beginning with the meeting this afternoon when he would drop the hammer.

He was now Ministre de l'Économie—would it be his legacy? For the moment at least, he was content, but who knew what would come his way in the future?

He thought of his ex-wife, Nichole, that unfaithful bitch, and smiled so widely his jaw cracked. At the time, rage had swamped him when a friend had told of seeing her and her lover in an out-of-the-way restaurant in the 5th Arrondissement, trading saliva over couscous. But no longer. Even though his teenage son, Jean, had blamed him for breaking up the marriage to his mother, the little pisshead, Marcel knew he'd been too young to understand, but someday he would.

His new office would be his private revenge. His ex-wife wouldn't be the woman on his arm at the elegant events that would make up many of his evenings—rather, he pictured a succession of beautiful women, perhaps more interested in his office than in him, but who cared?

His present lover, Elaine, was quite beautiful, and she basked in his new position as Ministre de l'Économie. Should he consider marrying her? There was no rush.

Fifteen Kilometers

He put portable headphones over his ears, tuned in to a streaming music service as he waited for his coffee. A mad song came on that only a French teenager could appreciate, but now he wrapped himself in the jagged dissonance of the notes as the two male vocalists wailed and screeched unintelligible words in his ears.

The vicious sounds made him think of his upcoming meeting that afternoon with Antoine Bardon at Marcel's office in Bercy. It would be their final meeting, and he was quite looking forward to it. He would ever-so-pleasantly tell Bardon about his new budget, about to be approved by the president. Marcel had cut off all the farm-equipment subsidies Antoine Bardon had received yearly and promptly stuffed much of the money into his own fat pockets, millions of euros he used to facilitate foreign bribes through his bankers and trucking businesses. Marcel had tracked down the paper trail of the stolen federal money, laundered through a small bank in Marseilles, and now he had the power to bring him down. At last. Marcel couldn't wait to see the look on Bardon's face when he showed him the proof. For all practical purposes, Antoine Bardon would be gone, perhaps to prison, certainly dead to the French government. So what if Bardon let it out that he'd been one of Marcel's ex-wife's lovers? Everyone knowing that would only make it sweeter. Maybe he could call his ex-wife, tell her what he'd done to her ex-lover, offer to tell her which prison he'd be spending his retirement years.

Marcel found himself tapping his fingers to the music and smiled. He held all the cards now.

It was all over but for the shouting, and he planned to shout really loud after the meeting with Bardon. He'd walk out of his new, beautifully paneled conference room in Bercy and into the glorious Parisian sun. And call the media.

He'd won.

Four Kilometers

An attendant recognized who he was, was properly deferential, bowing so low he could have fallen on his face, but the TGV ran too smoothly for that. Marcel nodded his approval and the attendant disappeared. He sipped the bitter, hot espresso. It was delicious. He bit into his warm croissant, frowned a bit. It wasn't quite as moist and fresh as the others he'd enjoyed on the TGV. No matter, he was too pleased with himself. Perhaps he would tease his friend, the Ministre de

Transportation, Jean LeMarc, about it when next they met.

Zero Kilometers

Marcel Dubroc had no warning he was about to die. His world disintegrated.

40

The Liberty Hotel
Boston, Massachusetts
Saturday morning

Samir Basara enjoyed the silk slide of Golden Slope chardonnay down his throat. He'd been surprised and pleased to find it in the small refrigerator in his suite, but he'd stayed at the hotel before and they knew it was one of his favorites. It was from a small boutique winery in Napa Valley, and very different from the heavy, overripe fruit taste of the Algerian wine he'd been raised with. He remembered his father striding through the family vineyard in Coteaux du Zaccar, fondling his Carignan and Clairette blanche grapes, whistling, giving orders, drinking a good amount of his profits. His preference had always been what they called their burgundy, but it wasn't burgundy at all, rather a heavy mongrel blend. No one ever pointed that out to him, they were too scared of the old man, as Samir had once been, a very long time ago.

He remembered his mother carping and whining after his father had struck her, Samir so used to it he paid it little mind. He couldn't wait for the day he left his family and Algeria, bound for Paris and the Sorbonne. He'd been unhappy in Paris as well, because his Algerian French accent was mimicked with a contemptuous twang, and he was looked down on, despite his family's money, his academic success, and his good looks. He practiced his English, anxious to leave the French bigots behind him, and went on to take his doctorate in economics at Berkeley, California. He'd found his home at this fascinating place where he could say anything he wanted—the more outrageous, it seemed, the more he was considered to be an intellectual and accepted, the women always eager to sleep with him. And the wine was good. At Berkeley, he hadn't been an outsider. He'd been embraced. He might have stayed on if he hadn't known he was destined for greater things.

His three sisters, the worthless cows,

had reveled in the rich lifestyle their father's lands provided and had all married money-eyed Frenchmen and enjoyed the fruits of Paris. But not Samir. He had chosen a different path. It had all come to him so gradually, it seemed, spawned in America, in the belly of the enemy, and there surely was irony in that.

Every year he traveled to Algeria to visit his father and mother, always during Ramadan. Last year Ramadan had fallen in July and a surprise awaited him. His father was lying in bed, his left side paralyzed from a stroke, and his mother now ruled the household. He was no longer a happy alcoholic who struck out when it pleased him, he was now a supplicant.

His mother glowed. Another irony. She'd talked mostly of wanting him to marry, about wanting grandchildren from her only son. All his father wanted was a drink.

Samir took another sip of his chardonnay, let it settle first on his tongue, then slide smoothly down his throat, and he smiled. Perhaps he would marry someday, perhaps Lady Elizabeth Palmer. He saw his dark hands on her smooth white flesh, heard her screaming his name when she came. What would their children look like?

His parents believed he was a big-shot intellectual, and he was, actually, a noted speaker and a professor at the London School of Economics. But he was much more than that. Neither of them had a clue that the man they called Hercule, the nickname his grandfather had bestowed on him, was also known as the Strategist, a shadowy figure, feared and spoken of in whispers, a man whose reputation continued to grow throughout Europe and the Middle East for the simple reason that he could always be trusted to fulfill a contract for any job desired, from an assassination to an exploded building. Jihadists believed him to be one of them, and Hercule knew his plan, his Bella, was a terrorist's wet dream and would make them admire him even more. What they didn't know was that the destruction of the West's sacred cathedrals, for him, the Strategist, was something else entirely. In the future, after three or four of the world's famous cathedrals had fallen into ruin from his hired bombers, all it would take was the threat of a specific target cathedral, and the payoffs would become a source of huge revenue to him.

He remembered Imam Al-Hädi ibn Mīrzā had christened him the Strategist after a particularly intricate plan he'd devised to kill a Shiite banker in Syria who was helping to fund Hezbollah. Hercule had profited handsomely from that plan, seizing a shipment of large bills before the man died in a hail of bullets. The imam never learned that detail. The imam thought of Hercule as a committed genius who would help him bring the world to Islam, a true believer to whom money meant little. So did dozens of hardened fighters who had worked for him and who feared his name. He'd heard one of his most trusted, skilled men, Bahar, call him the iron fist inside the imam's velvet glove. Until he decided otherwise, for the moment, he would continue to be tied to the imam.

He'd been based in London for seven years now, and each year he'd learned from his mistakes. Some had cost lives and, more important, cost him money. He had won the right to choose the targets the imam funded, putting Hercule in command of dozens of jihadists. He agreed with some of their grievances, but he saw them as misguided thugs who did as he asked for very little money. What better cover could he ask for than mindless acts of terrorism when there was an opportunity for profit?

It had been years since Hercule had allowed the imam to help plan an operation, but this time, against his better judgment, he had. Nasim Conklin had been a big mistake. Hercule wouldn't have used that kind of leverage. It was too uncertain, too unpredictable. You could always count on a true believer, but using a man's family as a sword over his head was taking too big a risk. The imam had been certain Nasim would make the perfect tool. He would give up his life for his family, the imam was certain. He had refused to approve Bella without his being used, and Hercule needed the imam's backing for this project. The stakes were too high. But there was more, Hercule knew it simply because he knew the imam so well, knew he hadn't told him his real reason for wanting Nasim

Conklin to give up his life at JFK.

He got up to ease his frustration. He cracked his neck and stretched as he walked to the wide suite windows that looked toward the Charles River. He couldn't actually see the water, not in the middle of the night, but knowing it was there was somehow satisfying. The endless flow, the gentle lash of waves against the docks, the water lipping the sloping grassy shoreline: it was like watching the Thames from his apartment window in London. It helped him think.

Hercule turned away from the window. He was tired but knew he couldn't sleep yet. It was time to meet the failures of the past few days head-on, to look at every step taken, every decision, and why each had failed. He had to salvage what he could of his meticulous plan, his brilliant project, Bella, named after a particularly inventive lover he'd enjoyed for several months in the South of France.

He'd even come to the States to oversee the details directly, his cover a lecture at Boston University, and that had gone well. But Bella's kickoff? It had dived headfirst into the crapper.

It was his thirty-seventh birthday and everything was cocked up.

Letting Al-Hädi ibn Mīrzā talk him into using Nasim Conklin to provide the grenade blast at JFK as a diversion was the obvious first mistake. Nasim had screwed up royally, was taken down by an FBI agent in the security line—a woman, of all things. It was a completely avoidable blunder, but not in itself fatal to his plan. It had worked as a diversion, in any case.

Then the wretched bad luck of the altar boy finding the bomb in the utility closet at St. Patrick's, the priest hurling the bomb out onto Fifth Avenue. No one had been killed, not a single stone ripped from St. Patrick's belly or even its newly shined-up façade. And worst of all, the vice president was still alive and well, a surviving hero. He would have to devise a new plan to remove him from this earth.

Two failures. The imam had consoled him that it was bad luck all around, but Hercule knew to his gut it wasn't bad luck at JFK. Out of respect, Hercule hadn't pointed out the obvious to the imam, that Nasim had been the **imam's mistake**. It was on Hercule's head nevertheless, because he hadn't said no. The imam would never make him go against his better judgment again.

As for St. Patrick's, yes, he would accept that every plan had risks, a small chance of failure, even if it was planned perfectly. But today in France, they wouldn't be so lucky.

He sat back down on the sofa, leaned his head against the soft cushion, and closed his eyes. He didn't even know for certain whether that idiot Nasim was dead, whether that irritating thread had been nipped.

He'd sent Jamil Nazari, his best sniper, a longtime friend in Algeria, to kill him. The GPS chip in Nasim's armpit would guide him, and Hercule had his family under his control. He surely expected Jamil to succeed, dangerous as it was for him. When Jamil called him on his business phone to tell him the FBI woman from the airport was there with Nasim at the safe house, Hercule happily gave the order to take her out as well. Surely the FBI hadn't gotten their hands on that burner phone— Jamil was always too careful for that.

Hercule had considered what would

happen if Jamil failed to kill Nasim—he always considered everything. He'd had Jamil followed to Colby, New York, with instructions for the follower to keep out of Jamil's sight, keep watch, and keep Hercule informed of everything as it happened. So he knew Jamil had been shot, knew he was out of surgery and expected to live in that Podunk hospital on Long Island. Hercule mourned losing Jamil even though he wasn't dead. He would be imprisoned forever, perhaps executed, and there was little chance of freeing him. He wasn't worried about Jamil talking—he was a true believer, not hired muscle. Hercule knew Jamil would never talk, not even if the FBI poured a truth serum down his throat.

What he didn't know for certain was whether Nasim was still alive, whether Jamil had succeeded in killing him. Nasim hadn't been removed from the safe house, not dead, not walking, in the several hours after the shooting, the GPS chip out of power or disabled. The FBI had made no announcement of any kind. Were they playing with him, hoping he would spare Nasim's family until he knew for certain?

Even if Nasim had talked before Jamil shot at him, it didn't matter much, because he didn't know about the whole, only his tiny part. He could tell him he'd met with the imam, but without proof, the old man was probably safe. Nasim knew nothing about Hercule, nothing about the Strategist. He really should stop worrying; Jamil had very likely killed Nasim.

There was a knock on the suite door. It was room service with fish and chips, his favorite, served up at the crack of dawn for his breakfast, served elegantly and without any smart comments. He would put everything right, back on track. He would give the FBI no more than a day to make an announcement about Nasim. If they didn't, he would eliminate Nasim's family and put the whole business behind him. It was too dangerous to let them live. Bella had more surprises than they knew of yet.

And there was France. He should find out very soon now.

As he chewed on a french fry dipped in mayonnaise, he wished himself a happy birthday and thought again of that redheaded female FBI agent who was there when they'd taken Jamil. She would be the woman who beat him twice. How would it look to let a woman do that to the Strategist? What could he accomplish if the primitive men who worked for him lost their fear of him, their respect? He decided to kill her—in public, if possible— with lots of smartphone videos running. It would be seen as an outrage, she'd be a martyr for some, but his own people would know the Strategist had the last word.

His cell rang. It was Bahar, calling from France. He listened and then hung up.

And smiled.

41

Plackett, Virginia
Saturday afternoon

Savich pulled into the driveway of an older one-story, red-brick house that looked settled in and comfortable, sitting in the middle of its large front yard. Flower beds filled with pansies and marigolds lined the front of the house and mature oaks hovered around its perimeter, their leaves rustling in the stiff breeze. As he walked the long flagstone path to the front door he smelled the sweet aroma of freshly mowed grass. He was glad to see a small white Miata in the driveway. Tammy Carroll's mother, Mrs. Stacy, was at home.

When he rang the doorbell, he was surprised to hear it play a similar chant to the Alcotts'. He heard hurrying light foot-steps inside, and when the door opened, he looked into what Tammy Carroll's face would become in twenty-five years. Mrs. Stacy was a beautiful woman, like her daughter, but there was character in her face, that only years could have given her. He saw grief there, too, saw it in her eyes. Like her daughter, she was suffering after the death of her son-in-law.

"Mrs. Stacy? I'm Special Agent Dillon Savich, FBI." He handed her his creds.

"I know who you are, Agent Savich. Tammy called me right after you and Agent Sherlock left." Mrs. Stacy gave him a small smile. "Agent Sherlock made quite an impression on my daughter, not because of her heroics at JFK, but because of her beautiful red hair." A smile that he imagined curved up her mouth most of her life quickly fell off her face. She said in a flat voice, "This is about Sparky."

"Yes," Savich said. "May I speak with you, Mrs. Stacy?"

She stepped back and motioned for him to enter. "This way, Agent Savich."

He followed her down a long hallway, past a formal living room on the right with heavy oak furnishings, an old-fashioned kitchen, and a half-bath painted pink, to a closed door at the back of the house.

"This is my own personal room," she said,

and opened the door. "Come in."

Savich walked into a Wiccan's fantasy. The room wasn't large, but still it felt light, airy, and spacious. It was painted white, and had a white sofa and chair, white curtains on the windows. An entire wall was covered with white built-in bookshelves with bottles of herbs lined up on one shelf, each jar meticulously labeled. There were dozens of books whose titles he skimmed, from **Dreaming the Dark: Magic, Sex, and Politics** to **The Spiral Dance** to **Wicca: A Guide for the Solitary Practitioner**. There were dried flowers in several vases sharing space with seashells and pearls and bowls of crystals. He saw a line of small, oddly shaped dolls on a long windowsill.

Mrs. Stacy said from behind him, "We call them poppets. They're tools to aid in working magic."

"How?"

"I can't do justice to that with you quickly, Agent Savich, but I will say that poppets help achieve what you wish for, and are an integral part of some of our rituals."

He didn't understand, but nodded.

She smiled at him. "They aren't voodoo

dolls, there's no evil intent. I will use them soon at Litha—our celebration of the summer solstice." She raised her chin, as if daring him to mock her. "And I will set the powers within myself and the powers of the gods we summon to discover why Walter Givens murdered poor Sparky." She shook her head, shrugged. "I doubt it will succeed, but I will have to try if you haven't found out the truth by then.

"I've heard Walter has no memory of killing Sparky, no memory of why he did it in such a public place. If this is true"—she raised raised her eyes to his face—"it's quite terrifying."

"Yes," Savich said, "it is." He pointed to a collection of small square cloth bags piled in a basket on the floor beside the sofa.

"Those are plackets." She fell to her knees and picked one up. "Yes, I know, it sounds like the name of our town, but it's a coincidence. I've already prepared a placket with Walter Givens's name on it. I will use that placket as well to help me." She gently set the placket back in the basket and rose. "Please, sit down, Agent Savich, and tell me how I can help you." She pointed to the white sofa. She sat in the single white chair facing him, placed her small hands on her jeans-covered legs.

"Tell me how Tammy is doing."

"She's a wreck, as you would expect. She'd been married four months and her husband didn't simply die, which would have been horrible enough, he was viciously murdered. In public. She refuses to come back home, though. She wants to stay where she lived with Sparky." Mrs. Stacy fell silent.

"Did Mrs. Deliah Abbott give you an Athame collection that belonged to her husband?"

"Why, yes, she did." She rose and walked to a glass cabinet, opened it, and lifted out a beautifully carved wooden case. She brought it back to the sofa and opened it. Savich looked at a dozen Athames, some similar to the Dual Dragon, others also with incredible carved figured handles.

"It was soon after Mr. Alcott died—well, Arthur was killed, too, wasn't he?" She sighed. "Deliah gave them to me about three months after he died, said he would have wanted me to have them."

"Do you know if there were any Athames missing from the collection when Mrs. Alcott gave it to you?"

She wasn't stupid. She swallowed. "You mean you believe Walter may have used one of Mr. Alcott's Athames to kill Sparky?"

He nodded.

"If it was one of Mr. Alcott's Athames, it wasn't in this collection. It's possible Deliah kept some of the Athames. I don't know. She never said and I never asked."

"Do you and Mrs. Alcott practice Wicca together, or in a group, to celebrate ceremonies like this Litha coming up?"

"No. Not for many years. I've become what Wiccans call a solitary practitioner." She nodded toward a book on the shelf. "I imagine Deliah still shares the circle with her own family."

"But she thought enough of you to give you Mr. Alcott's collection."

"Yes. Arthur Alcott and I got along very well. I thought he was a gentleman, a kind man. My husband liked him, too, trusted him. He was never mean about money like some folks get when they're lucky enough to come into a windfall like the Alcotts did.

No, Arthur always was down-to-earth and generous with what he had. I guess you could say my husband and I both loved him." She sighed again. "We considered poor Sparky's father a friend to us, too, until he started drinking so much. I don't remember Arthur ever drinking alcohol at all."

"I understand Sparky's father, Milt Carroll, owned the catering company that Sparky inherited?"

"Yes. Eat Well and Prosper—rather silly, but both Milt and Sparky liked it. Now, Milt was a big drinker."

"I understand Deputy Lewis was quite a drinker as well? Did they often drink together?"

She nodded. "Kane was an alcoholic; why, I don't know. He and Milt became drinking buddies, you could say. No one minded enough to get Kane in trouble for it. He never drank on the job, and most everyone liked him." She looked toward the small wood-burning stove in the far corner of the room. She raised her eyes to his face. "They're both dead, too. Like Sparky. Agent Savich, what is happening here in Plackett?"

42

Maple Leaf Inn
Colby, Long Island
Saturday, noon

Everyone's eyes were on the large TV on the wall behind the counter in the main dining room, where the news was report-ing at the scene of the horrific TBV train wreck hours before, thirty miles north of Lyons, France. A massive explosion had ripped through five first-class cars and derailed them, hurling flaming debris over a mile of countryside, some of it still burning and smoking. As the camera panned over some of the wreckage, a reporter was saying what incalculable loss of life and property might have resulted if a bomb that size had exploded under the train in a town or city. So far forty-eight people were confirmed dead, more than a hundred injured. The count would continue to rise.

Pip Erwin raised his head from his bowl of vegetable soup, pointed his spoon at the

TV. "I'm waiting for someone from the French government to even acknowledge that carnage was another terrorist attack. They'll have to, eventually. I'd be willing to bet the rest of my minestrone it's the same people who attacked us, that it was part of their Bella project. Not a cathedral this time, but certainly a national treasure, the famous French high-speed train. They were so proud of having built the fastest train in the world for the past thirty-five years."

Cal said, "They said the train was traveling at three hundred kilometers an hour, not anywhere near as fast as the TGV can travel—but that's a hundred and eighty miles per hour, fast enough to make that bomb a thousand times more effective. Can you imagine sitting in one of the last cars on that train and watching the front of it get blown off the track at that speed?"

Kelly's BLT and the lovely pile of french fries cozied up to it lay untouched on her plate. On even a mildly bad day, she still loved her french fries, but not today, not watching the horror unfold in France. She agreed with Pip, knew everyone else at the table did, too. It was terrifying. "Maybe someone in the group will take credit? Maybe this Strategist? We still have no idea who they are."

Cal's eyes were glued to the TV screen. "A couple years ago I rode on one of those from Paris to Geneva. **Train à Grande Vitesse**, they call it. They're amazing, some can travel up to nearly half the speed of sound. I remember we were hardly out of the station when the train was passing cars on the highway. It was better to be sitting as it picked up speed, one hundred kilometers before it even left the station, I heard. The French who rode the train already knew that, so only a couple tourists ended up getting slung into someone's lap.

"What was amazing to me was you couldn't tell you were moving that fast because the ride was smooth, and it was quiet, until you looked out the window and saw the world going backward. Eat your lunch, Kelly."

She picked up half of her BLT, studied it, set it back down. "Terrorist groups want to take credit. It brings them credibility, more support. I can understand not hearing from anyone after they failed to blow up

Saint Pat's, but this"—she waved a hand toward the TV—"vicious act was a massive success."

Sherlock was listening to a reporter interviewing a bystander who'd witnessed the explosion, and a passenger traveling second-class who'd survived it. An English newscaster interrupted him. "A French government spokesman has confirmed that French economic minister Marcel Dubroc was aboard the train and is presumed dead. President Dumas is expected to arrive at the scene shortly and to make a statement."

Cal said, "Dubroc had to be in first class, where all the cars were blown off the tracks. I wonder if that was by design or accident?"

Pip said, "At that speed, the timing would require great precision. They had to have wired an electronic detonator set off by the passing train itself. No way would you do that remotely by hand. A fraction of a second off and it would have been the second-class cars instead. They'd have to dig down deep under the ballast—"

Kelly shook her head. "The what?"

Cal said, "Ballast is simply the thick layer of gravel beneath and beside the train tracks. It's the bulk support for the train tracks, used for stabilization. For the TGV, I'd guess it would go deeper under the tracks than most, probably at least a foot beneath the tracks, and a foot and a half at the shoulders. The hard part would be digging down without being seen, without tripping any sensors, and plant what must have been a heavy load of explosives."

Sherlock frowned into her bowl of vegetable soup. Vice President Foley had been in St. Patrick's, as had a great many politicians and their rich and powerful friends. Was it people who were being targeted, as well as buildings and trains?

Kelly was picking the bacon out of her BLT when her cell rang. More bad news?

Pip, Cal, Jo, and Sherlock stopped eating and looked at her when she thumped her fist on the table. "That's amazing! Yes, by all means. We'll arrange air transport, be there as fast as we can—you're in operational control, Chris. If there's an imminent threat, it's your call. Otherwise, get your perimeter established and get those snipers in place, and wait for us."

She gave them a thumbs-up. "The Boston Field Office came through, they found Nasim's family." She turned back to her phone and punched in another call.

Pip said, "We'll get us a chopper in no time, knowing Kelly."

She punched off. "Yep, right now. Let's get to the SUV."

Fifteen minutes later, the five of them were strapped into their seats on an FBI Bell helicopter, and lifting off from the Jameson Mall parking lot. Maybe an hour, the pilot told them, and he'd set them down as close as possible to Lake Pleasant.

Kelly stayed in radio contact with Special Agent Chris Tyson from the Boston Field Office during most of the ride. Her voice was tinny through the headsets when she said, "Even though there wasn't any trace of the Conklins at Abdul Rahal's house, the Boston agents followed up with his phone calls, credit cards, bank records. Turns out the Rahal family spends a couple of weeks every summer at a rental house on Lake Pleasant, thirty minutes from Plover, on the Connecticut side. They tracked down the rental home's owner, learned the house was being rented right now by a James Lockerby and his family. They checked the name, found the address they gave didn't match. They positioned a drone over the house, eyes and ears, and saw three armed men patrolling the grounds outside the house. They dropped in a surveillance team and actually saw Mrs. Conklin and at least one of her children inside the house through their scopes.

"By now they've got a perimeter, but I imagine it's slow going getting the snipers in place without alerting the terrorists. They'll wait for us unless they're seen, or if it's too dangerous to the Conklins to wait."

Sherlock felt a surge of hope. She said into her mike, "They've got a good chance now, because of Nasim. I hope I can keep my promise to him."

43

Lake Pleasant, Connecticut

The helicopter set them down a half mile from the lake and the cabin, after flying in low to keep them out of sight. Agent Chris Tyson met them next to a stand of pine trees. He was wearing combat gear, Kevlar, a H&K slung over his shoulder. "We have vests for you at the operations site. As of two minutes ago, we've identified three targets, one of them moving in and out of the house, the other two stationed outside, patrolling. The family has been seen inside, eating, and that's very good news. We've got three snipers positioned overlooking the house in the surrounding oak trees. Two of them have eyes on the targets outside. I've kept most of the team well back. We'll be ready when the third one comes out of the house." And he grinned at Pip Erwin. "Long time no see, Pip. All of you look ready to rock and roll." He stuck out his hand to Sherlock. "It's a pleasure, Agent Sherlock. Okay, guys, let's get this done."

They jogged after him through the thick pine forest, thinning enough in places so they saw flashes of the lake through the branches. They all quickly broke into a sweat. It had rained earlier, leaving the air pregnant with moisture in the unexpected late spring heat. Tyson stopped, held up his hand, listened to his comm, and moved quietly forward to look through the trees. After a couple minutes, he jogged back to them. "All three targets are outside again, but they're not clear of the cabin and the Conklins. They're talking, arguing, in a combination of Arabic and accented English. We're trying to run facial recognition. Stay down, the command center is up ahead."

They followed him silently through the trees for several minutes, heard him checking in with the sniper team leader as they grew closer. The command center was well hidden from the cabin, and was nothing more than piles of communication equipment and weapons, and a half-dozen agents in combat gear. Everyone remained silent.

The five of them were each handed H&Ks, vests, and binoculars. They checked their weapons and magazines, shrugged on their vests, and covered them with dark blue FBI jackets. The team took them to the best nearby vantage point. Sherlock forgot the heavy humid heat and concentrated on the cabin in front of her in the distance. It was old, the wood weathered nearly black over the decades, but in good repair. It sat thirty feet from the lake and a dock that stretched out about twenty feet from the shore, where a single outboard bobbed easily in the gentle wind. The cabin was long and narrow, with a single window at the front that spanned nearly the entire main room. They'd made no effort to hide what was inside. Through the binoculars, she saw Marie Claire sitting in a faded old armchair, her three children close beside her. Two girls, about five and seven, were reading, and the third child, a small boy, was sleeping on a blanket beside his mother, his cheek cushioned on his hand. She saw the remains of their lunch on a nearby table. Marie Claire looked to be in her mid-thirties, her hair glossy black, twisted in a braid at the back of her head. She wore jeans and a white blouse that looked worse for wear. Sherlock couldn't see her face clearly from this distance, but she knew she had to be ready to close down, beyond tired from the fear she'd had to live with for four days, fear for herself and for her children.

Sherlock panned over to the three armed men. Two of them were very young, with short beards—stubble, really. Had they shaved off their beards for their flight to the United States? The third man was older, perhaps forty, smooth-skinned. He wore aviator glasses. They were dressed casually in dark T-shirts, faded jeans, and boots. All had AK-47s strapped to their chests, pistols hooked to their belts. Sherlock would bet her new pair of Nikes that the young ones wore KA-BARs strapped to their ankles. They looked tough, businesslike, even as they argued with one another. About what?

Agent Tyson handed her an earpiece, and then she heard them speaking, partly in British English. They were arguing, but she couldn't make out what it was all about with the Arabic mixed in. The older man, obviously their leader, pulled out a cell phone and dialed. He listened, then punched off, shook his head at the other two.

Sherlock turned to see Kelly conferring with three members of the Boston tactical team. One of them asked Cal a question, nodded at his response. Kelly met her eyes and nodded. She'd decided it was time to end it.

One of the agents cursed. He turned, whispered, "The leader has gone into the cabin." He said into his comm, "Hold, hold."

Sherlock turned her binoculars back to the cabin. The leader was leaning over Marie Claire, speaking to her, gesticulating with his hands.

She saw the young boy leap up, push himself against the man's legs. The man leaned down and shoved him away. The little boy began to cry. Marie Claire said something to the man, drew the little boy to her.

The man raised his fist, lowered it, turned, and left the cabin.

Good, the three were outside again, but they were clustered right in front of the glass window, arguing again.

Move, move, move. It was her silent chant.

One of the young men lit up a cigarette, tossed the match to the ground. The match flame didn't die, it smoldered against a piece of wadded-up paper, then burst into flames.

The leader yelled something, gestured for the man to put the flame out. As one of the young men moved away from the front window, Kelly whispered, "Bring him down. Execute!" Not even a second and the man was down, blood blooming on his chest.

The two targets fired blindly into the woods and juked and dodged toward the trees, away from the cabin. Two more sniper shots rang out, struck both men center mass. They dropped where they stood. Two more shots followed quickly.

It was over. Like that, it was over. Sherlock calmed her racing heart. No one of the team was hurt, and the Conklins were safe.

Kelly ran into the clearing with the tactical team, checked on each of the targets. When Sherlock joined her, she nodded toward the cabin. They both dropped their weapons and walked inside.

Sherlock had never before seen a face as pale as Marie Claire's. She'd pulled all three children tightly against her, covering their heads with her arms. Sherlock saw she hadn't pulled them under the table because her ankles were tied to the chair.

She met Sherlock's eyes. "We're FBI, Mrs. Conklin. It's over." Sherlock smiled at this woman who'd lived through so much. She said again, "All of this is over. Those men are all dead. You and your children are safe now."

Marie Claire stared at the two women. She said in heavily accented English, "Those shots—those horrible men are really dead?"

"Yes," Kelly said. "I'm Agent Kelly Giusti and this is Agent Sherlock."

Sherlock knelt beside Mrs. Conklin, slid a knife through the ropes around her ankles. She leaned back on her heels. "We'll take you all out of here to a safe place as soon as we can. Everything will be all right now." She said that for the children to hear, but of course nothing would be right. Their father was dead. Sherlock guessed Mrs. Conklin already knew that.

Marie Claire nodded, soothed her children. The older girl, the image of her mother, wiped her nose and stared at the two women. "How did you find us?" Her English came naturally to her, thanks to her father, thanks to Nasim.

Kelly patted her shoulder. "We worked hard to locate this cabin. We wanted to find you very much."

The younger girl had Nasim's eyes, Sherlock saw, and felt her throat clog. Marie Claire said, "My babies were so frightened. I could not help them." She took the little girl's hand. "All of us are very dirty. Those men didn't let us bathe, even though there is a bathroom."

Marie Claire raised her eyes to Sherlock's face. "Nasim," she said. "My husband. Where is he? I spoke to him only once. That was two days ago, Thursday night. Then nothing. Where is he?"

Sherlock couldn't say it aloud, not in front of the children, who were all staring at her. "We will speak of Nasim later, all right, Marie Claire? First, we want to make certain you and your children are safe."

She knew, of course, she knew. Sherlock nodded slowly, turned to smile at each of the children. "My name's Sherlock and this is Kelly. And you are?"

"I'm Gabrielle."

"I'm Lexie."

The little boy licked his lips, looked at his mother, and whispered, "I'm Thomas. I want to go to the bathroom," then pressed himself tightly against his mother's leg.

"Yes," Marie Claire said, "all of us will go to the bathroom, then we will leave this place." And she clapped her hands and herded the children out of the living room. At the door, she turned back to them, said quietly, "Thank you for coming." They watched her face tighten. "Nasim would thank you, too."

Kelly felt tears behind her eyes, swallowed. "I don't want to tell her, Sherlock, I really don't."

Sherlock drew in a deep breath. "We will tell her that Nasim was a very brave man, he sacrificed himself to save them, he led us to them. That is what we will tell her."

44

New York City
Saturday, early evening

As Pip drove the SUV into the garage beneath 26 Federal Plaza, Cal said, "After this press conference it seems to me we're done here. You ready to go home, Sherlock?"

Sherlock saw Nasim's face as he'd died in her arms, felt the familiar burn of tears. She didn't think she'd ever accept the unfairness of it all. She said, "I'm more than ready."

Kelly waited for Pip to pull into a parking space and turn off the engine. "The press conference is happening in about"—she looked down at her watch—"half an hour. Director Comey will be there himself. It's a big deal, puts the spotlight square on the FBI. This will be the first time the American people will hear about who Nasim really was and about how he was murdered by the terrorists, and how we managed to save his family. Afterward, well, sorry, guys, but neither of you is leaving. The change of plans came from on high."

She patted Sherlock's hand. "You'll be front and center, the face of the FBI on this one, the agent who fought off this terrorist attack, America's heroine. I wouldn't be surprised if they trot out Father Joseph Reilly and Romeo Rodriguez, too. So take a few minutes and think about what you're going to say." She raised her hand when Sherlock shook her head, started to open her mouth. "Director Comey doesn't want you to leave New York. He's very proud of you, proud you're an FBI agent, and that means after the press conference, he's not about to let anything happen to you. You've already been shot at and threatened by Jamil, on orders from his terrorist bosses. That means you'll be staying close to me until it's over, or until we have assurances you're not a target." She looked at Cal, and couldn't prevent a small smile. "As for you, Mr. Hotshot, you'll be staying on as her bodyguard. I've got to say you've come in pretty handy so far. You up for it?"

Exactly a half-hour later, Special Agent Lacey Sherlock stood next to Director

Comey on the dais set up outside for the press conference. They had a full media turnout.

Director Comey looked over the microphone at the sea of media faces. In his usual professional and organized way, he walked everyone step-by-step through each FBI action following the attacks at JFK and St. Patrick's Cathedral. He told them of the death of Nasim Conklin while in FBI custody, his murder enabled by Nasim himself, who sacrificed himself up in an attempt to save his family, and the shooting and capture of his murderer, Jamil Nazari, and he explained the reason for the delay in announcing his death— the FBI had been following critical leads obtained from Nasim Conklin by Agent Sherlock prior to his death.

Director Comey ended with their successes—the death of three terrorists holding Nasim Conklin's family in Connecticut and the family's safe rescue.

He thanked the New York Field Office, the Boston Field Office, and the New York Joint Antiterrorism Task Force for their efforts thus far, explained they would continue to pursue other members of the terrorist group but could not identify them definitively at this time. He did not refer to the Strategist specifically; that was to be kept close for now. He answered a number of the media's questions, clarifying what he could but giving away no other details of the investigation. He gave a rueful smile. "I don't pretend to believe you came here to listen to me." He turned to Sherlock, smiled at her, shook her hand, said to the sea of faces, "I'd like to introduce Special Agent Lacey Sherlock. The Bureau is very grateful to her for her quick actions at JFK on Wednesday afternoon, which saved many lives, and for being instrumental in securing the safe recovery of the Conklin family in Connecticut earlier today." He shook her hand and held it, smiling widely as dozens of camera flashes went off. He leaned down, whispered, "You're the face of the FBI. Get used to it. Smile for the world."

Sherlock stepped to the microphone. The sudden silence was unnerving after the constant buzz of voices from the overflowing plaza. She looked out toward a dozen vans hunkered up as close as they could park, paused when she recognized some of the media faces familiar from the nightly news. All of them were staring at her, restraining themselves, but obviously chomping at the bit to yell out their questions and, they hoped, get the sound bite of the day.

Sherlock wished Dillon were standing beside her, but he wasn't; she was on her own. She pulled the microphone close and said clearly, "I want to emphasize that Nasim Conklin was not a terrorist. He was a man forced by terrorists holding his family to do what he did. I don't know if I could have stopped him if not for his hesitation brought by the horror he felt at what he was being made to do. In the end, he helped us free his family." She couldn't help it, she blinked away tears. She was unaware that her hands, resting on the dais, were clenched into fists. "Let me say that the terrorists who did this to him, the terrorists who would not have hesitated to murder his family, would have succeeded were it not for the men and women here today who rescued them." She called out the names of Agent Kelly Giusti and Agent Chris Tyson of the Boston Field Office, nodded to them.

She raised her voice. "I hope the people behind this are watching, because they should know we will find them, and we will bring them to justice."

She stepped back. Director Comey looked at his watch, looked back at the large group of people, and said, "We have a few minutes for questions."

Martin Chivers from **The New York Times** had his own microphone and didn't have to yell. His deep voice drowned out the other voices. "Can you tell us anything more about who these terrorists are, what group is behind the attempted bombing of Saint Patrick's?"

Director Comey said, "You know I will not speculate. Nor can I give out any information that might compromise our investigation. There are many leads we are following, myriad details we are working through. We will share those with you as we are able." Comey knew he'd spouted the party line, no choice but to say everything and nothing at all.

Then came NBC's Lois Nedrick's little-girl voice. "Agent Sherlock, what are your plans now?"

Comey stepped aside and Sherlock moved close to the microphone. "The Bureau has asked me to stay on here in New York to pursue the investigation. After we have apprehended those responsible for these terrorist attacks, I plan to go home to my husband and son. For some R and R." That brought a few laughs.

There was a jumble of voices before Mark Allen of FOX managed to outshout everyone else. "Director Comey, do you believe the bombing of the TGV in France today is tied to the attempted bombing of Saint Pat's?"

There it was, the eight-hundred-pound gorilla.

Director Comey looked out into the sea of faces. His first inclination was to duck the question, but instead he said, "We are in contact with the French authorities and will continue to be. As yet we have no direct proof, but in my opinion, yes, there is no question in my mind the two acts are tied together."

Mark Allen picked it up before Director Comey had finished taking a breath: "A newly appointed French minister was killed in that explosion. Vice President Foley and dozens of other high-ranking officials were in attendance at the attempted bombing at Saint Pat's. Do you believe these terrorist attacks could have been intended not only to destroy national treasures, but to kill national leaders or specific individuals?"

Comey had expected that question, too. No one was stupid. "Let me say again that the FBI does not yet have information to tie the two attacks together. There has as yet been no credible announcement by any group taking responsibility for these attacks, or their stated goals. Both have the hallmarks of terrorist operations. But as you said, the attempted assassination of public officials in high-profile public venues goes beyond what we've seen from terrorist attacks in the past, and it raises serious questions."

Harold Carver from NPR started to speak, but a stout woman shoved him from behind. As he windmilled to regain his balance, she yelled out, "Agent Sherlock, what about you? What is your personal opinion?"

Sherlock shot a look at Comey, who nodded. She said, "I personally cannot imagine what a terrorist supposedly feels when he's managed to murder innocent people. Is he pleased? Is he dancing for joy at the sheer number of people he's robbed of their lives? Is he convinced he is fulfilling his duty to Allah? Is his hatred so great for those who believe differently that their destruction is all that matters to him?"

She paused, shook her head. "Whatever those people's motivation, they are not wise enough to represent God on earth. In my experience, many of them are violent psychopaths and self-serving egotists. I believe such individuals are behind these attacks." **Are you out there, listening?**

Director Comey finished it. "Thank you all for coming. We will keep you informed. If you have further questions, please submit them to my office." He stepped off the dais, ignored the loud tide of shouted questions. He paused to shake a few hands as he walked back into 26 Federal Plaza, surrounded by aides and all the agents. He looked back over his shoulder at Sherlock. "You just about invited the Strategist to come after you out there, Agent Sherlock."

Sherlock never broke stride. **I surely hope so.** "Someone had to say it."

45

Mulberry Street, Little Italy
New York City
Saturday night

Cal hadn't realized he was so hungry until he took his first bite of spaghetti Bolognese and his taste buds sang hallelujah. Kelly laughed. "Hey, is that a spiritual moment you're having, Cal? With your spaghetti?"

"I gotta say it's better than my aunt Millie's," he said as he took another bite. "And I use her recipe. Eat, Sherlock. I don't want to deliver a beanpole back to Savich."

Sherlock was picking at her chicken parmigiana, hungry but too wound up to eat much. "I've got to get myself calmed down. It's been an extraordinary day."

Kelly took a bite of her caprese. "What better place to decompress than right here? I've been coming to this place so long, the owner put me on his Christmas card list. Yes, I'm Italian, in case you were wondering."

Cal, who'd thought Kelly was as wound up as Sherlock, said easily, in a tone to invite confidences, "And here I thought Giusti was a famous Irish name."

"Har, har." Kelly tossed her napkin at him. He caught it midair, handed it back to her.

"Where in Italy do you hail from?" Sherlock asked her.

"Mind you, I'm not descended from the Napoli Giustis—they're a tough bunch, to put it nicely. My family comes from the Dolomite Giustis, most of us born not ten miles from the Swiss border. Great skiers, most of us. As you might guess, both sets of Giustis claim to go all the way back to Romulus and Remus."

At Cal's grin, she went on. "My great-grandparents immigrated to New York in the forties. You really should taste my mama's pizza—she makes the best pie, learned at my grandmother's knee."

Cal swallowed another bite of spaghetti, shared a silent moment with his taste buds. "I don't ever say no to pizza. I've found it goes great with my favorite Irish stew, from O'Flynn's in Foggy Bottom. I have a dog named after O'Flynn, a big Irish setter, my dog, that is. Sherlock, turn off your brain and eat your parmigiana. Kelly's now stuffing the caprese down her gullet. Both of you, we scored a big win today rescuing the Conklins. We deserve to celebrate."

Sherlock dutifully took a bite. "It's delicious." She shook her head sadly. "But no one's parmigiana beats Dillon's. Yes, you're both invited."

Kelly whistled. "That big tough dude makes parmigiana? Sherlock, don't let that man escape."

Cal said, "If he ever tried, I picture cement shoes and a deep body of water."

They both laughed, as he hoped they would. Cal raised his glass of Chianti. "Here's to your favorite restaurant, Kelly. And to our win today."

As they drank it down, Sherlock's cell phone sang out P. Franklin's "Ancient Wisdom." "It's Dillon." She rose immediately. "You guys go ahead."

They watched her walk past the beautiful mahogany bar with its dozens of liquor bottles lined up in front of its mirror, all of them glowing softly in the dim golden light of the main dining room. Cal watched her stop beyond the arched doorway to the restrooms. He scanned the restaurant again. No one seemed to be paying her any attention.

Kelly said, "I haven't spent so much time on the phone with someone since I was in college."

"That's because you aren't jointed at the hip like Savich and Sherlock. I think this is the first time they haven't worked a case together. It's tough on both of them, each worrying about the other. He reads her so well I don't see how she's going to keep her nearly getting shot from him. She'll try, though. None of us want him to come roaring up here."

"What would he do?"

Cal saw she was grinning. Good, she was staring to unwind a bit, like his uncle Mort's antique watch. "Lay me flat, maybe knock me in the head a couple of times, then he'd try to take over the case."

Kelly realized he wasn't going to stop trying to distract her. She also realized it was working. She said, "He's a good guy, isn't he?"

Cal nodded. "The best. He and Sherlock have already spoken half a dozen times today. Now they'll talk about the press conference and she'll try to calm him down about sticking her middle finger in the Strategist's eye in front of the world."

"If it were my husband who'd done that, I'd be upset, too."

"He'll deal with it, no choice. Both of them are sometimes in harm's way." Cal shrugged. "You either deal with it or the marriage doesn't last."

Kelly wondered if Cal had had a marriage go south on him, but now wasn't the time to ask him. She'd keep it light, like he had. "I still can't get over a married couple working together in the FBI. Savich has quite a rep." She paused, shook her head. "But now it's Sherlock in the spotlight, not Savich. There's one thing I couldn't deal with, though, if I was wearing her boots."

"What's that?"

She laughed. "The obvious. She has to report to him, right? He's her boss?"

"Sherlock calls him the Big Dog. We all

report to someone, so what's wrong with her reporting to him? After all, Savich is the one who started the Criminal Apprehension Unit."

"But what if they have an argument? How would you like to have to follow orders from the love of your life when you felt like smacking him on the head?"

"Savich says as long as she does what he tells her to at work, he's willing to pay for it at home." Cal gave her a fat grin. "Then he rolls his eyes."

As he did every few seconds, Cal automatically checked on Sherlock. She was still talking on the phone. She'd moved to stand directly beneath the arched hallway, in plain view. He looked back at Kelly. Despite the smiles he'd gotten out of her, she still looked bruised somehow, in spite of all the kudos for a job well done, in spite of the success of the press conference. So much had happened in such a short time. She had lost Nasim, and that had been a big blow for her, even though it was Nasim himself who'd led the killer to them. She wasn't used to losing, he thought, at anything. "How'd you get started in the FBI, Kelly?'

She took another bite of her caprese. "Not a big mystery. I'm third-generation law enforcement. The first Fed, though, much as it burned my granddad. He's retired now, but my dad's still a homicide detective in the Albuquerque PD, tells me he better not hear me bigfooting any local police."

"And your mom, who makes the great pizza?"

"My mom's the high achiever. She's chief of staff in Governor Turnbull's office in Santa Fe. No doubt in my mind that one of these days, she'll be governor."

"What does she think of your being a federal cop?"

"She'd like it if I were Director Giusti by the time I'm forty. She pushes me more than my brother, James, probably because I'm a woman. Pretty soon she's going to see I'm not cooperating."

"Your brother's FBI, too?"

"No, James is a priest. He laughs at her when she tells him he'd make an excellent cardinal. After all, he speaks Italian fluently, doesn't he? My mom never gives up. What about you, Cal? Why'd you sign up?"

"Unlike you, it had nothing to do with having cop in the blood. I was in high school when Nine-Eleven happened, already accepted into MIT. That day changed my life. I never looked back."

"Did you lose a relative? A friend?"

"No, nothing like that. I simply realized on that day what lengths terrorists would go to try to wipe us from the face of the earth. I wanted to help stop them."

"How long have you been in the counterterrorism unit?"

"I started there when I was nearly twenty-five, seven years now." He looked over to check on Sherlock, who hadn't moved, then back at her. "It's where I belong, where my talents lie. This terrorist operation—Bella—it's got me in overdrive, just like you. Thanks for letting me in, Kelly."

She tapped her fingertips on the table. "I took one look at you and wanted to boot you back to Washington. I've got to say, though, you've been pretty useful—well, so far."

He was out of his chair, moving fast toward the arched doorway. A man was moving purposefully, directly toward Sherlock, his hand going to his pants pocket.

Cal caught up with him, pressed his Glock against the man's kidney. "Don't move. I need to check what's in your pocket."

The man was jerking around toward Cal when he felt the gun. "What—what?"

"Take your hand out of your pocket. Slowly."

"But—"

"Now."

Cal patted his thigh, felt a cell phone. "I-I was coming back here to call my wife," he said, and looked nervously back at his table, where a very pretty young woman sat sipping wine.

Cal eased his Glock back onto the clip at his waist. "Okay, my apologies. Federal agent, doing my job. Enjoy your evening, although given what you're doing, I gotta say you're a jerk."

The man's mouth tightened and he started to say something more but thought better of it. He wouldn't make a scene while out with a woman who wasn't his wife. And with a cop. The guy wasn't entirely stupid.

"Yes, okay, but it's none of your business," the man said, and walked quickly back to his table.

"Thanks for moving so fast, Cal. I'm all right, go back to your dinner." He smiled, nodded and left her. She said into her cell, "Dillon, no worries, it was only some cheating guy who was going to call his wife. Cal was being careful." She'd seen the man's face close up, realized she wasn't even on his radar, but Cal hadn't, and he'd moved fast. She watched Cal walk between the tables back to Kelly, looking her way a couple more times, just in case.

She shifted the cell to her other ear. "Everything's okay, Dillon. False alarm. Yes, I promise. Now you want me to tell Kelly you spoke to your friend John Eiserly at MI5?"

"Yes, and he's keeping me up to date," Savich said, his heart still stuttering.

Sherlock wondered if Kelly would be pissed about Dillon sticking his nose under the tent. She realized she didn't care. She wanted this to be over, she wanted to go home. She wanted her life back.

He said, "You know, I'd really prefer to hear you were in a closet with four armed guards."

"Cal's been sitting right next to me, Dillon, one hand spooning his Bolognese sauce, the other an inch from his Glock. Everything's okay."

"Keep being careful, all right?"

"I promise. You were telling me about your visit to Charlie Marker's hospital room this evening." Finally, she had her own fear for him under control. He and Griffin both could so easily have been killed by a hypnotized man who didn't have any idea at all of what he was doing, much less why or who had convinced him to do it.

As he spoke, Savich pictured the young man propped up in bed, silent, pale, in some pain, and scared to death. He knew he'd done something bad but didn't remember what it was. His parents, an older couple, as scared as their son, were in his room, his mom continually patting his arm, watching him closely, as if afraid of what he suddenly might do, his dad pacing, neither understanding enough of what happened to know who to yell at. It was the dad's Kel-Tec that Charlie had taken from his locked gun box, his Silverado that Charlie had driven to the woods. Maybe Dr. Hicks could help Charlie remember what had happened, as he had Brakey. Savich told them what had happened, tried to explain the inexplicable. He'd already glossed over the attack when he'd told Sherlock about it earlier, assuring her that Griffin had everything under control. He finished with, "It was tough, for Charlie and his parents. At least Charlie hadn't killed anyone. I assured them he wouldn't be arrested and left it at that. Obviously they know all about what happened to Brakey and Walter Givens, as everyone in Plackett knows the McCutty woods where Charlie ambushed us. Ah, the woods, they were in Dalco's first dreamscape, so since he knew those woods, that's where he sent Charlie.

"Now, enough about my insanity. Was Mrs. Conklin able to tell you anything?"

There'd been more danger than he'd ever let on, Sherlock knew, and that was why he wanted to move right along. "She knew very little that's new, Dillon. Three men burst into her front door in Notting Hill in London, threatened her children and husband if she resisted. Two handlers she couldn't identify flew with them to Boston where they were put in an SUV, blindfolded, and driven she had no idea where. They let her speak to Nasim only once. The Boston agents had to tell her everything else that happened."

"Could she tell Boston anything pertinent about Imam Al-Hädi ibn Mīrzā?"

"Marie Claire believes the imam is involved, but she has no proof. And she's never heard of anyone called the Strategist."

"John said they have the imam under surveillance, but they're holding off bringing him in for questioning, hoping to identify his contacts."

Sherlock sighed. "Dillon, if you could have seen Marie Claire's face, her children's faces. It was a horror for her, believing finally that her children would die, having no reason for hope. When this is all over I imagine she'll go back to live in France. She'll be a wealthy woman, won't she, from the business Nasim inherited from his father?"

"Yes, the business will be hers now. I'm sure she'll sell it, and that she'll never want to go back to England again. She survived because of you, Sherlock. You gave her and her children a future."

She closed her eyes, so relieved and thankful everything had turned out as it had. Except for Nasim. "Thank you, but you know it was all of us working together. Now tell me how you managed to get Sean to bed tonight."

46

Thornsby, England
Saturday afternoon

Imam Al-Hädi ibn Mīrzā crossed his arms over his white-robed chest and sat back in his caned chair, well aware that the other dozen or so customers were eyeing him, not surprising because he looked so different from them, a foreigner they didn't trust or understand, a holy man who belonged in the desert, not in this time-warped little English village barely large enough to be on the map, in this middle-class little tea shop with its lace draperies and middle-aged serving women.

He looked with pride at the stylish man opposite him, the one he called Hercule, the name only those intimate with him were privileged to know. He dipped his almond biscotti into his cappuccino to soften it and chewed gingerly since one of his back teeth ached from a cavity again, a cavity he had to get taken care of but didn't want to. He saw Hercule was scanning the room from their small back-corner table to be sure no one would hear them before he spoke. The imam noted he didn't even look fatigued from his red-eye private flight back from Boston, not six hours before. **A privilege of youth and money,** the imam thought, and he wondered what the Strategist would look like when he'd reached his own age—if, that is, he was still alive.

"Thank you for coming this far so promptly," Hercule said. "Are you certain your driver evaded anyone following you on your way here?"

"You know my driver Sarkis is a wily old dog. He can sniff out an infidel no matter how they try to hide themselves. Stop your worrying, Hercule, you sound like an old woman."

The imam was being his usual dismissive self, not a good sign. "You should assume that MI5 has agents following you, listening in on your every word on the telephone. Listening as well to your followers, tracking where they go and who they see. Take this seriously, Imam."

"Naturally I take this seriously. I expect your pilot made good time from Boston?"

Hercule knew the imam hadn't been all that careful, regardless of his assurances, but now, he hoped, he would. "Mr. Picard always makes excellent time. It was nothing, less than six hours." Hercule gave an elegant shrug, lifted his cup of English tea in salute. "First of all, Imam, I wish to congratulate you on the spectacular triumph yesterday. Your funding and my planning, together as always. When our supporters find out you were responsible, your donations will flow like a river."

The imam smiled. The praise was his just due, and high praise it was from the man he'd nurtured and trained as a father would a worthy and beloved son, a man who'd earned the name the Strategist, a name now feared and respected. The man who sat across the table from him didn't dress as a devout Muslim. He wore Western clothes and exhibited Western tastes. He didn't pray five times a day, he drank alcohol whenever he chose to; indeed, he flaunted not being devout. Only the imam knew he was not just a master at planning, but a master of deception as well, appearing to those in his milieu as an adopted English gentleman, admired and accepted. Hercule knew lying to the infidels was not a sin, he had taught him that.

The imam raised his cappuccino to tap it against Hercule's cup. "In that you are right. It was a great success." The bombing of the TGV had succeeded beyond his wildest expectations. "Bahar executed your plan perfectly. The list of dead is growing. The French are beside themselves, and even more afraid of their Muslim population now after the bombing of their precious TGV."

The imam raised his cup again in a salute to a particularly nosy older woman who'd been staring at him, and smiled. She flushed with embarrassment and turned away quickly, the old crow.

Hercule witnessed this small drama. He understood both the woman and the imam, and realized he sided with her. Unlike the imam, he was dressed casually in a polo shirt, slouchy leather jacket, Armani slacks, and moccasins. He looked elegant and casual, a look he knew the English admired and instinctively trusted. He believed the imam a fool for shoving his differentness in the white English faces, particularly in this insignificant place where he wouldn't be forgotten.

As for the bombing of the TGV, yes, it had gone off exactly as he'd planned it, and he'd been very pleased. Five million euros from Mr. Bardon, to be exact, electronically forwarded to one of his untraceable Swiss bank accounts. Certainly the old man with the bad teeth and the white robe sitting across from him would never need to know that. It was time, he thought, looking at the imam's proud old face, so full of empathy one moment and sulking anger the next, hate always lurking behind those intense old eyes. He would let him know he would no longer tolerate his arrogance, his misguided belief that his position as imam would protect them both and that he would remain on Mohammad's all-time list of favorites.

Hercule leaned forward, said quietly, "You were wrong, Imam, about Nasim. Your assurances and blind faith in your plan for him brought us failure in New York. And for what? To protect a stream of money coming to the mosque and to you." There, it was said, and it sat squarely between them now. He watched the imam stiffen, imagined his thick white hair beneath its brilliantly white burnoose stiffening with him. Was he insulted? Afraid? Perhaps both. Hercule's voice had been like chipped ice.

Hercule took another bite of his chocolate croissant, being careful the chocolate didn't ooze out, and waited. The imam never believed it possible he could be wrong, and that's what made him dangerous. How would he deal with his most obvious blunder?

"Nasim brought us failure only at JFK," the imam said finally, his voice calm, as if they were discussing the light rain outside. He shrugged. "Nasim did no lasting damage. He knew nothing except his small part." He flipped his hand over, palm up. "He gave them nothing at all, so they continue to have no proof of anything."

The imam smiled then, crossed his arms over his white-robed chest. "If Nasim was my mistake, then you, Hercule, are responsible for our failure at Saint Patrick's

Cathedral. The end result of your plan in New York was a few broken windows on Fifth Avenue and the dead senator's hearse destroyed when the bomb exploded. Ah, but all the mourners inside the cathedral, and the cathedral itself, they were unharmed.

"Instead of blaming yourself or me, Hercule, for what has failed, let us enjoy what we've accomplished and move on to the next great task before us."

The old fossil had not only attacked him, he was giving him a sermon. Hercule realized the imam saw clearly he had managed to surprise him, and he was enjoying himself. Hercule said slowly, "You said yourself the boy finding the bomb, the priest hurling it away from the cathedral, was bad luck, that no one was to blame."

"There you have it. So was Nasim—simple bad luck. Who could have guessed that an FBI agent would be there in the security line? We both knew Nasim was not a trained fighter, and so it was possible for that woman with her sinful red hair to defeat him." Hercule saw his hand was now a fist on the table when he spoke of her, the veins riding high and thick beneath his flesh.

And that was why Hercule still admired the imam. He could turn on a dime, as the Americans said. It was well done. "Yes, and I saw the FBI press conference after they killed our men in Connecticut. The woman spoke directly to me, taunted me. On the flight I had time to plan. Everything is in place to rid us of her. She will become dust and bone for what she did."

"It is dangerous to play the hero in a holy way," the imam said, taking another sip of his cappuccino. "But why do you waste time killing this woman now when you have so many more pressing matters to settle? Sabeen Conklin has come to see me often since her son and his family disappeared. MI5 made accusations about me to her, and she had the gall to question me about whether I had anything to do with it. I had no choice but to lie to her, and assure her I was equally concerned and would look into it myself." He pictured Sabeen Conklin, a vain, rich, middle-aged woman, but still a true believer, despite all her Western extravagance. He'd been slowly turning her back to him again, comforting her daily in her time of grief.

Until the Conklins were freed. "What will happen now after her accursed daughter-in-law and grandchildren contact her? Marie Claire will poison her against us, and she will sell the business, just as her husband was doing."

Hercule took another sip of his Earl Grey tea, squeezed in more lemon. "Unfortunately, Imam, that is right, we will have to turn to other resources. The FBI has taken control of Marie Claire Conklin. They would not be so unwise to let her show herself, so there is little we can do. You should treat Sabeen Conklin as you always have and stop wishing for the impossible. Marie Claire now has all the control of all the money, not she.

"The bottom line here is that Bella will bring in more than Sabeen Conklin ever funneled illegally through her husband's business to you. What you need to do, Imam, is to eliminate all your records of her donations, and where that money went. Very soon now you can expect a visit from MI5, and this time they will have a warrant."

The imam said, "I do not understand why MI5 hasn't already come around to accuse me of all manner of mayhem in New York, but they have not."

Hercule was surprised, too, because it was not what he would have expected of them. And that worried him even more. "When they come, simply continue to tell them you know nothing of this. Destroy all files they shouldn't see. They cannot touch you without them."

The imam laughed. "They are fools. I have no fear of them."

The imam didn't understand his own enemies. Hercule wondered if his ignorance, his trust in the old barbaric ways, would be the end of him. He looked around the tearoom once again. "This is the last time we will meet. It will soon be too dangerous."

The imam nodded. "There is no need to take undue risks." He arched a thick white brow. "Is our next... effort to proceed? Has the Englishwoman given you what you need?"

"Yes. I am meeting her to confirm at lunch tomorrow." The imam hadn't called her his lover, though she was. She was also very good at it, for an earl's daughter.

Possibly because she had to pawn the gifts he gave her to keep her wastrel brother from living in a ditch because her family had finally cut him off. It was to her advantage to keep him pleased.

"It was well done of you, an inspired choice. Lady Elizabeth provides excellent cover, and entrée into the highest levels of London society."

"And to their politicians," Hercule said. "Her stiff-necked father is in the House of Lords and has the ear of a great many in government. He would as soon kick me in the teeth. I am a foreigner—an Algerian, no less—but I am well regarded in society and by his daughter, and so he's had to swallow his bile."

"Yes, you chose well. The cathedral will be thick with their kind."

Ah, that was true enough, but Hercule was interested in only one of them, which was why he'd chosen the time and place very carefully. He slowly rose, smiled down at the old man. He laid a ten-pound note on the table. "Watch the BBC tonight, Imam. I have been asked to give my expert opinion on the economic consequences if

the bomb had done great destruction to
Saint Patrick's. I imagine they will also ask
for my opinion about their precious Saint
Paul's."

"So the government looks to the wolf for
solutions?"

"They have no idea." Hercule left, aware
that every eye in the tearoom followed him
out.

47

Washington, D.C.
Sunday, early afternoon

Savich dropped Sean off at his grandmother's house for an afternoon at the park
and no doubt too many chocolate-chip
cookies. He'd have enjoyed staying and
throwing a football around with them, but
it couldn't be helped. He drove back
downtown and picked Griffin up at his
condo on Willard Street, an old established
area known in the summer for its thick
canopy of oak trees.

Griffin was waiting for him outside because
Anna had been up all night on a drug bust
and he didn't want to disturb her. He climbed
into the Porsche, turned to Savich. "Where
are we headed this beautiful day?"

"To see Walter Givens again, at the D.C.
Jail. I'd like to hear anything new you've
found on the Alcotts on the way over."

Griffin called up his files on his tablet.
"What I've got has to do with Liggert mostly.

He's a bully, Savich, no other way to put it—bar fights, had to be pulled in by Sheriff Watson and Deputy Lewis a couple of times. He spent a night in jail after assaulting Walter Givens. I wonder what that was about."

Savich said, "Liggert went after him at the bar after Walter called him out for hitting one of his kids. Teddy. Deputy Lewis arrested him."

"Good for Walter."

"I wonder, was that enough reason for Dalco to go after Walter, turn him into a murderer?"

Griffin's head snapped around. "You think Liggert could be Dalco?"

"I don't know."

"Doesn't sound like much of a reason. And to go after Sparky, have Walter butcher him? It would have to be something major."

"And that is the question. What did Sparky do to Dalco, or to his family?" Savich said, and stopped at a red signal. Traffic was as light as it got in Washington.

"There's something else interesting. Liggert's oldest girl, Tanny, ten years old—

she's got a juvie record. She was caught shoplifting condoms, of all things. Turns out she was selling them to all the teenage boys around town, cleaned up for a while until the pharmacy owner caught her with Trojans stuffed in her pockets.

"Sheriff Watson called her parents, and they paid for the condoms, took her home. The pharmacist insisted on a police report, but nothing more came of it, at least that I could find."

Savich had to laugh. "A ten-year-old isn't usually sent to Attica for stealing condoms. I do wonder, though, how Liggert punished her."

"We're not done," Griffin said. "That was when she was nine. She got slick enough to lift some watches from the general store. She tried to pawn some of them in Reineke when they were still brand new, and she was fingered. Get this, no charges again, they let her go."

Savich shot him a look. "I wonder if Deliah Alcott took care of the problem. Or maybe it was Mr. Alcott. Was she caught before he died six months ago?"

"Just after. Maybe she was acting out, as

the shrinks say, because of her grandfather's death?"

"We could talk to the people at the general store. Maybe Sheriff Watson knows something about it." He shook his head. When you came right down to it, what good would that do? Trying to find Dalco was leading them everywhere and nowhere. He was tired, his brain was tired.

"I spent some time looking into her grand-dad, Arthur Alcott. Nothing in the public record to suggest he was capable of anything hinky. After he died, there was a memorial service for him. The local paper gave it quite a write-up, said most people in town attended, so it seems he was respected well enough. Maybe that's how his granddaughter got off with hardly any juvenile record, out of respect for him."

Savich said, "But why Brakey?"

"He's not the sharpest knife in the drawer, Savich, doesn't take long to see that. Maybe Dalco used him because he was an easy target, he was handy? Malleable?"

"If so, it sure backfired," Savich said as he turned onto D Street. "After we speak to Walter, let's go over to Plackett to see

Sheriff Watson."

"Has he called you yet about Deputy Lewis's files?"

"Yes and no," Savich said as he turned into the jail parking lot. "All he said was there wasn't anything useful in the Alcott accident report."

"Do you believe him? He was, after all, Deputy Lewis's brother-in-law."

"Do you know, I'm inclined not to."

Savich had already gotten permission to meet with Walter again in the conference room. He was waiting alone when Savich and Griffin walked in.

"Agent Savich, do you know anything more about what happened to me?"

"We're getting close. Walter, this is Agent Hammersmith."

To Walter's pleased surprise, Griffin shook his hand, smiled at him.

Savage studied the young man's face. "Walter, we're working hard to find out who's responsible for all this. With your help, we're hoping to work it out so you can go free."

Color flooded Walter's face, hope shined from his eyes. "Thank you, Agent Savich. I'll help however I can, but I think I've told you everything I know." He paused, raised agonized eyes to Savich's face. "My folks, they look at me funny, you know? Even though they believed me when I told them I couldn't remember anything, they still gave me these looks when they didn't think I saw them. They're horrified by all this. They really don't know what to believe, and neither do I. But I really wasn't responsible, was I? Are you sure it wasn't some sort of fit?"

"No," Savich said, "no, it wasn't a fit. I'd like you to think with me, Walter. You called Liggert out last month, you told me, when you saw him hitting his little boy, Teddy?"

"Yes, sure. And then he laid into me when he got drunk at The Gulf. Deputy Lewis had to take him out of there."

"Did you have any other contact with Liggert at any time in, say, the last six months?"

"No." Walter frowned, tapped his fingertips on the conference table, made a decision. "Well, yes, once. He came to my shop about two months ago—a while after his dad got killed in that hit-and-run.

He asked me about cars I'd repaired since his father got killed, cars that had been in an accident. Sure, I told him, all those fender benders help keep my shop open, even in a small town like Plackett. I remembered right away that Sparky had brought in his blue Mustang. He was proud as punch he'd bought that car from an old dude in Richmond, said it sat in his garage for over twenty years. Anyway, Sparky said he'd hit a deer and needed work on a panel and his right front fender."

"You repaired it for him?"

Walter nodded. "I couldn't quite match the color, it had changed so much with age over the years, but I did the best I could." Walter paused. He looked a little guilty, Griffin thought, then he forged ahead. "I remember thinking it wasn't too long after Mr. Alcott was hit and I wondered about the damage. Hitting a deer, it didn't sound right, but Sparky was a real good friend, you know? Still, I knew I had to do something, so I called Sheriff Watson, but he was out of town, so I spoke with Deputy Lewis. He came over to see the car, told me he'd look into it. He didn't want me spreading any rumors in the meantime, though."

Griffin said, "Did Deputy Lewis get back to you, Walter?"

"Yes, the next day. He stopped at the shop, said he'd checked out Sparky and he couldn't have been the one who hit Mr. Alcott. He wasn't in town.

"Then, like I told you, Liggert came in asking about bodywork I'd done in the past months." Walter's eyes fell to his hands. "I wasn't about to say anything, knowing Liggert. I didn't want him blaming me, or accusing Sparky of anything, after what Deputy Lewis told me.

"Then he surprised me. He said he'd noticed a classic blue Mustang that had paint on the front bumper that didn't quite match, asked me if I'd done the job. I couldn't deny it, so I told him I did. Then I couldn't believe it. Liggert didn't try to hit me, no, he thanked me and left."

Griffin said, "Did you tell anyone else about this?"

"No, not even my dad or my girlfriend. I did tell Sparky, but he said Liggert didn't scare him anymore."

Finally, everything was falling into place.

Walter swallowed. "I wonder if my girlfriend, Debbie, will even want to talk to me anymore after this, even if you do let me out of jail."

Griffin was inclined to think Walter's girlfriend wouldn't want him within a mile of her. He said, "Hang tough, Walter, we'll get back to you soon."

48

Plackett, Virginia
Sunday afternoon

Sheriff Watson's big black Ford F-150 sat in the driveway of a small two-story white shingled house set back from the street. It was the last house at the end of an older established neighborhood, surrounded by oaks and maples, all gearing up for summer green, getting so thick they screened the houses from one another. A blue jay watched them, motionless on a low branch, as they walked toward the front door.

"Nice house," Griffin said. "I don't think I could get used to all this quiet, though."

Savich didn't think he could, either. He rang Watson's doorbell, heard movement inside the house. The sheriff himself came to the door, wearing a ratty old T-shirt and ancient jeans, his feet white and bare. He held a Diet Coke in his hand. He looked drawn, like he hadn't slept well lately.

"On Sunday? Really? What do you two

bozos want?" Hostility radiated from him. He stood squarely facing them at the open front door.

Savich said pleasantly, "We'd like to see Deputy Lewis's report on Mr. Arthur Alcott's hit-and-run."

The sheriff stiffened. "You asked me to look. I looked. As I already told you, it was a straightforward hit-and-run. No broken glass, no traces of paint, nothing there of any use at all."

"Yes, that's what you said. I assume you saw Deputy Lewis's note about Walter Givens doing some bodywork on Sparky Carroll's blue Mustang? Sparky said he'd hit a deer? Did you discuss this with Deputy Lewis?"

"Nothing to discuss. There's nothing like that in his report." He looked over his shoulder. "There's no need for you to come in. The house is a mess anyway."

Griffin said, "I don't mind mess, do you, Savich?"

"Not a bit. But I think I'd prefer if it the sheriff took us to his office and showed us Deputy Lewis's report on the Alcott accident. Is that all right with you, Sheriff

Watson?"

"No. It's Sunday, my day of rest. I've told you what there is and what there isn't. You can come by my office tomorrow if you want to look at it. So you're done here."

"I have to insist, Sheriff," Savich said, and he stepped forward, crowding him. "I strongly suggest you do not try to impede a federal murder investigation. It would not end well for you."

The sheriff eyed Savich, knew the man was serious. He threw the Diet Coke can as far as he could and hit an oak tree, sending the blue jay winging away. He was breathing hard and fast. "I'm not impeding anything. I have nothing to add, is all. You'll see tomorrow there was nothing in Kane's files. Now, would you mind going away?"

Savich said, "I thought you didn't like your brother-in-law, Sheriff. Everyone else seemed to like him, though, didn't even seem to care much when he drank too much. I'll bet you did, though. So why are you protecting him now?"

"Because he was my damned brother-in-law! Don't you understand? He was married to my only sister! There's no reason to stir this up now. It would break Glory's heart, she'd never speak to me again. And his daughters? They'd be devastated. Leave it alone."

"It's no longer up to you, Sheriff. You've done what you could to protect her and her daughters. It's time we go sit down and talk about this." Griffin put his hand gently on the sheriff's arm and pushed him back.

Sheriff Watson showed them to an ancient black leather sofa. After they were seated, he walked to the fireplace to stand, his arms crossed over his chest, and leaned against the mantel. Savich said, "Let me tell you what we pretty much already know, Sheriff. It was Sparky Carroll who hit Mr. Alcott, driving his Mustang. Sparky panicked and left the scene, but he told his father everything. His father, Milt Carroll, who died a couple of months ago, was one of Deputy Lewis's best friends. More than that, they drank together often, and both of them must have driven home drunk more than once. I imagine Milt Carroll asked his friend Kane for a onetime favor. Also, he knew he was dying at this point, and doubtless played the guilt card as well. He assured Deputy Lewis that it was an accident, that his son had panicked and left the scene, horrified at what he'd done but too afraid to come forward. So he'd tried to cover it all up, and that was wrong. Sparky knew it and was very sorry. Then Milt Carroll asked his friend to bury it.

The sheriff gave it up. Slowly, he nodded. "Yes, and Kane buried it deep."

Savich said, "It must have scared him badly when he got a call from Walter Givens, telling him that Sparky had taken in his blue Mustang for repair. Kane buried that, too, didn't he?"

"Yes. It was when I heard him speaking to Walter on the phone that I started putting it all together."

"But you said nothing, you didn't put a stop to it," Griffin said.

"I told you why. And by then it was too late. Kane had filed his report, there was no way to change that. It would be a felony and he'd have lost his job, even gone to prison. It was only an accident, and Kane's family would have paid an awful price. They didn't deserve that. People around here thought well enough of Old Man Alcott, but they don't like those witches very much, and they have good reason to steer clear of them. Who knows what Liggert would have done to Sparky, and to Kane, if he found out."

Griffin leaned forward. "You didn't know, did you, that Liggert went to Walter Givens's garage and figured it out for himself, did you? And that set in motion the murders of Sparky Carroll and your brother-in-law, Kane Lewis. It was all about revenge for the death of Arthur Alcott, and Deputy Lewis covering it up."

Sheriff Watson didn't say anything. He pushed off the fireplace mantel and sat down on the matching black leather chair, making it creak under his weight. "When they were both killed with those witch's knives, I figured it out," he said, and began rolling his big rough hands together. He raised his eyes to face them. "Look, it was obvious Brakey, an Alcott, killed Kane. Why he bungled it so badly I don't know. You had him cold, he was going to pay for it. I wasn't about to tell you why he did it—my sister, my nieces, deserved better than that.

"I have no idea how Liggert or some other Alcott got Walter Givens to stab Sparky. And then they set Charlie Marker in McCutty's woods to ambush the two of you." He jumped to his feet, unable to sit still, and began pacing the long, narrow living room. "I guess it had to be some sort of hypnotism, or some sort of witch's spell, is that right?"

Savich said nothing.

The sheriff continued his pacing. "Liggert gets my vote. He's the violent one, he's got a deep streak of it. I know firsthand he's got a short fuse, and he worshipped his daddy, took his death real hard. And he was mad when we couldn't find out who'd hit him and left him there lying in the road." He plowed his hand through his hair, making it stand on end. "Is there really a weird sort of hypnotism that could actually make those boys commit murder?"

"When we know for sure, you'll know, Sheriff." Savich eyed the man, saw the misery in his eyes, the guilt and grief that had been gnawing at him. He rose, stuck out his hand. "Thank you, Sheriff, for helping us. About your sister finding out what her husband did, I'm hoping we can keep it quiet, but I can't guarantee it, you know that." He paused. "I hope we can work together again someday."

When Griffin last looked back at Sheriff Watson, he didn't seem quite so huddled in on himself. If he wasn't mistaken, he saw a measure of relief on the man's face. He waved to them as they drove away.

Griffin said, "I think the sheriff might sleep better tonight. Are we going to confront the Alcotts?"

Savich turned back onto Main Street, shook his head. "Not yet, Griffin, not yet. We've got to have a plan first."

49

**FBI House
Brooklyn, New York
Sunday evening**

"So show me how you make pizza as good as your mom's."

Cal issued the challenge, Kelly punched him in the arm and told him he better be willing to help if he wanted any, and Sherlock shook her head at both of them and took herself and her cell off to the living room to speak to Dillon and Sean.

Cal unloaded the grocery bags while Kelly looked around the kitchen for what she needed: a big square cookie sheet that would make do as a pizza pan, and bowls for dough and sauce. She'd forgotten to buy yeast, but she found an ancient packet she prayed was alive enough to make the dough rise. The kitchen was vintage 1950s, tired, its cabinets saggy, but thankfully the oven worked and there was enough room for them to move around each other.

He'd set the table while she mixed up the pizza dough, listening to her hum the Harry Potter theme. Then they'd chatted while waiting for the dough to rise. "Hey, Giusti, you ever get yourself hitched?"

"Yeah, for about five minutes. He was— still is—a big professor at Berkeley, probably a department head by now, very likely still spouting that America is bad, you know the type. I can hear him telling the students that the bombing of Saint Pat's was all our fault, that we deserved it.

"The happiest moment of that marriage was when the divorce came through." She stopped tossing the pizza dough to wipe her nose, leaving a streak of flour. "I'll never forget the call I got from my cowboy uncle in Casper, Wyoming. When I told him, he yelled 'Yehaw!' I remember wanting to yell that, too. When I think of him now, I think he deserves a nice stay at a Siberian gulag." She moved to the stove to stir the sauce, the smell making Cal's mouth water. "We're going to make what my mom calls the carnivore's delight—sausage, hamburger, and a surprise: small hunks of ham artfully hidden beneath some artichokes and tomatoes. Your turn. You ever take the plunge? Any ex-wives in the closet?"

"Once, when I was a green lad, new at the FBI and working my butt off in the Philadelphia office. She left me for her country-club golf pro, who had a lot of time to work on her swing. I hear they've got a couple of kids and he's doing well on the pro circuit. Actually, Mandy's nice, I'm glad she's happy, so I don't wish any diseases on her." He clasped his hands over his belly, closed his eyes. "I've come to believe life is a crapshoot. People come into your life, some good, some bad." He straightened, breathed in the aroma of the pizza sauce. "The trick is to know when you've met a good one, and not let them go."

She eyed him, said slowly, "That's pretty much what I think, now that I'm at least a mature adult. The problem is there isn't much time for us to find a good one, is there?" She waved her hand. "We're usually up to our eyeballs in something. People depend on us—never, it seems, the other way around."

"There's always time, Kelly. I mean, here

we are, and we're making your mama's pizza together, rubbing along nicely, don't you think?" He watched her arrange the meat and artichokes on top of the sauce.

She stepped back. "What do you think?"

"You can never have too much sausage," Cal said. He sliced another half-dozen circles of sweet Italian sausage and artistically laid them on top of the big rectangular pizza.

"You're an artist," she said, grinning at the smiley face he'd made, and they both slid it into the oven. "Wait till that sauce bubbles up and melts the cheese, you'd shoot anyone who gets near your third of that pie."

While the pizza baked, Kelly checked with the agents guarding the house, parked half a block away. All quiet. Agent Larry Rafferty, the lead of the protection team, told her, "We're ready for anything." She phoned Gray Wharton, asked if they'd found Jamil's family in Algeria. He told her Jamil had been right, they were gone from their home and their town, simply disappeared.

Kelly saw Cal was also on his cell. Was he speaking to his girlfriend in Washington? Was she one of the good ones? Was he going to keep her? She rather hoped not.

Another fifteen minutes before the pizza was done, so Kelly called her mother. She saw that Cal had punched off his cell and he could hear her end of the conversation. "Yes, Mom, Agent McLain and I made the pizza together. He even sliced the artichokes just right to hide the ham. What does he look like? Hmm, well, he's not all that short, maybe comes to my nose, and the paunch doesn't show all that much. His hair? Only receding a bit," and then she ruined it by laughing. "He's very nice, Mom, and he's cute; in fact, I wouldn't kick him out of bed for eating crackers—well, never mind that. Looks like the crust turned out really well. I wish you could smell it, talk about a motive for murder." She paused, then Cal heard her say, "Yes, as a matter of fact, I'm still involved up to my eyebrows in the Saint Patrick's Cathedral case. It should push me right up to the director's chair, maybe next year, who knows?" She laughed again. "Love you, Mom. Gotta go. Pizza's ready."

"I don't ever eat crackers in bed."

"No, I never thought you did," she said,

and then Sherlock stepped into the kitchen, sniffing. "I've been smelling it for the past half-hour. Do you know I was ready to kick Sean to the curb—conversationally, at least —and he was in the middle of telling me about his checkers games with his grand- mother, in great detail. Oh, my, Kelly, that looks incredible. Mama's recipe, right?"

"Yes, the same recipe she taught me when I was twelve."

The house didn't provide anything as esoteric as wineglasses, so Cal filled three water glasses with Chianti.

Sherlock raised her glass to theirs. "Here's to our hard work today. I feel like we're close, it's only a matter of time. And here's to Kelly's mom's pizza."

They all sipped their wine.

Sherlock was on a roll. "Look at what we already know: there's no private plane registered to anyone named Hercule, so it's either not the Strategist's real name or the plane is registered to someone else. What good that does us, I'm not certain yet.

"I know we're going to get another hit soon, maybe on one of those terrorists holding Mrs. Conklin, or one of the handlers who brought them into Boston, or the man who placed the bomb at Saint Patrick's. None of them can be complete unknowns."

Cal said, "Maybe you're onto something, Sherlock. If Hercule isn't his real name, maybe it's a nickname."

Kelly nodded. "Something we can plug in to the mix in the morning. You know, guys, when I was growing up, there always came a time to shut it all down, and that was the time for **mangiare**, so let's eat."

When the three of them were eyeing the empty pan, all wanting one more slice, Cal looked down at his watch. "Okay, after we clean up the kitchen, it's time for some TV— the BBC, more precisely."

There might not be wineglasses, but there was a big flat-screen TV, about sixty inches, and Sherlock wondered who'd authorized the big bucks for a TV like that.

Kelly said, "Are you a BBC fan, Cal?"

"It's as good a way as any to catch up on breaking news on the TGV explosion, and I'd like to hear their take on what's happened. The world can look like a different place on the BBC than on CNN or FOX. Sometimes you can't understand everything they're saying because the Brits tend to swallow their words, when they're not trying to sound all upper-class and intellectual." He sat down, pulled off his boots, and raised his stocking feet to the coffee table. He placed his Glock on his thigh and waved to Sherlock and Kelly. "Plenty of room. Come on, Sherlock, it's too early to go to bed yet. Might as well see if the terrorists have come up with anything new before we black out the house."

Kelly eyed the ratty brown sofa. It didn't look comfortable, but Cal, who was sleeping here, would have to make do. "Okay, for a few minutes, then," Kelly said. Before she sat down next to Cal, she checked that the draperies were tightly closed, the doors dead-bolted, the chains drawn tight and hooked, then pulled the draperies aside for one final look to be sure the agents stationed outside were where they should be. As she settled in next to Cal, the program came on.

The camera zoomed in on a studio where two men sat across from each other, one of them a BBC newscaster Kelly recognized, Roland Atterley. He was hard to miss with his white hair, thick mustache, and magnetic voice. The other was a good-looking man in his mid-thirties, beautifully suited. He seemed to be an Arab, and wasn't that interesting?

Atterley looked directly into the camera. "I would like to welcome Dr. Samir Basara, professor at the London School of Economics, popular lecturer and writer on what he claims will be the coming economic destabilization of the Middle East. Thank you for being here with us this evening, Dr. Basara."

In a crisp upper-class British voice, Basara said, "It is my pleasure, Mr. Atterley."

"Dr. Basara, the terrorist attack on the TGV and the resulting large loss of life, as well as the failed attacks at JFK and Saint Patrick's Cathedral in New York City this past Wednesday, has come as a tremendous shock to the world. Do you believe these attacks were related, though no one group has yet claimed responsibility?"

"Yes, I do. I also believe the failed bombing attempt in New York has only fueled their hatred and resolve." Dr. Basara turned his head to look into the camera. He was darkly handsome, Kelly saw, and he looked very intense and intelligent. "Unfortunately, I fear these attacks may leave the United States and the Continent and move here to Britain. I believe it possible that Saint Paul's may be the terrorists' next target, or Westminster, or some other important symbol of our history. They seem to be targeting whatever they can destroy that we ourselves might see as defining who we are, and that includes our churches. For them, destroying our holy symbols means destroying our civilization itself." Roland Atterley hadn't expected Basara to leap to the guts of the situation so quickly, without his expert guidance. He wanted to ask him why an Algerian Muslim would care so much about Western cathedrals, but naturally, he didn't. He saw Dr. Basara was looking quite comfortable, sitting a bit forward in his chair, resting his hands lightly on its arms. It was time for him to take back control. "If you are right and these attacks continue, the economic consequences might be more far-reaching than the attacks of Nine-Eleven. Dr. Basara, are you concerned your predictions might cause undue alarm, even panic, in this country?"

Basara nodded, his face serious, his demeanor solemn as a hanging judge's. He had the look of an aesthete, Sherlock thought. "As well it should, Mr. Atterley. No sense tripping all over ourselves to avoid saying the obvious. In the short term, we must tighten our security measures, do our best to find the fanatics responsible. But that is only a partial solution. Much of this hatred is fueled by our own actions, our own omissions. I have argued for years that the key to fighting terrorism is to remove its economic causes, and that means providing more economic opportunities for our own disaffected Muslim minorities, and even more critical, providing far more focused and abundant economic aid to those governments we can work with in the regions of the world that are the well-springs of this hatred for us." He looked down at his fisted hand. "Until then, I have no hope we can put all this behind us, that we can, in fact, ever achieve a meaningful and lasting peace."

There was a moment of stark silence.

Roland Atterley cleared his throat but managed not to roll his eyes. "Some, shall I say, of the more enlightened members of our society—"

Cal's cell buzzed "Born Free," which got him an incredulous look from Kelly.

"McLain."

"Savich. Tell me exactly what you guys are up to, Cal, and don't even think of leaving anything out."

"We're hunkered down for the night now in the house the FBI picked out for us in Brooklyn, watching some big-time Arab economist on the BBC expound on why we're all responsible for the terrorist attacks." He paused. "Don't worry, Savich, we ain't gonna let anything happen to Sherlock tonight. All is good."

"I'm depending on you, Cal. Keep her safe."

"Has MAX made any progress on finding Hercule?"

"No luck yet with that name online or on the deep Web as either a moniker or a nickname. We'll keep trying."

When Cal punched off, he looked at Sherlock, who'd been waiting for him to hand over his cell. He grinned at her, shook his head. "Your husband only wanted to remind me my neck's on the line if anything happens to you. So let's take great care, all right?"

Kelly laughed. "Well, I guess a husband who's your boss at the FBI is better than a hysterical civilian cursing us for keeping you here, Sherlock. Sorry, Cal, the interview's over and we missed the big wrap-up. Lights out in five minutes, everyone. Cal, alas, you get the sofa. There are blankets in the hall closet and I even saw a couple of pillows. You can take the bathroom first, Sherlock and I are going to share."

Showering with a woman brushing her teeth not two feet away was a new experience, but Sherlock really needed that shower. As she washed her hair, she prayed a very simple prayer. **Keep me and my family safe.**

50

It was past midnight. Kelly and Sherlock spoke quietly as they sat in the dark in the small bedroom, both wearing jeans and sweatshirts, since they had no idea if anything would happen. But if it did, neither wanted to get caught in a firefight in her pajamas.

Candle Street was quiet, only the occasional sound of a car driving by. The air in the bedroom was still, with the scent of stale cigar smoke. Kelly waved her hand in front of her nose. "They should have sprayed after they let Butchy Remis stay here. He's a low-class hood who turned on his bosses. I remember those cigars."

"Part of the extravagant lifestyle we signed up for at the Bureau," Sherlock said, stretching. "You could be home in bed. So could I, for that matter. Do you ever regret signing up?"

"I always knew I wanted to be some kind of cop. I've got cop blood, as Cal put it, what with a dad and granddad in law enforcement. But I was kind of coasting, not really settled on a major. You're young and having fun and wondering what life is going to bring to you. Well, one night life brought me two local creeps who thought it would be cool to hassle a student coming out of the library. Maybe they were thinking rape, but they never admitted that. Mrs. Otis, one of the campus security guards at Northwestern, took them both on, arrested them herself. She told me I had to learn to protect myself unless I expected her to trail me around. I signed up for martial-arts training the next day. Turned out both of Mrs. Otis's sons were FBI agents. She said she wished she'd made the same choice when she was young enough to have the chance.

"We'd have coffee and I met her sons, talked to them about what they did. They were impressive. As I told Cal, one day I woke up and that was it. I'd be in the FBI. Did you join up before you met your husband, Sherlock?"

Sherlock remembered the now-blurred pain, finally at a blessed distance. She said only, "I joined up to catch my sister's killer, and oddly enough, Dillon and I did. I discovered it was my calling then and never looked back. Did Cal tell you why he became an agent?"

Your sister's killer? Kelly wanted to know what this was all about, but it was obvious Sherlock didn't want to give her any specifics. She said, "I know it all had to do with Nine-Eleven and how an eighteen-year-old boy responded to it."

"Yes, that was a big part of it. He also lost an uncle fighting Al Qaeda after the first Gulf War."

So he'd told her some, but not about his uncle. He'd been little more than a boy then. "Ah, Sherlock," she said, "Cal's not seeing anyone currently, is he?"

"Not unless it just happened. I expect Dillon or I would have heard it floating around the CAU." She grinned in the dark, even though she knew Kelly couldn't see it. "The CAU is like a big, clear Olympic pool—even if you try to sink something under the surface, most everyone still sees it."

"Same in New York. Everyone knows everything about you almost before you do." She heard Sherlock yawn. "Sounds like you're ready to hang it up. Think you can sleep?"

"Yes. I only hope I don't dream about terrorists buzzing around me like rabid wasps."

"I wonder if you have to get those nasty shots if you get bit by a rabid wasp."

It didn't seem like any time had passed at all. One moment Sherlock was deep in a well of sleep and the next moment she was jerked awake by bright floodlights pouring in through the window drapes and loud, piercing gunfire. Several bullets slammed through the window, sending glass shards everywhere; bullets hit the walls, and paint and drywall went flying. Kelly grabbed her and pulled her down between the twin beds. Cal came tearing through the bedroom door, Glock drawn, and quickly flattened himself beside the women. Kelly was on her comm unit. "What's happening? What's happening?"

"Stay down. We saw two men creeping around the side of the house. We surprised them and lit them up like the Fourth of July. Now we've got a firefight. Stay down!"

Kelly was reaching for her Glock when Cal's hand came down on top of hers. "Nope, we stay down, Larry's call." He tried to tuck both women beneath him, but it didn't work. There was no way either Kelly or Sherlock were going to lie quietly while the world exploded around them. More glass from the window came flying into the room, raining down on them. Cal reached up, grabbed a couple pillows, and dropped them over their heads. They waited, fighting floods of adrenaline, each wanting to be in the action, not lying between two beds.

"The neighbors must be lighting up nine-one-one," Kelly said, her voice muffled because Cal's arm was partially covering her mouth. "Never happened here before. Move your arm before I bite you!"

Suddenly, they heard a man yell, and the gunfire stopped. They waited, and Cal came up to his knees. Kelly's comm came on: "Larry here. Two men, both down, We got them trying to run out the front. Repeat, they're down, all is clear."

Sherlock looked at the digital clock beside the bed. No more than three minutes had passed.

Kelly said into her comm, "Anyone hurt?"

"No, all of us are good."

"Okay, we're coming out."

Kelly turned on the bedroom light. The room was a shambles, drywall all over the floor mixed with shards of glass from the broken windowpanes, the dresser chipped by flying debris and bullet fragments. "Probably sixty rounds sent in here," Cal said. "Let's go see what our guys have outside."

He turned to see Sherlock standing quietly in the bedroom doorway. She wasn't moving an inch. She turned and placed her finger over her mouth. "Stay here," she whispered. "I heard something. I'm going to check it out."

Cal's blood turned to ice. He whispered, "No, Sherlock, don't move, I'll do it," but she'd already disappeared into the hallway. He heard Kelly rack her Glock. "Let's go," she said low, and she and Cal followed Sherlock into the dark hallway. They didn't hear anything, only Sherlock's footsteps.

Then there was an ear-shattering blast that shook the house. "Sherlock!" Cal raced down the hall, Kelly on his heels. They ran into the kitchen in time to see a small figure leaping out the window. The kitchen was fast filling with smoke and flames, licking toward the cabinets. Sherlock was scrabbling up on the counter to go out of the kitchen window. The heat was suddenly incredible. Cal yelled, "Sherlock, we're going out the front. Stay on the kitchen side! Be careful!"

Sherlock dropped to the ground outside the kitchen window and into a yew bush, pushed herself behind it. She yelled, "Larry, it's Sherlock!" She felt the heat of a bullet pass by her cheek, and flattened herself to the ground, tasting dirt. She yelled again, "Larry, there's another one, he fire-bombed the kitchen! I'm pinned down!"

Sherlock elbow-walked around the yew bush, looked carefully past it. She saw a slight figure moving fast to hide behind a skinny oak tree on the far side of the yard, maybe thirty feet away.

She yelled, "Drop your gun and get your hands up. We won't shoot you. Do it! We have you surrounded, there's no way out. Your two friends are already shot! Don't make us shoot you, too!"

The figure's arm jerked up and fired toward the sound of Sherlock's voice. The bullet struck the house a few feet above her head. She heard the pounding of FBI feet coming closer, came up on her elbows, fired. There was a yell, and the gun went flying as Larry and four more FBI agents came racing around the side of the house, crouched over, fanning out into the backyard.

"He's down!"

She saw them approach the moaning figure, guns trained center mass, going to their knees to restrain the terrorist, who was crying and cradling his wrist.

The terrorist stopped crying and looked back toward the madly burning house, casting the inferno's glow on all of them. Orange flames gushed out toward them, and black smoke ate the oxygen out of the air, making it hard to breathe. The backyard looked like high noon.

"Hey, it's not a man, it's a girl!"

Sherlock ran to the fallen girl, who was clutching her hand. She was dressed in black, even her face blackened. She was trying not to cry now, doubtless it was humiliating, but still, tears seeped from beneath her lashes and trailed through the black paint on her face, cutting knife-like tracks. Sherlock knelt down beside her, saw another agent had applied a pressure bandage to the wrist. "You're going to be all right, lie still. An ambulance is on the way."

The girl raised dark pain-filled eyes to her face. "It was a trap."

"Yes, it was a trap," Sherlock said. She felt Cal's hand on her shoulder, heard Kelly speaking to the agents. Cal said, "You were sent in to set the bomb, right? Because you're so small? How'd you get into the kitchen?"

The girl turned her face away and didn't say anything.

Cal continued: "She didn't break the kitchen window, we'd have heard her. That window is too small for either of the men to get in, so she was elected. She cut a hole in the kitchen window and wriggled in, set the bomb, right?"

The girl looked up at him, said nothing.

"Her job was to set off the bomb between the kitchen and the living room, say, and then run as fast as she could and climb back out. If the bomb or the fire didn't kill us, we'd be forced out of the house and her two friends outside would be ready to mow us down."

"Didn't work out, did it?" Kelly said, standing over the girl with her legs spread, her arms crossed over her chest.

They heard fire engines and sirens in the distance. Soon, she knew, neighbors would venture out to see what had happened on their quiet street.

Sherlock sat back on her heels, looked at the raging fire. It didn't matter, a house was just a house, after all.

Everyone had done their job. One terrorist was dead, but two of them were alive, and one of them was this slight girl lying at their feet, cradling her shattered wrist.

51

Belamy Club
London
Monday, late morning

Dr. Samir "Hercule" Basara entered the sacred portal of the Belamy Club of Piccadilly Circus, nodded to the doorman dressed in the two-hundred-year-old club colors, deep blue with gold trim. Hercule always thought it looked ridiculous, a pretension that was a waste of time and money, but the upper class liked to cling to their old traditional ways. How else could they continue to regard themselves as different and above the rest? One of the only changes he knew of in the last decades was that women were now allowed to dine here for breakfast and lunch, but after two in the afternoon, no female was allowed through the door. Compared to White's and Boodle's, the Belamy Club was an upstart, but he liked the eighteenth-century building with all its gilded moldings, its impossibly high ceilings, its mahogany antique-filled rooms.

There were a dozen ladies and gentlemen in the receiving room, talking in low voices, all looking at home there. The majordomo, Claude, who looked nearly as old as the building, glided forward to give him a stingy smile. Dr. Basara was foreign, after all. He followed it with a small bow, another formal ritual that meant nothing. Then ancient Claude, his back straight as a Horse Guard's, his circle of gray hair hugging his skull, gave him yet another small bow, surprising Hercule.

"Sir, if you do not mind my saying so, I wish to compliment you on your superb commentary last evening with Mr. Atterley. Your discourse was spot-on. These are indeed difficult times."

"Thank you, Claude."

"Lady Elizabeth is in the Cloverly Alcove. If you would follow me, sir." Claude led him through the dining room, refinement and pride dressed in a shiny black suit, a red carnation in his lapel. The room's long, narrow windows rarely let in sunlight, since there was so little to begin with in England. The white-covered tables were elegant, glistened with silver, and were mostly filled, as usual, well-bred conversations low. They stopped at one of the dozen discreetly named alcoves, reserved for those diners who wished for privacy. Hercule wondered if Elizabeth was surprised to be in an alcove this gray Monday morning. He usually pandered to her wish to flaunt him to her friends, to her family's friends as well when the opportunity presented itself. An earl's daughter, after all, could allow even an Arab to court her and remain on the best guest lists.

He leaned down, kissed her cheek, and slid into the rich mahogany leather booth. "You are looking particularly fetching today, Elizabeth." She was wearing a stylish black Dior suit, her streaked blond hair in a severe chignon, which, oddly, suited her fine-boned face. She looked straight out of the boardroom, aloof, in control, indeed the epitome of cool English control. He wanted to laugh. She'd lost all her vaunted control in bed with him last night. And she would present yet a different face at the wedding she would attend with her father at St. Paul's this afternoon.

"Thank you." She scanned his Armani, admired its fit on his aesthete's body, wondered how much he'd paid for it, and thought of her brother, who'd texted her thirty minutes ago, begging for more money. After last night, she expected at least a diamond bracelet, which should keep her brother off the streets and in cocaine for a month.

To shock her, he said, "I also thought you looked particularly fetching last night with your hair tangled around your face, all your lovely white skin on display, your naked legs wrapped tightly around my flanks when you screamed my name." **And who wouldn't?** He didn't mind at all visiting Cartier's after lunch to buy her, say, a lovely emerald bracelet, perhaps even a diamond bracelet—they'd made love three times, after all. Perhaps she would wear it once or twice before discreetly pawning it and giving the proceeds to her brother. All in all, he'd made an excellent bargain, as he'd told the imam. She had no idea he knew about everything she did. Paying to have her followed, her conversations recorded, had kept him a step ahead. Hercule regarded the monthly outgo as protecting his investment. And today he would reap the rewards.

Elizabeth sucked in her breath at his crassness, saw his mocking smile. He did this to her every once in a while, spoke crudely to shock and embarrass her—she'd admit it, in public she would look around to see if anyone had heard what he'd said. But his being crass didn't change who or what she was—an earl's daughter—and so she said only, with a faint smile, "Thank you," and sipped at her sparkling Bavarian water.

Hercule nodded to Henry, their black-coated waiter, a stiff-necked old geezer who was as much a fixture at the Belamy Club as Claude. Henry placed a carafe of freshly squeezed orange juice in front of him, and beside it a bottle of François Montand Sparkling Brut, the Belamy sommelier Pierre Montreux's choice, Hercule knew, of the best champagne for a mimosa.

Henry himself mixed the mimosas, bowed, left their table to fulfill their order of croissants and espresso.

Elizabeth clicked her glass to his. "To an

excellent performance last night. You controlled the interview, left Atterley looking rather like a landed trout expelling gas."

It always amazed him how many euphemisms Lady Elizabeth and her kind could dish up. Never a basic Anglo-Saxon word that fit the bill for Elizabeth, far too common, except for her sex words when she hurtled into orgasm. He knew she was the product of weekends skiing in the Alps, vacations in Saint-Tropez, and a renowned Swiss finishing school. What she'd finished, she'd never said. But in this instance, about that ass Atterley, she was right. He smiled. "He is a smart man who has come to believe his own press. I saw your father this morning on my way here."

"You saw my father?" No doubt she was anxious to hear what her old man had said to him. It was subtle, but he heard the whiff of alarm in her well-modulated voice.

"I was visiting my banker this morning when Lord Thomas happened to come down from his office to congratulate me on the Atterley interview. He informed me I'd been succinct and astute, that my sympathetic attitude toward Muslims had stirred your mother. Then, he gave me this look, and I knew he thought both your mother and I were fools."

"That's quite amazing," Elizabeth said, and took another sip of her mimosa. "I can't recall my mother ever being stirred by anything—well, maybe a bit for Tommy."

Her younger brother, the earl's heir, was last year, on his thirtieth birthday, cut off without a sou. It was proper of the old earl, Hercule thought. Tommy was a useless git with a cocaine habit his doting sister, Elizabeth, could barely keep up with. If he were Lord Thomas, he'd have long ago drowned the little wanker in the Thames.

"Have you ever thought about arranging for a job for your brother, at one of the big banks in Italy, say?"

"Yes, right, certainly. Tommy would insist on traveling first class all the way, he would expect his address to be a suite in the Hassler, and to eat his meals at Alfredo's. And within the month he'd be back broke, and on his heels a dozen people extraordinarily upset with him, some of them, doubtless, with guns."

Her occasional show of wit pleased him.

He felt a tug of liking for her, a touch of pain for what was about to happen to her. He looked at his watch. "I have an hour, Elizabeth. I have meetings and a graduate seminar this afternoon."

"There's Henry bringing our croissants and espresso."

While Henry meticulously laid out their light midmorning breakfast, Hercule took another sip of his mimosa. It really was excellent. "You and your father are attending one of your friend's weddings this afternoon, aren't you?"

She smiled at that. "Yes, I'm one of her bridesmaids, six in all. The bride's family—you know the Colstraps, don't you? Lord Palister? He runs the Rothschild banks in London?"

"I've met him." Not really, but Hercule had seen him across the roulette wheel, surrounded by his drinking buddies, at one of London's private casinos. Florid and pompous, that's what Hercule had thought, looking at him.

"Ellie and I went to school together in Geneva. The man she's marrying, Ryan Gray-Murcheson, I don't think he deserves her. He gambles, you see, too much, like her father." She leaned toward him, lowered her voice to a whisper. "I've heard it said Ryan's father is a criminal, but his family is old and respected and he's rich as Croesus, so everyone talks about him behind their hands. Do you know anything about him?"

"I? How curious you'd ask me, a professor of economics. I've heard his name, is all."

Obviously she didn't care one way or the other. She spoke the moment he finished. "Ah, but trust Ellie's father, Lord Palister, to provide her with a specular wedding; it will be the event of the season." She shrugged. "We'll see how the marriage turns out. Ellie wants kids." She took a bite of her croissant. "Delicious, as usual. Will you accompany me to Lady Brecknell's card party tomorrow evening, Samir?"

"I would be delighted. Didn't you tell me Lord Harlow and Major Hornsby would be there?" His voice was light, only mildly interested. She couldn't know that Lord Harlow, actually an associate of the groom's father, was a kingpin in London's criminal underworld, far removed from the daily grind, to be sure, but he had a number of very rich, very determined enemies. It was hard to get to him. He wasn't stupid and was very well protected. But in two hours, when Elizabeth stood at the altar beside her friend and her parents were doubtlessly seated near Lord Harlow, it would all end.

It was a pity. He would mourn Elizabeth, sincerely. But the opportunity to once again combine a wonderfully paid assassination with a terrorist attack was too splendid to ignore.

52

Federal Plaza
New York City
Monday morning

The young man's fingerprints identified him as Mifsud Shadid, age twenty, younger than any of the terrorists at the Lake Pleasant cabin. He sat in an uncomfortable chair on one side of the table in a small white-walled windowless interview room. He was sitting very still, trying to look arrogant and unconcerned, but too young and too scared to pull it off. He kept rubbing at the sling on his arm. He didn't look to be in any pain. His lips were moving in repetitive Arabic phrases, probably repeating a prayer over and over.

Sherlock, Kelly, and Cal, along with a half-dozen other agents, stood in the next room, watching Shadid closely through the one-way glass. All of them knew he was their last hope to get any useful information. They'd spoken to the teenage girl who'd blown up the house in Brooklyn the night before, Kenza the name on her passport. They'd found her lying in her hospital bed under guard, her right arm elevated and her wrist wired, her arm swathed in bandages to her elbow. Without the cap she'd worn the previous night, her short dark hair stood in spikes around her face. She looked like a young East Ender. How strange someone so young had already been twisted into a terrorist. They'd hoped they could use her pain, or the drugs they'd given her. They'd tried shaming her, threatening her, lying about Mifsud, the young man they were looking at through the glass, but she'd stared out at them through large dark eyes, eyes that had seen too much in her seventeen years, and looked contemptuous. It was only when they told her Shadid had given up the Strategist that she'd said anything at all. "You're a lying bitch," she'd said to Kelly in a clipped British accent, and then she'd closed her eyes and turned away on the pillow.

"Zachery said to give Shadid a little more time to think about his sins," Kelly said to the other agents. "He'll be coming in soon, to observe." She waved a hand toward the muted flat-screen TV on the wall behind them that was tuned to an Al Jazeera newscast. "Isn't it amazing that Al Jazeera already knows our three terrorists are British citizens? According to that pretty young Arabic woman in her bright red Western suit, the American FBI brutally attacked three Arabs, killed one and injured the other two. Yet another racially motivated violent act is perpetrated by American law enforcement. Someone had to have leaked it last night. It was a zoo." She shook it off. "Okay, so how do we approach Shadid?"

Cal said, "Shadid's very young. He's never been arrested, certainly not for a terrorist act and not in the United States. We don't need him to talk about last night, we've got him cold on that." He grinned, said in a proper Oxford English accent, "Why don't I play the part of a British lawyer, sent from the British consulate to defend one of Her Majesty's put-upon citizens from the big, bad American FBI? I can at least try to keep him talking longer than he would otherwise."

She stared. "That's impressive, Agent McLain. Are you part British, like Agent Drummond here in our New York office?"

"Nope, pure mongrel American. I did some acting way back and my dad's an incredible mimic. I inherited his talent... well, some of it. You should hear him sing Elton John."

Kelly said thoughtfully, "Nothing he says would be admissible, but who cares? If you think you can pull it off, it can't make him trust us any less than he already does. I doubt he saw you at the house, Cal, not well, anyway. Let's try it. Sherlock, you up for being überbitch?"

"I'm up for anything now that I've had a shower and cleaned up. First, though, we need to get Cal dressed up a little, find him a fresh dress shirt and tie, and a briefcase, if he's going to be coming straight from the British consulate."

Ten minutes later, Kelly looked Cal up and down in his borrowed shirt, and Zachery's leather briefcase. "The shirt's a little tight, Cal, but it'll do. Keep on the suit coat to cover it. Here, let me straighten the tie." When she stepped back, she nodded.

"You'll do."

The three of them walked into the interview room together. Kelly sat down, crossed her arms over her chest, and introduced herself and Sherlock. Then she eyed Cal and dropped all warmth. "Mr. Shadid, this is your counsel, sent by the British consulate, Mr. Jonathan Clark-Wittier."

Good name, Cal thought. **Where did she come up with that?** "Mr. Shadid," he said, and nodded to the young man.

Kelly looked at the young man staring back at her, trying too hard to look uninterested. She turned to Sherlock. "Mr. Shadid and his imported fellow assassins tried to murder you last night, so why don't you speak to him first?"

"A moment, Special Agent Giusti," Cal said. "I would like to speak to this British citizen privately before you begin questioning him."

Kelly, not looking away from Shadid, said, "You can forget that, Counselor. The man tried to kill federal officers, here on American soil. You're here only as a courtesy."

Sherlock was aware Mifsud Shadid was staring at her, hate beaming out of dark eyes, for her specifically and for her as simply one of the enemy. She sat back in her chair, crossed her arms over her chest, and pulled a full-bodied sneer out of her bag. "Mr. Shadid, how old are you? Fourteen? Fifteen? Is that your sister in the hospital with a shattered wrist?"

"I am twenty-one years old, not fifteen!"

"No, you're not, you turned twenty a month ago."

"She is not my sister!"

Interesting, Kelly thought. His eyes fell to his hands, clasped in front of him on the scarred table, to the shackles encircling his wrists.

Sherlock shook her head, marveled aloud, "And you consider yourself a fighter? A professional? I don't think so. I've got to say, though, that young girl you brought with you to set the bomb in the house? To burn all of us alive? She was the only one of you who showed some grit and courage. Is that how a fighter behaves, cowering in the bushes after sending a little girl to her almost certain death?"

She lunged forward, banged her fist on the table, making him jump. His eyes flew to her face. "You expected to kill me? You couldn't kill this stuffed-shirt lawyer the British consulate sent to defend your wretched hide, not even if I handed you my gun."

Young Mifsud Shadid yelled, "I will kill you myself, you whore! You are an enemy of Islam, a blight to be erased and forgotten, cursed in life and in death."

What a lovely British accent, Kelly thought. It sounded to her trained ear straight out of Manchester.

"Yeah, yeah, quite your party line," Sherlock said, and looked like she wanted to yawn. Then her face hardened. "Mr. Shadid, why did you bring along your sister to do the dirty work for you?"

"I told you, Kenza is not my sister!"

"That is enough, Agent," Cal said. "You are bludgeoning this young man with accusations, insulting him—"

"We are not in a court of law, Mr. Clark-Wittier," she snapped out at him, without giving him the courtesy of a look back.

Mifsud said, "Kenza is well trained, and her heart is with us. Not even you saw her slip into that house. You should not have heard her slip out. She would have succeeded if you hadn't been waiting for us with those floodlights and so many guns."

Sherlock was shaking her head. "And you can't imagine why we were armed and ready for you? Did you believe us fools? Or didn't you question it at all? Did you believe the Strategist and the imam are very sophisticated, that they know what they were doing? I mean, they did manage to blow up that high-speed train in France, did they not? But then look what the Strategist did—he sent only the three of you to attack me, a well-guarded FBI agent; I don't think that shows much talent at all.

"The old man who died last night, Mohammad Hosni, was he your handler, your boss, your grandfather?" She paused for an instant, but got no reaction from Shadid.

"You spoke of Kenza being so quiet. Well, she wasn't, because I heard her. I'll tell you, Mifsud, I still can't believe you had to rely on a little girl to plant the bomb so that you and grandpa could shoot us dead if we managed to come running out of

the burning house." She gave him a contemptuous look. "Impressed by the imam
and the Strategist? I don't think so, look at
the three pitiful tools he sent."

53

If you had a gun you'd shoot me dead, wouldn't you, Shadid? But he kept himself silent. Sherlock gave a slight nod to Kelly.

Kelly picked it up. "Perhaps, Agent Sherlock, we've reduced the Strategist to using amateurs. I mean, after the three of you flew into New York yesterday, what did you do? Eat pizza and sleep in your rental car? Wouldn't the Strategist and Imam Al-Hädi ibn Mīrzā spring for a cheap hotel room?"

"See here, Agent Sherlock," Cal said, jumping to his feet, "enough of these puerile insults. You are not asking legitimate questions of this young man—"

Kelly snorted. "Maybe you'd better define **puerile** for him, Mr. Clark-Wittier, he doesn't look very bright. His actions sure prove me right, don't they? What will the Strategist say about you, Mr. Shadid, after seeing the three of you screw everything up?"

Sherlock said, "I don't know if you care, Mifsud, but Kenza will never use her hand again, too many bones shattered from my bullet in her wrist."

"The Strategist will kill you!" Mifsud yelled, and leapt to his feet, shaking his fist at them, his shackles clanging. "There was no way for you to know we would attack, we were very careful when we followed you." Tears came into his eyes, choking him. "It was a trap, you were waiting for us to come, you wanted us to come. We couldn't know there would be so many of you—"

Sherlock gave him another push. "Of course we knew you were following us. The Strategist failed you, didn't he? As did your precious imam. They sent you into a trap. Which one of those brilliant men selected Nasim Conklin to blow up the security line at JFK? Which one of them sent the three of you?"

Shadid flew out of control. "You shut your mouth, you accursed woman! Your laws are absurd, sending two useless women to insult me. As for the imam, yes, I know of him. So does every true Muslim in London. He is a great man, a holy man. The British will never be able to arrest him, he is too well protected by their own laws."

Kelly buffed her fingernails on her sleeve as she said in a bored voice, "Sit down, Mr. Shadid, calm yourself. You should know that Imam Al-Hädi ibn Mīrzā isn't going to be giving any more orders. We've heard the good news that the imam has been formally arrested in London. MI5 is providing his lodging now, no cell phones or visitors allowed. Your great holy man has had his teeth pulled. Next comes his head," and she made a chopping motion.

"There is no hangman's noose in England!"

"Oh, yes, true enough, Mr. Shadid," Kelly said. "But from where you come from, all you need is a knife, do you not, to cut off a hand, an ear, a head?"

Mifsud Shadid spat toward Kelly again, but Mr. Clark-Wittier's leather case was in the way. "No, you are lying to me. What you are saying is impossible."

Kelly shook her head at him. "Your counsel here can tell you it's true. As we speak, MI5 is searching the imam's office and home on Camden Street." She rose and slammed her fist on the table in front of Mifsud. "Your imam was as convinced as you that he was untouchable. I doubt he took all the precautions. They will find names, times, and places. They will find your names, too, won't they? Your precious imam will never again see the light of day, and neither will you."

Kelly leaned close. "In spite of her tender years, Kenza will be imprisoned for life, or, more likely, she'll get a shiv in her back within her first few months in prison. All civilized countries hate terrorists, and that includes their criminals in prison. Kenza won't be able to protect herself, not with a shattered wrist. She'll end up in a potter's field, a cheap gravestone to mark where her bones lie."

Mifsud was breathing fast and hard, his mouth working.

One more push, Sherlock thought, and said, "MI5 passed us a report that the Strategist has a young Muslim girl as a mistress. Is it Kenza?"

"No! That is a lie!" Mifsud leapt to his feet, chains banging against the table. Then he sank back down in his chair, lowered his face in his hands. "No," he whispered, "that is another of your lies. Kenza hasn't even met him. He is too important for the likes of her." He raised his face to Sherlock. "She would not sleep with anyone, Kenza and I—" He shook his head, shut his mouth.

Cal rose. "Mr. Shadid, I am here to advise you. If you wish to survive, if you wish that young girl, Kenza, to survive, you need to tell the FBI agents everything you know or suspect or have heard about the people whosentyouhere.Otherwise"—heshrugged— "I shall not be able to help you."

Sherlock sat back in her chair, tapped her pen on the tabletop. "Did the Strategist force her to sleep with him, Mr. Shadid? And did she tell you? Did it make you angry?"

Kelly said, "If you tell us what you know, I will personally ensure that Kenza is kept protected. I will not allow her to be killed."

Shadid was shaking his head, crying. He swiped a shackled hand over his eyes. "She said nothing to me because you are lying, it's all lies. Listen to me, the Strategist would never shame Kenza, she is honest and loyal, a fighter. He would never shame any Muslim girl, no, he consorts with an Englishwoman, a Christian noblewoman, he flaunts her in everyone's face."

Jackpot.

In the next room, the agents turned to their laptops and started pulling up London society pages and online social event calendars, looking for an English noblewoman on the arm of a rich Algerian who would turn out to be a terrorist.

54

Criminal Apprehension Unit
Hoover Building
Washington, D.C.
Monday morning

Savich reached out his hand to his phone, paused, drew it back. He wanted to speak to Sherlock, let her reassure him once again that she was all right, although he knew she'd downplay what had happened last night in Brooklyn. He'd let her get away with it, given that Cal was his pipeline. No way would he let Cal shade the truth when it came to Sherlock. He frowned. Could he trust even Cal to be totally up front? Or, like Sherlock, was he leaving out details, not wanting to worry him? Savich hated being apart from her, hated not knowing she was safe.

Was he being a hypocrite? He wasn't about to tell her what he was going to do to try to expose Dalco. He believed his logic was sound. There was nothing she could do to help him, so there was no point in worrying her.

Interviews and physical evidence couldn't tie Dalco more directly to the crime scenes, he hadn't even been there. And that meant there was nothing else left to Savich but to destroy Dalco. Then he would have to convince the federal prosecutor not to prosecute Walter Givens and Brakey Alcott because they hadn't been responsible for the cold-blooded murders they'd committed. A formidable challenge, but he was the only one who could save them. He had a plan, he was now ready to move, to face it head-on. He needed Griffin. He walked to where he was working on his computer, Ollie standing at his elbow.

Griffin looked up, met Savich's eyes, and nodded. He said something to Ollie, turned off his computer, and followed Savich into his office. Savich waved him to a seat, said without pause, "I have a plan, Griffin, but before we drive to Plackett to the Alcott compound, I want to make sure you understand what you're getting into. It could be dangerous.

"As you know, some of the Alcotts—or all

of them—have been lying, covering up who Dalco is, probably because they're afraid of him. There's anger and conflict in that family, there has to be, because of Dalco using Brakey to commit murder, and they've been covering that up, too. It's a front they've kept together, and it's gone on long enough. I'm going to blow it all up if I can. It's the only way forward, the only way to find out who Dalco is.

"I told you Dalco has already tried to kill me himself. If you come with me to the Alcotts' today, you might provoke him into targeting you, too. It's a risk you need to consider."

"I've already been in Dalco's sights, in McCutty's woods with you. We're in this together, Savich." He gave Savich a wide grin. "Hey, danger is my business."

Savich grinned back, but his voice remained serious. "Yes, but there's physical danger we risk every day, but then there's this. What did Anna have to say about the ambush on Saturday?"

"I haven't talked to her about it. I didn't want to frighten her, didn't want to have to try to explain the inexplicable. She'd believe me, but it would scare her and I don't want to do that. Maybe after we're married and she knows me better—we'll see. Right now, though, I don't want her involved."

Savich didn't understood that, but it was Griffin's decision. Anna was a DEA agent who could kick the crap out of a drug or gun dealer and whistle as she slapped on the cuffs. Savich thought she could deal with anything. She and Griffin had met when she was undercover in Maestro, Virginia, a couple months before, and had fallen for each other, a surprise to both of them.

"I ask because Sherlock woke me up when Dalco attacked me. She heard me moaning, thrashing around. I don't know what would have happened if she wasn't there."

"Anna's also a heavy sleeper. She'd be dead to the world even if I was lying there panting like a dog." His face split into a big grin. "But she claims her dreams are light and sweet since she met me—" Griffin broke off, embarrassed. "Well, it wouldn't be easy, telling her about a case like this."

"For what it's worth, my advice is to tell

her, Griffin. She might have some good ideas, like Sherlock. Use her."

Savich could tell Griffin wasn't going to say a word to her. Nothing more he could say. "You in?"

"Oh, yes, I'm in. You know what, though? I'll bet none of those agents out there have the slightest idea what we're talking about in here." He paused, looked straight at Savich. "Or maybe they could guess."

Savich shook his head, rose. "Let's do it."

55

Wyverly Place
London
Monday afternoon

Hercule stood in the center of his penthouse flat on Wyverly Place, sipping his favorite Golden Slope chardonnay, staring at the television as the BBC reported the incident the night before in Brooklyn, New York, a video of the raging fire in the background. The same FBI agent who'd saved JFK had shot one of the attackers, and that was headline news across the world. The BBC's report was, naturally, very different from Al Jazeera's. It was from an informant at the news desk at Al Jazeera that the imam had gotten the call telling him of what had happened in Brooklyn, minutes before the news broke in the media. It was the imam who'd called Hercule on his burner. The old man was upset, but Hercule had also heard the trace of a gloat in his voice when he told him that his own handpicked killers had failed.

What had happened? His contact in New York, Salila, was a man who owed Hercule his very life. Salila had provided the incendiary device and the automatic weapons. He'd sent over some of his best people. Mohammad Hosni, not as fast with a knife as he'd once been, perhaps, but still a seasoned warrior, competent with an automatic, and a leader. Mifsud Shadid, his protégé, too young to entrust with the planning, but eager, and ruthless as a viper. And little Kenza, Hercule's own prize, only seventeen. He'd seen her fight when she was fourteen, seen how she simply didn't give up even when she fell to her knees, her face turning blue because she couldn't breathe. Yet she'd kicked out with her foot and knocked her opponent to the ground, then leapt on him. He'd instructed the imam to give her over to his best trainer. With his guidance, she'd been fashioned into a guided missile, **his** guided missile.

Another big reason he'd selected the three was because none of them were on the watch lists, and they'd sailed through customs and security as he'd known they would, as British Muslims, an older man shepherding his two young friends. He didn't know who had been killed, who was being held in FBI custody at Federal Plaza. The woman, his Kenza, was said to be severely wounded and under guard at a New York hospital. No casualties were reported among the FBI: not their target, Sherlock, none of them. How should he have planned differently to change the outcome? In hindsight, he could answer that easily enough. The FBI had set a trap, and that meant he'd acted too quickly. He should have given the FBI time to grow confident and lax.

It was now in the past, over with. He'd lost that battle, but he would win the war. He always did.

At least he knew none of the three would talk with the FBI. Kenza would spit on anyone who asked her questions. He trusted them all implicitly, another reason he'd chosen them. But would Kenza live? He had no way to know, and none of his informants knew a thing. The FBI had put an immediate lid on her whereabouts. Not that it mattered how soon he found out.

Still, it was disconcerting to him to feel helpless. Hercule hated it. Who was dead, Mifsud Shadid or Mohammad Hosni?

He put it aside when his mobile buzzed. He'd been waiting for the call, from his man Bahar, who was to check in with him well before he entered St. Paul's. Hercule heard the London traffic in the background as he listened. It was understood they would always speak in English because Arabic coming out of a man's mouth tended to make Westerners pay attention. You could be holding a bomb in your hand, but if you spoke the Queen's English, Londoners would give you a smile and a nod. But today Bahar wouldn't be anything like himself. Hercule had planned out his appearance to the last detail, known exactly how he should dress for his role. It would be risky because they'd have increased security at St. Paul's since the bombing at St. Patrick's. But if he could get Bahar through the door as a plausible wedding guest, it wouldn't make any difference. No one knew who Bahar was, and even if they did, they wouldn't recognize him dressed as he was today.

Bahar sounded calm and confident. "I am standing across the street from the main entrance to Saint Paul's. Guests are starting to flow in, happy, chattering. I'll wait until there are more of them and then I'll enfold myself in amongst them, as you planned, Strategist. Security is thicker than usual. I can't tell if they're private, for the wedding, or added agents. But you were right again, they are not checking any of the guests' bags. But they are checking wedding invitations."

Hercule was pleased to hear Bahar call him the Strategist. The imam thought many years before that the name gave him a certain mystique. It had certainly added to his growing status. He thought it was one of the imam's better ideas. "And your disguise? Did you take your time, dress exactly as I asked? No one has seen Lady Durbish in years, but the dress I picked would suit her perfectly. And your makeup? You copied the photo I sent you?"

Bahar laughed. "Shall I send you a selfie, as the Americans call it? Trust me, Strategist, I am the very image of that wealthy, reclusive old lady herself, believe me. A faded beauty, as the English say. I am dressed exactly as instructed, with your large diamonds on my fingers. The powder on my face even lightens my skin to match the whey-faced English. Lady Evelyn Durbish's invitation is in my purse, ready to show security."

Hercule said, "If by chance someone who knows Lady Durbish comes up to you, they won't question you are. No one has seen her in the flesh for years. The old lady surely won't be there. She's very likely puttering about the family home, Durbish Abbey, an ancient pile of stones in Derbyshire."

"I believe I see Lady Elizabeth Palmer at the entrance with a group of young women. This is surely strange. They are all dressed alike."

"They are the bridesmaids, that is why," Hercule said. "I wonder why they aren't with the bride?"

Of course Bahar wouldn't know. Hercule wondered how Bahar knew of Elizabeth. Well, he had eyes, he'd probably seen photos of him with her in the **London Times** or the tabloids.

A pause, then, "It is possible she will be killed, Strategist."

"Death is but an instant away for all of us, Bahar. The C-4 is primed?"

"And carefully encased in our enriched plastic coating, flattened enough to slip into your selected spots for maximum destruction. It will not be noticed."

"Good. In forty-five minutes I will expect to hear news of our message to the West. Do not fail us, Bahar." Hercule slipped his mobile back into his pocket. All would go well this time, Hercule felt it to his bones. He thought of Elizabeth again. Could she possibly survive the blast where she would be standing?

Hercule had always been a fatalist, had never believed in the absurd rewards that supposedly awaited a devout Muslim upon his death. He wondered if Elizabeth was one of those who believed in an after-life, wondered if that would comfort her in the instant before her heart stopped beating. It was doubtful, though, that she would even have that. The explosion itself was an instant in time. Then he thought of Lord Harlow, seated on the groom's side, close to the front since the families were close, and of the eight million British pounds, half of which already resided safely in one of his Swiss accounts.

He poured himself another glass of chardonnay and walked to the wide window overlooking the Thames. He looked east, toward St. Paul's. He wouldn't see it explode from here, but he would hear the explosion, see the billowing clouds of black smoke rising about the buildings. And when St. Paul's exploded, or a goodly part of it came crashing down, he would hear the beautiful sound echoing around the city, and the sirens that would follow.

He raised his glass to Elizabeth and to Lord Harlow.

56

St. Paul's Cathedral
London, England
Monday afternoon

Bahar walked slowly along St. Paul's Church Yard, the wide busy street that formed the long south boundary of the rough triangle of land that enclosed St. Paul's Cathedral. The façade of the church wasn't set back from the incessant traffic or the encroaching buildings; it stood there right in the center of things, flanked on all sides by bicycles, big red tourist buses, and countless people scurrying about. Many small outdoor tables were filled with coffee and tea drinkers at the nearby London cafés.

He knew the real-time cameras of the state-of-the-art video surveillance system and people watching it from the on-site control room would pick him up when he entered the cathedral. They didn't know who they were looking for, in any case, so it wouldn't make any difference. No one would give the frail old lady a second glance.

They prided themselves on their Smart-cards, given out to more than two hundred of their staff. Like most security ideas, the Smartcards sounded like a good idea, the most effective way to have a solid handle on the cathedral's security, but it was so far from the truth, it was laughable. He hadn't even risked stealing one. The truth was St. Paul's allowed visitors to enter its sacred portals without even passing through an X-ray machine, and to an expert like himself, it was low-hanging fruit. The cathedral staff didn't have the space to run such a system, not when more than two million tourists flocked here every year into an area no larger than a quarter of a square mile. The great Christopher Wren couldn't have imagined what was going to happen to his grand creation.

Bahar felt blessed. He would achieve immortality today. He would forever be known as the man who destroyed one of the sacred shrines of the English, and of Londoners in particular. It would enrage them, they would yammer and yell, cer-tainly, but even more, it would scare them stupid. Ultimately, what could they do but change their ways, and he couldn't imagine that. The English mouthed every platitude of inclusion, praised diversity and tolerance, like the bloody Americans, but in the end they were certain of their own superiority, and that superiority made them objective and ethical. Hypocrites, the lot of them.

He smiled, thinking of what was to come. He wanted to whistle, but couldn't, not as he presented himself today. Their lovely wedding would begin soon in St. Paul's. The Strategist had expected as many as five hundred bejeweled and well-dressed nobs would be inside to witness the Christian union of these two old prestigious families. Bahar joined a crowd of sixty-odd wedding guests as they queued at the church entrance, past dark-suited men he thought now were added security. The Brits had moved fast since the attempted bombing of St. Patrick's in New York less than a week before. He imagined they'd added other security measures he didn't know about, and couldn't see. He would if he were in their shoes. What had they done?

Sadly for them, it wouldn't matter. He held up his invitation to the security guard, who merely nodded at him as he passed into the church.

He walked slowly, regally, as he'd practiced it, into the vast nave and down the aisle toward the magnificent altar. The couple would be joined there with great pomp beneath the magnificent dome, guests on three sides. The lovely dome would come down; the Strategist had calculated where to place the explosive to ensure it. Bahar split from the herd of guests to pay a visit to the chapels of St. Michael and St. George, blending in easily with a dozen other guests. He moved to the Wellington Monument and stood for a respectful thirty seconds before walking as stately as the queen toward the south transept. He stepped into the stairwell that led to the Whispering Gallery, the library, and the two hundred and seventy steps to the Dome. There were half a dozen people coming down the steps, another three waiting to go up, speaking, admiring. He'd been inside several times before, knew where the cameras were positioned. He dropped his ancient Chanel bag, shook his head at the two helpful gentlemen, and leaned down slowly and carefully to retrieve his belongings. He slid a packet of C-4 and its detonator beneath the stairs with his foot as he rose. He made two other stops before he moved back into the nave and turned toward the south transept, stopping beside the Nelson Monument. He leaned against it, looking at the rows of chairs being filled by wedding guests. He chanced to catch the eye of a pretty young woman with a young child sleeping in her arms. She looked all milk-and-white English, stylish in her pale blue dress. He saw a slash of dark hair on the babe. She was smiling at him, beckoning him to sit in the empty chair beside her.

He found himself smiling back. He checked his watch, not wanting to draw attention to himself as the remaining seats filled, and he would join her. He would say little, perhaps compliment her child and wish her a fond farewell when he left her in a few minutes. When he was clear of St. Paul's he would set off the detonators and enjoy the ear-splitting explosions and the chaos and the screams that would follow. A pity the Strategist wouldn't see the falling stone, the crumbling edifice, but he would see the flames and black smoke shooting above the skyline.

The young woman leaned close. "Aren't all the roses beautiful? I think the family must have emptied out all the florists' shops in London. You're a friend of the bride's family?"

The bride's family—the Colstraps, an ancient barony bestowed upon the family hundreds of years ago, later an earldom, still rich despite all the heavy taxes because they'd turned to banking and succeeded. He didn't know them personally. It was enough for him to know who and what they were.

He nodded and smiled at the young mother. She was pretty, a pity that in another twelve minutes she and the babe would be dead. From the blasts, or crushed beneath the tons of falling cement, flying glass from the smashed dome. All the cascading white roses wouldn't be very pretty then.

Mary Ann Eiserly was tired. Ceci hadn't

slept more than three hours the night before, napped for only an hour this morning. She was thankful that now was the time she'd picked to pass out. It meant Mary Ann wouldn't have to worry about her fussing in the middle of Ellie and Ryan's exchange of vows. Yes, Ceci was down for the count. She lightly kissed her child's head. Poor John was in worse shape, what with the terrorist red alert at MI5. She hadn't seen him in twelve hours. She smiled again at the proud old woman beside her, who smiled back but remained silent. Her clothes were antiques, at least fifteen years out of date, but they were designer and expensive. Mary Ann saw the old lady had an odd profile, a pronounced hawk nose, not uncommon, she supposed, among the old aristocracy, and she was wearing a heavy layer of powder. There was something off with this old matriarch, but in truth, Mary Ann was too tired to care. She would ask Ellie who the old lady was when she returned from her honeymoon on Crete—if she remembered, that is. She felt brain-dead at the moment from lack of sleep. She would witness Ellie take her vows to a man Mary Ann wasn't especially fond of, a gambler, she'd heard, then she'd haul Ceci home and pray John would drag himself in before midnight. She looked at her watch, wished they would get on with it. She wanted nothing more than to curl up next to her daughter and sleep the sleep of the dead.

John Eiserly, MI5, sat in the control room at St. Paul's with a half-dozen other agents and security staff, all eyes carefully studying the faces that passed into the cathedral. They'd been on high alert since the attempted bombing of St. Patrick's. In addition, St. Paul's deserved even more security this afternoon, given the number of very important guests here for the wedding. He'd heard the prime minister himself had spoken to John's boss, ensuring they were going all out. Other than strip-searching all the guests, there was nothing more they could do.

The guests were all well dressed and in a festive mood, laughing, talking among themselves, not a suspicious character in the lot. Strip-searching them would most certainly put a crimp in the jolly mood. He grinned at the thought, then yawned. "Another two weeks" was his and Mary Ann's mantra—the doctor said Ceci should sleep through the night in another two weeks. He hoped Mary Ann was finally getting some sleep. He chanced to look over at the monitor for the camera in the south transept and his heart stopped. There was Mary Ann sitting there, today of all days, Ceci hugged to her chest, sound asleep. She was wearing her beautiful blue dress she'd worn three weeks before when they'd celebrated their third wedding anniversary. For a moment he couldn't get his brain around it. She hadn't told him she'd be here today, had she? He remembered now. Of course she was here. She and Ellie Colstrap were friends, and her friend was marrying a man she'd told him she didn't like. He'd forgotten about it in all the chaotic urgency of the last four days, forgotten they had even been invited. Ellie and Mary Ann had been close in the days before he and Mary Ann had married; Ellie was one of her very rich friends, who, John knew, thought Mary Ann had married beneath herself. A copper?

John focused on his wife sitting in the south transept, away from her friends, who sat among a huge knot of people in the center, closer to the altar, in case Ceci woke up yelling at the top of her lungs, so she could make a fast exit. He never took his eyes off his wife. He felt sweat trickle down his cheek and brushed it off. She was here, Ceci was here. No, nothing would happen to St. Paul's. Nothing would happen to his family. Still, John couldn't bring himself to look at the other cameras; his eyes stayed locked on Mary Ann's face. He zoomed the camera in, saw a half-dozen people file in around her. A regal old woman stood near her, dressed to the nines, dripping with diamonds, her clothes out of date but screaming expensive. She was studying the Nelson Monument, moving closer, touching it. Then she turned, as if to leave, and Mary Ann smiled up at her and pointed to the empty chair beside her.

Wait. Wait. "Back up camera nine, now! The old lady, right there! Back up the camera!

"Stop, right there. That's her—she's

stopped beside Nelson's Monument. Okay, now go forward, half-speed." Three agents crowded around him. They saw the old lady had a flat package, maybe six by eight inches in her gloved hand. If you weren't looking closely, you wouldn't have seen it. They watched her press close to the Nelson Monument, pause a fraction of a second.

"Zoom in!" John pointed. She shoved the package into a small crevice. They couldn't see her after that, as people filed past her, blocked the view.

"Freeze it on her, full face!" John yelled. "Facial recognition! Quickly!"

The newly enhanced NCG homed in on the old woman's heavily powdered face. Seconds passed as the program juxtaposed hundreds of faces next to the old lady's. Then it stopped, narrowed her cheeks, removed the tight gray curls and her neck scarf. And there was the man Nasib Bahar, a fugitive wanted by the Algerians.

Bingo.

The agent at his elbow said, "John, there's Mary Ann and Ceci!"

"I know," he whispered. "I know."

John watched Bahar sit down beside a smiling Mary Ann. Was he going to blow all of them up, himself included? No, he was an operative. He had no intention of immolating himself in the process. He was here to set the explosives and escape. How many other packets had he positioned throughout the cathedral? John set them all to retrace Bahar's steps on the video recording. They counted as many as eight packets.

What if he was wrong? What if Bahar was going to stay, blow himself up sitting next to Mary Ann and Ceci? He'd never been so scared in his life. He had to make a decision. Then the old woman was getting up. She stood quietly, looking toward the altar, upward at the dome, and she smiled. She moved into the nave and slowly walked past several latecomers, back toward the entrance.

John and a half-dozen agents ran out of the control room, John yelling into his comm.

57

26 Federal Plaza
New York City
Monday

Agent Gray Wharton brought up a photo on his computer screen from the **International Herald Tribune**. "This is Sheikh Tamin bin Rashid al Amoudi. He's oil wealthy and is treated like royalty whenever he visits London, which is often, because he spends lavishly. From what I can find so far, he is what he appears: an aging playboy who's so rich he has not one but three jets." Gray flipped to another photo. "On his arm is Lady Pamela Sanderson, daughter of Baron Pembroke. They're on their way to a tony bash following a movie premiere, the latest James Bond."

Sherlock studied the sheikh's self-indulgent face, his dark eyes that saw nothing beyond his own desires. "No, not him, too old, too visible, too—pleased with all his wealth and what it brings him. What does he do with three jets?"

"Doesn't say, but he's got a good-sized family. I suppose you have to keep your relatives traveling happy." Gray brought up the next picture, pointed to the man. "Here's a British Muslim, Dr. Abbas Ghanbari, a professor at the University of Saint Andrews. The lady with him is the daughter of Viscount Pleasance. Look at him—stoop-shouldered, glasses, thinning hair, old. He looks too settled and content, doesn't really fit the bill."

Gray brought up another photo. "I'm thinking the next one's our best bet—Dr. Samir Basara, thirty-seven, English citizen, well-known international economics expert, a professor at the London School of Economics. He's Algerian, his father owns a large vineyard there. Samir was raised with wealth, left Algeria when he was eighteen to study at the Sorbonne in Paris, then went to the U.S. to Berkeley for his doctorate in economics, with emphasis on the Middle East."

Cal said, "That's bizarre. Kelly, Sherlock, and I watched him talk on the BBC last night. Bottom line, he said we share the blame for the attacks on JFK, Saint Pat's, and the TGV. Not so surprising a position, given where he was educated."

Kelly studied Basara's face. "Look at his eyes, guys, they're almost opaque, they give no clue what he's thinking, feeling. And that suit he's wearing, it probably costs more than I make in a month. He presents himself as a rich Western intellectual. Where does his money come from? His family? Middle Eastern contributors? If it's true he flies in a private jet, we're talking a lot of money. And that gorgeous blonde with him—"

"Lady Elizabeth Margaret Palmer, daughter of the Eleventh Earl of Camden," Gray said, looking up from his typing. "She's a popular society fixture and her daddy is a respected banker in London. Lady Elizabeth graduated from Oxford after returning from finishing school in Switzerland, active on the social scene. The tabloids say her younger brother is a cocaine addict."

"Lady Elizabeth Palmer," Kelly repeated her name. "Would you look at that smile she's beaming up at Basara? Yes, Gray, focus on him. I'll bet my Pink Panther knee socks Dr. Samir Basara is our Strategist."

Sherlock nodded. "Now our problem is to prove it. Gray, did you find the records of his commercial flights?"

Actually, Basara hasn't flown commercial in years, at least by his given name, which means he's flying private. Here we go, Dr. Samir Basara owns a two-year-old Gulf-stream, keeps it in southern England near Folkestone."

"I don't suppose you've, ah, ventured into the Civil Aviation Authority, you know, the FAA equivalent in Britain, to see if the good Dr. Basara files flight plans?"

"I'm going to the ICAO, the International Civil Aviation Organization. Any flights over international space are filed through them."

Kelly said, "Does Zachery want to know what you're doing?"

"Probably. Like you, I always tell him everything," Gray said, never looking up. "Okay, take a look. The jet has filed a number of flight plans—to Paris, Munich, Rome—most could be short vacations or business trips to other universities. No trips to anywhere questionable, like Syria or Iran." They all looked over his shoulder as he scrolled down. "It appears he travels once a year back to Algeria, at Ramadan." He looked at them. "Well, look at this. He flew to Boston last week, stayed two days, then back to London."

Kelly said, "So he was here not only when the Conklin family was flown in, he was close by when Saint Patrick's was supposed to be bombed. He's looking better and better."

Cal said, "You can bet he doesn't file flight plans for all his trips. That would mean his pilot is complicit. Can we find out his name, Gray?"

"Wait a second. I'm looking at his family in Algeria." He scanned, looked up. "Well, would you look at this. His grandfather's name was Hercule."

Sherlock pumped her fist in the air. "Yes!"

Cal said, "Kelly, you need to call your counterpart at MI5. Another thing—Shadid and Kenza are going to need protection. I have a feeling once Basara finds out we've outed him, he might try to have them killed."

Kelly picked up her cell and dialed. "John? Have I got something for you. What? **What**

did you say? Wait, I'm going to put you on speaker."

John Eiserly sounded higher than a kite, but with an odd slick of fear in his voice. "We nearly lost Saint Paul's. It was close, too close, but we got him in time. He's a wanted terrorist named Nasib Bahar. My wife and my daughter—they were in Saint Paul's attending a society wedding along with hundreds of the upper crust. If I hadn't been assigned there as extra security, if I hadn't happened to zoom in on my wife as he placed a packet of C-4 at the Nelson Monument, we would never have stopped him. He was dressed as a posh old lady, an incredible disguise."

"John, take Mary Ann out tonight, someplace really special, and celebrate. Congratulations."

"It can't be all that special, I mean, we'll have our baby with us, and believe me, Ceci can yell a house down. Well, maybe a Wimpy or Spudulike."

Laughter, then Kelly said, "And I've got some great news for you, too. We think we've identified the Strategist as Dr. Samir Basara, a British citizen. He's been in your newspapers lately as Lady Elizabeth Margaret Palmer's escort."

"You've got to be kidding me. I know the guy, seen him on the BBC, Roland Atterley's show. Lady Elizabeth Palmer? She was here at the wedding. She's still inside waiting to be interviewed. Let me go get her. Thanks. I owe you."

It never hurt, Kelly knew, to have a favor tucked in her pocket. She beamed at all of them. "Saint Paul's survived and now we're in business."

58

**Wyverly Place
London
Monday**

Hercule didn't look away from the skyline toward St. Paul's Cathedral. Where was the billowing smoke? But he knew he could no longer deny that Bahar must have failed. St. Paul's should have blown up at least twenty minutes ago. He had his television on and he turned when he heard the BBC break to a reporter standing near St. Paul's with news of an attempted bombing, and then they switched to a video obviously shot on a bystander's mobile, but clear enough. MI5 agents were hustling an old woman out of St. Paul's. She was struggling, trying to jerk away, when her wig fell off. He stared at Bahar. He watched wedding guests pour out of St. Paul's behind them, most trying to maintain their English dignity, but some yelling and pointing at Bahar, then the sharp voice of a man in a dark blue suit yelling at them to get the man into the waiting van. What had happened? They must have seen Bahar placing one of the C-4 packets at a site Hercule had chosen. Hard to believe because Bahar was a consummate professional. It was another failure. He found it hard to breathe, then forced himself to calm. He knew Bahar would never give him up. They'd worked together for nearly six years, brothers-in-arms in the jihad, or at least Bahar thought so. Hercule cared less about losing Bahar than the millions of pounds that would not be wired to his account in Zurich for the assassination of Lord Harlow.

His mobile buzzed. Was it Elizabeth? He grabbed it off the table and looked down at the name that filled the screen—it was the imam. Why was the old fool calling him on his private number and not on the burner? It was a long-standing agreement between them. Was the old man senile at last? He wouldn't answer it, it would be the height of stupidity to answer it. Then he realized the damage was done, the imam had already placed the call. He didn't bother to hide his irritation. "Why do you call me on my private line?"

The imam sounded old and afraid, his voice shaking. "MI5 agents have invaded my home. They have a warrant and are going through everything. They want to question me. **Me**, Hercule! They talked about Mifsud—your boy—they accused me of sending him to kill that FBI agent, and of sending Bahar to bomb Saint Paul's. They were gloating. Do you hear me, Hercule? They were gloating!

"They are confiscating everything! I told them I felt ill. I am in the bathroom, agents outside the door. They didn't realize I had my mobile to use because I destroyed my burner as they broke in on me and they didn't think to look for another. Hercule, what am I to do?"

Basara's heart was beating as wildly as the imam's, but he kept his voice calm and cold. "Get hold of yourself, old man. We have always seen to it they will find no evidence against you. You keep no papers, no computer files that can incriminate you or anyone we know." The old man stayed silent, and Hercule took it like a punch to the gut. "Do you have any incriminating evidence at the house?"

"No, no, I've always taken great care. I did not lie. All is safely hidden elsewhere."

Then why was he so scared? Ah, so that was it, the old idiot. "So you have damaging information at the mosque, then?"

Silence, then a strangled, "Yes, but they won't be able to get a warrant to search a Muslim place of worship. It is the safest place I could think of."

After the attempted bombing of their precious St. Paul's, they would have no difficulty at all even getting a warrant to search beneath the imam's precious prayer rug. "What records, exactly? The ledgers, our payments, receipts? Are there names mentioned? My name?"

"Yes! Some names, but not your own, not the name Samir Basara."

You old fool, you have left them the keys to everything, in your own mosque.

"Hercule, they are ordering me to come out. I must hurry or they will break the door down."

Hercule heard banging on the imam's bathroom door. He yelled, "Smash the mobile! Now! Keep your mouth shut. All will be well." Now, that was a lie of the first order.

Hercule heard the door burst open, heard men's voices. The mobile went dead.

The imam had had the time to destroy the mobile before the agents got hold of it. Not that it mattered. MI5 would find all the proof they needed at the mosque, probably right in the imam's massive ma-hogany desk. He should have known. As discreet and smooth as the imam could be in public, he never guarded his speech at all on his home ground, at his beloved mosque. He thought he was invulnerable there. Now he would pay for his stupidity in prison. **Good riddance, you old blighter.**

Hercule let the thought go. He prided himself on his intelligence, and he was smart enough to know his life as Dr. Samir Basara was near its end as well. How long would it be before the imam's paper trail led them directly back to him? A week? A month? Days?

He saw quicksand seething and surging everywhere ahead of him, knew if he didn't act, it would suck him under. He had no intention of being tried as a traitor; he couldn't imagine the humiliation, couldn't imagine spending the rest of his life rotting in prison. There would be no more television appearances for him, no more charismatic lectures at European universities, his views lauded and applauded. He could accept that—indeed, he'd planned for it. But what he couldn't accept was that all of his meticulous planning, all the options he had weighed so carefully, had left his life falling apart. It enraged him. He wouldn't, he couldn't, let that happen. The Strategist would have his last final victory, despite everything, and he would see to it himself. Then he would disappear where no one could find him.

He had his escape plan well in hand; he'd been preparing it for fifteen years. He would face what was coming head-on, not bury his head like the imam, who refused to see beyond his own veined nose. Most of his fortune was safely tucked away in Switzerland. He had several passports ready, plenty of cash, and a lovely small villa in Sorrento, Italy, owned by a Swiss corporation, waiting for him. He would at least continue to be the Strategist, even in hiding, as feared as before.

He turned off the television and dialed

Lady Elizabeth. She would be expecting him to call to show his concern, at any rate, now that the news about St. Paul's was everywhere. Perhaps she had seen why Bahar had failed. When she picked up over voice mail, he could hear her breathing, her fear making it fast, choppy. He schooled his voice. "Elizabeth? I saw on television they tried to blow up Saint Paul's. Please tell me you are all right."

"Yes, yes, well, now I am. Samir, it's been a nightmare, unbelievable—" And she told him the ceremony was about to begin when a man ran up the aisle, waving a badge and ordering them out. "He said a man had been placing explosives inside the cathedral and we were all to leave as quickly as possible. Now they've brought me back inside one of the cathedral anterooms. An MI5 agent said he needed to speak with me, that it was urgent, and I was to wait. Before I could ask him why me in particular, he rushed off. Why would MI5 want to speak to me, Samir? I mean, what could I possibly know about any of this?"

He'd stopped listening, punched off his phone. Why indeed? They knew he was seeing Lady Elizabeth Palmer. But how was that possible? Mifsud—he must have known about Lady Elizabeth. Had the imam boasted of her in his hearing? But why had Mifsud betrayed him in that way? It didn't matter any longer. He had, it was done. He knew then he had no time left to prepare his leaving. It was time to disappear.

Dr. Samir Basara didn't pack a bag, only took time enough to empty his safe before he closed the door to his penthouse on Wyverly Place and walked to the private garage off Bond Street to fetch the nondescript beige Fiat he kept there under the name of a man who didn't exist.

59

**Alcott Compound
Plackett, Virginia
Late Monday morning**

Savich's Porsche purred to a stop directly in front of the Alcott main house. He sat a moment, marveling at the peaceful setting, the three houses set in the middle of nature, vibrant and green, the scents of grass and flowers everywhere. Hard to believe a monster lived in that house.

There was no sign of the Alcotts, but Savich knew they were inside, waiting for them. He'd called earlier, made it an order that they would meet while the children were still in school. He wondered what they saying to one another, what they were thinking. One thing for sure, they had no idea what he had planned for them.

He turned to Griffin. "You ready?"

"Oh, yes. Let's do it."

They'd stepped onto the porch when the ornate front door opened and Deliah Alcott appeared. She was wearing her usual, a long flowing skirt and sandals on her long, narrow feet, a white blouse tucked into the skirt. She wore no makeup, and today she looked pale. Was she afraid? He hoped so.

She looked from him to Griffin, stepped back. "Everyone made the effort to be here, as you ordered. I don't know what you expect to accomplish by disrupting our lives again."

They stepped into a living room filled with Alcotts. Brakey stood in his favorite post near the fireplace, his head cocked to one side, looking at them with—was it hope?

Jonah was standing by the window, no doubt watching them as they drove up. He followed their every move, wary about what kind of ax would fall, but certain it would fall.

Liggert looked at them with frank loathing, his stance aggressive, and Savich couldn't see a spark of fear in his eyes, only the threat of violence, barely leashed.

Savich turned at the sound of the clack-clack of knitting needles, loud in the stark silence. Ms. Louisa appeared to be humming softly as she knitted what looked like the same scarf Savich had seen when he'd first met her, paying them no attention. She clamped her false teeth together when she dropped a stitch and frowned over at them. "Our honored lawmen are here to protect us? Or are you two here to string someone up by his heels? Believe me, they've all been jabbering on about it. As for Morgana, I think she's afraid to know. I don't suppose you've found out who made our poor Brakey stick that Athame into Deputy Lewis's chest?"

Brakey took in those words and looked like he was ready to faint.

Savich looked at each of them again. It was a face-off, all of them standing stiff and silent, looking back at him and Griffin. He said, "We've asked you here today because we know why Stefan Dalco wanted Sparky Carroll murdered and in such a spectacular way. Some of you already know Sparky's murder was revenge because Sparky struck and killed Arthur Alcott six months ago."

Brakey blinked, started forward. "Sparky killed Dad? But that's crazy, Agent Savich! Sparky knew my dad all his life, spent lots of time here. Dad played football with him. He really liked my dad."

Savich nodded. "He didn't mean to, Brakey, it was an accident. He struck your father and then he didn't know what to do. Like you, Brakey, Sparky panicked. He drove away, too afraid to say anything. Except to his father."

He studied each of their faces. "Then Sparky made a bad decision. He went to see his lifelong friend Walter Givens to fix the dented bumper on his Mustang and Walter put it together and called Deputy Lewis." He paused, nodded to Griffin.

Griffin said, "Everyone in Plackett knew Deputy Lewis liked to drink. One of his best friends was Milt Carroll, Sparky's dad. After Walter told Deputy Lewis about the damage to Sparky's prized Mustang, we believe Milt Carroll begged Deputy Lewis to protect his boy. It was an accident, after all— Mr. Alcott had wandered into the road. Sparky couldn't avoid hitting him. It wouldn't be justice to ruin his son's life because of an accident. So Deputy Lewis became complicit in Mr. Alcott's death."

Liggert said, "It wasn't like that! The little

sod was drunk and he was driving and he hit my dad!"

Savich said, "We'll never know now one way or the other since Sparky's dead. In any case, Deputy Lewis buried the information Walter Givens gave him about the dent in Sparky's Mustang. He called Walter back, told him to forget about it, that it wasn't Sparky.

"Then you, Liggert, noticed that the paint job on Sparky Carroll's Mustang didn't quite match and you wondered. You went to Walter's shop and asked him about it. An innocent question, and so Walter told you about the dent in Sparky's Mustang and how you had had such a hard time trying to match it. Walter didn't realize he was painting a target on himself, as well as on Sparky.

"You were furious, weren't you, Liggert? You wanted to see your father's death avenged."

Liggert yelled, "The little bastard murdered my father! He left him to die! Yes, I could have killed him for that. He deserved what he got."

"But you didn't want to get caught for it,

did you, Liggert? You're fast with your fists, everyone in Plackett sees your wife's bruises, everyone knows you smack her around. I imagine you wanted to beat Sparky to death in the middle of Plackett, watch him die, and walk away, like he did to your dad."

Liggert was breathing hard, his hands clenching and unclenching at his sides. "You can imagine what you want. You have no proof I was involved in any way. Why don't both of you leave, before—"

"Before you what, Liggert? You want to try to throw us out?" Savich flicked his fingers toward Liggert in invitation.

Liggert took a step toward Savich, his face a picture of rage, his hands fisted so tightly his knuckles bulged. Deliah yelled, "Liggert! You stop now!"

He wanted to fight, to pound them into the ground, but his mother's voice reined him in. He flicked her an uncertain look. So Deliah still exercised some control over her son. Savich wished she'd kept her mouth shut. But at least he might get Liggert to keep talking.

Ms. Louisa sang out, "Let the boys have

some fun, Morgana. Why not? What's a little blood on the floor?"

Deliah turned on her. "Be quiet, you old witch!"

Savich never turned his eyes away from Liggert. He said, "Liggert, did you make Walter murder Sparky in front of all those people?"

"Don't be an idiot," Liggert said. "It was Walter who killed Sparky. I was here in Plackett. I have witnesses. And that little murderer Sparky deserved it, but I had nothing to do with it. How could I?"

Savich ignored Liggert, said to Deliah Alcott, "You know who Dalco is, Mrs. Alcott. I imagine you're furious that Dalco made Brakey a murderer. I think you're not saying anything because you're terrified of what else Dalco might do. To you, to your sons, your grandchildren, to your life."

Deliah stood in the middle of the living room, looking utterly disconnected from all of them, utterly alone. She shook her head.

"Liggert is your son, but you know he can be vicious, ungoverned. He beats his wife. He beats his children. Does he have the power to frighten someone into doing whatever he wants? Is Liggert Dalco, Mrs. Alcott? Has he threatened to kill you if you say anything? Threatened to kill Brakey or Jonah? Perhaps even his wife, his children?"

That got her. Deliah yelled, "That is ridiculous! Liggert has a bit of a temper, that's all. He rarely hits his wife—"

Brakey said, "I saw him hit Marly, Mom. He smacked her so hard he knocked her out of her shoes."

"All right, I know, I know. Liggert, you promised me you'd stopped. You don't hit your children, do you?"

Liggert said nothing.

Deliah looked devastated.

Griffin said, "Walter Givens said he did. He said he had to stop Liggert from beating his little boy in public." He turned to Liggert. "Is that why you sent Walter to murder Sparky Carroll? He'd be labeled a murderer? And you'd have your revenge?

"And then we came along and were getting too close. You wanted us out of the way. Why did you pick Charlie Marker to ambush us in McCutty's woods? What did he do to you? Or was he just handy? And you knew he could get ahold of his dad's gun. Come on, Liggert, aren't you man enough to own up to that?" Savich could see the pulse in Liggert's neck pumping from eight feet away.

Griffin said, "Charles Marker said he did." He turned to Liggert. "He said he had to stop you from beating your little boy in public. Is that why you sent Charlie to ambush us in McCutty's Woods? After all, you must have known he could get ahold of his dad's gun. You wanted to punish him for crossing you, simple as that, and get rid of us at the same time. Come on, Liggert, aren't you man enough to own up to that?" Savich could see the pulse in Liggert's neck pumping from eight feet away.

Jonah took a step toward Griffin. "Stop it. You're wrong, both of you. This Dalco character you say forced Walter Givens and Brakey to kill people, forced Charlie to come after you two—it can't be Liggert. He has no ability to convince anyone to do anything at all. That's why he's so pissed off all the time. He hits his wife because he can, because she puts up with it and won't listen to me when I tell her she should leave him. She only shrugs and waits for him to smack her again." Jonah looked at his brother and continued, disgust thick in his voice. "Liggert's common. He's a good old boy with more rage than brains. I didn't know he'd fallen so low to hit his kids. You actually hit little Teddy? That sweet little boy? You hit him again, Liggert, and I swear to you I'll call the sheriff. You hear me? He'll toss your ass in jail, and you'll pay for that. Imagine the shame you'll bring on the family then. Liggert Alcott beats his kids."

They were getting off the tracks, though Savich was pleased Jonah was taking a stand. He hoped Jonah would follow through. In his experience, someone like Liggert would never stop hurting those weaker than him. Savich said, "Is it you, then, Jonah who has the ability to control what a person does? Do you have more luck with young men? You find they're more malleable, easier to control? Did you avenge your father's death by manipulating Walter and Brakey and Charles to do it for you? Your own brother? Are you that cowardly?"

Savich was surprised when Jonah

laughed. "Nah, I'm not Dalco. Don't get me wrong, I loved my dad, his death hit me hard, hit all of us hard, made me really mad, but the thing is I've known Sparky Carroll his whole life, watched him learn how to make meatballs from his dad. Sparky was always a nice little wuss who wouldn't squash a bug on his nose. He was sweet, you know? It's really sad if he did hit my dad. I can see him standing there, frozen, not knowing what to do. I can see him going to his own dad. He wouldn't have gone to Tammy, she's sweeter than he was."

Jonah looked at them, shook his head. "It isn't me who's this wild-haired Dalco. It certainly isn't Brakey. I mean, Brakey's such a good criminal, he put Deputy Lewis's body into his own truck in his own OTR. And Liggert?" He turned to his brother. "Have you learned some things I don't know about, Ligg? Have you been dancing around a fire in McCutty's woods, learning spells? Come on, Liggert, out with it. You saw the mismatched paint on Sparky's fender and that turned you into a mad psychic?"

There was cold pounding hard silence. Liggert was looking at his brother like he wanted to cut his brain out. He shook himself, sucked in a deep breath, and turned back to Savich and Griffin. "You two clowns done here?"

Savich said, "I haven't said the most important thing I came to tell you all. Dalco tried to kill me last Thursday night. He tried to terrify me in my sleep, as he did to Brakey, and Walter Givens, and that boy Charles Marker, just as he's trying to terrify some of you. He tried, but he failed. I was stronger than that madman. I took him to my own ground, and I scared the crap out of him. He hasn't come again because he's afraid of me. He knows I'll kill him.

"He's so afraid of me he didn't come after me in McCutty's woods. No, he sent a boy, Charles Marker, with his father's gun to ambush us. He's a coward, not man enough to come at me head-on again. Worse, look what he did to Brakey.

Deliah, you've got to give him up. I can protect you. If you don't, Walter Givens will spend the rest of his life in jail. Brakey will be indicted. Every shred of evidence points to him, and the federal prosecutor will even have motive, revenge for the cover-up of his father's murder. Aren't you more afraid of that than what Dalco might try next?"

Deliah Alcott didn't move. Slowly, she shook her head.

Ms. Louisa cackled, raised her arthritic hands, and waved a finger at Savich. "You waltz in here, boy, and you make your threats and try to get poor Liggert to lose his temper, and what have you accomplished? Nothing. Who is this Dalco? What is he? You claim he's tried to kill you. You know what I think? I don't think he even exists."

The old lady looked at each member of her family. "All I know for certain is that Morgana isn't Dalco. She isn't strong enough. Even if she were, can you imagine her making her precious Brakey into a murderer?" She picked up her knitting needles, dismissing them all, and lowered her head to the interminable scarf that looked like it had grown another foot.

Savich looked from Brakey, who was standing behind Ms. Louisa's wheelchair, to Jonah, leaning against the windowsill next to an oversized pentagram, to Liggert. Savich smiled at him. "Are you Dalco, Liggert? Will you come to me again when I'm sleeping and try to kill me? Do you think you can?"

Griffin watched everyone's faces as Savich goaded Liggert. Their expressions didn't give anything away, but he smelled fear, ripe and dark, and a deep, smoldering rage that heated the very air. From Liggert? Probably.

"You don't want to wait until I'm asleep, do you, Liggert? You want to have a try at me right now, but not here in your mom's living room. You want to come out-side? I'm not weak and small like your wife or your kids. I can fight back.

Liggert roared and lunged at Savich. His mother yelled.

Savich kicked out, no muss, no fuss, got Liggert square in the belly, sent him flying backward to fetch up against a table leg, gasping for breath.

Deliah ran to stand between them. "That's enough, Agent Savich. Leave my house, and don't come back without a warrant. Liggert is not Dalco!"

Savich said, "Dalco should know it's over now. He should give himself up, for Brakey's sake, or he should come try to get me. Those are his choices, and yours."

He said nothing more. He and Griffin turned and left the Alcotts in their living room.

60

26 Federal Plaza
New York City
Tuesday morning

The speaker was blasting out John Eiserly's voice when Special Agent in Charge Milo Zachery walked into the conference room that smelled of old bitter coffee and over-ripe pizza, but the agents focused on the MI5 agent's voice didn't seem to mind.

John was saying, "Kelly, as you know, we obtained a warrant to search Samir Basara's flat—excuse me, the penthouse —on Wyverly Place within minutes after you called yesterday. He was gone, which means he was already prepared to make a fast getaway. The safe was open, and empty, probably missing his private papers, money, and another passport. He may have several passports, we don't know, but he'll have trouble accessing any accounts in his own name in England at least. We're working on freezing any accounts he may have in Switzerland. Naturally he could have accounts in other names, in other places. Our forensic people are neck-deep finding that out. We've mobilized all our resources, alerted ports, airports, private airstrips. Still, it will be difficult to catch him if he's intent on leaving England. He's obviously spent a long time thinking it all through."

"Sherlock here, John. You didn't find anything to help us with a possible destination in the imam's papers at the mosque?"

"Unfortunately, no. Basara isn't mentioned directly, always by his moniker the Strategist, but there are a great number of financial reports to sort through. We found a set of books with enough illegal funding to put the imam in prison for a very long time. Once he stopped screaming about the sacrilege of our invading a holy place, he swore he knew nothing about anything. Not his fault. That bit will not fly, obviously."

"Any idea where Basara went immediately after he left his penthouse?" Kelly asked.

"He left his Bentley, didn't take a taxi, so we can't be certain. He could have taken the Tube or a train to just about anywhere inside England."

Sherlock said, "Or had another car. Didn't you say, John, that he was obviously prepared to pick up and leave very quickly if his house of cards came down?"

"Yes, that's probably what he did. No idea how we'd trace that."

Cal said, "What about Lady Elizabeth Palmer? Was she helpful at all?"

John paused briefly. "She was horrified, at first simply refused to believe he could be an assassin or a terrorist. When I told her he'd set up to bomb Saint Paul's, and wouldn't you know she was standing right under the big dome as a bridesmaid, she very nearly fainted. Unfortunately, she wasn't helpful with possible destinations. She knows a great deal about his personal habits, but knew nothing about his life as the Strategist. You know the last thing I heard her saying as I was leaving the room?"

"All right, John," Sherlock said, "this better be good."

"She should have listened to her father after all, should have known better than to take up with a man who liked to watch himself on the tele. Obviously he could have no sense of honor or fair play. And what would you expect from a commoner?"

Kelly said, "That wasn't bad, John. Now, you spoke about Lady Elizabeth being surprised he was an assassin and a terrorist. We've been discussing this and believe, like you, that Basara was using terrorism as a cover to murder individuals, but we have no idea who he could have been after in Saint Patrick's or the TGV or Saint Paul's."

John said, "If we don't find him I'm afraid we'll never know. But all three recent targets had highly placed government officials present."

Sherlock said, "Okay, we know Basara hasn't bought a commercial ticket, and you have his private Gulfstream and his pilot under wraps. If he took a boat, we may be out of luck. Private boat hires aren't well monitored, and cameras at yacht harbors are few and far between. So we've been focusing our efforts the last few hours on contacting private jet charter companies to see if any male in our age range bought a ticket within the last twenty-four hours out of England to anywhere in the world. Many of them have been surprised to hear from the American FBI, until we mention

Basara is a prime suspect in the attempted bombing of Saint Paul's. That's been getting their cooperation fast."

John said, "Thanks for helping us cover those. What worries me is that if he managed to get to France, there are scores of European private jet outfits available to him—"

"I've got him!" It was Agent Gray Wharton, who'd burst into the room, waving his laptop. He was so excited he was nearly jumping up and down. "Twelfth on my list was Manchester Private Jet Hire—they had three international bookings in our time frame. They were pissy at first about warrants and customer privacy until I told them who we were looking for. They couldn't move fast enough.

"They e-mailed the eight passport photos of their clients. I wasn't sure any of them matched our guy until I ran them through facial recognition. Even with the beard, this one is a good match for Basara." He put his laptop down on the conference table. "Take a look. His passport's under the name of Bruce Condor, supposedly born in Caldicott, Maine, some thirty-five years ago. He told the woman at the counter he was an American businessman, returning home. Get this, no one with that name and birth date has ever filed a U.S. tax return and he has no Social Security number. It's got to be him, I know it to my boots."

John said, "Where did he book to, Gray? Timbuktu?"

"No." He shot a look at Sherlock. "That's what's unbelievable. He arrived nine hours ago at Baltimore Washington International Airport."

Zachery was almost out the door when he said over his shoulder, "I'll call Mike at the Baltimore Field Office, tell him the situation, and he can marshal his troops. Kelly, Cal, Sherlock, you guys head down there right now. I'll have the helicopter waiting for you at Thirty-fourth Street."

John was shaking his head in disbelief. "Amazing. He could have flown to safety, but instead he's flying right into the maw of the beast. Why would the Strategist do something so foolhardy? Has he gone entirely lunatic?"

Sherlock said aloud what everyone was thinking. "I can think of only one reason he'd come here. He wants to kill me."

John was silent, remembering how close Mary Ann and Ceci had come to death in St. Paul's. Was Sherlock in his sights now? "If that's his plan, he's gone crazy enough. You be careful, Sherlock." Sherlock knew he'd be calling Dillon right away.

61

Four Seasons Hotel
Baltimore, Maryland
Tuesday

The Baltimore Field Office called them before the helicopter landed with the news they'd found Samir Basara. Sherlock called Dillon. "I hope you can hear me over the rotor. He checked into the Four Seasons last night, Dillon. We're nearly there. We're landing on the Pier 7 Heliport on Clinton Street, not more than two miles from the Four Seasons. What are you up to?"

Savich said, "I'll let you know if it works. This is all I need. Remember, Sherlock, you're my wife and Sean's mother. Take care of yourself."

Four Baltimore Field Office agents were standing next to two large FBI SUVs at the helipad. Giusti assigned each of them an exit as soon as they arrived. "I called up the plans in the helicopter. This should cover all the ways out. Everyone okay with this?"

The agents were hyped, wanted to be in on a possible takedown of a major-league terrorist and assassin.

Cal, Kelly, and Sherlock walked through the resplendent lobby and presented themselves to the clerk at the registration desk. They showed the young man their creds and asked about one of their guests, Mr. Bruce Condor, businessman. The registration clerk hemmed and hawed and said he would try to find the manager.

"Take us to his office," Kelly said. "Now." The clerk looked at her and nodded. While Kelly and Sherlock went to the manager's office, Cal made the rounds of the lobby, speaking to bellboys, parking attendants, and the concierge on duty. He showed each of them Basara's photo. It was the day shift, and no one recognized him.

Kelly and Sherlock followed the clerk through the beautiful gold marble lobby with its three huge chandeliers and artfully arranged flowers, to the manager's office, to the right, beyond the concierge's desk.

He rose, eyed the two women behind the scared-looking registration clerk, and frowned. "What seems to be the problem,

Jeb?"

Sherlock and Kelly simply stepped forward, introduced themselves. The man only stared at them, not pleased. Kelly raised her eyebrow.

"I'm Mr. Gibson," he said at last, but he didn't move around from behind his desk.

"FBI? Why are you two **ladies** here at the Four Seasons?"

Both of them heard the snark, knew what he would have liked to say was **two bitches**. What a joy, Sherlock thought, to be a female and have to have this idiot for a boss. A pity this was so urgent, there wasn't time to dismember him.

"We need to know the room number of one of your guests, Bruce Condor."

Up went the chin, his shoulders squared. "You will need a warrant for that, Agent. We value our guests' privacy."

Kelly told him this man was the prime suspect in the attempted bombing of St. Pat's. Mr. Gibson was not moved. He thrummed with attitude.

"As I already said, you will need a warrant," he said, and Sherlock would swear he smirked.

Kelly stepped around his desk and right into his face. "Mr. Gibson, this is a matter of national security. If you do not allow us immediate access, I'll call my brothers at the Baltimore FBI Field Office back and tell them to arrive in full SWAT gear, ready to search the hotel. I can't imagine that would make your guests very happy. Has it occurred to you that your company might find fault with you for trying to harbor a known terrorist?" She leaned in close. "I hope he was happy with your room service, by the way, otherwise, given who and what he is, he might come back and pay you a personal visit." She held out her hand. "Give me the card key. Now."

Mr. Gibson dropped the snark and called up the data on his laptop. He buzzed the front desk, and when another clerk arrived, he handed Sherlock the card key. "Suite 613," Gibson said, attitude back in full force. "Mr. Condor is not here. And before you ask, he did not register a car in our parking garage, nor do we have any record of his destination today."

Kelly asked, "How long ago did he check out?"

Gibson looked at the registration clerk. "Less than an hour ago."

"Has the room been cleaned yet?"

"I don't know."

"Probably not, Mr. Gibson," the clerk said.

They left Mr. Gibson and headed across the lobby. Kelly saw all the agents were in place. Cal joined them as they headed toward the bank of elevators. He waved the photo. "Day shift, no luck."

They rode to the top floor and walked to the end of the long corridor to a set of locked double doors, suite 613. They drew their Glocks, stuck in the key card without knocking, and pushed both doors open. A young woman who had folded clean towels draped over her arm let out a scream.

Luckily, she'd just arrived. They hustled her and her cart out of the suite and started searching.

"Even on the run, our guy likes his pleasures," Kelly said, looking around at the luxury suite with a view of the Inner Harbor.

The three of them split up the big suite and went to work. They were about ready to hang it up when there was a knock on the door. It was Jeb from the registration desk. "Mr. Condor ordered room service after midnight last night. A bottle of Golden Slope chardonnay and some food. I checked with the kitchen, and the employee who delivered the order is still here."

Sherlock wanted to kick herself. She hadn't thought to ask about room service. She wondered if Mr. Gibson knew Jeb had brought them this information.

Elena Wisk was tall, thin, and pretty, and looked both tired and excited. She nearly bounced into the suite, then suddenly yawned right in front of them. She flushed with embarrassment, told them she was just going off duty from the night shift. Evidently, Jeb hadn't told her Mr. Condor was a terrorist—yet, at least.

Yes, she'd brought Mr. Condor a tuna salad sandwich with potato chips and a bottle of chardonnay. He was good-looking, she said, but he looked tired. He told her the chardonnay would help him sleep, and he had a big day tomorrow—today, now— and he wanted to be ready. "I uncorked the chardonnay for him and told him I was from northern California. I said something about Golden Slope being a good choice. It's from a Napa winery I'd visited some years ago. He said it was better than anything he'd ever tasted from his family's vineyard. I asked him where that was, and he frowned and got me out of the suite real fast. I guess he didn't want to talk about it. I don't know why. He gave me a big tip."

Slipped up there, didn't you, Hercule? Cal showed Elena his picture of Samir Basara. She nodded. "Yes, that's him."

They asked her more questions, but the well was dry. Then, on her way out of the suite, Elena turned in the doorway, "I guess I'm really tired. I forgot, Mr. Condor was talking on his cell phone when I arrived."

All three of them went on red alert. Kelly asked, "Did you hear anything he said, Elena?"

Elena pursed her lips. "I wasn't really listening, you know? But it was something about the person he was talking to doing a good job and he knew he could always count on him, something like that. That's all I got. What'd he do? Something really bad?" She shivered.

Sherlock merely patted her shoulder.

"Thank you, Ms. Wisk, we really appreciate all your help." She called Dillon on speakerphone, told him about the call Basara had made.

"Yes, that checks out," Savich said. "I pulled up the cell data from the cell tower that services the Four Seasons Baltimore, looking for outgoing calls after Basara arrived there last night. One single call was made from an unregistered phone, a burner phone, and it was activated yesterday. The number that cell phone called was right here in Washington, D.C., and it was also unregistered. We've either found ourselves a pair of drug dealers, or Basara called a henchman."

"The room-service clerk said it was about midnight," Sherlock said.

"Yes, that's it. Good to have confirmation even though we thought he would be heading toward Washington." He added, "You live here. Now I'm working with the carrier to try to locate both of those phones in real time." He paused again. "Well, maybe I'll use a shortcut."

Cal took the phone. "Keep us in the loop, Savich. We're finishing up here and we'll be heading to Washington to join you. That call means someone arrived here ahead of Basara to see to his needs, like parking a car at the airfield, with that burner cell left in the glove compartment. It means he's very probably got a gun."

"I know," Savich said, "I know. I'll see you soon. Be careful, all of you."

Sherlock took the cell back from Cal. "Dillon? Are Sean and Gabriella out of the house?"

"They're at my mom's already. No worries there, Sherlock."

62

**Interstate 95,
en Route to Washington, D.C.
Tuesday afternoon**

Samir Basara pressed the gas to pass a beer truck that had slowed to thirty miles per hour for no reason he could understand, then slowed immediately back to exactly fifty-five and eased smooth and easy into the right-hand lane. He wasn't going to let his excitement for what was coming affect his driving. He wanted no trouble from the state police. The car Salila had left him in the airfield parking lot was perfect, a three-year-old light tan Toyota Camry that would draw no attention. A Walther P99 semiautomatic was on the seat beside him, Salila's own weapon, he'd told Samir when they'd spoken on the phone briefly late last night. Everything else they would need, his nephew had driven down to Washington. Everything was ready for him in the condo Salila had rented, and enough C-4 to blow the FBI woman's house in Georgetown into a pile of rubble, her and her family with it. She would return to her home soon enough. Basara would simply wait. He couldn't fault Salila for the debacle in Brooklyn. Salila had been so mournful about the failure of his "soldiers"—Salila called everyone he worked with his "soldiers," no matter how young or how old—that Samir had felt moved to comfort him, but still he'd had to make it clear that his soldiers had mucked it up, gotten themselves wounded and caught, and the oldest comrade in arms, Mohammad Hosni, had gotten himself killed. Salila had told Basara he feared the two younger soldiers, Mifsud and Kenza, whom he thought of as his children, would never be released from the American prisons. He assured Basara neither of them had anything to fear from the young ones. They would never talk. His children were loyal to the cause, as he was loyal to Basara.

A pity the FBI agent hadn't roasted to death in that house in Brooklyn. It was a royal cock-up, but it wasn't Basara's fault, he'd planned it well, given clear, concise instructions. Salila's soldiers had somehow given themselves away, alerted the FBI. Best not to think of it now. It was no longer important.

It was time to move forward, to focus on the woman, and Basara trusted Salila to handle the details, trusted him to do whatever it was Basara wished. He'd trusted Salila since he'd saved his life in Syria when a bomb exploded next to their car outside Damascus and Basara had pulled Salila to safety. Salila wouldn't fail him in this, his final assassination, unlike Bahar, who'd failed him miserably. He planned to reward Salila handsomely for this day's work.

Traffic thickened and he was forced to slow down. He wondered if MI5 had found the papers in the imam's office yet that listed out the huge donations Mrs. Sabeen Conklin had made to the imam with funds she'd embezzled from her husband. That alone would be enough to send them both to prison. Nasim Conklin's widow, Marie Claire, who had survived, would no doubt press charges. He felt rage build because he didn't know how the American FBI had found her and her children, but he knew that damned woman Sherlock had taken part, and she would pay for that as well. Thinking of how he'd make her pay calmed him.

He wondered briefly if he would ever see his family again. His sisters could rot in hell for all he cared, but he admitted to himself he would like to see what his mother did to his father in the months and years to come, and how long his father would survive her endless tender care.

He laughed, wondering what Elizabeth thought of him now that she knew she'd defied her parents and shared her secrets and her quite lovely body with a terrorist. And not just any terrorist, but the mastermind who'd planned to blow up St. Paul's and her along with it. What would her father have to say now? Poor Elizabeth, there would be no more jewels to pawn for her wastrel brother, but more than that, the London **Times** might print the whole sordid story and ruin both her and her noble family. He would watch from afar and enjoy the media free-for-all.

His stomach growled. He realized he

hadn't eaten after that late-night sandwich from room service and a bottle of wine, his favorite, which always made him sleep like a baby. He looked down at his watch. Nearly noon. He'd eat after he met with Salila.

He started whistling an old Algerian song, as he added up all the money he'd put aside into the several accounts he knew no one would ever find, buried under a tangle of intertwined corporations. It reminded him yet again that he had more than enough to relocate to Sorrento, Italy, when all of this was done, to the villa he'd bought there four years ago. It sat right on a cliff overlooking the sea, and he would put up his feet on the exquisite railing, sip his wine, and settle his soul. Only then would the Strategist slowly return to his business. It would be more difficult with the imam in prison, but his reputation as the Strategist would be enough. Their followers would fear and respect him still. Blowing apart the FBI agent who had helped send the imam to prison, along with her family, would help convince them.

He knew she alone wasn't responsible for

his lost career as one of the greatest assassins of all time, his lost jet, his lost penthouse, but killing her was a start. He hummed, picturing the bitch blown to hell.

63

Criminal Apprehension Unit
Hoover Building
Washington, D.C.
Tuesday afternoon

Savich sat in his office in the CAU, waiting for his cell to ring as the half-dozen agents outside, ready with their assault gear and their Kevlar jackets, waited for his word. The wireless carrier wouldn't locate the phones the FBI was looking for without a warrant. So he'd thrown a Hail Mary and called his friend Clint Matthews at the District Court U.S. Marshals office. The Marshals Service owned a Cessna they flew over the District when they needed to find a fugitive by tracking his cell phone. The plane carried its own imitation cell tower they called a dirtbox, which could trick cell phones below it into giving up their unique identification codes. Matthews has bragged he could find any powered-up cell phone in the area to within three feet.

Savich's phone rang seventeen minutes after his call, and Clint was on the line, nearly hyperventilating. "We found the phone, the one that was called here in Washington. It's in Georgetown, Savich, not a mile from where you live, in that new condo complex, the Gilmore. We got the address on Nyland Drive Northwest, even the unit number—338. You want some of our guys with you or do you have to settle for your FBI wussies?"

Savich laughed. "I owe you, Clint. Big-time."

"Nah, if this helps net the lowlife terrorist who tried to blow up Saint Pat's, this'll be a huge win for all of us."

Savich was out of his office before he'd punched off his cell.

64

The Gilmore
1188 Nyland Drive NW
Georgetown
Tuesday afternoon

Everyone called the three side-by-side identical buildings on Nyland Drive the **new** Gilmore condos, though they were, in fact, built in 2003. Each was three stories high and done in mellow red brick, with parklike, beautifully landscaped grounds to attract the upwardly mobile young professionals who had bought up most of them.

There were single residences across the street, with no space between them for parking. Their owners' cars usually lined the street, but now in the middle of the day when nearly everyone was at work, the street was mostly empty and quiet, with very little foot traffic. Savich assigned four agents to the grounds near the building and across the street, asked them to stay out of sight or blend in, though he knew it would be difficult for them to remain unnoticed for very long. He walked up three flights of Berber-carpeted stairs with Ollie and Ruth and down a long hallway to the end unit, 338. Savich hadn't called the manager to try to bludgeon him into giving up information about who'd rented unit 338. He'd decided it was too risky. He couldn't spare an agent to stay with the manager to make sure he didn't call his wife or his girlfriend, or anyone else who might surprise them by showing up. They'd know soon enough who was waiting for Samir Basara.

They met no one on the stairs or hallways, heard nothing from the condos they passed, everyone was at work. Still, they walked as quietly as possible when they neared the door. Savich pressed his Glock to his side, smiled into the peephole, and knocked on the door. "Pizza delivery."

A deep voice with a light Arabic accent mixed with pure Brooklyn called out, "You have the wrong address. I did not order pizza. Go away."

Savich nodded to Ruth and Ollie, stepped back, and sent his foot into the doorknob. The door flew open as Ruth yelled, "FBI, don't you move!"

They saw a dark-skinned man dive for cover behind the sofa in the living room to their right. He fired three quick shots toward the door, but they'd pulled back behind the wall in the doorway entrance. They heard movement down the apartment hallway in front of them. Someone else was there.

Savich called out, "Both of you, including you in the bedroom, come out now. There's no way out of here. You're surrounded."

They heard a window open and the metallic clang of someone jumping onto the fire escape.

Ollie said into his comm, "Dane, a perp is headed your way down the fire escape."

The man in the living room poked his head out again around the other end of the sofa and emptied his magazine in their direction. They heard him slam in another magazine. That was too bad, no choice. Savich nodded to Ollie, who pulled a flashbang from his jacket, pulled the pin, and tossed it into the living room. The three of them pulled back into the hallway and pressed their palms over their ears against the shattering blast to come. The explosion of sound and light was horrific in the small space.

They heard the man wheezing and coughing. He rolled on the floor, his hands covering his face, his gun on the floor beside him, forgotten.

Ruth ran into the living room, flipped him onto his stomach, and cuffed him.

He was gasping, tears streaming from his eyes. "I'm dying, I'm dying."

Ruth swatted his head. "No, you're not. It was only a flashbang, no shrapnel, so stop your whining." She dragged him to his feet and shoved him onto a chair. As Savich and Ollie checked the back of the condo, she PlastiCuffed him to the chair. He was still wheezing, tears running down his face. She imagined he hadn't heard a word she'd said, his ears still ringing from the flashbang. She walked to the living room window and saw Dane hauling a man out front toward Griffin. He was very young, not much older than her stepson Rafe. She turned back and stared down at the man in the chair. He had something of the look of the young man downstairs, wide-set eyes, a strong chin, hair black as ink. "You want to give me your name?"

He tried to spit at her.

"That was rude," Ruth said. She gave him a wide berth and came up behind him, stuck her hand into his back pocket. She pulled out his alligator-grain wallet.

Savich and Ollie searched the condo together, a room at a time. The first bedroom had a king-size bed and clothes strewn around on the floor. It looked like both men had slept in there. The bathroom was a jumble of dirty towels and smelled of toothpaste and musty aftershave lotion. The second bedroom was neat as a pin, except for the open window that gave onto the fire escape.

Was this bedroom waiting for Basara? While Ollie checked the fire escape, Savich opened the closet door and found a stash of handguns, six of them, all of them Glocks. He knelt down and picked up several packets of what looked to be C-4, the same explosive that had blown the TGV off the tracks and that they'd used at St. Patrick's and St. Paul's. He stilled, felt rage surge. **So you bastards were going to bomb us? Our house?**

He and Ollie met Dane coming through the front door with the young man he'd jerked from the fire escape, cursing non-stop. Savich pointed to the sofa. "Ollie, cuff him. Dane, those shots and the flashbang are going to pull police and fire here any minute. Call nine-one-one, cancel the calls. Tell D.C. Metro to keep their squad cars well away from here. Find the manager, have him help you clear the street of any onlookers. Basara could be close now."

Savich looked at the freshly shaved young man and smelled the same aftershave lotion in the bathroom. He was still cursing softly, repeating himself now. Savich stepped up to him and said, "Shut your mouth."

The young man was so startled, he shut his mouth, looked up at Savich. "What are you going to do, hit me? American police-men can't do that."

Savich said, "I can do anything I want to you. What's your name?"

The young man shut his mouth.

"Let's see what your dad has to say about bringing his son into this."

"I'm not his son, I'm his nephew."

"Good to know." Ruth handed Savich a

well-worn alligator wallet. Inside was a New York driver's license, three credit cards, five hundred dollars in cash, and a photo of a woman with three children surrounding her. "So, Mr. Salila," Savich said, looking at him, "you're Samir Basara's advance man. I don't see this young man in the photo, so I guess he didn't lie, you are his uncle. What is his name?"

Salila didn't say anything.

Ollie shook his head. "No wallet on him. Ruth, keep an eye on him. I'll check the drawers in that pigsty of a bedroom."

"You will not call us pigs. We are men," Salila said, and spat at Ollie.

"It won't help you if you continue to be rude," Ruth said, and punched him in the arm. "You're already in very big trouble."

"You are nothing but a stupid woman, you mean nothing. Look at you, dressed in your trousers, playing at being a man."

She smiled, patted his blackened face. "You need to rethink that, Mr. Salila. I'm the one who has you handcuffed to a chair."

Salila stared at each of them, at his nephew sitting on the sofa opposite him. "I demand you let us go. We have done nothing wrong."

Savich raised his eyebrow. "Would you like to explain the six Glocks in the bedroom closet, or care to tell us what you're doing with all that highly illegal C-4?"

Salila shook his head.

His nephew said, "We know nothing about firearms. Perhaps the last person who stayed here left them."

Ollie came back into the living room, holding a wallet. "I found this under a dirty shirt. We've been talking to Mr. Asad Salila. So your uncle here, Husam Salila, has a brother. Is your father in the terrorist business, too?"

Salila said nothing. He frowned at his nephew when he started to speak, and Asad lowered his head.

"When is Basara to arrive?" Savich asked him.

Salila started, then grew very still. "I do not know any Basara."

"Is that a fact? I see you live in New York. Did you help him with trying to bomb Saint Patrick's? You were the handler for those three who tried to kill Agent Sherlock?"

He stayed silent, but his breath quickened.

"They sure mucked that up, didn't they, Mr. Salila? Did Basara have no one else left to help him after he flew into Baltimore?"

Salila looked at Savich. "It is all impossible what you say. How do you know all this?"

"I also know Basara called you from the Four Seasons hotel at midnight last night."

Salila's mouth fell open. "That is impossible. You are lying to me."

Savich reached his hand into Salila's shirt pocket and pulled out his cell. He waved it in Salila's face. "Your cell phone came to me and whispered all its secrets. Now let's see what you've been up to since you arrived in Washington."

Savich scrolled through the call list. There were only three. One from Basara and two to a number in New York. His family?

"Tell me, when Basara arrived here, were you planning to plant the C-4 around Agent Sherlock's house and blow her up? You see, it's also my house, and that of our five-year-old son."

Savich saw the pulse pounding wildly in Salila's neck. Savich knew he was afraid, he knew failure was staring him in the face, but he managed to hold himself together.

"If that is so, what happens to your house is her own doing. Your fate is in Allah's hands."

"Whatever that means," Ollie said.

"We are all in Allah's hands," Salila said. "And those who commit evil, Allah will see that they pay for their sins."

Ruth said, "I can't imagine Allah encourages you to murder innocent people, like the hundreds of people at that funeral in Saint Patrick's in New York. So will Allah make you pay, Salila? Will Basara pay? Basara will come and we'll catch him, you know."

Savich knew he couldn't ask Salila to call Basara, even if Basara was expecting him to call. Salila would warn him if given the chance, no matter how Savich threatened him. He also realized he could make as many threats as he could think of and Salila would never give him up. What had Basara done to earn such loyalty?

Salila closed his eyes and his lips moved in a prayer. Asad stared at his uncle, fear bleaching his newly shaved face bone white.

Salila's cell phone rang. And rang.

65

Sixteenth Street NW

Cal turned off the siren and flashers and seamed back into traffic as he turned right off Sixteenth onto U Street. "We're close, maybe five minutes to Nyland."

Sherlock's cell sang out "Born to Be Wild" and she put it on speakerphone. "Dillon, we're five minutes out. What's happening?"

"Salila's cell rang with a call from Basara, probably to confirm their meeting, so he could be close. I didn't risk letting Salila answer it. Keep a low profile as you approach. We still don't know what kind of car he's driving. Hurry, guys."

"Turn left here on Pritchert, Cal," Sherlock said, after Savich punched off. "It's the locals' way to Nyland and the Gilmore."

When Cal turned right onto Nyland, Sherlock said from the backseat, "The condos are two blocks up, on the left. There's Griffin now, trimming bushes. He looks good. Basara wouldn't spot him for a Fed."

Kelly sucked in her breath, not wanting to believe it. "There he is! Ten o'clock, Cal, a Toyota Camry. He's driving slow, studying the street. Let's get him!"

Cal hit the gas only to see an ancient Chevy Impala pulling out of a driveway directly in front of him. He slammed on the brakes, barely missing the driver's door. At first he thought there was no one driving the Impala, then a curly gray head and a terrified white face appeared above the steering wheel.

Basara looked back at the sound of screeching brakes and spotted them. He threw his cell phone out the window and hit the gas, barely avoiding an elderly man with a walker who'd stepped out onto the street. Griffin dropped his cutter and took out his cell as the Toyota two-wheeled around a corner and headed south, toward 29.

Kelly yelled, "I don't know Washington, where's he going?"

"Don't know yet," Sherlock said. She unfastened her seat belt and sat forward between the front seats, her Glock in her hand. "No, wait, he could take 29 east into

D.C. or try to cross the Key Bridge into Arlington."

Cal turned on his siren and flashers again as he swerved past a dozen cars and a Silverado flatbed stacked with tires, to the sound of blasting horns and shouted curses. He was only three cars behind when the Camry swerved around a Cadillac onto the Key Bridge. "He's not a bad driver," Cal said, "but he's at a big disadvantage because he doesn't know Washington."

Kelly said, "What's this way?"

"Arlington National Cemetery, if he keeps heading south," Cal said. "He'll see the sign soon enough and realize he doesn't want to get caught in that maze. Hang on!" He swerved around a black limo with government plates, two startled faces staring at them as they whipped past. Cal slipped back into his lane with feet to spare to the horrified face of the Mustang driver headed directly at him. "No," Cal said, "Basara's not going to the cemetery, he's headed onto 66 and that'll take him back across the Roosevelt Bridge into D.C. I wonder if he knows that. Hey, isn't that Dillon's red Porsche behind us?"

Sherlock looked back. "It sure is. Ruth's with him." She looked back to the thick traffic ahead of them. "Basara has no idea what he's getting into once he gets to the other side, Cal. If he exits out of this traffic, he could be dumped onto the traffic circle at the Lincoln Memorial. He won't get through there without stopping, not with all the cars circling, not to mention all the tourists around it." She started to tell him to be careful, but she didn't. Cal was in Dillon's class. She turned to see Dillon's red Porsche on their bumper, Ruth leaning out the passenger window, her Glock in her hand. Dillon was letting them take the lead.

This is madness, Kelly thought, as she shot a look down at the Potomac flowing fast beneath them, to what the sign had informed her was Theodore Roosevelt Island on her left. She looked over at Cal, saw his eyes were focused and calm, his hands relaxed on the steering wheel. He knew what he was doing. She felt her heart pounding loud and fast, not in fear, but in exhilaration, and saw herself at seven years old, skiing down a black diamond, her mother screaming at her from behind. She stared again at Basara, weaving in and out of bridge traffic six cars ahead of them.

Cal followed the Camry off onto Constitution Avenue, watched it veer right again toward the river at the first access road. Sherlock was right, he had no idea he was headed straight for the Lincoln Memorial and its traffic circle right up ahead. Cal roared up behind the Camry, barely missing an oncoming car, sitting on his horn in the circle. There was a construction site up ahead, cut off from traffic with big concrete blocks. He forced his way past two cars on the inside of the circle, calculated the speed he needed, and struck the Camry's left rear panel. The Camry careened sideways into the concrete blocks and went airborne into the construction equipment. A couple workers nearby dove for cover. The Camry struck a backhoe, rolled once, and once again, spraying mud and splintering a construction horse.

"Hold on!" Cal slammed down on the brakes, sending them into a spin. The SUV slammed into one of the construction blocks, sending smoke pouring from under the hood. They all stared beyond at the overturned Camry. The driver's door was shoved open and Basara, blood streaming down his face, rolled out and came up to his knees. He saw them on the other side of the concrete blocks, cars stacked around them at an angle, their blaring horns filling the air.

He raised his gun but saw they were blocked in, and ran across the traffic circle toward the Lincoln Memorial and its crowds of tourists.

Sherlock and Kelly were out of the SUV, running after him, weaving through tourists and traffic. Kelly held up her creds and yelled, "FBI agents!" every few steps, but a father didn't jerk his small child out of Kelly's path fast enough. She tripped and went down. Sherlock was ahead of her, saw Basara running toward the Lincoln Memorial, people parting in front of him at the sight of his gun and the blood running down his face.

Please, don't let him grab a hostage.

She yelled, "Everyone down!"

Basara heard her, stopped, and she knew he was going take a teenage girl standing on the steps, but in the last instant, he turned, deaf to all the screaming people, and his eyes met Sherlock's. He fired three shots, and the last one hit her in the chest. Sherlock staggered back with the god-awful pain. For an instant she couldn't breathe. She fell to her knees, wondering blankly if her ribs were broken under the Kevlar. She flattened herself onto her stomach and forced herself to calm, held her Glock steady with both hands, her eyes never leaving him. Before he could fire again, she got off three shots. She watched them strike his neck, his shoulder, his chest. He froze on the wide step for a moment, his eyes locked to hers before he collapsed and tumbled down the steps.

She jumped to her feet and yelled, "Stay back!" as she ran to him, kicked away his gun that had fallen to the first step. He was lying sprawled on his back, at an angle on the steps, his chest heaving, blood fountaining out of his neck. She dropped to her knees beside him.

She heard Dillon shouting, but she didn't look away from Basara.

His eyes were filming over, but still he

whispered, his words thick with blood, "I wanted to bomb you to hell."

"That didn't work out for you, did it?"

He licked the blood off his lips. "I can't die. It wasn't supposed to happen like this."

His head fell to the side and his eyes stared up at the sky, seeing nothing now. He was dead. It didn't make up for Nasim's murder, but it was all they'd get. Sherlock stared down at him, aware now of a dozen people beginning to crowd around her. She heard Dillon's voice ordering them back. Kelly came running up to fall on her knees beside Sherlock, Cal on her heels.

Sherlock rose slowly, Basara's blood covering the front of her white shirt, and felt Dillon's arm go around her.

It was over.

66

Savich House
Georgetown
Tuesday night

By the fourth verse of their sing-along of "The Little Kid with the Greatest Mom," Sean was finally down for the count. It was a country-and-western song Savich had written for him when he'd been two years old. The words weren't all that good, but then again, neither was Sherlock's voice. It wasn't a problem. Sean didn't know any better. They stood together, looking down at their sleeping son. Savich kissed her temple. "Welcome home."

She turned in his arms and pressed her cheek against his neck. "I hated being away from you and Sean." She gave a little laugh. "I've told you that half a dozen times since I walked in the door."

"Keep saying it, makes my heart settle down. I don't know who was happier to see you, Sean or Astro. It was me, actually." He pulled her tight against him again.

"I always had agents around me, Dillon, you know that."

"You could have been under a blanket of agents and I'd still feel the same way."

She reared back, touched her fingertips to his face. "I feel the same way about you, but it's over now, finally over. Basara is dead." She blinked. "Hard to believe it all started less than a week ago at JFK." She saw Nasim's face, Marie Claire's face, and turned it off. "The thought of Basara using terrorist acts to cover up his assassinations —murdering hundreds of people for the sole purpose of murdering one—and all for money. I think about all those people now dead because they happened to be riding the TGV in France. And what if he'd succeeded in bombing Saint Patrick's and Saint Paul's? I wonder how many years this goes back? How many people he killed? He was a psychopath, Dillon, evil to the core."

"He's dead now, his evil with him," Savich said, and thought of how close she'd come to being his next victim. "As to the millions of dollars he's got stashed in accounts in

Switzerland, we'll find them.

"You know what I can't get over? Basara would still be alive, still be in business, if he'd used his money and his contacts to disappear when he had the chance. But he couldn't accept losing. He needed someone to blame, and he picked you, Sherlock—a woman, no less—and made you into his nemesis." He shook his head, felt the fear for her well up again from deep inside him, tamped it down. He kissed her, held her tightly. "Welcome home, for the twelfth time. You're exhausted, sweetheart. You ready for bed?"

He was right, she'd been so tired she'd thought she would pass out, but not now. No, not now. She gave him a slow smile, took his hand, and led him to their bedroom. He was big and warm, and she loved him to the ends of the earth.

Savich stripped down to boxers and a T-shirt in under thirty seconds, but when he turned he saw she was lying in the middle of the bed, fully clothed, sound asleep. She never woke up when he undressed her, slipped her nightgown over her head. He looked at her beloved face for a very long time before he turned out the lights and went to sleep.

Savich dreamed he was freezing. Frigid water was pouring over him, drenching his T-shirt and boxers, hitting his face. Powerful waves were slamming him back against something hard and unyielding—a rock. The water receded, only to roar back against him, pounding at him, freezing him to his bones. He tried to get away from the waves, but he couldn't move. Thick ropes held him tight against a huge rock that jutted out from the sea. **What sea?**

He was dreaming he was strapped down to a rock? He pulled and jerked with all his strength against the ropes, tried to work his hands free from beneath the thick hemp, but he couldn't. The ropes were wet from the freezing waves, and growing tighter.

It was no dream. It was Dalco.

Savich heard a loud sweeping noise and looked up to see a huge black eagle with an enormous wingspan circling above him. It swooped low until its black wings covered him, and it dug its beak directly into his side. The pain was so unspeakable he nearly passed out. The eagle pulled out its bloody beak and soared upward, then dove down at him again the next moment. Again it sent its beak into him, digging deeper, pulling and ripping, until he screamed from the horrendous pain. When the eagle pulled its beak out of his body again, Savich looked at its black opaque eyes. The eagle returned his stare, looked back down at him for several seconds. Its eyes weren't opaque after all. Dalco was behind them.

The eagle sent its beak into his side yet again, burrowing deeper, hollowing him, gashing out parts of him. He nearly passed out. He caught himself. No, it was Dalco, he couldn't let that madman win. He had to fight the pain, had to figure out what was happening. He was tied to a rock, couldn't get free. A huge eagle was digging its beak into his side. What was this all about? Who was Dalco playing this time? Was he playing out the Prometheus myth with himself as the eagle? Zeus sent an eagle every day to tear out and eat Prometheus's liver only to have it grow back again every night, and repeated the cycle endlessly, at least until Hercules saved him, eventually, maybe, depending on who was telling the story. It was Zeus's punishment because Prometheus had dared to give mankind the gift of fire.

Dalco imagined himself as powerful as Zeus? Savich yelled, "What's wrong, Dalco? Can't you come up with anything original?"

The eagle sent a tearing cry into the heavens, but then it hovered above him, apparently in no hurry. Talking to it would do no good; the eagle wouldn't talk back. And Dalco had seen to it he was physically helpless. He pictured Winkel's Cave in his mind, focused as hard as he could on sending them both into the large chamber again, but nothing changed. He pictured Dalco standing on a huge alligator, lazily cruising through the green waters of the Everglades, its jaws slowly opening, its black eyes staring up at him. But he was still on the rock, the eagle above him. He pictured a purple sea, a wooden raft riding the waves, and he set Dalco on the raft, alone and in an open sea.

Nothing happened.

The relentless waves were still pounding him, washing into the open wound in his side. Remarkably, the water was so cold it numbed the pain, but for only an instant.

The eagle screamed as it dove at him again, covering Savich's head with its wings, digging its beak deep into the gaping wound in his side. And again it lazily took flight, hovering over him, flapping its black wings, staring down at him, his blood dripping from its beak.

He yelled to be back in his bed, but nothing changed. Why couldn't he change anything? Would he die in this dreamscape, tied forever to this rock? He screamed, "Griffin, help me!"

Griffin stood on the rock above him, nearly hurled off the rock by the ferocious wind. Waves splashed around his legs, pulling at him. His eyes were wide with shock. Savich watched him grab the thick ropes to steady himself.

He scrambled down the side of the rock, using the ropes that bound Savich to brace himself. He began working a knot. The eagle dove toward them, Savich's blood still dripping from its beak, then, suddenly, it pulled back, its wings flapping madly, screaming at them. It slammed into Griffin and sunk its beak into his shoulder, nearly knocking him off the rock and into the sea. Griffin managed to hold on. He whirled around and struck the eagle's head with his fist. The eagle screamed and pulled back, keeping its distance. "It's watching us," Griffin said. "It doesn't know what to do now that there are two of us."

Griffin felt warm blood on his shoulder, running down his arm. He ignored it, didn't slow. He'd been in a deep sleep when he'd heard Savich's shout, and the next instant he was on this huge rock in a nightmare he understood quickly enough.

Dalco.

Griffin managed to loosen the rope enough for Savich to pull an arm free and help him. The eagle shrieked, preparing to dive again, but now Savich was nearly free of the ropes. But where would they go? The frigid water below them was filled with jagged black rocks, violent waves spuming over them.

The eagle continued shrieking at them, its huge wings flapping, hanging in the air, as if uncertain what to do. The skies burst open, hurling down a torrent of icy rain on them, nearly dragging Griffin off the rock and into the sea below.

Savich tried to talk, but it was beyond him. He couldn't bring himself to look at his side. He knew he'd see his mangled flesh. The pain was so crippling he couldn't seem to draw a breath. Everything was blurring, he was going to pass out. Griffin would be helpless with him, and they would both die. He saw blood dripping off Griffin's shoulder, knew there was nothing he could do to stanch the blood. Griffin was wearing only a soaked T-shirt and pajama bottoms.

The violent rain slammed against him, filling the wound in his side. He heard Griffin shout, "Hang on!" He saw Griffin bend down and pull up his pajama leg. He was wearing an ankle holster with a Glock 380 pistol in it. Then he saw it was in Griffin's hand. The eagle came through the cascading rain, diving down at them, its wings flapping wildly, shrieking, and Griffin waited until it was nearly on them and then shot it square between the eyes.

Its head flew off, feathers and blood mixing with the torrential rain. Still it hovered, still flapped its wings, as blood streamed from its neck. It flew away and disappeared into the sheets of thick, gray rain.

"Dillon! Dillon! Wake up, you're moaning, wake up!"

He heard her voice, felt hard slaps on his face, and she was yelling over and over, "Dillon, wake up!"

His eyes flew open. He sucked in a breath and stared up at her, saw her her outline in the predawn light. "Sherlock," he said, and stilled, waiting for the crippling pain, but it didn't come. There was no gaping wound in his side, his flesh was smooth, he was whole. He felt pain from the ropes, but it was fading, and when he looked at his wrists, his arms, there was nothing. He felt cold, but he wasn't freezing. Sherlock pulled him against her, stroking his hair, kissing his face again and again. "It's all right now, Dillon, I've got you. It was Dalco, wasn't it? He can't get you again now. It's all right, you're safe."

He managed to say against her neck, "Griffin was with me. I have to call him, see that he's okay."

She scrambled over him, grabbed his cell, and speed-dialed Griffin.

Griffin answered on the first ring. "Savich? Are you all right?"

Savich closed his eyes against his relief at hearing Griffin's voice. "Yes, I'm all right. Sore, cold, but no open wounds. Your shoulder?"

Griffin worked his shoulder. "Like you, I'm sore, but there's no wound, no bruise, nothing at all. It's like it never happened, but it did." He paused, then, "That was a hell of a thing, Savich."

Savich smiled. "It was that exactly. Thank you for coming, Griffin. Thank you for saving my life. A gun, I couldn't believe it when you pulled out a gun and shot the eagle's head off."

"After what you told me, I've been wearing it to bed with me for three nights now. Do you think Dalco's dead?"

"I guess we'll find out when we visit the Alcotts tomorrow. Try to get some sleep. I'll call you."

When he hung up, he realized he was cold again. He pulled Sherlock close until he was warm. She said against his shoulder, "You can tell me all about this, but not now. Now you need to sleep."

And he did.

67

Alcott Compound
Plackett, Virginia
Wednesday morning

"It doesn't look like anyone's home," Griffin said as he got out of the Porsche into the fresh morning air. It was so quiet he could hear a crow cawing high in the air above him.

Savich knocked on the front door. He heard the coming footfalls, recognized the steps as Deliah Alcott's. When she opened the door, she looked at each of them, and nodded. "Agent Savich, Agent Hammersmith. I've been expecting you. I thought it best I be here alone when you arrived, after that scene between you and Liggert yesterday." She suddenly smiled. "Thank you. Finally, it's over. Come with me, see for yourselves."

Savich and Griffin followed her past the pentacle hanging on the front door and down a long hallway fragrant with the scent of lavender, to the very end room. She stopped in front of the closed door, drew a deep breath, quietly opened it, and stepped inside.

It was a large room with old-fashioned furniture, lace curtains on the windows, rag rugs on the polished maple floor, an old person's room. There was an ancient iron-framed bed against the far wall, and on it lay Ms. Louisa, utterly still, deeply asleep or unconscious. She was wearing a white high-necked nightgown, a white bedspread drawn to her neck. Her hair was in a skinny braid over her shoulder, as gray as her still face. The nightstand beside her was ablaze with lighted green, white, and gold candles surrounding a plate overflowing with herbs and dried flowers.

Deliah looked down at her. "I heard her scream after midnight. When I came running in she was on the floor, clutching her head. Then she fell over unconscious. When I touched her I knew she was gone. How strange it is, but do you know, I miss the sound of those infernal knitting needles of hers?" She turned to them. "You know now, don't you? You know what she was?"

"Until this moment I wasn't completely sure whether she was Stefan Dalco," Savich said.

"You thought I was this Dalco character?"

"Perhaps, for a short time. I quickly realized how much you loved Brakey, how you'd go to any lengths to protect him. You would never make Brakey a murderer."

"She came after you again?"

Savich nodded. "She would have killed me if Griffin hadn't shot her. I was helpless until then."

"Actually," Griffin said, "a huge black eagle was attacking Savich. I shot its head off."

Deliah picked up a large book from under the bedside table, handed it to Savich. "She liked her Greek mythology. She was studying this." He and Griffin looked down at a painting of a naked Prometheus chained to a rock over a violent sea, an eagle hovering above him, wings flapping madly. Savich nodded, handed it back. "Yes, that was what she fashioned for me." He turned to stare down at the still figure who'd had so much power. He remembered the horrific pain in his side.

Deliah said, "She was always bragging

how she was the most powerful witch who'd ever lived. But you beat her, Agents, you beat her."

"What she was," Savich said, "was a powerful psychic who used the symbols of witchcraft. And she was quite mad. I've known a couple others like her, both of them terrifying."

"Why isn't she in a hospital, Mrs. Alcott?" Griffin asked, looking down at the slack face.

"It would do absolutely no good."

"They could monitor her, feed her intravenously."

She shook her head again. "As I told you, I knew the moment I touched her that she was no longer there. Come with me to the kitchen. We can have some tea." She turned and left the bedroom. Savich and Griffin followed her through the lavender-scented hallway to the kitchen.

Savich and Griffin remained silent, watching her prepare the tea, giving it all her focus and attention.

When at last she sat at the table with them, spooning sugar into her tea, she said, "Looking back, I realize she'd been hovering on the edge of madness for a long time, or maybe she always was and I simply refused to see it. After Arthur and I were married, she liked to mock me for being a Wiccan, for my foolish and meaningless rituals, she called them, but never when Arthur could hear her. He held her in check. You see, my husband knew what she was, knew what powers she had, knew she had no compunction about using them. She was his mother, after all. Then a car accident put her in the wheelchair a few years ago. Arthur was driving when a drunk slammed into the passenger side at an intersection. That man died a month later. He killed himself. We didn't know if she was responsible, but sometimes I would look at her and she would look very pleased with herself. But when her injuries healed, she changed. She was angry all the time. Arthur was worried he couldn't control her. When he realized he had no choice, he bound her. Binding is a powerful spell that holds a witch's power in check. After that, she didn't harm anyone for several years."

"Or perhaps, Mrs. Alcott," Savich said,

"she respected him enough to listen to him?"

Deliah rolled her eyes. "Believe that if you like, but I strongly doubt that. It is true that she loved Arthur more than anyone in the world, more than her two dead husbands, more than any of us. She admired his strength, you see, probably envied it, continually begged him to free her. She thought he was weak not to use his power, and she blamed me.

"When he died six months ago, she said she was free to do as she wished. That's when her madness surfaced for all of us to see, and the chaos began." Tears sheened her eyes. "Arthur was a fine man, a good man. He didn't expect to die and leave us in her hands.

"After he died, I tried everything I knew to control her. I tried cajoling her, making her feel a central part of the family. I tried ritual prayers, even repeated the binding spell Arthur had worked to control her, but none of it was enough. I wasn't strong enough, not like Arthur was."

Deliah looked down at her tea cup. "I confronted her one night after I overheard her speaking to Liggert, encouraging him to punish his wife because she thought Marly had insulted her."

"What did she do?" Griffin asked her.

"She laughed at me. She did that a lot, said I was a silly weakling, a sham who couldn't stop her from doing anything she liked. She started threatening my children, making them do bizarre and dangerous things to amuse herself and frighten me. She told me if I didn't behave—her word—she'd make Tanny, Liggert's daughter, sorry she'd ever been born. I believed her. I think now that if I'd had a knife in my hand I'd have tried to use it, I was that afraid for my children.

"When Liggert told her about Sparky Carroll's damaged Mustang, she didn't scream and yell and curse him, she went silent, didn't say a word for hours. Then she made Walter murder Sparky because she thought they both deserved it. She picked Brakey, her own grandson, to kill Deputy Lewis. In her mind he was as guilty as Sparky—he'd buried the truth. I believe it's my fault she used Brakey. She was punishing me for trying to control her. She wanted me to see how powerful she was—she could make Brakey murder someone, and her silent threat was that she could make me kill someone, too.

"It's been a reign of terror, and she's held us all prisoner. Until you came, Agent Savich. What will happen to Brakey now?"

Savich said, "Brakey will be fine. As for Walter, that will be more difficult. He stabbed Sparky Carroll in front of dozens of witnesses, but I hope I'll be able to convince the federal prosecutor to send him for psychiatric evaluation and, I hope, a stint in a federal sanitarium, not jail."

"When you left that first time, do you know she sat rocking in her chair, and she laughed, knitted and knitted and laughed and laughed. She said she was going to have some fun tormenting you, teaching you what was what, she said. We all thought she would kill you.

"Thank you for what you did," she said simply. "Last night you and Agent Hammersmith ended six months of terror for us."

She smiled. "Most of us Wiccans are cremated when we die and return our life force to the Goddess. I think I'll have her cremated when she takes her last breath. She would have hated that, you know."

Epilogue

Savich House
Georgetown
One week later

"You can be sure I've given it a lot of thought," Cal said. "My boss, Marvin Conifer, told me this morning my transfer's gone through. I'll be starting in New York in two weeks."

Sherlock looked from Special Agent Kelly Giusti to Special Agent Cal McLain. Kelly looked pleased. Sherlock knew she and Cal had discussed his relocating to New York, but now Kelly was shaking her head sadly. "You won't be reporting to me, or I'd already know about it. Too bad—I could whip you into shape in a week, two on the outside." She turned to Sherlock. "Actually, I'm glad he'll be in New York, part of the team. He now knows that's where the action is, where boots hit the ground, not like down here in nerdland, analyzing everything to death. When all's said and done, I've got to admit, he was pretty useful." She smiled at him. "We'll have to try to keep you from driving like a maniac race-car driver in Manhattan. Hey, if you're nice, I'll let you stay at my place until you find your own digs."

Cal took another bite of Dizzy Dan's pepperoni pizza, chewed, and looked thoughtfully at Kelly. Maybe if things worked out between them, he wouldn't need his own digs. He wondered how she would react to his real news. He patted her knee and dove in. "Ah, Kelly, I'm real glad to be coming to New York, and I know I'm really going to like staying with you at your apartment, but I gotta tell you something first."

That got her attention. "You already told me everything. What something?"

"Well, not quite everything." He took a drink of his beer, swiped a napkin over his mouth, and prayed.

"What? You're going to try to snag that last piece of pizza?"

"Maybe, but I think Sherlock's going to nab it. Okay, here's the thing. I did get the transfer to the New York Field Office like I told you. But there's more. I also got a promotion. Director Comey said something about being impressed with my part in bringing Basara down. He, ah, seemed impressed by my driving, particularly in that FBI SUV. Good advertising, I guess."

Kelly looked surprised again and blinked at him. "A promotion for that? You didn't really do anything," she sputtered. "Well, yeah, your driving was okay, well, amazing, really, but it was Sherlock who brought Basara down. I'll even admit you have a good brain, yeah, maybe they should promote you for that." She cocked her head to one side, studied his face, drilled him with a look. "What kind of promotion?"

"It turns out," he said, eyeing her, "that your boss, Vince Talbot, is transferring here to Washington and I'll be taking his place in New York." He sat back, folded his hands over his belly, and gave her a big smile. "You know what that means, Giusti. I'm going to be your boss."

"No," she said, waving her pizza slice at him, shaking her head. "I don't believe it." She looked at the slice, looked at him, and threw it, hitting him in the face. Cheese dripped off Cal's chin. He wiped off the cheese, grinned at her, picked her slice of pizza off his lap, and took a bite. He turned to Savich. "I hope you'll give me advice on how to handle the potholes. I mean, you're Sherlock's boss. Given what a tiger she is, there's lots of potholes, right?"

Savich threw back his head and laughed. Sean, who'd been positioning pepperoni slices up in a straight line across his paper plate, raised his head. "Papa, what's so funny? Is it a joke? Why did Kelly throw her pizza at Uncle Cal?"

Savich said, "It's what you'd maybe call a cosmic joke. My first piece of advice, Cal, is to know when to stop talking. Raise your glass so Sherlock and I can congratulate you."

Sean clicked his iced-tea glass to Cal's beer can. "Maybe you should have a reward, Uncle Cal. I'll play Flying Monks with you after dinner. Kelly said she didn't know how, but you're a guy, you have to know."

Cal, who'd never heard of Flying Monks, high-fived Sean. "Prepare to go against the master, Sean. Maybe you'd better play with your parents first; they can get you warmed up for me. Maybe you should call me Special Agent Doom."

Sean cocked his head to one side, the picture of his father, and blinked. "I think you'd have to warm up to play with my dad. My mom, too."

Sherlock ruffled Sean's black hair. "You're right, Sean, no matter what he calls himself, your uncle Cal is a distant second to us."

"What does **distant second** mean?"

Kelly said, "It means Cal thinks too highly of himself, Sean. He won't be able to compete with the big kahunas in New York, either, no matter how great he thinks he is."

Cal scooped up the last slice of pizza, sat back against the seat cushion, and looked pleased with himself and the world. "At least I won't have to do anything by myself. I've got you to pave the way, Kelly, whip those cowboys in line, and get them to admire me."

Kelly looked from Cal to her coffee and back again, picturing how a big coffee stain might look on his white shirt, but she saw his big smile and something else in his eyes, something warm and filled with promise. She smiled back and threw up her hands. "Oh, all right, I'll have your back if you have mine, Cal."

Sean looked at each of the adults. "You're smiling, Kelly, so I guess it's true, what Mama says."

"What does Mama say, Sean?" Cal asked.

"When the queen is happy, there's peace in the kingdom."